PLATEAU

N

Hill

ravine

steep drop

and Panjim

steep rise

wooded slope

Bamboo & cashews

sharp drop

3

Mango Grove

8

11

7

5

6

13

4

14

To the coast →

15

16

Rice Fields

To Mapusa & Aicona →

17

Nullah

18   19 20

Fields

21

Jivolem

Rice Fields

Bridge →

1

Church of St. Cornelius the Contrite, March '33.

Tivolem

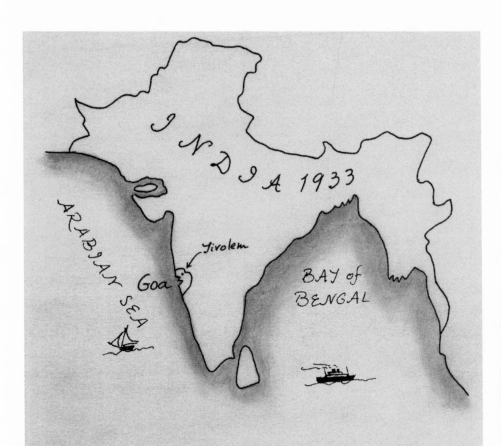

ARABIAN SEA

INDIA 1933

Goa

Tivolem

BAY of BENGAL

Cartography by Fr. F.X.A.C. Pires
Tivolem, March '33.

Tivolem

VICTOR RANGEL-RIBEIRO

MILKWEED
EDITIONS

The characters and events in this book are fictitious. Any similarity to real persons, living or dead, is coincidental and not intended by the author.

Published 1998 by Milkweed Editions
Printed in the United States of America
Cover design by Adrian Morgan, Red Letter Design
Cover painting by Subodh Kerkar. Printed with permission of Victor Rangel-Ribeiro.
Interior design by Will Powers
Maps by Victor Rangel-Ribeiro

98 99 00 01 02   5 4 3 2 1
First Edition

Epigraph on p. vii is from *A Flight of Swans: Poems from Balaka* by Rabindranath Tagore, translated by Aurobindo Bose. Copyright © 1962 by Visva-Bharati. Translation copyright © 1962 by Aurobindo Bose. Reprinted with permission from Visva-Bharati.

Milkweed Editions is a not-for-profit publisher. This Milkweed Fiction Prize book was underwritten in part by a grant from the Star Tribune/ Cowles Media Foundation. We also gratefully acknowledge support from Elmer L. and Eleanor J. Andersen Foundation; James Ford Bell Foundation; Cray Research, a Silicon Graphics Company; Dayton's, Mervyn's, and Target Stores by the Dayton Hudson Foundation; Doherty, Rumble and Butler; Ecolab Foundation; General Mills Foundation; Honeywell Foundation; Jerome Foundation; The McKnight Foundation; Andrew W. Mellon Foundation; Minnesota State Arts Board through an apropriation by the Minnesota State Legislature; Creation and Presentation Programs of the National Endowment for the Arts; Lawrence and Elizabeth Ann O'Shaughnessy Charitable Income Trust in honor of Lawrence M. O'Shaughnessy; Piper Jaffray Companies, Inc.; Ritz Foundation; John and Beverly Rollwagen Fund of the Minneapolis Foundation; The St. Paul Companies, Inc.; Star Tribune/Cowles Media Foundation; James R. Thorpe Foundation; Lila Wallace-Reader's Digest Literary Publishers Marketing Development Program, funded through a grant to the Council of Literary Magazines and Presses; and generous individuals.

Library of Congress Cataloging-in-Publication Data

Rangel-Ribeiro, Victor.
    Tivolem / Victor Rangel-Ribeiro. — 1st ed.
        p.   cm.
    ISBN 1-57131-019-3
    1. Goa (India : State) — History — Fiction. I. Title.
    PS3568.A566T58 1998
    813'.54—dc21   97-43264
                                                                 CIP

This book is printed on acid-free paper.

To the long-departed
Dona Maria Julia Gomes Vaz e Pinto,
my dear maternal grandmother,
whose stories have continued to delight our family
for four generations

ACKNOWLEDGMENTS

Several chapters in this novel have been previously published as short stories—some of the Lazarinh' capers as "The Miscreant" in the *Iowa Review* 20, no. 2 (Spring/Summer 1990); Pedro Saldanha's story as "Angel Wings" in the *North American Review* 278, no. 3 (May/June 1993); and chapters 43 and 45, dealing with the monsoon, as "Madonna of the Raindrops" and "The Day of the Baptist" in the *Literary Review*'s special International Nature Writing issue (Summer 1996).

The author gratefully acknowledges the support and encouragement provided by the New York Foundation for the Arts, in awarding him its Fiction Fellowship in 1991 while the novel was just stirring into life.

Special thanks go to Subodh Kerkar, M.D., noted Goan artist, for his depiction of Tivolem for our cover.

My special thanks go particularly to my caring and insightful editor, Emilie Buchwald; to the ever helpful and perceptive Thomas F. Epley, and his Potomac Literary Agency; to David Hamilton, Robley Wilson, and Walter Cummins, editors, listed in the order in which they came into my life; to Dorothy Rouse-Bottom, and to Lester Goldberg, and my other peers in the Two Bridges Writers' Group; all of whom provided support and nurturing above and beyond the call of reason, friendship, or duty.

I hear the countless voices of the human heart
Flying unseen,
From the dim past to the dim unblossomed future.
Hear, within my own breast,
The fluttering of the homeless bird, which,
In company with countless others,
Flies day and night,
Through light and darkness,
From shore to shore unknown.
The void of the universe is resounding with the music of wings:
'Not here, not here, somewhere far beyond.'

Rabindranath Tagore, *A Flight of Swans*

Tivolem

SPRING

1933

JANUARY

1

As the big ship that sails down the coast from Bombay steams past the fortress of Aguada on Tuesday mornings, that ancient stronghold greets her arrival with a one-gun salute—a single shot fired from an antique cannon. Three centuries earlier, from atop that same stark promontory in Goa, that venerable muzzle-loader, guarding the jewel of Portugal's Indian empire, twice kept an entire Dutch fleet at bay, but to the villagers of Tivolem, nestled in a valley six miles to the north, its noble greeting—puff! thud!—is lost in the raucous cawing of crows and the soughing of bamboo clumps swaying in the wind. What they listen for instead is the deep vroooom-ooomm-mmmmm with which the *Lilavati* announces she has rounded the fort and safely slid past the broad sandbar at the mouth of the Mandovi River; that lingering sound, skipping over hills and bouncing its echoes around valley walls, seems to say, "Rejoice! A son, a daughter, someone you love and are waiting for, is coming home today."

Marie-Santana stood at the rail of the main deck, her scarf fluttering in the wind, as the *Lilavati,* still a good half hour from the fort, plowed past the Baga headland at a brisk eighteen knots, sending a foaming wake skimming over eight-foot breakers toward the Pirate's Well at the foot of the bluff, and the white-sand beach beyond. Marie-Santana had climbed that cliff as a child, and raced wind-blown tumbleweeds along those dazzling sands. The sun in her eyes, she sought, among the fishermen's shade-flecked houses scattered amidst the coconut trees, the one cottage where, each May till she was twelve, she had romped with her parents and Angelinh' Granny, and their neighbor's son, Mottu. She remembered the cool of the rented home, the ocean breezes wafting through open doors and windows; remembered too how ember-hot the sand had grown each afternoon, and how, wanting to go down to the beach to play, they had had to race from the shade of one coconut tree to another, their bare feet on fire, digging down with their toes to cooler sands to ease the stinging.

Angelinh' Granny had been playful then, Marie-Santana remembered; and she wondered about that, since her own parents had tended so much to value decorum and respect-ability. Granny could climb the low-branching cashew trees that grew on the hillslope behind their house, and once, when no one was around, even climbed halfway up a coco-nut tree in their garden, though she had looped no rope around her ankles to help her grip its trunk. It was Granny who taught her how to smell rain an hour before it arrived. It was also Granny who, with her father at the seashore, took her crabbing on moonless nights, taught her how to cut a reed from a dune without being stung by a cactus, how to fix a candle in a coconut shell and face it into the wind so that, once lit, the flame would flicker but not die. The giant crabs, when they saw the light, would scuttle swiftly to the water's edge; you had to be quick to cut them off, whipping your reed along the wet sand to flip them on their backs. Then you had spicy-hot crab curry for lunch the next day, using even the red lacquer scraped off the crab's underbelly as part of the sauce.

Marie-Santana wished her parents were with her now, going home. In her mid-thirties, and on this trip, she felt more orphaned than when they had died in Mozambique,

6

in Portuguese Africa, within months of each other eight years ago, leaving her there alone. She had buried them in accordance with her mother's wishes, side by side in Quelimane's Catholic cemetery by the River of Good Omen. Coming home like this, even coming home to Granny, was itself a wrench; it was she who was leaving them behind, abandoning them. The thought that she could no longer visit their graves, bringing flowers and prayers and love, filled her eyes with tears.

A flurry among her fellow passengers finally snapped her out of her reverie, and she saw they were almost abreast of the Aguada fort, the great round bastion thrust into the sea now a mere empty threat, its gun ports empty, but the weathered turrets and battlements on the heights still manned by a scattering of troops, and the ghosts of the past. The *Lilavati* cut her speed, and Marie-Santana felt her stomach heave as, turning due east, the ship began breasting the breakers that fought their way into the river's narrow mouth. Beyond the last great foaming crest lay the broad and sometimes ill-tempered Mandovi itself, its banks lush with vegetation, the waterway alive with launches and dinghies and multioared river craft, and sleek Arab dhows still furling their sails. The hubbub on deck increased as the deep blast of the ship's siren scattered the circling gulls. Around her Marie-Santana heard the familiar sounds of English and Portuguese interspersed with the babble of more ancient tongues—Konkani, Marathi, even the elegant Hindi of the north. Already the dock and customs shed, gaily festooned with welcoming red, green, and yellow bunting, were drawing closer. Gathering up her rolled-up bedding, and keeping her one large steamer trunk in view, she prepared to debark.

Water churned and bubbled along the stern and sides of the ship as, with bells ringing and engines alternately driving forward and reversing, the captain balanced tide and thrust in a slow ritual courtship of the dock. Seamen stood poised fore and aft, hawsers in hand. From a good twenty feet away they sent the lines snaking through the air, smartly lassoing iron stanchions on the dock. At last, the *Lilavati* firmly secured, the gangplank barely in place, coolies came swarming on board, reaching for baggage even as the press of passengers surged to the rail to greet relatives who were eagerly awaiting their debarkation.

Despite the growing excitement around her, Marie-Santana's mood remained pensive. She became concerned at the prospect of facing her grandmother. Would she find her in good health? Bedridden? Half-blind? Senile, even? She had written home only intermittently over the years, as had her parents. Should she have shared her fears and failures with her aging grandmother, even though she knew that these bad tidings could have caused great anguish? Still . . . she could at least have written ahead this time, even wired, to say she was coming, yet she had chosen not to. Had she herself perhaps become more selfish? Self-centered?

With her eyes once again tear-laden, she needed a kerchief. She checked her purse.

2

THE EIGHT-FOOT-WIDE STREAM that rustled and
rippled along the rock-strewn *nullah* under Tivolem's
only bridge was the same brook that, minutes earlier, starting from a spring up in the woods, had burbled behind Bald
Uncle Priest's long-vacant house on the north slope of the
south hill, then curled behind Dona Elena's, and Angelinh'
Granny's and Senhor Eusebio's, on its way toward the
fields. At the height of each monsoon in July and August,
following an unusually heavy downpour, it would turn into
a raging torrent; cattle were sometimes swept downstream,
and, more often, pigs both large and small, since they foraged
along it daily where the outhouses lined its banks. But the
stream dwindled as the monsoon waned, and by January
the water level dropped low enough to form a series of well-
stocked pools, keeping the kingfishers fat and happy.

The bridge spanned the nullah where the lane, leaving
the houses and the Goregão road behind, turned toward the
church and the outlying government primary school and
the Tivolem-Mapusa road. The bridge was hence somewhat
isolated; the only vehicular traffic was an occasional bullock cart that came that way, and sometimes a taxi from the
city, and every other week or so Dona Esmeralda's gaily
painted yellow wooden carriage in which she rode to

Mapusa, with Ramu the old retainer perched on the driver's box up front and singing to the bulls that pulled the carriage smartly along. The bridge was thus a quiet place, and though set apart from the village proper, was yet as convenient to the church as to the gentlemen on the hill; and since the knee-high stone parapets on either side were just some ten feet apart, the vicar and his friends could sit comfortably facing each other, discussing pressing local issues and matters of international moment without ever coming to blows.

It was on the parapets of this bridge, therefore, each afternoon after the children had gone chattering home from school, that mighty councils convened. Besides the learned Father José Mascarenhas, vicar of the Church of Saint Cornelius the Contrite and pastor of Tivolem, the other regulars included the local justice of the peace, or *regedor,* Gustavo Tellis; the principal of the local English high school, Prakash Tendulkar; the postmaster-for-life, Cajetan Braganza; and two out of three returnees—Eusebio Pinto, back from the Persian Gulf, and Teodosio Rodrigues, back from Africa. In this cabal of Catholics, Tendulkar was the lone Hindu. Each subscribed to one or more of the Portuguese-language dailies being published in Panjim; Eusebio subscribed also to the *Times of India,* brought in by train, a day late, from Bombay. Together they comprised the local male intelligentsia, and they knew it; they alone in all the village cared to debate the state of the world, and they did this without fail during the hour they spent together on the bridge. In deference to Eusebio, they carried on their discussions in English, the language in which he was most fluent, with forays into Portuguese and Konkani as necessary in search of the mot juste.

The morning of Marie-Santana's return, as the *Lilavati* was sliding past the sandbar and easing into Panjim's harbor, the vicar had just finished mailing a letter at the village post office when the echoes and re-echoes of the ship's arrival caught him in midsentence.

"Ah, Cajetan, the siren call of the outside world," he said to the postmaster. "How subtly it impinges upon our consciousness. A single sound and its reverberations—quite insubstantial in themselves—yet reminding us of oceans ever to be crossed, of events beyond our control."

"But we cope, we cope," Postmaster Braganza said. "We keep that world at bay, as best we can."

"Thank goodness. But over there," the vicar waved a hand, vaguely, in the direction of the sea and Europe, "there's always something doing, some of it good, some bad. Gives us things to discuss, at least. We'll meet at the bridge, then, at the usual time?"

"At five, yes. We'll have much to talk about. There's some news out of British India, about those thousands thrown in jail."

"Gandhi's men?"

"Political prisoners, yes, about fifteen thousand, through December."

"That's a large number, but it may not stop Gandhi. Of course, there's unrest everywhere. Just look at Germany."

"The trouble over the coming elections, yes, of course. This new fellow, this Adolf what's-his-name," the post-master said. "What do you make of him?"

"An unknown, but he claims Germany needs him, and who's to tell? He hasn't won yet, has he? And even if he does, he'll have the crusty old field marshal to cope with. Hindenburg. A onetime corporal challenging a field marshal —it's like me challenging the Pope. Hardly a contest, now, don't you think?"

"If only the world would listen," the postmaster said, laughing. "We solve as many problems as the League of Nations—and possibly more."

"The 'League of Knaves,'" the vicar said. "Cajetan, I tell you, there's a Latin phrase that sums up some of the people who go up there and make all those fancy speeches. *Anceps imago.* Two-faced."

"Did you know we'll be better informed from now on? Eusebio tells me he has a new toy—a shortwave radio."

"Imagine! A radio! And what can he get on it?"

"So far, mostly yowls, howls, whistles, crackling, sputtering, and grunts. Sometimes, music, which comes and goes like the waves of the sea. And he gets news from the BBC in London, their new worldwide broadcast. And when Eusebio hears that 'London calling!' and the sound of Big Ben, he thinks he is in paradise."

"Always the Anglophile."

"Well, the British were his masters in the Gulf; he liked their ways," the postmaster said. "And, it seems, their accent."

"So now he gets the news, told with a British accent? Most certainly the voice of authority."

"Indeed. But as to how much of it is really intelligible, with all that static and caterwauling going on—it would be easier for him to invent it."

"Hardly a novel concept," the vicar said. "Well, we'll have to match what he says against what we read in the papers."

"A day or two later."

The vicar turned to leave, but the postmaster stopped him with a gesture. "I've asked the new man to join us," Cajetan Braganza said. "Simon Fernandes, back from Singapore. He's known about our sessions the couple of months he's been here, but since he's held aloof, I felt perhaps he was waiting for a formal invitation."

"Kuala Lumpur," the vicar said. "He's back from Kuala Lumpur, not the Straits of Singapore. If we're going to solve the world's problems, old friend, we'd better get our world geography straight. Now there's a pun, though not one I'd intended. But you're right in asking him—he's been here all these weeks and still does seem rather lonely. And I'll bring my new curate—there's another lonely fellow, though at least you see him in church, which is more than one can say for Simon; but that's neither here nor there. Coming from Malaysia, he'll bring some fresh insights into our discussions. Perhaps, even, a British accent." He laughed. "Well, pip-pip, cheerio, toodle-oo, and all that bosh."

3

A T THE FOOT of the gangplank a white-clad official
held out his hand, and Marie-Santana, taking this as
a gesture of welcome, reached out and shook it.

"Well, well," he said in Portuguese, bowing gallantly and
raising her hand to his lips, "that was a pleasant surprise.
But I was merely trying to take your pulse."

Puzzled and somewhat embarrassed, she gave him her
wrist.

"Cholera, typhoid, diphtheria," he explained. "Can't let
any of those bad germs get into Goa, even if they're accompanied by so charming a lady. Heh heh!"

How can he laugh so heartily, Marie-Santana wondered,
when it's a joke he probably tries out on every woman
passenger he meets? Nevertheless, she smiled, hoping this
would reduce the chances of evil germs being discovered
hiding in her pulse beat. Apparently none were, for he
directed her to the customs shed.

Marie-Santana took her time going through the *alfândega;*
she saw that the mestiço official on duty there had brusquely
ordered a couple from British India to unlock and open all
their luggage. He turned a scowling look on her as well, but
finding she was returning home from Mozambique, like Goa
a Portuguese colony, he stopped her as she was stooping

14

over her baggage, wished her a good day, and waved her on. Nevertheless, she found she had missed not just the big coal-burning launch that would have taken her to Betim but the new and much faster little *gasolina* that would have sped her across the broad river in minutes.

Not wishing to wait, Marie-Santana paid a coolie to take her things down to the beach where the large river canoes were plying; but the man was old and slow, and by the time she got there, a boat, half-full of passengers, was already pulling away from shore. She turned to find the coolie standing unsteadily under his burden. "Put it down here," she said, holding on to one end of the trunk as he slowly squatted to get the load off his head. There was nothing to do but wait until enough passengers had gathered for another boat to make the trip.

A graying but muscular boatman, who had been watching her with intense curiosity, now approached hesitantly.

"I'll take you across, *bai,* in my *orrem.* I could leave at once," he said, pointing to an empty canoe bobbing in the water.

Remembering the aggressiveness of river boatmen, the way they seized your luggage and hustled you in, she was struck by his gentleness. Nevertheless, a trip on her own could cost more than she wished to pay.

"I'm sorry," she said, "but I don't want an *especial.*"

"I won't charge you extra," he said. "I'm going across anyway. Rather than letting me go empty, you might as well come along."

He helped her in, steadying the boat against her weight, then loaded the trunk and the bedroll. She sat on a bench in the middle, with an arched bamboo awning shielding her from the sun, while he sat facing her, his back to the bow. The tide was sweeping in, and he rowed strongly against it, keeping the boat pointing diagonally toward the ocean, while the current pushed it steadily toward the abandoned Fort of the Three Wise Kings. She wondered why he rowed this way, when she could see others rowing directly across;

it stirred vague memories. Twice they passed Arab dhows at anchor, with their cargoes of dates and smuggled gold. Progress was slow; a hundred yards upstream, a canoe that had left some minutes after them had already seemingly drawn abreast, and was rapidly pulling ahead.

"You are rowing against the tide," she said. "Doesn't that make it longer and harder?"

He laughed. "Longer, yes, but harder, no," he said. "You see that boat over there, and you think, they're moving faster. And they are, for now. But in a minute, I'll turn our boat around, and then with the tide behind us she'll swoop to the landing place like a gull to a fish."

Marie-Santana looked at the far shore, still almost a mile away, remembering past crossings. He broke into her thoughts. "You're returning from Africa," he said.

The *Lilavati* only sailed between Bombay and Goa. What made him guess Africa?

"Your trunk," he said, noticing her surprise. "The labels say 'Mozambique'. You've been away a while?"

"Twenty-three years."

"Twenty-three years," he echoed, then fell silent, straining to the task at hand. Deftly, he eased up on one oar, and the bow swung with the tide, pointing now diagonally upstream. Though the far bank with its tree-covered cliffs did not seem appreciably nearer, on looking back Marie-Santana could see they had traveled quite a distance. And now, with the tide in their favor and the boatman rowing strongly, the craft indeed sped swiftly for the distant shore. She could not remember a canoe ever moving so fast in such a tidal river. The other boat, now left far behind, was already wallowing in their wake—its boatman frustrated, its passengers disappointed, bested in an undeclared race they thought they had been winning handily.

By the time Marie-Santana's canoe had made the northern bank of the Mandovi, however, the tide still had not risen enough for her to step to shore. Instead, the boatman drove the canoe hard aground; then, with Marie-Santana cradled in his arms, he waded to dry land. Sloshing back, he eased both steamer trunk and bedroll onto his back and brought them to her, saying, "Follow me, bai, I'll get you a taxi."

"Tell me what I owe you," she said, fishing anxiously in her purse.

"No charge, bai," he said.

"But," she protested, "you did row me across!"

"You have no reason to remember me," he said, "but I believe I know you. I was watching as you came down from the dock to the boat beach. You must be Angelinh' Granny's grandchild, who went to Africa with your parents. I see it in your features—you look the way she did when she was about your age."

"Yes, she is my grandmother," Marie-Santana said.

"And your father—he is well?"

"Both my parents are dead."

He turned to face her. "Your father was highly respected," he said. "He did me a great favor once, a long time ago— I was never able to repay him. It is my good luck that I saw you this morning. This way, at least, in a very small way I can say, 'thank you.'"

"You knew my father, then?"

"Bad things were happening with me," he said. "When no one else would help me, your father did. He said that in life, as in crossing a river, one sometimes has to row against the tide, turn a hardship into an advantage. I was young, and didn't know what he meant, but he showed me. All these years later, I still row through life and across the river the way he showed me."

By now he had found her a taxi, and while the trunk was being tied to the roof, she once again turned to thank him.

"It was nothing, bai," he said. "It was really nothing."

She was touched. "At least tell me your name," she said, but he was gone even as she spoke.

4

SIMON FERNANDES, on his return from Kuala Lumpur
in November, had expected to fit easily into the flow
of village life; he had been born in Tivolem, had lived there
as a child, and, on revisiting his native village once in the
forty-odd years he'd been away, he found it much to his
liking. The family had migrated to the Malay Peninsula
when Simon was just five; his father Michael, a violinist,
had found employment there at the otherwise all-white, all-
male Selangor Club, leading a nonwhite trio that performed
waltzes, polkas, marches, operatic arrangements, and von
Suppé and Rossini overtures for scotch-and-soda-swigging
burra sahibs and mustachioed empire builders; the pay was
adequate and the tips were good.

Two years into their stay, Simon's mother, Faustina, once
again grew big with child, and great was the anticipation
as the projected birth day approached. "He's pink!" the delighted midwife said, holding the baby up by the feet for the
glowing mother to see. "Oh, look how pink he is!" Michael,
noting the healthy color, was also pleased, expecting the
pink in time to fade away into a more normal brown. But
baby John, drawing on who-knows-what distant aberrant
genes, retained the color in his cheeks and his light brown
hair, so first-time visitors cooing over the crib had to play

for time, saying, "What dainty little fingers!" and "Oh, look at that cute little nose!" before remarking that the long dark eyelashes were just like Faustina's and the mouth and chin were definitely Michael's. Which they weren't.

Michael, loving his wife, trusting her, could not help but notice the sly looks, the unspoken speculation, and at moments was tempted to ask, merely to end the torment, "Faustina, did you?" even though they had few white acquaintances and absolutely no white friends. And she, loving her husband and her first-born son, loving the baby, noticed the hidden smiles as well, suspected her husband's anguish, and was sick at heart.

The needs of the family grew, and to cope with the extra bills, Michael played "Light Cavalry" or the "Triumphal March" from *Aida* for an encore if the mood at the club was more than usually bellicose, or "Poet and Peasant," or even some Waldteufel, if it was romantic. This loosened the patrons' purse strings, and as their generosity increased, so did Michael's family become more than merely solvent. Wishing, therefore, to ensure for Simon a future as financially secure as his own, Michael taught the seven-year-old to play the violin and taught him well. By the age of twelve the young man became proficient enough to join his father's trio on demand; as a quartet they could more easily do justice to some Wagner arrangements, and even to John Philip Sousa; but if ever they played "Stars and Stripes" to please an American visitor, loud calls would promptly arise for "Rule, Britannia." In the good old Empaah, even visiting Yankees had to be put firmly in their place.

Lucrative though Simon's occasional stints at the club were, his bent was for serious classical orchestral music, and at sixteen he auditioned for the Kuala Lumpur Philharmonic, was admitted, and in eight short years became its youngest concertmaster ever. That the KLP was an amateur group and paid its musicians no money mattered not at all; Simon had done well in school and obtained a job in the civil service when he was twenty-one, and the pay, though not on the lavish scale granted to Englishmen, was still better than that paid the local Malays.

John grew up on a different path. He clung to his mother, shied away from his father, resented Simon, and in school played only with the Eurasian children, even though they taunted him because his parents were "black." He was silent at dinnertime. Simon, newly ensconced in his civil-service job, kept his parents laughing with stories of his day at work; John, asked what had happened in school, invariably answered, "Nothing." To avoid having to speak, he kept his mouth continually stuffed. "His hand and mouth coordination are unbelievable," Michael remarked to his wife. "If my bow arm worked as smoothly as that, I'd be another blooming Paganini."

At fourteen, grown tall and muscular for his age, John wanted to quit high school, and when his parents refused, he played truant. His father caught him and slapped him; John slapped right back; he was sent hungry to bed that night. His mother sat staring at the food on her plate, then burst into uncontrolled weeping. Michael put his arms around her to comfort her and get her to eat; when she would not, he spooned his own food into the garbage can, spilling some on the kitchen floor. The servant mopped it up; it was days before husband and wife spoke to each other again.

Nine years after that incident, Simon returned to Tivolem as a poised but quiet young man of thirty, alone. His mother had been dead three months of a cancer that had gone undiscovered until it was inoperable. In Tivolem he stayed at the family home, where an elderly cousin was living as caretaker. His memories of the place had been washed clean; when neighbors pointed to various sites and recounted incidents relating to his childhood, he listened with rapt attention, and sometimes with embarrassment. He spoke but little; his silences the village attributed to his grief. To those who enquired after the family he gave news of his father and, with some difficulty, of his mother's passing; of his brother he would say only, "He's fine," which was probably true. He was not sure. He did not say, "I'm not sure he was ever really one of us," a thought that was sometimes at the back of his head, so oddly hostile was his brother's usual behavior. Nor did he add what would have been true: "He's run away, he's been gone three months, we just don't know where he is." Instead, the answer, "He's fine," seemed to satisfy those who asked. They never pressed him further.

The breakup had been as brutal as it was unexpected. After the funeral, the three of them left alone in the strangely empty house, Michael had sought comfort with his weeping sons, but John had pulled away and run out of the house. Michael and Simon had looked for him for hours, unsuccessfully; when they returned, they found him stretched out on the living-room settee, flushed and asleep, a nearly empty whiskey bottle by his side. Together they carried him to his room. Next morning, while Simon was showering and Michael was sitting shirtless and bleary-eyed at the breakfast table, John brushed past him, a rucksack on his back. Michael half-rose to stop him, crying out, "Son," but John, at the door already, turned and shouted, "You're not my father!" and ran into the street, leaving Michael desolate.

This time John did not come back. Notices in the agony column of the *Kuala Lumpur Times* brought no response. Friends and strangers that Simon and Michael spoke to denied having seen him. At the railway station, too, they drew a blank. They described him—tall, fair, light brown, almost sandy hair, just twenty-three but looks more like thirty. "It's too busy a place," the stationmaster said. "And there are so many Anglos around; can't keep an eye on them all. Have you tried the police?"

They had. The police had come up with no better news.

Although Simon's trip to Tivolem had been planned for some time, as the date of sailing approached he had wished he could cancel it, fearing scandal might have preceded him. He need not have worried. The visit was uneventful, but the warmth with which he had been received impressed him deeply. "Come back!" the neighbors cried, pressing around the taxi as he was leaving. The cousin ran alongside, giving Simon a last-minute message for Michael, a message Simon could not hear because of the rattling of the engine and the hubbub outside. "Come back!" the voices said, fainter now with the distance.

Returning now for good, some sixteen years later, Simon savored an added dimension. The tradespeople like Govind and Atmaram and Kashinath all called him *baab*. Dona Elena and Dona Esmeralda, when they met him, called him Senhor Fernandes. Postmaster Braganza, who loved to flaunt his English, addressed him as Mr. Fernandes. He had earlier been met with affection; now his money and his age—he was approaching fifty, Angelinh' Granny said, recalling he was born the same year her own grandmother died—gained him some added respect.

The village had changed, but not by much. Senhor Eusebio's new house, however, dominated the lower landscape. To Simon's dismay, his own childhood home now stood half-ruined. The cousin to whose care it had been entrusted had taken off for parts unknown, leaving no one else in charge. (Had the man been trying to tell about his impending departure, the day he ran mouthing alongside the taxi as Simon was leaving?) Eventually, under the battering of the monsoons, the roof had caved in. Red fire ants then took over the mud castles that termites had built along the crumbling walls, and in time even the ants moved out, surrendering the red earth turrets with the gaping holes to a slithery nest of cobras. For a while Simon considered rebuilding, but finding the plot too small, decided against it, seeking to rent instead. The vicar referred him to Pedro Saldanha, an upright man and favorite parishioner. Together they looked at several houses, the most promising among them Bald Uncle Priest's old home, which had been rented briefly only once in the many years since the old priest had died. But the place, Senhor Eusebio warned him when Simon mentioned he'd looked at it, had a bad reputation. "Remember the woman!" Senhor Eusebio said.

"What woman?"

"What woman? You've been away too long. The woman who, after Bald Uncle Priest had died, came here one evening thirty years ago, from another village, and failed to return home at night. The woman who was found next morning sitting on the topmost tip of a tamarind branch in Bald Uncle Priest's garden, and the twig not even bending with her weight."

"A village tale. Did you see it?"

"Me? I was in the Gulf."

"And you still believe it?"

"What's there to doubt? The tree's still standing; anyone can show it to you. Other people saw it happen, people I trust, and everyone believes it."

"So. What happened with the woman?"

"They tried to get her down, but nothing worked. They sent for the old vicar then, not the one we have now but the one before him, and he brought holy water, but she was too high up, and, try as he might, he could not sprinkle her with it. Then they called the *bhott,* the Hindu priest from the temple, and he made *puja* in Sanskrit and burnt some incense; when the smoke curled up into the branches, the great tree bent right over and eased the woman onto the ground."

"Unharmed?"

"Unhurt, but not unharmed—she went stark-raving mad. Didn't utter one word after that, not that anyone could understand. Except curses. Those she spat out in profusion."

Simon fell silent.

"Would you like to see the place again?" Senhor Eusebio asked.

"To look at the garden," he said. "I want to see the tree."

"It's way past Angelinh' Granny's, toward the spring."

It was a tiring walk. In the sunlight the garden slept; the tamarind tree's branches, lightly touched by a breeze, feathered tall against the sky.

Simon was disappointed. "It looks like any other tamarind."

"What did you expect—witches on every twig? That branch there was the one she was found on, incidentally, that big one high up on the left."

"And that great limb just bent down to the ground."

"You sound skeptical. Ask anyone, anyone at all—they'll tell you the same thing."

They strolled up to the gate.

"And the house?" Simon eyed the structure, still in good repair.

"Oh, people feel it's haunted. And there's a *casró* tree in the back."

"And that's bad?"

"It's not a good tree to have around. The fruit is perfectly round, like a big mouse-colored Ping-Pong ball. No other fruit is quite as round. Strange? Hindus say it brings bad luck. They also hold the tree sacred—things happen around casró trees. People believe demons live in them. Sometimes demon lights are seen dancing and floating away, up into the hills."

"Well, that settles it, then. I don't want the house."

"There's one more place you should see, though it's not as large as this one."

"If it's too far down in the village I won't consider it. I value my privacy."

"Then it may be right for you. It's on this lane, but somewhat further down. In fact, we walked by it on our way here."

They stopped by a house three doors from Granny's, but on the opposite side of the lane, fronted by a miniscule garden, its distinguishing mark a weather vane that spun merrily on the roof. Though the man who had had it installed had sold the property and moved permanently to Bombay, people still referred to it as Weathervaneman's house. Simon liked what he saw: The house, which one approached by a steep flight of steps, had a view from its *balcão*—that pillared porch, open on three sides, that shaded the front door and overlooked a garden ablaze with colorful crotons. He saw, too, that he'd have fewer neighbors to cope with than if he found a house closer to the road, but he was a cautious man and not about to make up his mind on impulse.

"It's been well kept," Senhor Eusebio said. "Before I decided to build, I considered renting this place for myself."

They pushed open the gate and walked into the garden.

"Crotons," Senhor Eusebio said. "Crotons everywhere. You've got fantastic colors year-round, and minimum upkeep."

"And no roses, thank God."

"You don't like roses?"

"They don't like me. Once, a thorn pricked my left index finger; it became so sensitive I couldn't play for days."

Simon climbed the steps to the open porch and stood before the closed door to the house, looking about him. The gardens on either side were well tended, but Granny's farther down to the right—what he could see of it across the lane—seemed sere and yet overgrown in parts, badly in need of care.

"The old woman lives alone," Senhor Eusebio said, reading his thoughts. "The neighbors do what they can."

"Overall, I like it," Simon said.

"Then you'll take it?"

"I'll think about it," he said.

But he had almost made up his mind. He found the balcão particularly attractive; while traditionally it was used for informal entertaining of friends and neighbors—its stone benches stayed cool even in the hottest weather, and the absence of walls invited each passing breeze—Simon saw another use for it: he could practice or play his violin there, for hours on end, while enjoying the serenity of the outdoors.

"Don't think too hard," Senhor Eusebio said. "The absentee owners not only want no rent, but they're offering a sack of rice per year, and a two-gallon tin of kerosene every other month, to whoever stays at least a year and keeps the house in shape."

"I'll take it," Simon said. "An offer like that—I'd be a fool not to take it."

5

IN THE BACK SEAT of her taxi, Marie-Santana drank
in the sights and sounds at the boat landing while a
mechanic cranked the car engine repeatedly to get it to
start. While the great crush of people from the steamer had
long gone, there were still some who were looking for transportation. Several buses were waiting to complete their
complement of passengers, the drivers standing bareheaded
in the sun, calling out their destinations—"Mapusa!
Mapusa! Mapusa!" "Bicholé! Bicholé! Bicholé!"—while
passengers already on board sweltered in the heat. "Hurry!
Hurry! We're leaving!" called the bus drivers, as potential
customers still lingered around a banyan tree closer to the
water, haggling with the vegetable vendors and fisherwomen who had squatted in its shade. The engine now
having caught, the taxi began a long and tortuous climb.

From the top of the hill Marie-Santana caught a momentary glimpse of the harbor—the *Lilavati* moored at her
dock, dwarfing the river shipping; the dhows anchored mid-
stream; the customshouse now deserted; the ancient white
church sparkling against the backdrop of pink and blue
pastel houses of the capital city rising on the hill beyond it.

"Can you stop?" she asked the driver, but he, changing
gears and coping with an uncertain engine, pretended not

to hear, not wanting to take the chance of stalling. They drove for a while on the tarred Betim-Mapusa road that runs the length of a plateau from that point on, but halfway across, at the crossroads known as the Savior of the World (though not a soul may be seen there, waiting to be saved), the taxi followed a fork to the northeast, in the direction of Goregão. The cashew trees and mango groves that had crowded the highway on either side now thinned out to grassland, where goats and cattle could be seen grazing— a richness of green split by the mud red road, pockmarked and deeply rutted by rains and the metal-rimmed wheels of lumbering bullock carts. Though the driver slackened his speed, Marie-Santana had to hold on to the seat in front of her to cushion the jolts, and lessen the risk of being tossed about. She felt increasingly the nearness of home; it was not the wind alone that brought her eyes to tearing.

Three miles later they had reached the end of the plateau, and the driver shifted abruptly into low gear for the steep descent. Marie-Santana, jolted back into reality, took in the familiar landscape now unfolding before her. Almost there. She remembered that a squat stone cross part-way down the hill stood facing Angelinh' Granny's gate, and she could see it now, low and over to her right, as the taxi eased into a higher gear for the final looping run into the village. The house facing the cross was hidden by trees, but her heart leapt as she glimpsed a patch of brown-tiled roof. Farther down and off to the right, Dona Esmeralda's expansive mansion faced a stretch of fields; to the left, the sight of a sprawling new house where none had stood gave her pause—the village had changed. With her own memory of Tivolem's byways now cast in doubt, she asked her driver to stop at the post office for directions.

Though the man at the far desk busily dealing with the mail was no longer the dapper person she as a child had known, but was now white-haired and grown quite plump, she recognized him by his mannerisms. He picked each letter from a stack with his left hand, placed it in front of him, hit the stamp squarely with the postmark twice, then flipped the envelope over and hit it twice again before tossing it to one side. Thump-thump, pause. Thump-thump. He had not heard her come in.

"When I postmark something, I make sure it gets postmarked," Marie-Santana said softly.

Postmaster Braganza spun around, saw a woman silhouetted against the light, and squinted in a vain attempt to make out her features.

"My father used to tell me that that was your motto," she said teasingly.

He took a step forward. "And you are?"

"A voice from the past."

He came round the counter then, took her by the shoulders, and turned her gently to the light.

"Angelinh's granddaughter!"

"Yes, I'm Marie-Santana."

"You're back!" he exclaimed, stepping back to get a better look at her. "Wonderful! You came by the ship?"

She nodded. "My taxi's outside."

"Just this morning our old vicar was here, and when he heard the ship's siren, he said it reminded him of oceans to be crossed. Wait till I tell him who has crossed the oceans, ha!"

"My grandmother," she said. "How is she?"

"She is well, for her age, but we rarely see her down here. Is your coming a surprise, then?"

Before she could answer, a short, broad-shouldered man walked in the door, and the postmaster seized on him with enthusiasm.

"Mr. Fernandes, do you know who this lady is? Marie-Santan' Pereira, your neighbor Angelinh' Granny's granddaughter, just back from Africa! This moment she has arrived!" And to Marie-Santana he said, "This is Mr. Simon Fernandes—he has rented old Weathervaneman's house. He's a returnee like you; just retired from the civil service, from Singapore."

"Kuala Lumpur," Simon interposed. He nodded to Marie-Santana, smiling, then held out his hand. "So glad we'll be neighbors."

"You must be enjoying Weathervaneman's house," she said. "I remember it well. That tiny garden—I'd go there every day. Are those crotons still there?"

"Rooted in place, and nowhere to go. But I'm glad— they're that beautiful. You must come see them."

She excused herself and, having got directions from the postmaster, headed out the door before news of her arrival spread and half the village came to greet her.

Out on the road, she found a small group of street urchins already clustered by her taxi. As she prepared to get in, a man who had just ridden up jumped off his bicycle and let it fall to the ground with a clatter as he moved to intercept her.

"Mar'-Santan'!"

She knew him instantly. "Martin?!" She felt the color flooding her cheeks.

He stopped a couple of feet away, letting his hands fall to his side. They faced each other awkwardly, neither of them moving. The years had changed him. The once gangly but handsome boy, her childhood friend and neighbor, now a man of thirty-seven, had turned much darker, thinner, gaunt almost.

"You left a girl-child, and you're back a woman," he said.

She smiled. "But you still recognized me."

"You're still you. Should I have forgotten?"

She smiled again. "You have married," she said, indicating his ring.

He cleared his throat before replying. "Eight years already." He cleared his throat again. "And I have a son, just six years old; Little Arnold—you'll like him. You'll like Annabel, too. My wife."

She wanted to ask, "Are you happy?" but heard herself say, "I'm happy for you. We're still neighbors?"

He nodded. "But my parents are dead. Is Angelinh'

Granny expecting you? I think not. We would all have known. . . ."

"Mr. Braganza tells me she does not come down much anymore. Is she all right? I've had no news."

"Oh, she's getting to be housebound, but Annabel helps." He hesitated. "And your coming home, what a wonderful surprise. I know you didn't write. I'm the mailman now, and would certainly have seen your letter."

"I must go now," she said. "I'm anxious to get home, it's been too long a time. I must meet your wife, Martin. Little Arnold, too."

He stood by, holding the cab door open as she got in. "You used to call me Mottu," he reminded her, smiling. "So did everybody else. They still do, and so should you. If you asked anyone for Martin, they wouldn't know whom you meant." They laughed. "You remember the way?"

"Mr. Braganza just told me." She waved good-bye.

"It's a very sharp right," he warned. To the driver he said, "Go slow, or you will miss it."

"I'll show them the way," one of the street urchins said, and he ran down the road to the corner, beckoning to the driver to follow him. The taxi groaned as it lurched along the lane that wound steeply uphill, while the small band of curious urchins skipped alongside, delighted to be escorting the unexpected visitor. The houses were built helter-skelter along the slope, and lanes to the left and right wound in between them like miniature ravines. Like ravines, too, during the two annual monsoons they drained off the water after each blinding downpour, feeding it into the nullah.

She remembered many of the homes now, the yellow pillars on one, the red front on another, but could only guess at the identity of the men and women who lounged in the open porches or looked up curiously from their labors in the gardens. A half smile on her face, she leaned out the window, waving excitedly when she spotted a familiar face; and it did seem that some of them recognized her, flashing a delighted smile after the first shock of surprise, dashing out into the lane to wave after her, or rushing into their homes to spread the news of her arrival. The one alien structure was the large house she had seen from the hill. The long flat roof had no tiles at all, but a terrace on top; it would have fit better in a Bombay suburb than it did in Tivolem.

"It's been built by a man from the Persian Gulf," her driver said, admiringly. "I saw it go up. There's money there."

A minute later, she saw the familiar garden wall come up and asked the man to stop. Overcome by emotion, she stood by the cross, facing the old wrought iron gate and the scraggly stone steps that led up to the family home. The house seemed much smaller than she remembered it; and so, too, did the garden, and the guava tree, whose crisp green-turning-yellow fruit had once seemed so out of reach they made her mouth water. She looked up at the house again, expecting at any moment to see the door swing open and her mother step out onto the pillared balcão. With memories tugging at her heart she fought to regain her composure. The children, now uneasy at her delay, whispered among themselves; but the boy who had led the way raced up the steps ahead of her and waited for her to come up and knock.

When she did, there was no answer. Marie-Santana could have pushed open the unlatched door, could have gone in, calling out the customary "Oh, good people in the house!" to announce her presence, but she preferred to knock again and wait outside so her grandmother could see her, and she her grandmother, in full sunshine. She heard the soft dragging of slippers on bare floor, watched the door creak inwards, and then saw Angelinh' Granny standing in the doorway, not the Granny she had known, but a woman quite bent, quite old, peering at the cataract-blurred figure before her.

"Who stands there, bai?" she said.

"Grandmother," said Marie-Santana, her heart pounding, "don't you recognize me?"

Angelinh' Granny peered closer then, took Marie-Santana's face in both hands, ran palms and fingers over cheeks, ears, forehead, nose, mouth, chin, then fell to weeping, "Lord, my God! Lord, my God! My Mar'-Santan', you have come back to bless me in my old age."

6

THE MORNING AFTER her arrival, Marie-Santana was walking back from the village store when she espied the owner of the new house as he walked among the coconut palms and mango trees in his garden. She was pleasantly surprised; she had imagined a stout, indolent, ill-kempt man, the popular caricature of a village *bhatkar;* instead, she saw a thin, wiry, well-groomed individual, whose very walk conveyed a sense of purpose.

"God give you a good day, Senhor Eusebio," she called from the middle of the lane. "Are you enjoying your garden?" She had fallen easily once again into the conventions of time and place; elsewhere, one began a conversation by commenting on the weather; here, one began by asking whether people were doing whatever it was one saw them doing.

He returned the greeting. "God grant you grace. You know my name?" She could see dirt on his hands; he had been digging.

"Who doesn't, around here? I'm Marie-Santana, Angelinh's granddaughter. She told me about you."

"Of course! I heard you were back. You find things changed?"

She laughed. "Only by your house. Time stands still here. But your house, it's quite a place."

"I'll take that as a compliment. It's too much of a place, for some people, but it's mine. If you'd care to see it, you're welcome to visit. Bring Granny along. I'll show you around."

"Thank you, but I'd have to carry her here. She rarely leaves the house now."

"Well, that won't be a problem," he said. "I have a car."

"A car!" Cars and taxis in Mapusa and Panjim and at the river crossings, yes, but a car in Tivolem? Things had indeed changed.

"A Model T. The latest. You've been to the market?"

"To Atmaram's—we were short of flour. Well, I must go."

"Any time you'd like to visit," he said, and she nodded, continuing on her way.

Eusebio Pinto, a man of modest beginnings, but now "Euseb' baab" to his social inferiors and Senhor Eusebio to his peers, had gone to the Persian Gulf at the end of the Great War in 1918, having heard that the Turks had been ousted and great things would be afoot. Then aged forty, he had wound up accepting a position as a low-salaried clerk with a British oil company prospecting in Mesopotamia, but the word that his fond mother spread around Tivolem was that he was there because the *feringhee* had sent for him. From his modest paycheck he unfailingly sent his aging parents a monthly stipend, intending they should spend it on their food or other essentials; instead, his mother bought a candle a day, which she burnt at the altar of Saint Cornelius, imploring his blessings on her son. Her prayers bore fruit; Eusebio's diligence earned him promotions, though not large salary increases; however, as he had found no place in which to spend his earnings, and he had absolutely no vices, his savings mounted. When his parents died, he transferred to his now substantial bank balance both his attention and his affections. He retired and returned to his native village thirteen years after he had left it, saw the cramped house he had been born in and the small plot on which it stood, and was dissatisfied. At the vicar's suggestion he turned to

Pedro Saldanha. When none of the houses they looked at met his needs, Eusebio, shrewd manager that he was, looked about for land he could acquire and build on. A lot of land.

The search did not take long. A great stretch of the village, running alongside the nullah, caught his eye. "Who owns all this?" he asked Pedro Saldanha.

"Dona Esmeralda. But it's not for sale."

"It's a lot more than she needs."

"People need as much as they have, and usually want much more."

Senhor Eusebio, uncertain whether this was a barb directed at him, looked sharply at his companion. But Pedro Saldanha's expression was stolid; the vicar had said he was a taciturn and plainspoken man. Eusebio decided to say no more.

Through Postmaster Braganza he found that Dona Esmeralda's tenants included Fortunato the tavernkeeper, known popularly as Forttu, he who sold not only choice coconut-palm liquor but also Johnny Walker Scotch ("Born 1820, still going strong," a jaunty sign proclaimed); the shopkeeper Atmaram and his family; Govind the carpenter, his wife Amita, and their five small children; and Kashinath the barber, with his wife Rukmini and four children. Dona Esmeralda had been their landlady since the 1890s, as her husband's family had been for generations before that; with the Great Depression, however, the old widow had fallen on hard times, and it did not help that, like their ancestors before them, her tenants paid no rent, but gave payment in kind—in produce, in loyalty, and in services.

Armed with this knowledge, Senhor Eusebio looked for an intermediary. Neither Pedro Saldanha nor the postmaster would do for that purpose; instead, he decided that Dona Esmeralda should be approached through someone of equal social status, and late on a Sunday morning called on Senhor Marcelo and Dona Elena.

He was met at the door by the maid. "The master's not in," she said immediately, standing squarely in the doorway.

"Actually," he said, embarrassed, "I'm sorry to have missed him, but I've come to talk to your bai."

Reluctantly she ushered him into the vast living room, inviting him to sit while she went to fetch her mistress.

Hat in hand, he sat somewhat nervously on the edge of a heavily carved chair. His childhood home, too, had had old chairs that his parents had prized, but the one he was sitting on was a precious antique, made of the finest ebony, and, like the rest of the furniture here, a couple of centuries old at least; he was not sure how it would hold up under his weight. A large crystal chandelier that hung in the center was used, he gathered, on rare social occasions, as were the sconces high on each wall, light being usually provided by the ornate oil lamps that were placed around the room. Six tall windows overlooked the garden; from the facing wall the portraits of bearded ancestors glowered down at him with fierce intensity. He had seen that same type of portrait in other homes; even the women seemed grim. That was the generation Dona Esmeralda belonged to; he hoped Dona Elena, whom he knew but slightly from meeting her casually at church and on the street, would be more accommodating.

He found Dona Elena to be pleasantly sociable. She apologized for her husband's absence. She remembered both of Senhor Eusebio's parents, though they had lived on the other side of the village and had been dead some years. She asked him about his years in the Gulf. And she offered him tea that the maid brought in in elegant diminutive china cups, and raisin cake on exquisite dishes.

He had to wade through minutes of small talk before Dona Elena allowed a moment of silence to develop. She was sitting upright in her chair, cup in hand, waiting for him to speak.

He decided to come right to the point. "I'd like to build myself a bigger house," he said, "and I need land."

"That could be a problem. The village is heavily built up, and all land around here is already owned."

"I realize that. People will not easily part with what they hold."

"There are sentimental attachments that develop," Dona Elena said. "And reluctances. Status—you'll understand. . . . It's not like selling off a bit of furniture, though heaven knows that, too, can be traumatic. But there are roots, and memories. . . . Quite aside from which, none of our properties are up for sale."

"Your land is working for you, and that's not the land I'm after," he said. "But your friend Dona Esmeralda has the largest tracts around here. Perhaps on my behalf you could ask if she's willing to sell, all or at least part."

"Dona Esmeralda is more attached to her land than I am to mine," Dona Elena said. "Besides, she is deeply involved in the lives of her tenants, and they in hers."

"With all the respect due Dona Esmeralda, the times are hard," he said. "The Great Depression—it has not treated people kindly. Me, I've been fortunate; I had nothing, and went where the oil was. I saved up some money. She, on the other hand, is in dire straits; that's common knowledge, but she need not know that I know. Sooner or later she'll have to sell. In telling her I'm interested, you'll be doing your old friend a favor. I've looked into the land; I'll pay five thousand rupees for it. That's a fair price, and in these times, it's quite a lot of money."

As Dona Elena had foreseen, Dona Esmeralda's initial reluctance to sell ancestral lands to a nouveau riche was compounded by concern for her tenants and fears for the future.

"My son, I'm thinking of my son," Dona Esmeralda said.

"Of course," Dona Elena said.

"Artistic, but shiftless. No, don't protest," Dona Esmeralda said, as her visitor made a move to interrupt her. "The whole world knows it is so. Barnabé has a wife and child, has been married ten years, lives in Goregão, is almost fifty years old, and still he comes to me for money. You've

38

seen his business—antiques and clutter, that's what I call it. Nobody buys the stuff he has. Without land to fall back on, what will he do when I'm gone?"

"You still have vast properties in Aiconá," Dona Elena said.

"But that's a far-off village."

"Maybe so, but the land there is valuable. More valuable than any of the parcels you have here."

"If only Romualdo were here!" Dona Esmeralda cried. "What a mess. What a mess! You have your Marcelo, but I? Why do our men die and leave us with a mess?"

"You need time to think," Dona Elena said, embracing her old friend and comforting her. "I'll come back tomorrow."

When they met again, Dona Esmeralda was visibly perturbed. "Word has gotten around. My tenants are greatly distressed."

"That's understandable. Over the years you have been more than generous with them."

"No more than Romualdo would have been. Or his parents and grandparents before him. But the truth is, they can't hold on to me forever."

"Fortunately, most of them have grown children."

"Except for Govind and Amita. Of their five children, the oldest is just six years old. And all those goats! Govind and Amita depend on me for everything. They came to see me yesterday, bringing their little ones, pleading that the land they were on not be sold. Govind fell at my feet. 'You are my father and my mother,' he said. 'Do not abandon us.' The children began crying. What am I to do? Eusebio's right—I need the money, and if I don't get it today I'll need twice as much tomorrow. But those children! I hugged them, and they cried and clung to me, not knowing why they were crying. On this I am adamant—I will sell Eusebio the rest of the land, but not Govind's patch. No. Those children. . . . Never."

Senhor Eusebio was upset. "I'm from this village, too," he said to Dona Elena. "I feel for the people here. What makes her think I'll be rough with her tenants? Does she think I'm an ogre? That makes me angry."

"But do you see her point?" Dona Elena countered. "She has known their parents and their grandparents; has celebrated their weddings, rejoiced at their births, mourned each passing. She has been their protectress and their benefactress far longer than you and I have lived."

He would not be mollified. "And probably spoils them rotten, while they rob her blind. If I can't have Govind's plot, I must reduce my offer. Or withdraw it completely."

"And then you won't have your house. The five thousand you offered, and she gets to keep Govind's plot."

"You're as tough as an Arab sheikh," he said.

"And, alas! not quite as unctuous."

"Tell the old bat I agree to her terms," he said. "She can keep her Govind, her Amita, and all the kids, both two- and four-footed."

The deal concluded, on an extended idle lot he set about building himself the second largest house in the village, a bit larger than Dona Elena's, though neither as large nor as grand as Dona Esmeralda's, and certainly not quite as elegant. Her house, after all, was three hundred years old; people knew how to build houses in those days, as she once remarked to a visitor, the gossip Josephine Aunty, under rather extreme provocation.

Senhor Eusebio knew just the kind of house he wanted. Not for him the sloping roofs with interlocking rows of curved mud-brown tile found in every village in Goa; those tiles tended to break if any hard object fell on them; but even if they didn't, they had to be removed and reset each year, since they shifted with the action of the wind and the sun and the rain. Besides, he wanted a house that would be unique—made not just out of red laterite rock but with outer walls made of poured cement concrete, a flat roof to match, and a terrace on top that would be open to the skies.

Tivolem had not seen so much activity in decades. The

laborers worked in long lines, the men picking up the large red rectangular stones as the lorries brought them in from the quarry to the mouth of the narrow lane, then carrying them on their heads to the worksite; the women sometimes carrying stones, sometimes mortar, sometimes sand, but more often two large gleaming copper potfuls of water, one on their heads and one at the hip, for the mixing of the concrete. Like so many busy and conscientious insects, they then retraced their steps, picking up yet other burdens to deliver.

People came from as far away as Vasco da Gama in the south and Pernem in the north to gawk at the work in progress. Reaction in Tivolem itself was mixed. Senhor Eusebio's new tenant families showered it with praise, but were inwardly concerned, wondering whether their new landlord would take some of its cost out of their hides.

Dona Esmeralda felt no such contraints. It was her habit to go on a ritual stroll through the village each evening, with her three black wirehaired terriers running ahead in single file, to receive obeisance from her former vassals. As the new house took shape, she was disturbed by the style of construction. Yet she kept her own counsel, confiding only in Dona Elena when the latter paid her a visit and they both sat down to tea: "An ugly monstrosity—it does not belong. The man has much money but absolutely no taste."

Dona Elena agreed. "But there's good and bad in everything," she pointed out soothingly. "Let's thank God for the money and blame the bad taste on the devil."

Dona Esmeralda was not amused. She was even less amused when a bustling Josephine Aunty stopped by, demanding an audience, soon after Dona Elena had left. After a proper wait, Dona Esmeralda met her on the balcão; not everybody got to see the inside of her house.

Josephine Aunty wasted no time: "Wonderful news! Senhor Eusebio is enlarging his plans. He now wants the terrace on the roof to be large enough so a dance band can fit in one corner."

"A band!"

"Not a very big band. But he says he finds the village is much too quiet. Once in a while, he'd like to see some dancing and revelry in the evenings."

So shocked was Josephine Aunty by Dona Esmeralda's emotional reaction to this bulletin that she reported the conversation verbatim to Senhor Eusebio, adding a few turns of her own.

Senhor Eusebio was in a charitable mood. "Let her be," he said. "I'm not troubled by her criticism of my plans. She should talk! Her roof leaks."

"He says your roof leaks," Josephine Aunty reported to Dona Esmeralda, salvaging what mischief she could out of the mild response. It was a damaging blow, because true. Come the monsoon rains, Dona Esmeralda's roof leaked not just in one place but in several. No sooner had a servant placed a bucket to catch the rainwater dripping through in one spot than others had to scurry to place pots and pans where more leaks began to sprout. "I'm told that in her house the drumming of raindrops on various metals is like a percussion concerto," Senhor Eusebio had added. This, too, Josephine Aunty had reported.

Dona Esmeralda stopped speaking to Senhor Eusebio, and Senhor Eusebio continued to provoke her by raising his hat and bowing slightly each time she passed the construction site. Her dogs, sensing the mood, bared their teeth and snarled at him. In time, she passed that way less and less often.

The house was completed in January of 1932, and Senhor Eusebio moved in immediately. Josephine Aunty revisited Dona Esmeralda. "New furniture in every room," she reported happily.

"Couldn't afford antiques?" Dona Esmeralda wanted to know, her eyebrows arching over the top of her lorgnette.

"Now he's added some," Josephine Aunty came back to say a week later.

"Probably fakes," Dona Esmeralda said. "One does not know antiques until one has lived with antiques. All of one's life."

"Dona Esmeralda should know—she has lived with herself all her life," was Senhor Eusebio's somewhat ungallant reply.

Josephine Aunty, while fearing for her own safety, reported that sally.

"I do not trade personal insults," Dona Esmeralda said, retreating to moral high ground. But in time she got her revenge. In the monsoon that year, one of the most severe in memory, her roof leaked water like a squeezed sponge, but Senhor Eusebio's leaked worse still. The flat roof and open terrace with its retaining walls acted as a cistern where rainwater accumulated; it seeped through the ceiling, and ran in great streams down the insides of the walls, continuing to come down into the house long after the squall itself had passed.

"If my house is a percussion concerto, his is a *perpetuum mobile*," Dona Esmeralda quipped, when Josephine Aunty told her of the floods in the enemy camp. "A movement that never ends—and the worst is yet to come."

Dona Esmeralda resumed her leisurely walks through the village, preceded by her feisty terriers. Senhor Eusebio now did his best to avoid meeting her in public, but this became difficult, since each time they saw him the dogs rushed furiously at him, barking until she chose to call them off. She herself, however, remained the model of propriety, forcing him to acknowledge her presence by lifting her silver-knobbed cane in salutation and nodding her head in a most gracious manner.

7

THE GARDEN drew Marie-Santana outdoors. The rose patch her father had planted alongside the square balcão demanded special attention; the bushes had not only survived, but now, unkempt, resembled a thicket. On her first day home, she cleared the debris; the next morning, after she had tended to Angelinh' Granny and returned from the bazaar, she was out in the garden again. She had pruned and watered the roses and begun trimming the flowering jasmine when she heard a violin softly tuning up; by the time she had tied the shrub onto its trellis, the lilt of a Viennese waltz filled the air. She could not pinpoint the source; floating and ethereal, the sound could have come from anywhere. When the music stopped, curiosity got the better of her, and she went out into the lane, but by then the unseen violinist had disappeared. Back at her tasks, she was watering the brilliant-leaved crotons and the hibiscus when she heard footsteps in the lane. "I can smell the jasmine once again," a voice said, admiringly.

Startled, Marie-Santana looked up to see a smiling, elegantly dressed woman at the gate. In the glow of the pink parasol she was carrying, the face, lightly lined and in partial shadow, was vaguely familiar.

"Maria-Santana, isn't it?" the visitor gave the name a

Portuguese inflection, changing "Marie" to "Maria," and tasting every syllable. "Back just one day, and already I hear you're working miracles. I'm Elena de Penha Fonseca. Since I was passing by, I thought I'd welcome you home and see for myself what the excitement was about."

"Come in, do come in, Dona Elena," Marie-Santana said, her voice conveying her surprise and pleasure, as she wiped her hands on her hips and bustled up to the gate.

"I can only stay a moment. Marcelo will be back from Panjim shortly, and I must see the servants about lunch. You remember my husband?"

"Senhor Marcelo? Of course!" Marie-Santana said. "I was going to visit you both. I remember your wedding, though I was only a child, and we left for Africa, I think, the very next day. You made a handsome couple! Do you have children?"

"A daughter, Maria, just turned sixteen. You know how it is—an awkward stage. She needs company her own age, and there's none, not in our village. Our youngsters, they finish their schooling and off they go to college in Bombay. We've kept her home and babied her, our only child. Perhaps that was a mistake. Time will tell."

"Has she been to Bombay at all?"

"I may send her there for a month or two later this year," Dona Elena replied. "Right now, she will not leave my side. But we have relatives there, and the break will do her good." She sighed.

The church bell struck the noon Angelus and, beyond the garden, the village suddenly grew still. Even the birds seemed silent. Dona Elena crossed herself and Marie-Santana quickly followed her example, the two of them standing a full minute in silent prayer.

"It's been long since I last said the Angelus at this hour," Marie-Santana said. "I had forgotten it rings here three times a day."

Dona Elena nodded. "You'll get used to it. Ours is a sleepy village, and change comes slowly, when it comes at all; sometimes, as you can well imagine, it's change of the sort we'd rather not have."

Marie-Santana, following her gaze, found herself looking down the lane toward Senhor Eusebio's new house. "I met the owner not an hour ago," she said. "A charming man."

"I'll grant you that—he has his moments. Besides, your garden will make that thing more bearable," Dona Elena added, laughing. "Your garden, and the sound of a certain violin."

"I meant to ask—who's the violinist? I thought the best musicians around here were the songbirds that woke me up this morning."

"Aren't they wonderful? He, too—our new neighbor, the man from Kuala Lumpur. You haven't met him yet?"

"I did, briefly, at the post office. Mr. Braganza introduced us. But he said he was a retired civil servant, not a musician."

"Well, Simon Fernandes is both. But he's a shy man, has made few friends. Marcelo met him once, but my husband speaks no English, and Simon speaks nothing else. Perhaps you can help draw him out?"

Marie-Santana looked at her quickly, but said nothing.

"Just a neighborly thing," Dona Elena said. "You'll see, not he alone but lots of people here will need you. From what I see, Tivolem itself needs you."

"Perhaps, but not as much as I may need Tivolem."

"In that case," Dona Elena said, "everybody wins."

Marie-Santana's devoted caring for Angelinh' Granny became the talk of the village. Granny's neighbors, who had shopped for her, cleaned for her, cooked for her, every day of the week, found Marie-Santana doing all this and more. She bathed Granny daily, first heating the water she drew from the well, then mixing hot and cold to the right temperature before passing each jugful to her grandmother. Daily, she massaged her grandmother's scalp with coconut oil, and was allowed to comb the hair, but not to tie it back in the traditional knot; Granny insisted on doing this herself. "I'm not yet that old," she said.

Though the spacious rooms Marie-Santana remembered roaming in as a child now seemed to have shrunk, they still took a lot of cleaning. Her parents, when they had lived there, had maintained a staff of three—a maid to look after her and do general housework, a cook, and a factotum. Granny in her old age had had to let the domestics go, relying instead on occasional cleanings by one of Atmaram's daughters, and the daily ministrations of willing neighbors.

What furniture was left was utilitarian: a cupboard for clothes, a chair, and a bed in each bedroom; four rickety chairs at the oblong dining table, and a cupboard for the dishes and what was left of the silverware; a bookcase, three armchairs, a carved sofa, an easy chair in the living room; and a rocking chair, creaky but still serviceable, placed in the balcão, where Granny liked to sit of an afternoon, inhaling snuff. There had been more chairs, more tables and bookcases, more furniture overall, Marie-Santana remembered; some ornamental vases, a half-dozen ornate lamps. Granny said she had given some away to people who needed them; she could not recall what had happened to the rest.

A chore Marie-Santana had particularly liked as a child was drawing water from the broad, deep well. Standing on tiptoe by the kitchen window, she still had had to stretch to snare the noose that dangled just outside; then, the pot securely fastened, she would send it swinging outward and let it drop into the well, the spiny rope scorching her palms as it spun over the pulley, the heavy pot hurtling downward till it smacked into the water, burbling as it sank. She'd count the bubbles and wait, until the rope itself, bearing dead weight, dared her to pull. With one leg well back of the other, front foot braced against the window wall, she would heave and lean back, reach up on the rope and heave and lean back, with gasps and grunts of joy and occasional yelps that always brought one or other of the servants, or even Angelinh' Granny, to her rescue. "I'll do it, Granny," she'd insist, gritting her teeth, until the gleaming copper pot would swing into view, and she would need help hauling it in.

It had been a game back then, as a child, but drawing water now, these many years later, was a different matter altogether. She had to draw three potfuls for Granny's bath and two for her own; six or seven to water the garden sparingly; another three for cooking and for the scouring and washing of utensils; still more when there were clothes to be laundered. Since at this time of year the level in the well was low, drawing this much water took time and considerable effort. Her arms and shoulders ached, as did the small of her back and her stomach muscles and the whole of her body. "Get the rhythm right," Annabel said encouragingly, "and then it will no longer be such a tug-of-war."

8

FROM WHERE Marie-Santana stood on the brow of the hill, if she put out her left hand to blot out her view of Senhor Eusebio's house, Tivolem was the way she had left it twenty-three years earlier, at the age of twelve. It was still an hour to sunset, and the hilltop around her was alive with goats; but from this height—five hundred feet, her father had said—the village seemed asleep. At the market-place, however, she saw some signs of activity; more rarely, she saw a stray figure or two entering or leaving the church. Saturday evening: confession time.

Unlike the tarred highway that ran due north from the river to Mapusa, bypassing the village, Tivolem's lifeline to that town was a narrow country road, a raised strip between fields, lined for almost its entire length by coconut trees. At this hour the road added to the sense of an endless and languorous siesta—Marie-Santana could hear but not see a lone lorry chugging up a bend in the hill, but along the miles laid out in front of her she saw only a solitary bullock cart and, in the far distance, a speck of a car trailing a comet's cloud of dust. Here on this hilltop, with the wind blowing in from the west, she could smell the salt of the sea, a scant ten miles away. A familiar breeze, a familiar smell. Home. Granny's house she could barely see, but the cross was visible, and the roof of Mottu's house in the dip beyond it. They had stood here as children, she and Mottu, she twelve and he a year older, a day or so before she had sailed off with her parents to Africa. And Mottu, teary-eyed and anguished, had said he loved her. So now he was married; she could see he was happy and she was happy for him; but if it was true, as some philosophers and scientists so stoutly maintained, that nothing is ever lost in the universe, then surely those tremulous words he had spoken were still pulsing there, somewhere around her, swirling in the evening breeze. All she had to do was reach out into the air, and they would settle as softly as butterflies in the palm of her hand. How sweet, she thought, do one's childhood memories grow as one grows older.

Even some memories of Quelimane. In that tiny provincial town, where the family had settled on first arriving in Mozambique, she had found a wider world by far than the Tivolem that had been her universe. British traders and German colonists continually crossed the border, from the west and the north, to sell their produce and replenish their supplies, as did the occasional Boer farmer from far-off South Africa; while the men haggled with Arab and Indian merchants, their wives shopped and the children tagged along. Rosy-cheeked or pale-faced, blue-eyed, hair running to gold, those children stopped to stare at Marie-Santana and her friends at play but made no effort to join in the fun. So she played with Luisa from Lisbon, and Elsa from Mossamedes; with Marco from Lourenço Marques, Mushtaq Ali from Yemen, and Kamat from Mangalore, all of them her classmates at the Portuguese school she attended, and the color of their skin ranged from pale luminous olive through light and dark cinnamon to deepest ebony. Perhaps it was this rich harmony of colors that made the Boer, the British, and the German children stop and stare, just as it was this same harmony that made their distraught mothers seize them by the hand and drag them away. Marie-Santana had wondered at their reaction; she had not, at twelve, learned to recognize in young eyes the fears born of adult prejudices, nor had her parents seen any reason to enlighten her just yet.

In those first months away, Mottu had drifted in and out of her waking world. Occasionally she wrote him a letter that she never mailed. By the time she was thirteen he was seldom in her thoughts. On her thirteenth birthday, her classmate Luisa, a year older than she, brought along an older brother, fresh out of Lisbon. Strumming a Portuguese guitar, his inseparable companion, Alfredo languidly caressed its dark, slender, and beribboned neck while he sang plaintive songs of unrequited love. With the very first *fado* her heart ached suddenly for Mottu; she should have kissed him that last evening on the Tivolem hill the moment he said he loved her, instead of running foolishly home, leaving him to follow slowly, kicking at stones all the way. Ah, this desperate, unrequited love that Alfredo sang about, surely that love was Mottu's! But as Alfredo sang on, Mottu's image faded. She realized then, with that flash of intuition that comes so easily at thirteen, that Alfredo and his guitar were singing directly to her, and that it was Alfredo's love, too, that was truly hopeless. Perhaps it was hopeless because Mottu's image suddenly reappeared; perhaps because Luisa at that moment whispered in her ear that Alfredo had to return to Portugal that week to complete his baccalaureate studies at Coimbra. Later, she had confided her thoughts to Luisa, on promise of utmost secrecy; Luisa, consulting Alfredo, had said he concurred. This left Marie-Santana both pleased and mystified. Concurred in what? That he was in love with her, or that his love was hopeless, or both? It baffled her for days; then she asked Luisa, who didn't know. Since Alfredo by then had sailed for Lisbon, the mystery lingered. She started a secret diary, that only Luisa was allowed to read, and that too at infrequent intervals. When Luisa herself sailed off to Lisbon, the entries ceased.

Late in 1914, with the Great War raging in Europe, Portuguese troops arrived in Mozambique, and although Portugal was officially neutral, skirmishes with German contingents broke out on the northern frontier. At sixteen, Marie-Santana was both excited and troubled. "I thought we were at peace with Germany?" she said to her father, anxiously.

"We are," he replied, "but the world has gone mad. Whatever happens in Europe, let's hope the fighting here ends soon."

It didn't. In 1916 Germany finally declared war. Then came the Portuguese military expeditions, the parades through town with bands playing and flags flying, a nervous but excited populace cheering them on, Marie-Santana among them. She remembered her father humming the national anthem as he tacked a large map of southern Africa to the wall:

Heroes of the sea, noble people, valiant and immortal nation,
Lift up again today the splendor that once was Portugal.

With tiny green flags he marked the Portuguese positions on the south bank of the Ruvuma River; "I'll use red for the Germans," he explained. A few green flags on the north bank showed where inroads had been made into the German colony of Tanganyika.

Then the Germans struck back in November of 1917, chasing the Portuguese troops pell-mell across the border. "A temporary reverse," her father said, placing a red flag on the captured town of Ngomano. He hummed some more:

From the depths of her memory the Fatherland hears
the voice
Of your valorous forebears, guiding you to victory!

By May, red flags sprouted on the north bank of the Lurio River, two hundred miles closer to Quelimane, but still two hundred miles away. "The line will hold," her father said evenly, but she saw his hand tremble as he fumbled to position more green flags between the enemy and Quelimane.

In June he was placing red flags along the coast. Her mother had begun packing their things. "We must go," Marie-Santana heard her mother say. "I don't care where to—Beira, Lourenço Marques, the farther off the better. Even back to Goa."

To arms! To arms! On land and on sea.

Her father's voice now had an edge to it.

To arms! To arms! To fight for our country.
Against the cannons we shall march!

On July 1, he placed one last red flag on Nyamakura; the Germans were just twenty miles away.

She remembered the hurried departure, her father's insistence on saving one last armful of books, the agonizingly long trip to Lourenço Marques, where mustachioed officials huffily insisted the enemy dare not advance any further. In Lourenço Marques tall tales were told of Portuguese bravery; that did not explain why the Germans were now roaming almost at will inside northern Mozambique.

Only after the armistice just four months later, after the family had returned to Quelimane and her father had revived his briefly abandoned business, did she learn from a new employee how the fighting had gone. Almost six feet tall, blond and fair-skinned, John Fernshaw spoke in an accent more exaggeratedly British than any she had heard. In one of the last engagements, he said, Portuguese forces had been reinforced by British troops; there were problems of leadership. The British officers, though outranked and leading a smaller contingent, yet wanted their man to command. It was a desperate situation, he said: the Germans in front, the Lugela River at their backs. With the Germans shouting hurrahs as they attacked, demoralized Britons and Portuguese alike dived headlong into the murky, crocodile-infested waters; he alone, John Fernshaw said, had worked his machine gun until he ran out of ammunition. The Germans, capturing him, had recognized his bravery and let him go. That, too, was what John Fernshaw said.

There were other stories that Fernshaw told, stories she did not quite know whether to believe, of years he had spent in the civil service in Kuala Lumpur with another Englishman, his crazy boss, Old Bartlett, before emigrating to Mozambique.

"Were there Goans there?" she asked.

"Yes, but we Brits kept our distance." When she made a face, he said, "Nothing personal. Civil service code, running the Empire, that sort of thing. Not personal at all."

His stories amused her father vastly and often left him speechless and teary-eyed from laughter.

"Do you believe him?" she had asked.

"Sometimes. At other times he reminds me of Münchhausen."

"You mean he's lying."

"That's one way of looking at it. He's inventing the truth to amuse us. Well, sometimes he does it to impress us. For example, claiming to be British. With his coloring, and his overly British accent, I think he's an Anglo."

"Anglo-Indian?"

"Yes. Does it matter? Not to me, anyway. He's a good employee, and I'm promoting him to assistant manager."

"You're what?"

"You heard right. He's very efficient."

"He's still in his twenties, and he's just joined the firm. The older workers will resent the promotion."

"He looks older than he is," her father said. "And at twenty-five he's seen more of the world. It'll work out, you'll see."

When seven years later her father died, John Fernshaw

was a comfort to the family. He saw to the funeral arrangements and, with the manager out sick for weeks, kept the business running smoothly. He spoke with authority; the men respected him. Her mother responded by giving him greater responsibility in a commercial venture she barely understood. Marie-Santana, thrown into deep despair when her mother died four months later, remembered turning to John Fernshaw as a source of strength. It was then, as he held her close and bent down to kiss the top of her head, that he told her that despite being orphaned she was not alone, that she would never be alone, that he loved her. That is what John Fernshaw said, and this time, without reservation, she believed him; believed him enough to say candidly that she did not love him back, and also enough to place the family business increasingly in his hands. Finally, she found herself falling in love, deeply in love. . . . How was she to know?

Strange, that when in coming home to Granny she had placed an ocean between herself and the dark clouds of her final years in Quelimane, the first man she had been introduced to in Tivolem, the retiree Simon Fernandes, had also, like John Fernshaw, been with the British Civil Service in Kuala Lumpur. John's stories had been about his boss, who like him was an Englishman; but though he had never mentioned a Simon Fernandes by name, it seemed clear to her that they must have been contemporaries, and, despite the racial divide, perhaps even friends. If, then, finding out she had just returned from Quelimane, Simon should ask about his former colleague, what should she say? Admit she had known him, and then be faced with a flood of unwelcome questions? Fernshaw was the last person in the world she'd want to talk about; those memories were too bitter. If Simon asked, she'd say no, she'd never met the man, never even heard of him.

Brusquely she erased Quelimane from her mind, focusing instead on the new phase of her life—this sheltering village below her, older than remembered time. Dona Esmeralda's house, so plainly visible down there with its massive walls, its long twin roofs, its gnarled and ancient guardian trees, reputedly the oldest dwelling in Tivolem, three hundred years old—surely such a palatial structure would not have been built unless the village had already been solidly there, waiting for a master, waiting perhaps for centuries. And yet the village was measured in terms of Dona Esmeralda's house, rather than the other way around. Dona Elena's, built a full century later but with walls almost as thick as Dona Esmeralda's, denoting privilege, rose this side of Granny's, right at the point where the lane forked—one branch going east down a gentle slope toward Dona Esmeralda's, the other winding uphill. But though the two houses were thus connected by sharing a common lane, Dona Elena's was built far enough away that it could not have been considered an intrusion, and on a scale modest enough not to be a threat.

And now, in addition, there was Senhor Eusebio's. Its very outlandishness invited attention; one could not long keep from looking at it—his monument to new money, his gesture of defiance in the face of privilege. And the contrast went deeper: He alone had a car; Dona Esmeralda used a coach drawn by bulls; Dona Elena, having neither, had to send for public conveyances. It's the outside world, Marie-Santana recognized then; that's where the changes were coming from, changes that would alter, for better or worse, her beloved Tivolem. On one side, the Eusebios, the Teodosios, the Simons of the world, returning with a car, a gun, an expensive violin, and, above all, with money; on the other, the Esmeraldas and the Elenas, the vicars and curates and regedores, clinging to stability; she herself, who could have returned comfortably off but hadn't, somewhere in the middle. But are they the village, she asked herself, these people who already have and are struggling to hold or struggling to gain what power there is? After the Eusebios supplant the Esmeraldas, will they not be supplanted in turn and in time? But by whom?

"It will be getting dark soon, bai, and the jackals will be out. Would you know the safe path back to the village?" a voice asked at her elbow. Looking down, she saw a boy of perhaps ten, chewing on a straw, the goats crowding at his side.

Touched by his concern for her safety, she reached out to stroke his head, and he, puzzled and disconcerted, pulled back.

"I'll come with you," she said.

The boy turned the lead goat around, and on impulse she said, "Give me the stick. I'll help you drive them down."

A little apprehensive, he said, "This twig's not for beating. They don't need it. We don't have to drive them—they know the way, and they're anxious to go home. All we have to do is watch over and follow them. If we drive them too hard, or beat them, they'll run and scatter."

"I'll be careful," she said.

"Hutt!" the boy said, prodding the lead goat lightly in the ribs. "Hutt-hutt!" He handed her the twig.

The goats followed the twisting path down the side of the hill at a pace so brisk Marie-Santana had to take off her sandals to keep from sliding. It was a long and steep descent. As they neared the first houses, the goats quickened their gait; then, ignoring the barking dogs, began to peel off in small groups, each heading down a different alley toward its own home. By the time they neared the cross, the flock had been reduced to eight.

Marie-Santana was quite out of breath. She could see Simon in his balcão, as she had seen him on other days at this hour, in white undershirt and khaki shorts, violin nestled against his cheek. His eyes were fixed on her garden, but his mind was engrossed in the music; he had neither seen nor heard them come from the other direction.

"We can stop now, bai," the boy said. "These last few are Amita's. They'll find their way home."

Together they watched the goats head down the lane and turn into Amita's compound.

"Do you go to school?" she asked.

"In the mornings," he said. "Whenever I can. When I'm not helping. Will you be going to the hilltop again?"

"Sometimes."

"I'll let you drive the goats down again if I see you."

"That will be nice."

"I must go now," he said. "My mother's waiting."

"You and Amita," she murmured softly to his retreating back, as he faded into the dusk. "You and Amita—you are the heart of the village, and its future. You will outlast us all."

Over the next few days, Marie-Santana not only transformed the flower garden but planted vegetable seedlings as well. Simon, playing the violin in his usual spot, idly noted her slow but methodical progress: rows of beans and okra, tomato, onion, cabbage, row upon row of hot red chilies. People marveled at her gardening skill.

"A woman such as she deserves a husband," said Annabel, Mottu's wife, who lived directly across the lane and had quickly become a good friend. Josephine Aunty, standing within earshot, felt a needle under the skin.

"But then, Annabel," she said, "you want everyone to marry. Think how many times you tried to arrange a match for me, and that too in spite of my protests. And the men you were trying to help! Not that there was anything wrong with them, but sometimes a woman just has to wait for the right man to come along."

Annabel bit back a tart reply. "A pity," she said, "that we have three wealthy bachelors in our midst, and every last one of them is much too old for her."

"What bothers me," Josephine Aunty said, "is not why she has never married, but why she has come back poor from Africa. And it's not as though she has known starvation, or anything."

"What makes you say that?" said Annabel.

"Well, just look at her. She may not be as plump as you, but she's no bag of bones, either."

"So why don't you ask her?" said Annabel. "Why not come right out and ask her, 'Why are you not rich?'"

"She will not talk about her life over there," Josephine Aunty grumbled. "Not even to me, though when she was a baby I dandled her on my knee. Lord knows I've tried to draw her out. Why the mystery? What went wrong? She says to me, 'That's the past. This is the present.' All the while, I'm thinking: Look at our people who went overseas, the same bachelors you mentioned, all came back with money put away. Senhor Eusebio now has built himself a fine palace; Senhor Teodosio spends his time hunting, not a care in the world; Mr. Fernandes is busy with his stamps or out in his balcão playing the violin. That's all I'm thinking. But others are making comparisons, some saying, 'All those years in Mozambique, and she comes back with just a steamer trunk and a bedroll? That's no more than a college student brings home after ten months in Bombay.'"

"Some of those same people," said Annabel, "when they first heard she had returned, felt she would be one of those returnees who put on fine clothes and fancy airs, and look down on the likes of us."

"I never said that!" said Josephine Aunty, indignantly.

"You may not have, but your mouth certainly did," Annabel retorted.

"She came back from Africa wearing a dress, but has switched to a sari," Josephine Aunty said. "Don't you find that strange? We single women here wear dresses until we marry—Hindus and Christians both! Then we wear a sari. That's the custom. Look at me! Do I wear a sari? If I did, it would confuse everybody."

"Her wearing a sari, that bothers you?" Annabel asked. "You follow custom, that's fine; she has chosen to break it. And if married women must wear saris, as you say, why are Dona Elena and Dona Esmeralda still wearing dresses?"

"It's different with the gentlefolk," Josephine Aunty said.

"They have the land and the money, they can do as they please. They speak Portuguese and dress Western style."

"And that's what I like about Mar'-Santan'. She speaks Portuguese, too, and English, and yet puts on no airs. Look how she's adapted to our ways. She is, truly, one of us."

"Well, then, Annabel," said Josephine Aunty, "now that she's such a favorite of yours, I suppose you'll go from saying Mar'-Santan' this, Mar'-Santan' that, to just calling her Mariemana."

"Marie-my-sister!" said Annabel. "Thank you for suggesting it. I like the sound. Yes, I'll certainly call her Mariemana."

9

MARIE-SANTANA looked forward to hearing the soft sound of Simon's violin as she worked each day in her garden. The mellow throbbing notes lifted her spirits and made the chores lighter. At times she would break off from her planting and weeding entirely and just stand there, long minutes, letting the music surround and soothe her. But lately the pattern had changed. What was now heard in the village of Tivolem was a harsh and strident sound that began each morning some four hours after cock-crow, and continued with hardly a break until the sun rose high enough overhead to all but wipe out one's shadow.

The sound troubled her. With the hillslope itself acting as a natural reflector, it could be heard right down to the fields—so strongly and so jarringly that when Pedro Saldanha's poultry began laying fewer and fewer eggs each day, some neighbors insisted on blaming the violin, when otherwise they would have said it was caused by the evil eye. Pedro Saldanha himself did not complain; instead, he added an extra half hour to the time he spent in church each day, a fact that was duly noted. Was he praying for more eggs, sweeter music, or for a certain bow arm to fall off at the elbow? Pedro smiled, refusing to tell.

Simon did not mean for his playing to be jarring; not at

all. All he wanted to do was prove a point. In Kuala Lumpur, his violinistic skills had helped fill the concert hall; in Tivolem, he could play only for his own pleasure, although lately as he drew bow to string he was well aware of Marie-Santana's voluptuous presence bending over the roses, especially bending over her roses. His playing seemed to have the power to draw her into the garden. But an audience of one, even if appreciative, was not enough; he craved again to share his art with a wider public. And he recalled that from the Middle Ages, and perhaps even earlier, music had been one of the chief glories of the Church. There was music to be made during Mass, and also at the various litanies and vespers that marked the feast days, and though he was an indifferent Catholic, tending even to agnosticism, the prospect of playing fine religious music enthused him. The Church of Saint Cornelius the Contrite, however, already had a violinist on its payroll, a retired and much-loved music teacher from the parochial school who had grown deaf and whose fingers now rarely dropped on their appointed places on the strings. What's more, the man controlled the choir, and their singing matched his playing. Strangely, nobody complained of the cacophony. Simon at first had decided to bide his time; it would not be long, he felt, before people found out how especially fine a violinist he himself was, and turned to him to provide more inspiring and better played music on Sundays.

Weeks passed. Finally, tired of waiting, he had boldly suggested to the new curate that the old violinist be asked to retire because he played so out of tune; to which the priest had gratuitously responded that God looks beyond the outward out-of-tuneness to the grand celestial music surging within.

Now Simon's sole intent was to prove to himself, to the village at large, but most of all to the curate—Father Francisco Antonio Xavier or Antonio Francisco Xavier or Francisco Xavier Antonio Candido or whatever—that he was a violinist, yes, a violinist, and a violinist of the finest

calibre, good enough to be concertmaster of the Kuala
Lumpur Philharmonic, and therefore good enough to be
heard at Mass and other services at the Church of Saint
Cornelius the Contrite, no matter what the curate or anyone else thought.

The way Simon set about proving his point was by practicing scales, and arpeggios, and double and triple stops,
and glissandos, and double-stop glissandos—hideous slides
performed on two strings simultaneously; a sound that
reminded the villagers not of music as they understood it,
to be played and digested one sinuously unsteady note at
a time, but of the day some years earlier when Rukmini's
she-buffalo was trying to deliver herself of an oversized
calf. Or so they said. But they also remembered that once
the calf had been delivered, that had been the end of the
bellowing; while the scraping on the violin. . . .

Senhor Eusebio had not been in Tivolem—in fact he had
been a couple of thousand miles away in the Persian Gulf—
at the time the she-buffalo's historic delivery was taking
place, but he could still empathize with the villagers. He
liked to sit on his rooftop terrace of an evening, enjoying
the breeze blowing in from the ocean, but at the first sound
of the violin being tuned he would head for the stairs like a
crab scuttling into its hole. The vicar and the curate, early
risers both, shared Senhor Eusebio's feelings. In the still
morning air, each stroke of the bow, each slide of the fingers,
was magnified and heard in the rectory not just through the
ears but through the nerve-endings themselves.

"It's enough to curdle the milk in one's tea," Senhor
Eusebio said to the vicar, but with him it was just a figure
of speech, since he always drank his tea black. "I much prefer Teodosio; at least, when he plays the mandolin, he plays
what I consider real music. Music I can listen to, music I
can sing." He stretched out the "s" in "sing," and made the
"ng" resonate.

The curate was even more forthright, as Josephine
Aunty found when she sought his opinion. As the vicar's

right-hand man, he had been restudying his Latin idioms, and had come up with one that he felt fit the situation perfectly.

Josephine Aunty promptly conveyed it to Simon Fernandes: "He says your playing reminds him of an *asinus ad*—an *asinus ad lyram,* a donkey sitting down at the lyre."

The violinist berated her for interrupting him in the middle of a passage in double stops, but made no other reply. Instead, he set about applying fresh rosin to his bow, using full, steady, controlled strokes that displayed admirable bow-arm technique. Disappointed at his apparent refusal to join battle, Josephine left, as slowly as she could, even lingering at the gate before finally slamming it shut.

When Simon finally found the answer he had so desperately been seeking, he put down his bow and his little cake of well-rubbed rosin and rushed to the edge of the balcão.

"It reminds him of a donkey because he has the ears of a jackass," Simon shouted into the lane; and though there was no longer a soul in sight to hear him, he felt very much better.

10

"You did not write," Angelinh' Granny repeated. "I can't understand why you didn't write."

It was a conversation Marie-Santana dreaded, a circular conversation, and it kept recurring. This was the third time since her return.

"I've told you—because I had no news that would be pleasing to you."

"Just knowing you were well, that you were alive, would have been pleasing enough."

"I was wrong not to keep in touch, Granny, and I'm truly sorry. But it happened, and now I can't redo the past. So please let's not talk about it anymore, all right?"

"Then let's talk about the future. The money your father had set aside, that would have taken care of your future—what happened to it?"

"Once Papa died, the business ate it up as fast as it had once earned it."

"That happened to a lot of people. Why couldn't you have written and told me just that?"

"Because I was ashamed of having been cheated," Marie-Santana said. "Cheated by a man Papa had trusted; I trusted him, too." She did not add, Had I written, with your bad eyes you would have taken the letter to Dona Elena or to Dona Esmeralda to be read, and sooner or later the village would have learned what had happened.

"Did he cheat your father, too?"

"No, the cheating began after Papa and Mama died. I wasn't trained to run the business, and he duped me. He told me that together we could increase my little fortune. Instead, he cheated me out of everything, leaving me in debt. I owed a lot of people. Should I have dumped my troubles on your head? Perhaps, but I wasn't going to. Instead, I sold the house and stayed on, working where I could until I had repaid everyone and saved enough for my passage home. I came to you as soon as I could."

She rose and went to her grandmother's side, dropping to her knees. "Granny," Marie-Santana said, "knowing I have hurt you, that's been punishment enough; but if you still feel like scolding me, I will understand."

"I was concerned for your sake," Angelinh' Granny said. "What use do I have for money at my stage of life?" She pulled Marie-Santana to her and held her close. "I may be a cranky old woman, but there are limits even to my cranki-ness. We can talk about this again some other time."

The question of why Marie-Santana had never married— a question that Josephine Aunty had put to Annabel—was an issue that Annabel herself had raised with Mottu a week after Marie-Santana's arrival. "You've known her from childhood," she said. "Such an attractive person. Dark eyes, light skin. Not skinny either. So why is she single?"

Mottu had wondered about that himself, then put the matter out of mind, but now that Annabel had turned to him for an answer, he recalled his first meeting with Marie-Santana the day of her return, when she, noticing his ring, had observed that he had married. He remembered feeling uncomfortable about that; in the light of Annabel's ques-tion, he tried to recapture the mood of that moment. Marie-Santana's pleasure at seeing him had revealed itself in the way she had pronounced his real name. To call him Martin when with everybody else it was "Mottu this, Mottu that," showed respect, even affection. But when she noticed his ring, had her tone changed? Had she said, "You are married?!" in pleased surprise, or had her voice been tinged with disappointment? Could it even have been an accusation? He thought perhaps it might have been; one of her last memories of Goa, one that he himself had carried a long time in his heart, must surely have been of that evening on the hilltop, the day before her departure, when he had plucked up the courage to tell her he loved her.

For months after she had sailed, he had lived and relived those moments on the hill, wondering why she had fled so suddenly? Would she have stayed if he had kissed her? (He had seen that once in a movie; overcome by emotion, the girl had fainted.) Perhaps she had run because she hated him; this was the thought that had filled his mind as he watched her running madly down the hillslope; but in time he became convinced that, strange as it might seem, she had run because she loved him. Looking back on that episode so far removed in time, he could see he had been right. She had run because she loved him. Had she then loved him all those years she'd been away? Saved herself for him? Come back in hopes of marrying him, only to find him married, and not just married, but raising a son?

Though modest by nature, Mottu did not rule out that possibility. He went into the kitchen, where a tiny sliver of a mirror hung on the wall, and under the pretext of combing his hair he took a good look at himself. He needed a shave, but that aside, the face that peered back at him, with the intense eyes and strong bushy eyebrows, was at least passably handsome.

Annabel's question he answered with a shrug. Theirs was a good marriage, and he had no wish to disrupt the tenor of their days. He would be watchful, lest Marie-Santana be unable to control her feelings for him. Still, her plight, he decided, merited some consideration. Annabel would probably try to find her a husband; Annabel's mind ran that way. He would encourage her to try, might even scout around among his bachelor cousins, if only to play fair by Marie-Santana, and to ease some of the guilt he was beginning to feel lying coiled upon his shoulders.

11

THE MORNING Marie-Santana went to pay a courtesy call on Dona Esmeralda Graça de Menezes, she had barely reached the gate when a fierce barking within the house announced her arrival. Seeing the three black terriers that now came racing down the steps, she was glad she had not actually gone into the garden before they sensed her presence. But the bark was a welcome; they stood on their hind legs and yapped merrily in her face, then turned and ran back into the house and back out again. She loved animals, and they seemed to know it.

From where she stood, Marie-Santana could see the great house stretched out in front of her—east wing, west wing; instead of the usual open balcão, where neighbors could sit on stone benches and pass the time of day face-to-face, it had a wide and ornately pillared veranda that ran the entire width of the house. Inside lay sumptuous riches she had been told about, but had never seen; carved furniture far finer even than could be found in the Portuguese governor's palace in Panjim; curtains of lace, and drapes, and cushions and coverlets and table linen to boggle the mind. Angelinh' Granny had told her this, for Angelinh' Granny had been to the house to help when Dona Esmeralda had gotten married.

A woman in her sixties came down the steps and let her into the garden, pushing the dogs away. "They won't bite," she said. "They're just noisy. Go! Go!" She prodded them again with her feet. Marie-Santana let the dogs smell her hands before she followed. The woman looked at her with barely concealed curiosity. "Are you Angelinh' Granny's granddaughter?" she asked. And without waiting for an answer, "We heard you'd come. Have you been well?" They were climbing up a long flight of marble steps and Marie-Santana wondered how Dona Esmeralda coped with these during the monsoon, when the slightest drizzle would make them slippery. On reaching the veranda the woman turned. "Wait here a moment," she said. "I'll go tell bai you're here." And she closed the door behind her as she went.

Marie-Santana expected a very long wait. The dogs had chosen to stay near her, and followed her as she strolled about. From a corner of the veranda to a *chikku* tree overhanging the nullah, a great ugly spider had slung a deceptively silken web that stretched tautly in the wind. Marie- Santana watched as monarch and other butterflies flitted perilously close to the trap; yet despite the stray gusts, all that the web had collected thus far were droplets of morning dew. Still the spider waited, anchored to a strand in the upper right corner, silent and malefic, for the first visitor of the day. The first visitor! That would be the Marie-Santana of the insect world, she thought, and chuckled, though Dona Esmeralda, for all her eccentricities, could hardly be considered rapacious.

"Bai will be with you shortly," the woman said, emerging from interior darkness. "Come with me. She's just finishing her breakfast." They went through a dark anteroom into a cavernous drawing room that stretched interminably to the left.

Marie-Santana stopped in awe. The room, in semidarkness, seemed even bigger on the inside than it appeared from without; close to a hundred feet long, at least. The eight tall arched windows that faced out onto the garden were closed, as were another three on the side that promised a view of the hill rising steeply behind. Since the windows went back to the time the house had been built, in the mid-sixteen hundreds, whatever light came in had to filter, not through clear glass panes, but through translucent seashells arranged in overlapping, two-inch-wide strips set between vertical wooden slats.

As Marie-Santana's eyes adjusted to the light, more of the room's details emerged. The walls, carrying a heavy load of portraits, rose some twenty feet or so; the ceiling soared to a barely-seen central ridge some eight feet higher still. Three elegant chandeliers hanging from the central beam seemed to be floating in space, as the crystal and silver caught and reflected stray hints of light. But the lace curtains had vanished, as had the other signs of opulence Angelinh' Granny had talked about; far from vying with a governor's palace, this room was furnished sparsely indeed.

The woman came into the room again, this time to throw open a window. "Bai will be with you soon," she announced cheerfully. "Now she's getting dressed."

"At least," Marie-Santana thought, "I am inside the house." She had reason to be thankful. The old house had been built with walls like a fortress, as much to keep people out as to shelter those within, and although there were no longer armed enemies about, it was Dona Esmeralda's custom—the custom of almost every gentlewoman—to have visitors who were not of her station in life wait outside on the veranda. They would stand there for long minutes as she went about her routines—giving instructions to the servants, supervising their chores, scolding the dogs, checking the laundry brought in by the washerwoman, taking an account of the money the cook had spent at Atmaram's shop or at the bazaar—until she felt the time was right to grant the visitor an audience. And this was not a matter of caprice or idle whim. Dona Esmeralda was drawing on the tradition of generations of bhatkars and *bhatkans;* villagers and sharecroppers alike had long learned that the minutes they spent waiting on their landowner's veranda or balcão bore a direct relationship to their status in the community; or rather, in the present case, to how Dona Esmeralda viewed their place in the scheme of things. They had also learned that Dona Esmeralda's view of their place in life soon became, for all intents and purposes, their reality.

From deep within the house Marie-Santana heard a grandfather clock strike the three-quarter hour; she had been there almost fifteen minutes. Still she chose not to sit. She expected Dona Esmeralda to come out at any moment to greet her; they would spend some minutes engaged in small talk; then the ancient would reappear to offer her a cup of tea, which she would accept, and a piece of cake, which she would also accept; and she'd be offered a second cup, which she would be forced by convention to accept after first having declined it; and a second piece of cake, which she would also have to eat; but a final polite offer, and an equally polite rejection of it, would set the proper stage for her leaving. Marie-Santana knew the process well, having witnessed it from childhood: The rituals of politeness held meanings beyond meanings, and one worked one's way through each ritual as carefully as though peeling an onion.

With brilliant sunshine burning an arch into the room and light reflected onto the facing wall, Marie-Santana found herself drawn to a large daguerreotype of a strikingly beautiful young woman. She had been portrayed from the waist up, dressed in the Victorian style, with a ruffled, high-collared blouse and her hair drawn back from her face. Marie-Santana had been regarding it pensively for quite some time when she sensed Dona Esmeralda's presence in the room. The old woman had entered without making a sound, and had been regarding her visitor as intently as Marie-Santana had been looking at the portrait. Though older by far than Angelinh' Granny, Dona Esmeralda stood tall and straight, as tall as her five-foot frame would allow.

"I must apologize for my servant," the old lady said.

"Maria-Santana"—again, as had been the case when Dona Elena had uttered her name, Marie-Santana noted the Portuguese inflection—"you see I remember your name. Do sit! Graciela is getting old and no longer hears all my instructions. I had told her to have you sit, then throw open all the windows. All—and I see she opened only one." Dona Esmeralda went to the door and called in a high-pitched voice, "Graciela! Graciela?" In the reflected sunlight her hair was a cloud of silver and gray. She called again, tilting her head to catch an answer that did not come.

"Let me open them," Marie-Santana said, but Dona Esmeralda would not hear of it.

"Graciela will do it," she insisted. "Please do sit."

Marie-Santana moved toward a straightbacked chair but Dona Esmeralda said quickly, and Marie-Santana thought a bit anxiously, "No, no, not there. You'll be much more com-fortable here," indicating an ornately carved chaise longue facing a settee.

Marie-Santana lowered herself onto the ultralow chaise, but finding that it stretched too far back, and that the old cane seat began to give beneath her weight, she sat up straight, her hands gripping the low curved arms. Her hostess, placing herself not on the settee but on yet another straightbacked chair next to it, genially urged her to relax.

"Lean back, lean back," she said repeatedly. "You can't sit on a chaise longue and expect to be comfortable leaning forward or sitting upright. Stretch your legs, Maria-Santana, stretch out, lean back, go on, far as you can. To be comfort-able you must let go, lean back. There—that's much better."

Marie-Santana eased herself backward and found she was lying almost horizontally, as if in a hammock, but hammocks at least felt snug. Lying helplessly supine like this, uncomfortably settled in an unstable chaise with its cane seat sagging, she remembered the web in the garden. Did spiders tell insects where to sit? she wondered. Was this what an insect felt like, waiting for the spider?

Pulling herself quickly out of the chaise, Marie-Santana

walked over to the daguerreotype she had been looking at. "This portrait, Dona Esmeralda," she said, "I don't know when it was taken, or how young you were, but it's still very much you."

Dona Esmeralda smiled. "You think so? Age has been kind to me. I was beautiful once—that's a fact, no point in being falsely modest about it—but to hear you say you still find me so, that's very gratifying. But I can't mislead you— that's not me, that's my mother. She was the reigning beauty of her time, and if you think I have some part of her magic, why, that's a very great compliment, and I accept it with pleasure."

"From your tone, you must have been very close."

"Oh, we were. Unfortunately, she died when I was still quite a little girl—barely six. So when I think I remember the things she used to do—how she walked around a room, how she carried herself—I'm not sure whether these are actual memories, or whether I'm bringing that portrait to life." Dona Esmeralda paused, striving to keep her emotions under control. "And the incidents linking her to me, things I love to recollect—am I remembering things as they actually happened, or just what I've been told? I'd like to think that I do remember. It gives me pleasure; it's as though my mother had never left me."

She rose and came to stand beside her visitor. "And in a sense she didn't. Her eyes—look at her eyes, how they look back at you. As a child, after she had gone, I felt those eyes never left my face. At night I'd leave my bed to come and stand here, in front of the portrait, and then I'd move about the room; but no matter where I stood, her eyes were on me. They follow me still." Her voice turned husky.

"In a way, one never loses one's parents," Dona Esmeralda continued. "No matter how long they've been dead, in times of trouble you feel them by your side."

"I had my parents with me until I was twenty-seven," Marie-Santana said somewhat diffidently. "And yet, I feel I did not get to know them well enough. Like you, I have questions and am groping for answers. Did you know my parents at all well?"

"Well? I cannot say that I did, but I did know your father better than I knew your mother, because he was of the village. He was kind and well regarded."

"That much I know. But do you remember any stories about him? Specific stories? Anything at all?"

"I'm afraid not. I remember only that he treated the poor with respect; he had a rare gift for making even the lowliest person feel important. He listened to them, actually listened, and cared about their lives. That much I can tell you. But surely Angelinha can tell you more?"

"She has grown old, Dona Esmeralda, and she remembers very little. Stray facts here and there, odd pieces of a fragmented jigsaw puzzle, when I'm looking for a life. I find it sad and frustrating."

"And I feel with you."

"The day I arrived, a boatman rowed me across the Mandovi, in an especial, and would not charge me even a single *paisa* because he remembered a kindness my father had done him. There must be others like him, whose lives my father touched. I want to know where, when, how? But I find few answers."

"And you may never find them. But remember, Maria-Santana, the history of one's parent is the precious memory one carries in one's heart. The boatman treasures your father's memory as well. Everything else—reputation, the 'facts,' or how the world perceives them—becomes irrelevant, when the heart recalls its memories. No one can take them from you except age, and that, too, thank God! only sometimes."

Graciela walked in with a tray laden with tea and thinly sliced raisin cake. The dogs, trooping in at her heels, flopped down in front of Dona Esmeralda, heads on their paws.

"Graciela, Graciela, the windows, Graciela," exclaimed Dona Esmeralda, loudly. "The windows! I've told you to open the windows! How many times must I tell you the same thing! Windows first, when visitors come. Then the tea."

"Yes, senhora," Graciela said meekly. "I'll open them right away, senhora." And she set down the tray and served the tea.

"Deaf," said Dona Esmeralda. "And stubborn. What did I tell you? Old and deaf and stubborn." She leaned toward her visitor, tapping an earlobe with her forefinger.

The dogs came to their feet, facing Marie-Santana.

"I hope they haven't been bothering you too much," Dona Esmeralda said. "Sometimes they're a bit over-zealous."

"Not at all. In fact, they rather welcomed me."

"Oh? I'm sorry to hear that. They're supposed to act ferocious and scare people away. Well, scare men away, at least, and especially take a bite out of Lazarinho, if that rascal ever shows up."

"Who's Lazarinho?"

"An infrequent and uninvited guest of the government. If you don't know about him yet, you'll find out soon enough."

Graciela had opened the last window, and the room was ablaze with light. "My!" Dona Esmeralda exclaimed, placing her hands on Marie-Santana's shoulders and holding her at arm's length, "you're certainly a pretty one! We'll have to see about getting you married!"

Marie-Santana felt herself flush with embarrassment. "Dona Esmeralda!"

"Well, no use being coy about it, is there? I'm a plain-spoken person, Maria-Santana, as you may have heard, and you might as well get used to it. How old are you now, thirty at least, I think? Some people would say too old to marry, but I don't think so. There are plenty of respectable bachelors around who'd jump at the chance, and not just in this village."

In the lane, a jingling of bells and clatter of hooves came closer.

76

"Ramu is here with the coach, senhora," Graciela said, as a vehicle creaked to a stop by the gate. "And Pedro Saldanha has brought you six eggs."

"Tell Ramu to wait," Dona Esmeralda said. "Tell Pedro we will pay him on Monday." To Marie-Santana she said, "You should get your eggs from him; they're expensive, but worth every anna. Oh, why am I talking to you about eggs! We should be talking about your future, but we'll have to do it later. Ramu's taking me to Mapusa to see the *administrador*. All these property matters to be taken care of, at my age. Or perhaps because of it. I have heirs, you know—my son Barnabé, his wife Rosa, my little grandchild Angelo. Well, it'll be a comfortable ride—Ramu has trained the bulls well, and they know the road. Come with me, Maria-Santana, but first finish your tea. We can talk on the way. Would you like to come?"

"Some other time," Marie-Santana said, glad of the chance to leave. "You are very kind to offer. But Angelinh' Granny. . . ."

"I understand—the infirmities of age, that I'm no stranger to. Some other time, then. Well, I see you've finished already. Good, I musn't keep Ramu waiting too long. Everybody else has learned to wait, but he gets so cranky, he won't sing to the bulls. I love to hear him sing, and so do they. Why should the bulls be deprived, just because he's cranky?"

She laughed, and held out her hand, and Marie-Santana helped her to her feet. "About your father," Dona Esmeralda said. "I often think the parent resides in the child. You remind me of your father. Have you ever wondered what makes you behave the way you do? Or where your values come from? To understand your father—which is what I think you are trying to do, in every way you can—try to understand yourself. Look inward, Maria Santana, and you will find him." She turned to the door. "Graciela," she called. "My cane. My cane, Graciela."

With her free hand she waved Marie-Santana good-bye.

12

AT NIGHT Angelinh' Granny's house was plunged into
darkness. Nights were the times Marie-Santana
dreaded, for then she found loneliness crowding in on her.
Angelinh' Granny, alone these many years, was set in her
ways. She retired early, soon after her dinner, which she
took around eight o'clock; but even while awake, to stretch
her meager funds, she lit just one kerosene lamp, which she
carried around as she went from room to room. As a further measure of economy, the wick was turned down low.

Marie-Santana tried to change the pattern. She lit a second lamp, and endured a scolding; Granny wanted the lamp
put out. "We are not totally destitute, Granny," Marie-
Santana protested mildly. "I have some funds; you need not
worry. I'll buy the oil." It took days for Granny to agree,
reluctantly. Still, when Marie-Santana turned the lamp on
again, Granny had her turn the wick down. Marie-Santana,
who had grown accustomed to reading late into the night,
now found it almost impossible to read at all. In despera-
tion she snuggled closer to the lamp and held her book up
against it. "You'll ruin your eyes," Granny said from the
door. "Why don't you read in the daytime?"

Relief lay in the garden. Marie-Santana took care of
Granny's needs by day, and read in the afternoons, but took

to working the garden in the early morning and in the relative coolness of the evenings, often lingering there until twilight. Those were the hours when Simon played the violin. The sound took away the loneliness; she listened, as almost to a conversation. And perhaps it was; she knew Simon had begun to play for her.

He had started doing so on the day Josephine Aunty had told her about the curate's ill-natured comment. The remark had upset her; those technical exercises grated on the nerves, to be sure, but comparing it to a donkey at the lyre? She had talked to Simon, then, as he walked past her garden later that day, not to add to the flood of criticism, nor even to refer to it, but to ask why she no longer heard the sweet-sounding melodies he had been playing earlier in the year?

"I'll play you something special when I come back in a few minutes," he promised, smiling. "The 'Meditation' from Massenet's *Thaïs.*" He kept his word.

She wished she could talk to him at leisure about his music, but the constraints of the village kept them apart. People would talk; the most she could do, without causing comment, was exchange a pleasantry or two as he strolled past each afternoon. But those exchanges were almost always quite formal; he being her senior by a few years, she addressed him as Mr. Fernandes.

On one such stroll he promised her Schubert's "Serenade," and, having played it, asked next morning, "Did you like it?"

"I loved it. It was beautiful."

"It's even more beautiful if you know the words."

"Which unfortunately I don't."

"Then I'll write them out for you," he said. But before he handed her the handwritten sheet that afternoon, they both made sure nobody was watching.

He had the German and the English versions side by side.

"Did you translate this yourself?"

"Oh no, I got it from a friend in Kuala Lumpur. He had liked my playing."

"A love song," she said, glancing down the sheet. The text seemed to her to be unduly cloying and sentimental. "Thanks, Mr. Fernandes; the words certainly add depth to the music. Or do I have it backward?"

He laughed, and continued down the lane. She read the words once more as she climbed the steps to the balcão, and then she folded the sheet and put it away in a drawer.

It became routine for Marie-Santana to sit out after dinner, with Granny asleep, and watch the stars drift slowly across the sky. Over at his own house Simon would still be playing. Every night, he ended with the "Serenade," then put his violin away. He could not see Marie-Santana where she sat in the shadows, but it was his way of saying, to his audience of one, good night.

FEBRUARY

13

"WELL?" the men sitting on the bridge parapets said, as Senhor Eusebio approached.

"I don't know what you'd do if I didn't have my radio," he said. "You remind me of fledgling crows sitting on a branch, mouths open, waiting to be fed. Thank God what you crave is tidbits of news, not worms."

"Some of your tidbits are no better than worms," Postmaster Braganza teased.

"I don't make the news," Senhor Eusebio said. "When I get trivia, you get trivia. But today, the BBC has confirmed Malcolm Campbell's land speed record—two hundred and seventy plus miles per hour—set in America last week. That's like driving from Goa to Bombay in one hour and a half, flat, instead of forty-eight, which is what it would take me in my Model T. *If* I could coax it over the mountains. Boggles the mind, what?"

"It certainly does," the vicar said. "To go that fast— much faster than even an aeroplane—is pointless. And think of the danger. You're better off with the tortoise you've got."

"Model T for tortoise," Teodosio said. "I like that."

"Speed is of our age, friend vicar—from this there's no

turning back," Principal Tendulkar said. He turned to Eusebio. "What news of the London talks?"

"Independence for India is not in the cards. There's much talk of 'England's civilizing mission'—of the 'white man's burden.'"

"The only white man's burden I can see is the sacks of loot they go home with," said Tendulkar. "Poor fellows—it bends them quite in half. And that goes not just for the British but for another nation I need not name."

"And you'd better continue not naming it, at least not too loudly," Senhor Teodosio said. "When a student from Bombay shouted 'Viva Goa' at a rally in Panjim, the police tossed him in jail and shaved his head."

"I'd like to keep my hair, for as long as I can," Senhor Eusebio said. "Tendulkar would, too, I guess. But I have two more bits of news—in Germany, the Catholics have refused a seat in Hitler's government, and some fool set fire to the parliament buildings."

"The Reichstag set on fire? What on earth for?"

"I don't have the answer to that, Father Vicar," Senhor Eusebio said, "but arson by Communists is what they say it was."

14

As the echoes of a distant gunshot ricocheted around the surrounding hills, Dona Elena, at ease in her balcão with her husband, paused in her tatting, head tilted to one side, listening. A second shot broke the silence, and she smiled. "He has missed the first time," she said, "as usual."

Senhor Marcelo grunted. "Does it on purpose," he said. "Told me so himself, when I asked him about it. Doesn't like to shoot a sitting bird, so he fires a shot just to get them in the air. Then, bam! He's got one."

There would be more shots to be listened for that cool February morning, perhaps two, perhaps four, for wisps of mist still lazed around the fields at the outskirts of the village, and the white paddy herons would be there waiting, long-legged, long-necked, and weasel-eyed, to strike with their long sharp beaks at frogs, snails, insects, and whatever else moved. There, too, would be Senhor Teodosio, dressed all in khaki, with his broad-brimmed felt hat, knee-high boots, cartridge pouch, and double-barreled shotgun. Dona Elena knew the hunter's habits well, for he was her husband's crony and a frequent visitor to their home, often bringing the family dinner with him—sometimes a rabbit, or a brace of quail, and, even in this skimpy northeastern monsoon season, a paddy heron or two. This day he had been specially invited because she and Marcelo had a matter of some importance to discuss with him, and it involved music lessons for their daughter, Maria.

Teodosio Rodrigues had spent ten years in Mozambique and another ten in Tanganyika, entering it when it was a German colony and staying on when it became British East Africa. He retired in 1931 at the age of forty-five. Though born in Aiconá, he had made his home in Tivolem, with an aged sister who had married into the village and been widowed. A year after his arrival she, too, had died, leaving him the house.

Teodosio was comfortably off. The villagers liked him. They liked his dashing air; "he walks as though he were being preceded by a mirror, admiring himself," Senhor Eusebio said. They liked, too, his unflappable good humor, the white egret feathers with which he adorned his hat, the scalpel-sharp knife that he wore in a sheath at his belt. "A hunter can never be without it," he would say, smiling enigmatically, then add, "in case the gun misfires." In his listeners, this conjured up visions of a crouching Teodosio carving up charging lions with his knife. He wore it even when he'd left his gun at home. "It's a *kukri*," he would explain to people he met for the first time. "Gurkhas wear it all the time." He'd unsheathe the knife so they could admire the wicked curve of the large blade, see the light glint along the polished, finely ground steel. "Of course, once a Gurkha unsheathes his kukri, traditionally it must taste blood, so he must deliberately prick himself before sheathing it again," Teodosio would explain, holding the point of the blade a fraction of an inch above a fleshy fingertip. "Fortunately," he would add, "I'm not a Gurkha." The remark always provoked a smile, and Teodosio's fingers went unmarked.

His past was an enigma. He had made his fortune in Mozambique, some said, in sisal and cotton; but around

Forttu's tavern—where, being egalitarian, Senhor Teodosio defied social taboos by sometimes stopping by for a warm beer, a hunting trophy dangling from his belt—the word was that he'd been a big-game hunter in Kenya, or Uganda, or Tanganyika. Yet others said he'd been a poacher, shooting rogue bull-elephants and selling their tusks to white settlers and British tourists, who then went home claiming they had shot the enormous beasts themselves. Senhor Teodosio denied neither rumor; indeed, he contributed to both.

In his life of leisure the villagers soon detected a developing pattern. Tuesday mornings and Monday and Thursday evenings he joined the vicar and Senhor Eusebio in a brisk round of three-handed bridge at the rectory; Saturdays and Sundays he visited—occasionally with Dona Esmeralda (whose husband Romualdo in the 1880s had been posted with the Portuguese Army in Mozambique, where he had been the first colonial to attain the rank of major general), but more often with Dona Elena and her husband Marcelo, who were closer to his age, and their teenage daughter Maria. His nights he spent working on his memoirs. Or so he claimed. No one had actually seen the memoirs, nor even seen him working on them, and no information could be pried out of the only servant he had, a taciturn, cross-eyed woman. Even Josephine Aunty had to admit she knew precious little about him, though she did claim she had heard him playing the mandolin late into the night, very late into the night. This was no surprise, since he took the mandolin with him to parties, and accompanied himself and others in all manner of Portuguese folk songs.

He had also acquired a reputation as an excellent pianist, and that too without ever playing a note, because on entering a parlor for the first time, if he saw a piano there, he invariably asked the hostess, "Do you play Balakirev's 'Islamey'?" This was his opening move in a carefully planned verbal chess game, where question and counter-question led to a desired result. To the invariable response "Balakirev's 'Islamey'? What's that?" he'd answer, "It's the most difficult piano piece in the world." "Oh! Won't you play it for us?" "Oh, I haven't looked at it in years. I couldn't possibly." "Please! Please?" "Oh no, it's much too difficult." And word got around: "Did you know that at one time he played Balakirev's 'Islamey'? It's the most difficult piano piece in the world. He must be a fantastic pianist."

For most of the year, Teodosio spent his days hunting for rabbit up in the hills and woods, except for the rainy months of June through August, and the far milder secondary monsoon extending from November through February, when an abundance of waterfowl lured him to the paddy fields. It had been some years since Dona Elena herself had stalked both the white and gray paddy herons in those same fields, to the dismay of her indulgent parents (she was an only child), not in high boots and with a shotgun, as Teodosio did, but barefoot and armed with a slingshot, the pockets of her dress weighed down with pebbles that had been rolled smooth and round by the waters of the nullah. Dona Elena had been the best in her time; not till she was nearly in her teens had she given in to the pleadings of her parents and turned from her wild tomboyish ways, but by then she had supplied impromptu fare for many a family dinner. Whether baked or roasted or served in a piquant curry, the herons she brought in tasted good; sometimes tough and always gamy, "but all in all," an aunt privately conceded, "they make a tasty dish."

Time works its magic, and caterpillars turn into butterflies. The girl-child Elena, an imp at eight, became a beauty at twelve. Even at that tender age, through aunts, matchmakers, even distant cousins, marriage proposals began coming in. Two years later, to the allure of the de Penha Fonseca name—already much sought after in the highest social circles—Elena's parents added the lure of piano lessons. By the time she turned sixteen, the trickle of proposals became a flood. Politely, after rich servings of tea and cake, and talk about the weather, the go-betweens would broach the subject and request a formal meeting on behalf of the hopeful suitors. Proffering more tea, more cake, to be politely refused and proffered yet again, her parents deflected the requests, citing her extreme youth, and her need to complete her education, taking care not to say she has a will of her own, she has told us outright she never will agree.

But at twenty she was married. An arranged match, to be sure, but she liked young Marcelo da Silva Pinto, liked his people, felt there was enough in common that they could make a go of it. Dona Elena's parents bestowed on her a substantial dowry; and the groom, in a gesture of unprecedented generosity, presented her with a handsome Blüthner upright piano, purchased and brought down by rail from Bombay at no inconsiderable expense. The elders of Tivolem remembered the wedding as being a grand affair, even though few of them had been able to attend—the ceremony after all had been held at the Church of the Immaculate Conception in Panjim, the bridegroom's parish, as tradition demanded. The church stood partway up a hill overlooking the harbor and had to be reached by a series of zigzagging flights of steps. "Had it been night," a reporter wrote enthusiastically for the *Correo de Pangim,* a Portuguese-language paper widely read for its society column, "enough luminaries of Goan society could have been found on those steps to light up the entire city."

That night those same luminaries gathered at the bridegroom's home for the wedding reception. The center of the garden had been spread with waxed bamboo matting, and on its slippery surface the guests whirled to the waltzes of the Strauss family, a colorful cloth *pandal* above their heads shielding them from the dew. With barely a pause to catch their breath they then danced the quadrille. After the toasts—including one to the health of His Majesty the King, the young and vulnerable Dom Manuel II, teetering on his throne in far-off Lisbon—they danced the traditional Goan *mandó,* the men and the women facing each other in two long rows, the men flaunting white linen handkerchiefs in their hands, advancing, wooing, retreating, and advancing again as bidden by that haunting music, those tender voices, those fluttering fans, those so coquettish eyes. The mother of the bride and the mother of the groom both wept, and they did not weep alone. The *Correo,* in noting this fact, balanced it by dwelling on the bride's "continued radiant effulgence," the groom's "controlled sense of *panache,"* the guests' "untrammeled surrender to joy." Such was the night of the first of October, of the Year of Our Lord 1910.

On the night of the third, again in accordance with custom, a lavish *tornaboda,* or counter-reception, was held in Tivolem. It was hosted by the bride's parents, and it held more than normal significance—since they had no male heir of their own, the bridegroom would now set up house in their home. Elena de Penha Fonseca would retain her maiden name, but the bridegroom would change his— Marcelo da Silva Pinto would henceforth be Marcelo da Silva Pinto de Penha Fonseca. "He is the *ghor-zaoim,"* the villagers would now say, referring to Senhor Marcelo, "the son-in-law who is going to live in and inherit the house. The de Penha Fonseca line will continue."

On that third night of October, the carriages of the well-to-do—some of them horsedrawn, others drawn by bullocks—converged on Tivolem from all directions, clogging the main road leading into the village and spilling over into the alleys and bylanes. Several guests arrived by *machila,* a type of *palanquin,* especially those who had to come over the hill from Goregão; the sharply articulated iss-iss, iss-iss with which the machila-bearers, the *boís,* synchronized the rhythm of their breathing and of their bare feet could be heard well before each conveyance itself arrived at the gate. Marie-Santana, age twelve, and her neighbor and playmate Mottu, a year her senior, stood side by side and wonder-struck among the crowd of eager onlookers. Just hours earlier, on the hill overlooking Tivolem, Mottu had told her he loved her. Now he leaned over and whispered, "Our wedding will be grander than this." Their hands brushed.

She, aglow with her own imaginings, warmed to the touch, but barely heard him.

Marcelo felt joy as he never had before. At the height of the dancing he looked into Elena's eyes and saw great happiness there as well. But the joy in his heart was different, a joy so intense that it brought with it its own inner core of sadness. It had happened to him before, this feeling of a happiness too complete: in the midst of revelry with friends, at a party or a dance, or even when he was just with family. "He has a strain of melancholy in him," his mother used to say, using the Portuguese term *tristeza,* but he knew she had not understood. "Melancholy is a predisposition to sadness," he told her once. "Tristeza is a sadness that pervades the soul. I am, most times, very happy. It's just, at those times when I'm almost deliriously happy—"

"Yes?"

Unable to finish the thought, he said, simply, "Never mind."

When he was normally enjoying himself with friends, and this sadness came on, he would find a way to be by himself, if only for a minute or two, to collect his thoughts and wait for the mood to pass. But in the midst of his own wedding celebration, while dancing with his bride?

"Something wrong, Marcelo?" Elena asked, sensing his unease.

He wanted to say, when I'm this happy, at a moment like this, I dread the moment when the moment will end. He wanted to say, at times like these, my mind races ahead, thinking of the finality of all the things we treasure—all music eventually ends, all laughter ceases, loved ones pass away, friends scatter. Words that should have been uttered remain unspoken. He wanted to say, I'm holding you in my arms and the music fills our veins and it is paradise, but the same crescent moon that shines on us tonight will some night shine on this spot and not find us here—not me, not you, nor yet the children we hope to bear. In my dreams our ecstasy lasts for ever. Because it won't, and only because it won't, I'm sad. But understand this, please—I'm only sad because all of this day I've been so sublimely happy.

"Is anything wrong?" she asked again, deep concern in her voice.

He took a deep breath, and shook his head. "It was only a little fatigue," he said, smiling. "See, you have chased it away already." The longer explanation could wait.

Since the festivities continued well into the night, many of the guests had to be accommodated at least until the next day. Far too many relatives on both sides had shown up for Dona Elena's ancestral home, large though it was, to house any but the nearest kin; others accepted Dona Esmeralda's generous offer of hospitality. In both homes the older adults got the bedrooms and the beds; others slept on endless eight-foot-wide bamboo mats that had been unrolled and spread out end to end wherever space permitted. Although they had no mattresses, no padding at all except the thin hard mat between themselves and the cold tiled floor, the children seemed to think they had the best sleeping arrangements of all—they laughed and giggled through the night. In the adjoining rooms their elders slept. Some snored. Others stayed awake, seeking traces of meaning in their lives. Some sighed. Others found their love rekindled; yet others, inflamed by wine and passion, embraced in their spouse an imagined partner. No muffled cries, no shrieks of climax disturbed the tranquility in either mansion, but between the snores of the weary and the sighs of the troubled and the tittering of the very young, one could hear the discreet rustling of sheets. Eventually, one heard only the snores.

Even though Dona Elena rarely played the piano her husband had so lovingly given her, he did not take it amiss, and their arranged marriage worked out as they both thought it would. Companionship and caring blossomed into love. When, six years into their marriage, she became pregnant, Marcelo was elated; but when Sara Maria Fulgencia was born—named after maternal aunt, paternal aunt, and a great-great-grandfather—he could not quite hide his disappointment. His father-in-law buoyed his spirits, quoting an old Portuguese proverb, *"Primeira filha, maravilha."* And it had come true—the first-born girl-child was truly a marvel. At the birthing the midwife had predicted a bright future; and after the christening—the godparents having been nudged forward, Satan having been abjured, the little head dowsed with water, sacred chrism placed on the forehead and lips and heart, and salt on the protesting tongue—the old priest had remarked, "This little angel has a most musical cry," thus forever endearing himself to Dona Elena while offending the other young mothers at the baptismal font.

Maria indeed showed musical talent from an early age. Though, being a girl, she was not allowed to sing in the church choir, by the time she was twelve her voice soared above the congregation at each heartfelt alleluia. Angelinh' Granny declared that when Maria sang, the sparrows so busy flitting around the church apse would fall silent and come to rest, to burst out in a frenzy of chirruping as soon as she had finished. Angelinh' Granny herself had not seen such a thing, she said, since she had first begun coming to this church as a new bride, and that had been the year a falling mango tree almost knocked down a corner of Weathervaneman's house. Since few people in Tivolem had been around when that event took place, but all had heard of it, Angelinh' Granny's memory was considered phenomenal, and her word carried weight.

Not for Maria, then, the scraped knees, the well-aimed stones, the mud between the toes. Even the low-branching trees in the family garden went unclimbed, the birds nested undisturbed, and red-crested chameleons by the hundred—those "bloodsuckers" whose ancestors Dona Elena and her group once had hunted almost to extinction, knocking them off even as they spiraled up the tallest coconut trees—watched her indolently from low-growing palm trees, dreaming of flies.

Senhor Teodosio by then had settled in Tivolem, and become a family friend. Senhor Marcelo and he would sit on the balcão for hours, nursing warm foamy beers in tall glasses while Teodosio regaled his host with tales of hunting in Mozambique, particularly in the regions of Téte and Zambezia.

The evening that Senhor Teodosio came to discuss Maria's music lessons, they all sat in the balcão savoring the softening evening breezes. With three hours yet to dinner, the maid served tea and raisin cake. Maria reported seeing a garter snake in the rose garden. That gave the hunter an opportunity to describe yet another exploit. "I'm hunting along the banks of the Zambezi," he said. "I see a pair of hippos feeding in the water—dangerous creatures, very territorial. Fast on their feet, despite their bulk; can carve up a human with their huge teeth. Not to eat, just to kill him. I raise my rifle, just to be safe, when something makes me turn—providence, God, perhaps even my guardian angel. Imagine now a large python on the ground almost at my feet, its head lunging toward my waist and its body rising swiftly to encoil me." The teacup wobbled perilously on its saucer as his arms described the reptile's encircling move.

"A python does not crush your bones, as people think it does," he explained, setting down his cup. "It just wraps itself around you tight, and tighter and tighter, until you cannot breathe. So you die. Then," here he shaped his hands into a python's open jaws, "it swallows you whole, beginning with the head."

Senhor Teodosio had told the story elsewhere with great success; at the point where he so graphically described the swallowing, the ladies present invariably shuddered.

"Another moment, had I missed," Senhor Teodosio would then say, "I would not be here talking to you, enjoying this magnificent cake." Grateful for that fact, they would offer him another helping.

Dona Elena and Maria reacted as expected. The hunter, a great lover of cake, accepted the proffered slice with alacrity.

"Teodosio," Senhor Marcelo said, "you tell the most wonderful hunting stories. It's a world of adventure I'd love to enter. Why can't I join you on one of your trips?"

"You'd like to be a *shikari?* You'll be more than welcome," the hunter said. "But now, let's talk about Maria."

15

"GRANDMOTHER," Marie-Santana said, a month after her arrival, "I'm curious about that boatman who helped me. I've been thinking about him a lot lately, and all day today. You're sure you don't know who he is?" They were relaxing on the long stone bench in their balcão, enjoying the cool afternoon breeze and waiting for the sun to set.

"Your father helped so many people, child, half of Goa probably knew and respected him."

"But the man knows you—he said that I look the way you did when you were younger."

"Ah, that flatters me, Mar'-Santan', but more people in the world know me than I can remember! We traveled much in those days, crossing the river by canoe—where were the gasolinas then? The big launches, yes, but they were few. So we took a canoe instead. And so did your father. And yes, there was one that we particularly liked; when your parents were just married, a young boatman ferried us all across. He was so happy to see our party—your mother was glowing. But he was just a boy; we were his *bonee,* he said, his very first passengers, and we would bring him luck. His own father having died, he had taken over the boat. So after that we always took his canoe, sometimes even waiting for him if he happened to be on the opposite bank. Your mother and I sat on one side, and you and your father sat facing us. That much I recall. However, remember the boatman's name? Almost housebound for years as I have been? But we'll find him some day, I promise you."

"But when?" Marie-Santana asked, holding on to her grandmother's hands.

"When next we cross the river, we'll look for him."

"Will that be soon, you think?"

"Soon? I go to Panjim just once a year, child, at the feast of Our Lady of the Immaculate Conception—and that's in December! It's a three-hour walk over the hills just to get to the river; can I do that at my age? So now I must share a taxi to the landing, and you know how much that costs. Plus the launch, and a horse gharry when we arrive to take me to the foot of the church. Even so, once there, climbing all those steps to the church itself is a penance that takes me half an hour and lasts me a good twelve months. But we'll go, we'll go; at least we'll go just up to the river. I'll not forget, I tell you."

Some days after they had had this talk, well past cockcrow but much before the sun had risen, Marie-Santana was putting their frugal breakfast on the table when Angelinh' Granny hobbled in and remarked, fretfully, "You're fully dressed."

"I must go to the river crossing at Betim. I had a bad time sleeping last night. Dreams—"

Carefully, she added buffalo's milk to the bowl of cooked ground millet sweetened with brown jaggery and handed it to her grandmother.

"I'll have crossed the hills before it gets too hot," Marie-Santana said.

Angelinh' Granny tilted her bowl and slurped at the gruel, saying nothing.

"You're angry with me," Marie-Santana said.

"I am. You could have told me yesterday of your plans to go."

"I didn't know I was going." She kissed her grandmother on the forehead. "Besides, I've cooked for the day. But I'll be back as soon as I can, Granny."

"You're going to look for him, aren't you? You're going to look for the boatman."

"Yes, dear Granny. I want to know what he knew about my father, and what my father did for him."

"If you must go, go. You're taking some food?"

"More than enough. I'm going, Granny."

"God guide your way." She shuffled behind Marie-Santana to the doorway. "You're all I've got."

"Me and the entire village," said Marie-Santana. "How they love you. I'll stop by Annabel's and ask her to spend the day with you." And with a hug and a kiss she was gone.

Angelinh' Granny was expecting Annabel, but the voice at the door calling out "O good people in the house!" was Josephine Aunty's. Josephine marched right down the hall into the kitchen where Granny was standing.

"Annabel tells me Mar'-Santan's gone to Betim," she said. "I thought I'd drop by and sit with you a spell. I've brought you some snuff."

Granny ushered her back into the balcão. "It's the best snuff in Bombay, my sailor cousin told me," Josephine Aunty continued, seating herself on one of the smaller stone benches. "And he should know, seeing how much he knocks about. Here, try some."

Angelinh' Granny, seated in her rocker, took a generous pinch and inhaled deeply up her right nostril. Josephine's cousin had been right—the snuff was good. She sneezed, and sighed with satisfaction. "I'll treasure it," she said. "But you've really brought me much too much. Keep some for yourself."

"No, no, you keep it all. I know how much you enjoy taking a pinch now and then."

"I do. It clears the brain wonderfully."

"My mother—may she rest in peace—used to say the same thing. She'd say, 'Angelinh' *mana* and I, we know what good snuff is, and what it does for you.' But she never wanted me to try it then; said I was too young."

"Your mother was good company," Granny said. "Sometimes I still talk to her in my mind. I'll say, 'Simplu, forget what others said, this is how it is.' It's an old habit; and then I'll remember she's not with us anymore. Which I regret, but that's life, isn't it? We're always in transit, it seems to me; only, some of us get off the bus before the others do, sometimes even without the chance to say good-bye."

She paused in her rocking. "At other times," she said, "I get the sudden feeling that it's all right to say, 'Simplu, O Simplicidad'! See this!' And 'Simplu, look at that!' because I feel her presence right there beside me, listening; it's so real I can almost reach out and touch her."

Her visitor, visibly moved, said nothing.

"It's mighty lonely, getting old," Granny said.

"That I can understand. You are therefore blessed, having Mar'-Santan' back."

"Until she came, my life was nothing but sleep and eat and eat and sleep, with a little puttering about the house in between. Now she has me moving about, being useful, even helping a little in the garden. After lunch, we sit on the balcão a spell, I on my rocking chair, she with a book in her lap. She reads, you know; she reads a lot, but not when I'm awake. When I'm awake, she talks." She took another pinch of snuff.

"Of course."

"But when I start to doze, she opens her book. Now I sometimes pretend to nap just so I can watch her read."

"She's good company, then. Tells you wonderful stories?"

"Ah, yes, truly wonderful."

"She was working over there?"

"Working, in Mozambique? Ah, yes, certainly. Working."

"Government service, I suppose?"

Angelinh' Granny seemed distracted. "No, I don't think so. Or maybe it was. You know how it is. Sometimes this, sometimes that. Anyway, one or the other."

"A girl as bright and healthy as Mar'-Santan', you must be disappointed she didn't get married."

"Disappointed? With someone else, perhaps I would have been. But Mar'-Santan' has a mind of her own."

"So she did get offers?"

"More than one could count." Granny chuckled, interrupting her rocking once again. "You asked me about stories—Mar'-Santan' told me one I simply must tell you."

Josephine Aunty leaned forward in her chair.

"She met an old African there, a Makwa chief, very old and bent and very wise. Mar'-Santan' had been asking him about local customs, and he told her an extraordinary story. 'My grandmother used to tell me,' the old African said, 'about an enchanted lake. All it held was one single enormous goldfish. Every fisherman for miles around wanted to catch that goldfish.'"

Granny stopped rocking to take another pinch of snuff. She wrinkled her nose and Josephine Aunty waited, but the sneeze was a long time coming. Then Granny took a deep breath and puffed up her cheeks and blew out and in and out and in but said nothing.

"About the goldfish," Josephine Aunty prodded gently.

"What goldfish? Oh, that goldfish! The chief told Mar'-Santan' the men would come with their long bamboo poles and coconut-fiber fishing lines, and some of the fishers were Makwa and some were Maua and some were Medo; and they would bait their hooks with live earthworms and sometimes with golden butterflies and drop them into the water. Then the goldfish would swim out of the depths and take their bait, but they could not take the fish. The more they tried the more bait they lost, all to no purpose. Must have been very frustrating, don't you think?

"Then Mar'-Santan' asked the old chief, 'Why did your grandmother tell you this story?'

"And he said, 'I don't know. I don't know what the story means. But I do remember, anytime I asked too many questions that my grandmother did not want to answer, she'd say, "You still fishing for that goldfish?" And that would shut me up right away. She was a very wise old woman, my grandmother was.'"

Josephine Aunty, flustered, rose to go.

"Why, Josephine," Angelinh' Granny said, "We had just begun to talk, and you have to go? Why don't you come back when Mar'-Santan' returns, and you can ask her directly?"

"Seeing how busy she is?" Josephine Aunty seemed aghast at the idea. "She's here, there, everywhere—at the well, in the garden, at the market, most of all by your side; for me to visit and take up her time with idle questions would be unfair. I was just passing a pleasant moment or two with you, that's all."

When the noise of Josephine's going had brought silence back to the house, Angelinh' Granny dozed off in her chair. She was still dozing when Annabel came hurrying in, apologizing for being late.

"But I had company," Granny said. "Thank you for sending in Josephine. We had a little talk."

"She was here, saying I'd sent her? That's not true! I merely told her I'd promised Mar'-Santan' I'd stop by later to be with you. Did she pump you for information?"

Angelinh' Granny nodded. "But first she gave me a present of snuff. The best in Bombay, given her by a sailor cousin, she said."

"Given her by me, last year. She got nothing out of you, I hope?"

"Only a story Mar'-Santan' had told me, about a magic goldfish in an enchanted lake. Surely you know it?"

Annabel laughed. "But of course! Mar'-Santan' told

me the very same story when I too was asking too many questions."

"Ask, ask, ask," Granny said, in mock seriousness. "I sometimes think that's all we women do."

16

SIMON FERNANDES had saved assiduously, but not as
much as Senhor Eusebio, simply because in the Persian
Gulf there was no place where Eusebio could have spent
his earnings. In Kuala Lumpur, on the other hand, Simon
could have squandered his money anytime he chose to.
Even on women. Instead, he invested a portion of his salary
as a civil servant each month in postage stamps of the
British Empire. "It's my only vice," he'd say, "aside from
music." In fact, he divided his leisure time equally between
his stamps and his violin, spending hours with his instrument each day, practicing scales and arpeggios and running
through orchestral studies—Beethoven, Brahms, Dvorak,
Wagner, and even this barbarous newcomer Stravinsky,
whose music was too difficult for the rest of the orchestra
to play. One didn't get to be concertmaster of the KLP,
Simon would quip, just by fiddling around. He was equally
passionate about his stamp collecting. At the monthly
chapter meetings of the Federated Malay States Philatelic
Society, his friends—some of whom had built up vast worldwide collections—tempted him with other prospects:
Portuguese Colonies, Spain and Colonies, the French
Colonial Empire. Single-mindedly he resisted them all.

The printed British Empire album Simon had started

with soon proved to be unsuited to his needs. He switched therefore to looseleaf binders, and devised elegant displays for each and every set of stamps, carefully ruling in squares and rectangles in which to place each item, and including squares for the stamps that were missing. And he practiced calligraphy, so whatever details he wrote in—dates of issue, perforation varieties, watermarks, and whether or not the stamps were issued to commemorate a special event—would be not only clear and legible but also pleasing to the eye.

Michael, a practical man, chided his son for letting a hobby ride him. The last time this happened, when Michael was enduring his final illness, Simon pulled out the latest Stanley Gibbons Stamp Catalog, where he had painstakingly marked in red the price increases of every stamp he owned. The value of his collection was increasing steadily, he pointed out. It brought him hours of pleasure every day; it kept him out of the bars and the whorehouses; and what's more, it would provide him with an extra nest egg in his later years. Was that so bad? His father, convinced, had approved.

But the old man had clearly had other concerns as well. "Between your stamps and your practicing," he had often pointed out, "you have no time to socialize." He had wanted to see his son married, and married well. "Your mother would have seen to it, she was such a capable woman, so good at these things." Hadn't she arranged marriages for half the Goan young men in Kuala Lumpur, and for those Goan girls in Johore and Singapore that everybody said would never find husbands?

"Time's flying," his father would say. "You're already— thirty-five? Thirty-six. Your mother dead already all of six years. What are you waiting for? For me to go, too?"

"I know of a young woman," the father said, on Simon's thirty-seventh birthday, "Patrick's daughter. You know Patrick, second violinist in my trio. She arrived last week from Bombay, and he brought her to the club last night— beautiful young woman. Well-behaved. Modest, too. Wears long dresses. Not bold, as so many of these young things are. There were some European young women there, and some Anglos and Eurasians, and you should have seen the difference. All overly made-up and brassy; flappers, every one of them, but not Patrick's girl. I wish you'd been there to see her—nice Goan girl, one of ours. Perhaps you can come tomorrow, I'll call Patrick and ask if he'll bring her again. You two could dance, talk a while, get to know each other."

Simon said, "I wish you'd stop pushing me. I'm not much for dancing. I don't know how."

"What's there to know? It's like playing the violin, only much easier. You count two, or you count three, or you count four. If they're playing the rumba, you lean forward and shake your behind. For the waltz you get up on your toes. The more you dance, the faster you'll marry."

"I'll marry when I'm ready," Simon retorted, angrily. "Someone I really want to marry, someone I love, not someone I just danced with."

"Before I die," the old man said. "Please God, it should be before I die. Don't wait much longer! Thank God, I still have my health, can still play the violin better than Patrick or almost anybody else in these parts. But I'm getting on in years. It's time you got married. Our line must continue."

Simon became upset enough whenever his father spoke of being one of the best violinists around, without acknowledging his own role at the Philharmonic, but it was his father's closing comment that made him really angry. "Our line? What line? You sound as though we were kings or nobles, or something."

"One doesn't have to be a king or a lord to want that," Michael said. "We are the Fernandes's of Tivolem. Small people, from a small village, but. . . . People know us. You want our name to die out? We live on through our children and grandchildren. All of creation renews itself this way."

Simon said nothing.

"You're the one son I have," Michael said, when the silence had become unbearable.

"You are forgetting John."

"Don't talk to me about John," Michael said. "You're damned right I'm forgetting him. To me he doesn't exist."

"He's my brother."

"A bad seed. *Sheesh!* To hate us that much—"

"He must have hated himself, too."

"So he looked like an Anglo. What did I have to do with that, or your mother? A freak accident of birth, that's all! And the day he ran out on us, the day after your mother's funeral, that day I was glad—yes, glad—that your mother was dead and not, like us, living through the shame."

"I've got things to do," Simon said abruptly, and went to his room, where he took out his albums, his catalog, his magnifying glass, and other paraphernalia, and a batch of glassine envelopes full of stamps to be sorted through, and kept himself busy sorting by color and shade, checking perforations, poring over watermarks, looking for potential rarities and finding none, until the wall clock struck twelve, and the lure of sleep precluded any need to think about the things that bothered him most—the foolishness and mortality of parents, family pride, nuptial bliss, the pretended and probably dubious lures of posterity.

When Simon's father eventually died, some three years after Patrick's daughter had married a Eurasian who drank too much and abused her, so Patrick said, Simon at forty-one was still unmarried. Michael had been conscious on his deathbed, but had not verbalized the question Simon did not want to hear; instead, he had looked at his son, and looked at him, until Simon had blurted out, "Yes, I'll marry. I promise you, I'll marry. A girl you'll be proud of. Our line will continue." And the old man had propped himself up on his right elbow and raised his shrivelled left hand to caress his son's face in blessing and gratitude, but the hand had not quite made it, Michael dropping back exhausted as Simon leaned forward to kiss it.

A month after his father's death, Simon received a letter from Mozambique, a brief note, with an enclosure. "I am well," it said. "I hope you are, too. I've struck gold. Add these to your hoard." It was signed, simply, "John." Simon checked the postmark: Quelimane, September (date undecipherable) 1927. There was no salutation, no return address, no hint of an apology, no mention of their father. The enclosure was a commercial packet of seventy-five stamps from Mozambique. Simon tossed the stamps into his wastebasket, but held the note a long time, staring at it till it was just a blank white space in his mind; then abruptly he crumpled it and tossed it, too, into the trash. Moments later he fished it out, smoothened it, and replaced it in its envelope; he retrieved the packet of stamps as well and placed them both on a corner of his desk. "Damn!" he said, drawing his forearm across his eyes. He did not get much done that day.

Now back in Tivolem and embarked on a life of leisure, Simon found loneliness pressing in on him. By nature reclusive, he had not realized how much he had come to depend on the occasional concerts of the Philharmonic, and the monthly stamp-swapping sessions of the FMSPS, to provide him with some measure of human interaction. While, in Kuala Lumpur, his stamp collection had helped provide him with companionship, in Tivolem it could no longer fulfill that function. He had shoeboxes full of duplicates, and no one to trade them with. The only other stamp collector in the village was the vicar, and all he collected were stamps from the Vatican. The vicar's entire Vatican hoard—and it was practically complete, lacking only two values—consisted of just twelve stamps, stuck down with rice paste on one single well-thumbed page of a lined notebook; Simon's British Empire collection, in contrast, now took up two bulky Stanley Gibbons albums, and each stamp was expertly hinged on the back, an eighth of an inch from the top. Glassine envelopes by the hundred, all neatly stacked, held stamps yet waiting to be sorted and mounted. Despite the great disparity in size and value, the two collectors derived equal satisfaction from their bits of colored paper. Unfortunately, they had absolutely no interest in each other's collections.

The vicar, of course, did not depend on his stamps to provide him with social contacts—he routinely met a great many people either in the fulfillment of his priestly duties or during his daily strolls through one or other sections of the village. Simon, on the other hand, felt quite frustrated. What use was his magnificent collection if he could not show it to admiring and even covetous eyes? Adding to his sense of isolation was the fact that his agnosticism made him even more of a misfit in a village in which the population—whether Catholic or Hindu—consisted of various shades of believers.

Language became yet another barrier. Having left Tivolem at the age of five, he now spoke English and Malay, but had forgotten much of the Konkani and the Portuguese he had spoken as a child. True, he remembered the garlands of polite phrases that eased one's path through the day, including the "God give you a good day" and "God give you a good night" used when passing even total strangers, the "God grant you grace" that was the standard response to either greeting; but his lack of fluency inhibited him. His social contacts were thus restricted to chance meetings with Senhor Eusebio and Senhor Teodosio, with the vicar, the curate, Gustavo Tellis the regedor, Postmaster Braganza, and Principal Tendulkar, a tightly knit group of cronies, all of whom, besides speaking Portuguese and Konkani, were more or less fluent in English; and he could of course talk to the two ladies, Dona Elena and Dona Esmeralda, who were also trilingual. To these he finally added the recently arrived Marie-Santana, his neighbor, whom he could see, from the vantage point of his balcão, tending a now thriving garden while he played the violin each morning and evening. Granny he hardly saw at all. But while Marie-Santana soon seemed aware equally of his music and of the fact that he was watching her, he for the first few weeks had maintained a cautious distance, fearing entanglements.

Simon's first break from loneliness came on the day of Marie-Santana's arrival itself, when Postmaster Braganza invited him to join the group that met each afternoon at the bridge; yet another break came when he found that Eusebio and Teodosio played cards with the vicar two evenings a week, and also on Tuesday mornings, and that they lacked a fourth. He offered to join them, pointing out he had never played contract bridge before but was willing to learn. To his relief, his offer was promptly accepted.

His time was now more fully filled, yet his life remained shallow. Even the daily journal he so carefully kept was devoid of profundities. Where others might have set down philosophical ramblings, or even attempted a poem or two, he meticulously jotted down the trivia of the day: "Played bridge with the vicar; lost half a rupee." On another page: "To Panjim by bus and gasolina in the morning. Two annas. Back at four. Splurged on lunch and a bottle of St. Pauli Girl beer, Rs. 1–8–0." That was it: where he went, at what time, what he bought, what it cost. Nowhere did the name of any woman appear, even in a passing reference. Despite his growing friendship with Marie-Santana, his heart was a mighty fortress, and it was very secure.

17

MARIE-SANTANA did not go down to the main road
but instead turned immediately to the right, following the lane uphill past Dona Elena's house. Beyond Bald
Uncle Priest's house, that section of the lane petered out entirely, but in the early dawn there was light enough for her
to make out the goat path that would take her to the crest.
Drawing a deep breath, she set about climbing the steep
slope with long deliberate strides; she had no time to lose,
and besides, at that hour, though the jackals had long re-
treated to their lairs, there might still be cobras about. Seeing
she was quite alone, she made a great deal of noise as she
climbed, and not just to bolster her own courage; an occasional rustling up ahead told her that her warning had been
noted, and a snake or some furry creature was scurrying
out of the way. It was hard going, the uncropped grass being
slippery with dew, but in half an hour of scrambling she
had reached the top, and from then on there was no more
climbing to be done—hill abutted flat-topped hill to form
one long plateau all the way to the river. Now she could
breathe easier; yet, though she quickened her pace, within
minutes small groups of fisherwomen twice passed her at a
trot, baskets balanced on their heads, leaving behind a trail

of smells—mackerel and sardine and swordfish—that blotted out the cool scent of dew-dampened hill grasses.

Descending to the river bank at last, Marie-Santana saw few of the boatmen around, and the man she was seeking was not among them. In the early morning hour, with the ebb tide nearing its end, the river lay steel gray and shrouded in mist. The river traffic picked up as the sun rose higher; Marie-Santana now went closer to the water's edge, her hopes alternately soaring and falling as each new canoe pulled in, propelled by a stranger.

"I'm looking for an older boatman, gray-haired and well spoken," she said to all who would listen. "Perhaps in his fifties."

"Does he ply his boat from here, at Betim, or over there, from Verem?" they asked, pointing downriver to where it broadened into a bay.

"Between Panjim and here," she answered.

"That could be Jacki," one said. "He's over on the Panjim side right now. He could be the one."

"Then he's the one I want to see."

"Shall we call him?" the man said, and she hesitated, thinking they would have to send a boat across. But without waiting for an answer, he cupped his hands around his mouth and let out a long "Ooooeh! Jacki!"

Faintly, from across a mile of rippled water came an echo and an answering halloo.

"Over here," the man called. "Someone to see you. Hurry!" And to her he said, even before Jacki had answered, "He's coming, he'll be leaving soon."

Marie-Santana watched the boats come and go. Finally, the man pointed, crying, "That's him! That's Jacki—in the boat on the right."

Watching closely at that distance, even though all she could see was Jacki's back as he rowed toward them, Marie-Santana had a growing sense of unease—he, like the others, was rowing almost directly across the river, cutting across the tide. But her hopes rose again as he neared—he was gray-haired, and he worked the oars with a will. She began walking down to the water's edge as, easing his canoe onto the sand, he discharged his passengers with brisk efficiency. Then he turned; she saw him full-face, and he was not the man she was looking for.

"I need your help," she said, as he walked up the bank toward her. "I'm looking for a boatman who rowed me across a couple of months ago. Your height, but thinner, quite gray."

"Alas, many of us are growing old," he said, smiling, "and I know several who would fit your description. Do you remember his name?"

"No," she said. "I asked, but he did not answer. He had already turned away."

"Then that could have been Louis," he said. "He's a little hard of hearing. He—he—"

"Yes?"

"He—became spoiled, bai."

She reached back into the recesses of her mind, searching vainly for the meaning of a phrase she once may have known.

"Became—spoiled?"

"He died, bai, a month ago already. That's his boat I have now."

A month ago! That was around the time the boatman had been much on her mind. She walked down to the boat and he followed, looking on as she ran her hand back and forth over the gunwale.

"Louis was a good man," he said gently, as her eyes filled with tears.

"Do you know where he lived?" she asked.

He waved a hand upriver. "Near Sanvordem. He had no family, if that's why you're asking. Was it important, your seeing him?"

"To him, no; to me, yes. I was going to ask him about my father." She was silent a moment, looking across the water.

"Your father?"

"Yes. When Louis rowed me across, he did something unusual. He rowed against the tide before running with it. He said he learned that from my father."

He looked at her, surprised. "Your father was a boatman, then? Or a sailor?"

"No, no! But this man—"

"It's not Louis," he said hastily. "If he rows against the tide, it's not Louis. It's Shankar, and he'll be here in an hour." He looked quickly away from her tear-stained face. "I did not mean to give you bad news about Louis," he said. "It made you sad. But I can tell you that he died at a time when he was happy. He had a good fate, and may mine be as good as his."

"God will surely grant your wish," she said.

"You won't have to wait too long for Shankar," Jacki said. "He should be here in an hour, or at most two. If you'd like to sit a while, and rest your feet, you'll get a good cup of tea at that stall over there. Or you could rest in the shade of the banyan tree. I'll make sure Shankar knows you are waiting."

When he left her, Marie-Santana strolled along the square overlooking the quay, watching the launches and gasolinas come and disgorge their human cargo and take on another boatful, while the canoes still pulled slowly across the river with their load of passengers. It was not yet a losing battle, but she wondered how long the old mode of transportation would survive the intrusion by the new. The launches crossed the river every twenty minutes; two had already made the trip; a third was about to leave. An hour gone, she might still have another hour to wait.

And then she saw him. He was pulling in from up-stream, empty, and she waved, but he had the canoe turning, and was preparing to beach it; mindful of the dock's pillars and other obstacles, he did not see her. She saw people waiting for him on the bank and ran down to the water's edge. Several of them, both men and women, had already taken off their sandals and, pulling their clothes up above their knees, were in the water waiting for Shankar to help them clamber aboard.

"Bai!" he exclaimed, surprised and pleased as he reached out to pull her in. "My lucky day! My very first trip, and you're on board." He turned to find her a seat. "Make yourselves thin," he said to the others, smiling yet officious. "Don't take up so much space! Make room for the lady." She found a spot on the front bench.

"I need to talk to you," she said, as he shoved the canoe into deep water and climbed aboard.

"I'm listening."

"Not now. On the way back—an especial. But this time you must let me pay. Please. An especial. It's important."

"If you wish," he said. He seemed uncomfortable. "That will cost two rupees, bai; I mean no offense, but it is a lot of money. While I wait for passengers in Panjim, we could easily talk on the riverbank."

"I'll give you the fare, and more," she said. "On shore we'll be interrupted. I want to talk about my father, and the time you knew him. But we must talk on this boat, alone, on the river. In the boat, where it brings back memories."

He nodded. Busy with her own thoughts, she let him row the rest of the way in silence. On the Panjim shore he let off the other passengers and made his excuses to the ones who were waiting there. "Jacki and his canoe will be here in minutes," he said to them. "He left Betim soon after me. Now I've got an especial to take care of." Nobody grumbled.

He pushed the canoe back into the river. Before the current had quite seized hold, he bent to the oars.

"I want to find out more about my father," she said. "He died too soon, and I remember too little of my childhood. You said he helped you once, when nobody else would; exactly how did he help you?"

He did not answer her immediately. "I had been thrown in jail, arrested for something I did not do," he said at last. "The man from whom my father and I bought this canoe claimed we hadn't paid him. He lied, but nobody believed me. I would have lost the canoe and the money I had paid for it. Then your father came forward as a character witness. He told the magistrate I couldn't have done it; that I was an honorable man. And he offered to stand bail. It was on his word that the magistrate let me out, and next day my accuser confessed. You can imagine, I fell at your father's feet."

"Had he known you long, then, when he vouched for you?"

"Long? No. Only from riding in my boat, and talking to me."

"He had faith in you."

"I think he had faith in all people," Shankar said. "He would talk to others in my boat, my passengers, and no matter who they were—they might be the lowest laborers in the fields—he spoke to them with respect. If only for that moment, the moment he was talking to them, he made them feel important."

"Someone else said that about him," Marie-Santana said. "And I saw that happen myself, in Mozambique; I can vouch for that, I can vouch for it firsthand. As for his faith in people, he had that, too. In your case, thank God, it was not misplaced."

He looked at her quickly, but she would not meet his eyes. "Do you remember anything else," she asked.

"I remember one other incident," he said. "I had been helping a man get off the canoe, and he tripped and fell into the water. It was not more than ankle-deep there, but he got his clothes wet, and he got up screaming curses and rushed forward to hit me. I could have broken him in half, but your father stopped me. 'You heard his insults,' I said, 'and still you come between us?' 'I have heard him say many harsh things,' your father said, 'but I didn't think they applied to you. Do they?' 'Of course not,' I said. And your father said, 'An insult is only an insult if you accept it, and I'm glad you didn't.' To the man he said, 'You see, you were mistaken about Shankar. You must have been thinking of someone else. Why don't you go now?' The man went, without another word. He never took my canoe again, but I would have welcomed him back, had he tried."

A stiff ocean breeze was stirring wavelets that slapped smartly against the bow. Marie-Santana dipped her hand in the warm salt-laden water, reaching back in time. The river was like the past, slipping away between her fingers, leaving little behind but seaweed and traces—of what? She was seeking to fill the gaps in what she knew, of herself, her childhood, her family. Her parents—what had they really been like? After having lived with them for twenty-seven years, why did she feel, looking back, that she hardly knew them? She had not even a letter to treasure, since she had never been away from them until they had died. Her father—Granny had told her a few stories about him, yes, but Granny was biased, he was her son, she had to say good things, treasure the good in him, especially since he was dead; but her memory was gone, and the stories changed with each retelling. What was she, Marie-Santana, to believe? She was grateful for the boatman. In a minute Shankar had made her father real, given him a dimension in a new and different world, beyond family and friends. The boatman was certainly one of those whom her father, in her neighbor's words, had made feel important. She recalled Dona Esmeralda leaning toward her, saying, "Everything is irrelevant when one holds precious memories in one's heart." Memories! A gull screeched overhead. The boat rocked. The spray in her face, her cheeks already wet with tears, she was a child again, hearing her father's voice, above the slosh of the oars and the liquid lap-lap-lapping of the waves, urging Shankar, boatman, protégé, and friend, to buck the incoming tide.

MARCH

18

THE CONCLAVE at the bridge was in full session, and Senhor Eusebio was holding forth. "Big news from America," he said. "This Franklin Roosevelt—became president just last week, shuts down the banks a couple of days later. All of them, and I mean, all."

"America's in very bad shape," Teodosio said. "Stock market down, fortunes lost overnight, people jumping out of windows. The threat of revolution. Roosevelt had to do something! Thank God we haven't reached that stage here yet."

"We came close enough that I got me some land," Senhor Eusebio countered. "Too many of our old land-rich families are in real money trouble."

"That may be true, but we'll never see suicides," Tendulkar said. "And I'll give you three reasons why: One, as a society, we've never been money-mad, thank God! We lose our money, so what? Life goes on. Two, economically we're down so low, we can't go any lower. Three, even if things got worse, we've got no windows high enough to be worth jumping out of."

"Well, things will get worse, if our governor gets his way," Simon said. "This Craveiro Lopes, that Salazar has sent from Lisbon—he's an army man, so he holds the

Military Recruitment Act over our heads like a sword—
we serve in the army, or else. Serve in the army, for what?
Who will we fight, the British in India? Drive them back
into the Himalayas? Or will we be shipped out to put down
an African rebellion, as happened once before?"

"There's always the 'or else'," Teodosio said.

"That's my point," Simon said. "The 'or else' being, we
buy our way out of doing military service. If that's not a
tax, I don't know what is."

"By the way, have you seen the latest *Prakasha?*" Senhor
Eusebio wanted to know. "There's a funny piece here about
a king—obviously our esteemed new governor—who decides
his peasants—that's us—should sow and present him with
a third harvest of rice. He gets his way; the seed is sown.
But when the harvested grain is piled up at his feet and the
threshing begins, the king finds the husks are empty."

"I'm amazed that *Prakasha* was allowed to get away
with that, when even *O Heraldo* is censored," Tendulkar
said. "Anyway, I'd like to hear what our vicar thinks of the
military tax."

"That question was answered centuries ago," the vicar
said. "To Caesar what is Caesar's. Eusebio, what else have
you heard over the radio?"

"The repression continues in Germany, and it's getting
worse. Not just Jews and Communists are being beaten
and killed, but now Hitler's police have begun persecuting
Catholics as well, and his storm troopers are beating them
up on sight."

"*Argumentum baculinum*—the argument of the stick.
And this is the same Hitler who last month told the world
nobody wants peace and tranquility as much as he does?"

"No inconsistency there," Teodosio pointed out. "That's
why he's killing off his opponents. Once you've killed them
all, you have total peace."

"Dragon's teeth," Tendulkar said quietly.

"Absolutely right, Tendulkar," the vicar said. "Killing

off opponents may cause a general uprising. Could be the end of him! Eusebio?"

"Japan has quit the League of Nations," Eusebio said, "and its troops have strengthened their hold on Manchuria."

"Manchukuo," Tendulkar said. "No longer Manchuria. The Japanese have killed off Manchuria and given us Manchukuo instead. The world map is changing, before our very eyes."

19

LAZAR, as not just Dona Esmeralda but the entire village of Tivolem knew, was a bad lot, and Annabel took care to warn Marie-Santana about him. Not just ordinary bad, she said, like Lallu, the cobbler's son, who had taken to drinking coconut-palm toddy and to general shiftlessness before becoming Senhor Eusebio's chauffeur, but bad bad. Though Marie-Santana had not yet met him, she had already developed her own suspicions: for whenever she had overheard the villagers mention his name—even though they used the diminutive, and referred to him as Lazarinh', dropping the final o—they had not used the tender tone of voice that so closely ties in with the diminution of first names; instead, it came out with the kind of rasp that generally precedes the act of expectoration. And in fact Kashinath, the barber, when Lazarinh's name came up at all, always took care to avert his face and spit into the dust.

It had been Kashinath who, years earlier, had burst into Forttu's tavern one forenoon to say he'd seen Lazarinh', then just turned fifteen, terrorizing and scattering a brood of Pedro Saldanha's fledgling chicks, while the anguished mother hen fluttered and squawked about in helpless rage. "I cuffed him, I cuffed him really hard," Kashinath had said, still shaking with anger, and Forttu and his customers had approved. Even in retrospect, years later, discussing Lazarinh', they would hark back to that chicken incident. There, it was agreed, in that one episode one could see the incipient seeds of badness, because one cannot grow up in a place such as Tivolem without knowing that on the care and love bestowed on helpless creatures depends the life and well-being of the village. "Perhaps he wasn't slapped hard enough," Forttu said, time and again, as Lazarinh' went from bad to worse. "To scatter tiny baby chicks, to drive them away from their mother so they can be swooped down on and carried off by crows and shrieking kites, is to go beyond the pale. Way beyond. We should have known what was to come."

"I would have slapped him so hard, it would have broken both his eardrums," Annabel said to Marie-Santana in recounting the chicken incident. "Maybe that would have made a difference."

"Annabel, what else did he do?"

"At first he just stole fruit—mangoes from Dona Elena's garden, cashews from the trees up on the hill. That was nine, ten years ago. Now, much bolder, he gets into people's houses and steals."

"While they're there?"

"Makes no difference."

"And the police?"

"The police! Things haven't changed in the years you've been away, Mariemana. The nearest police station is still in Mapusa, five miles away. By the time we get a messenger over there, on foot, and the police get here, also on foot, do you think? . . . Besides, Lazarinh' is a great talker; he can think up more excuses and alibis than a monkey has fleas. No, we have our own way of coping with Lazarinh'—if we catch him in the act he gets a sound thrashing. That keeps him in line for a little while."

"And is he quiet now?"

"Yes, but only because the police finally caught him

on an old charge and threw him in jail. He'll be released tomorrow—so be careful."

"Me? What can he take? I have nothing to my name."

"He doesn't know that. When he finds out you're back from Africa, he'll figure you have gold, jewelry, ivory, something."

"Thanks. I'll bolt the doors and windows at night."

"No need to be sarcastic. Bolting doors and windows won't help much, anyway. He climbs up onto the roof, removes a few tiles, and lowers himself into the house. People sleep through it all."

"Remind me not to sleep."

They laughed, and parted company.

The smiling young man standing expectantly by her gate next day had to be Lazarinh'. Marie-Santana put down the pickax with which she had been digging up a neglected patch of ground and turned to face him. He made no move to enter.

"You've come back to our village, bai, after all these years, and I hope things are going well with you?" he said.

"As well as they can be," Marie-Santana said. She sized him up—mild-mannered, slender, neatly dressed in blue-striped white shirt and shorts (his fresh-out-of-jail outfit?), not at all a villainous-looking type. "You're a neighbor?" she asked, feigning ignorance.

"I'm Lazarinh'."

"Oh! So you're Lazarinh'!"

"People don't say good things about me. You must have heard reports?"

"What reports! I have no time for gossip. In any case, I'd pay no attention."

"Still, some people have evil tongues."

"Certainly; and others have larcenous fingers. You, I can tell you're an honest man."

He seemed pleased. "If ever you need help, bai, send for me. I'm good at odd jobs. I—"

She cut him short. "So am I. In Africa, where I was all these years, one learns to fend for oneself. Still, if I need help, I'll be sure to let you know."

She smiled and prepared to turn away, but Lazarinh' would not be dismissed.

"You should still let me dig up that patch for you," he said. "That looks like a tough piece of ground—probably rocks under the surface, too, hasn't been worked in years. It'll take a lot of deep digging, and you shouldn't be doing all this yourself, certainly not, seeing how hard you have to work to take care of Angelinh' Granny and all."

She hesitated. His sudden burst of loquacity surprised her. Perhaps he was genuinely offering to help. But Annabel's warning came to mind; she decided to be careful. "Thanks, but I think I can manage." To lend weight to that assurance she swung the heavy pickax high above her head. "But if I need your help I'll be sure to send word."

As Lazarinh' turned to go, she drove the pickax smartly into the ground, and the sharp expulsion of breath that went with that blow served notice, if notice were needed, that here was someone he should not ever tangle with.

20

Senhor Eusebio had not known Marie-Santana when she was a child, because he and his parents had lived in the farthest outpost of the village, a clump of houses beyond the paddy and sugarcane fields and right next to the one-room Portuguese primary school. Nevertheless, in his changed circumstances, he welcomed her on her return for the same reason that, some months earlier, he had welcomed Simon Fernandes—like himself, they too had spent a large portion of their lives in the outside world, and so would have much to talk about, aside from the state of the crops and the price of fish. Talking to Marie-Santana at length, however, was a problem; she was a woman, after all, and single at that, and he a bachelor; tongues would wag. They would wag even more if, like Simon, she joined the conclave at the bridge, a lone woman no doubt flirting with the men at hand, one of them a priest.

Marie-Santana's skill at gardening gave him the excuse he needed. Although he had lavished a great deal of time on the construction of his house, he had given little thought to the plot of land that stretched out in front of it, other than to give orders that the fruit and coconut trees should not be cut down. But a luxuriant flower garden, he felt, would add a touch of distinction, and who better to advise him than

Marie-Santana? To avoid arousing gossip, however, he took an oblique approach, letting word drop in the bazaar, at Atmaram's, and at the post office that he was looking for a gardener. He then spent his mornings puttering around the garden and screening the applicants who showed up.

Lazarinh' was among the first and, had it not been for his record, might have been the most promising. But Senhor Eusebio, besides having someone else in mind, would have none of him. Knowing that Mottu and Annabel were close friends with Marie-Santana, he tried another tack.

"Most of those who showed up are field hands," the landowner complained to Postmaster Braganza later that day, loud enough for Mottu to hear as he was sorting through the mail. "They know about rice and onions and string beans; what do they know about flowers?"

"Senhor Euseb'," Mottu said, "what about Mar'-Santan'?" It seemed to him absurd, although he could not say so out loud, that this one or that one, and in this case specifically Senhor Eusebio, should forget so easily about so lovable a neighbor, when he himself could hardly put her out of his mind.

"Marie-Santana!" Senhor Eusebio exclaimed, slapping himself on the forehead. "Of course! How could I have forgotten about Marie-Santana! Such a fine gardener! Do you think you or Annabel could ask her to see me?"

21

Mottu's concern over Marie-Santana's state of mind became more acute when Annabel told him Marie-Santana had refused to meet a prospective suitor he had suggested. The man was a cousin of his, a clerk in a government office, and therefore assured of a steady if not overly lucrative employment for life. Being parsimonious, he had even saved up a tidy sum of money. Yet Marie-Santana had refused to consider him.

"What does she have against him?" Mottu asked. "That he's a little deaf in one ear? People get that way. That he's bald? That happens, too."

"It's not him," Annabel said. "She won't consider any-body. No matter who."

To Mottu, this was bad news. It proved to him that his instincts had been right—Marie-Santana had remained sin-gle because she was in love with him; so much in love that now she would not consider any other man, would accept no substitute. As he thought about this, he suddenly realized its true significance—he had gone through life underrating himself. Here was proof, if proof were needed, that he was desirable. Not just his wife, but another woman—a woman who had been overseas, and no doubt had had her pick of suitors—another woman loved him. He looked in the mirror again, as he had done when first Annabel had asked him why Marie-Santana had remained single. He stuck his chin out and moved it from side to side and narrowed his eyes. Once again the mirror did not lie. He was truly handsome. He decided he'd look even better if he grew a mustache.

That night, when Annabel joined him in bed, she was surprised by the urgency of his lovemaking. When they had finished he did not fall asleep as he usually did. Instead, he caressed her, and she snuggled up against him. In the warmth of that closeness he began to think of that other being who lived directly across the lane, just a few paces away, yet was no doubt tossing forlornly in her bed. He contrasted his own situation with hers. Annabel and he were comfortable with each other; no fireworks in their lovemaking, but deep comfort. At any hour of the night, if he turned, she turned. And if she turned, he turned as well. It was a spontaneous response. Who could Marie-Santana respond to? A pillow? He wondered what it would feel like to make love to her, who had been alone for so long. On the one hand, she might be all afire; on the other, she might be like ice.

She was, of course, vulnerable. Of that he was sure. A clever man, an unscrupulous man, could take advantage of that. Three names came to mind, and he examined them closely. Two he dismissed almost immediately: Forttu the tavernkeeper as unscrupulous, but stupid; Teodosio the hunter as clever but much too involved in himself. That left only Senhor Eusebio, who was both clever and unscrupulous. Clever, unscrupulous, and rich. He regretted now having suggested that the landowner consult Marie-Santana about his garden. It had been an act of helpfulness, a spontaneous gesture, and he saw how it could backfire. He imagined Marie-Santana being seduced, Marie-Santana in Senhor Eusebio's arms. And then he inwardly laughed: the man was old, his hair was already turning white. She would never fall for him.

Having dismissed Senhor Eusebio as a threat, Mottu

focused on another. Also old, it is true, but a man of recti-
tude. Hardworking, like her; a churchgoer, like her. Pedro
Saldanha, a good match, although poor. But the poor part
might not be true; some said he had money stashed away.
On the other hand, his sister Geraldine, who lived with him,
would never let him marry, never allow another woman
in that small house of theirs. No, for Marie-Santana, he,
Mottu himself, though married, was the only solution.

Between fire and ice, he decided that she was now a
combination of the two, a volcano gone cold. That would
explain why, in all these weeks, she had not pursued him,
as he had feared she would. Either way, he might have to
teach her to let go, to love, from having been so long alone.
He thought again of how she had wasted all those years,
saving herself for him. A tragedy! And now, even with a
proposal from a good man, a man of means though bald and
a little deaf, she was still waiting—for what? For him,
Mottu, to leave Annabel? For Annabel to die? He did not
want Annabel to die. That aside, Marie-Santana would be in
for an extremely long wait, for Annabel was as healthy as
a—but whatever animal he thought of as healthy, whether
ox, or buffalo, or tiger, he immediately saw that animal dying; sometimes, even, from unnatural causes. The possibility of Annabel's death became real. He remembered a cousin
who had been widowed in his twenties. Why should his
own marriage be immune? Shuddering, he began to imagine
a life without Annabel, a desolate life, a barren life, filled
with loneliness. Mottu's face contorted; his eyes filled with
tears as he pictured himself weeping. He saw himself being
comforted by neighbors, but most of all by Marie-Santana,
ministering to him day and night. Although she did this
willingly and untiringly, her face was a mask. He saw at
once that he had been right, she would have to be taught
the arts of love, step by step. He lingered over each step,
deliciously, until she, now an expert, was providing him
endless hours of connubial bliss.

"Day and night," he said, half-aloud. "Isn't that amazing!"

"Isn't what amazing?" Annabel asked, stirring sleepily by his side.

"That's amazing," he said hastily, not knowing what else to say. "I was dreaming." She threw a comforting arm around him and once again drifted off to sleep.

Mottu, however, found sleep evading him. His wife's trusting touch had shamed and humbled him; he became aware that he had committed a grievous sin against her, if only in his mind; now that he thought about it, he had committed a whole series of sins in his mind, he a married man, against her and against God, in the lustful way he had pictured himself and Marie-Santana tumbling about. Tumbling and rolling. All that wild moaning—and in recollecting it he was sinning yet once again. This was March, this was Lent, the middle of Lent, when the vicar in all his sermons was calling attention to sin and the need for repentance. And he, Mottu, had committed adultery, had even killed off his wife. In his mind, true, but had the vicar not said, impure and sinful thoughts were often worse than deeds? With Easter around the corner, he would be expected to go to Communion. To receive Communion, he would have to go to confession. That meant having to confess either to the vicar or to the curate, and though a wooden screen would shield him from being seen by the priests, either of them would recognize his voice. They always did, he knew, even though they gave not a hint of it when assigning penance: three Our Fathers and three Hail Marys, and three Glory Be to the Father, Son, and Holy Ghost. This was the sentence imposed on him most often because, in the past, all his sins had been venial. Could he face them now, loaded down as he was with mortal sin?

At last the solution came to him: he would simply receive Communion without first going to confession; each priest would think he had confessed to the other. "Thank you, Lord!" he cried inwardly, ecstatic. But then he felt, not God's grace, but God's frown. Instantly the thought of receiving Communion while not in a state of grace appalled him; that would be adding a far more grievous sin to those he had already committed. So grievous that for that alone he could rot in Hell. Had the Devil gotten him already? He crossed himself as well as he could with his left hand, for his right arm was pinned under Annabel's waist and he dared not move it. And no sooner had he crossed himself than a far better solution suggested itself—he did not need to go to the vicar at all, nor even to the curate. All he had to do was walk over the hill to Goregão, a very long and tiring walk up that steep and unforgiving hill, but there at the end of it all he would find a most welcome sight—the centuries-old Church of Saint Martha of the Miracles, where the vicar was so new and so old and so troubled by cataracts that he could not recognize his own parishioners, let alone a stranger making the long trek from Tivolem.

22

SIMON SLEPT FITFULLY. The night was hot and he was sweating, but his window stayed closed. Each time he awoke, he lay wondering what time it was. The ticking of the wall clock irritated him—he wished the minute hand would get to the hour, and the clock would strike. He determined now to stay awake, only to drift off into sleep. He was half-awake once again when the clock whirred and struck one. That could mean anything—half past twelve, one o'clock, one-thirty, half past some other predawn hour. The sound reverberated until the ticking returned. The noises outside offered no clues other than that it was still deepest night. There were no footsteps in the lane. Jackals howled up in the hills; other jackals called back from the sugarcane fields, and were answered each time by the dogs in the village, a ragged and futile challenge that only provoked the jackals to mock them once again. Normally, Simon, like his neighbors in the village, would have slept through the cacophony, but not that night. His unease was too great.

He roused himself and sat up in bed, his feet groping for his sandals. The translucent strips of seashell in his windows hinted faintly at starlight. He sat long moments in the dark, considering his immediate options—if he chose to get up, he must first find the box of matches under his pillow, and then the candle (no big problem; that candle was always by his bed, he'd just have to feel around a bit), then light the oil lamp. Perhaps he could then work on his stamp collection; that would set his mind at ease. But he'd have to wait hours for a hot cup of tea; it was too early for him to awaken his maidservant.

Fists clenched in frustration, he threw himself back on his pillow. His thoughts turned to long walks he had taken past all those houses, all that domesticity. Couples, with families. Sometimes just couples, older couples, whose children and grandchildren had grown and married and migrated to far-off countries to earn a living and send some money home. Family gatherings. A sharing of sweets; arguments and laughter. And he? Alone, out there by himself, standing by the gate.

The irony of it was, he could afford a bride. He thought of other men in the village. He was not quite alone in his situation, after all—Eusebio and Teodosio were also bachelors, though Teodosio was at least as well-off as he was, and Eusebio was even rich. And he reminded himself that, for those who were married, life was not always paradise. On the other hand, it was not always purgatory, either, though there was hardly a love match among them. Nor were there any shotgun weddings, but instead, marriages carefully arranged through go-betweens, each move and its repercussions thought through in advance, the only excitement generated by disputes over dowry and the total number of bridesmaids and who gets what share of the house. His own parents? Their marriage, too, had been arranged, "till death do us part." And it had lasted as scheduled. Strange, how the arranged matches seemed to have worked, most of them. Enough to create a home, to procreate. To produce the continuity of line his father had sought, vainly. His father! He had promised. . . .

But who to marry? He had, it is true, received proposals since his return, for word had gotten out that he was a bachelor with means; but he had been taken with none of them. Too old, too young, too fat, too thin, and, above all, too much after his money. "She will come with a handsome dowry," one man had said. "Fifty thousand. With that and your own money, you and my daughter could live like kings." He did not want to live like a king; too many kings in his lifetime—George V and the Japanese emperor aside— had been shot to death or toppled like banana trees in a high wind, Tsar Nicholas and Kaiser Wilhelm included.

And in Tivolem? Marie-Santana? Yes, she was kind. Alone of all the people in the village, she had comforted him after the curate's acid comment, asking why she was no longer hearing the wonderful pieces of the previous weeks? And when he had played her the "Meditation" that very evening, from the depths of her garden she had rewarded him with a wave and a smile. Indeed, he had played for her each evening since that day. Especially the Schubert "Serenade." He found himself getting sentimental, and decided to tick off the points in her favor, dispassionately: she had been abroad and, though plain, had a certain air about her, was well-spoken, neat, a hardworking and wonderful housekeeper, with a ready smile. Remembering her smile, Simon caught himself smiling. He recalled then that she was poor— Josephine Aunty had made sure to tell him—too poor.

But did that matter, he asked himself? It would have, had she been impressed with his money, which she was not. He liked that. But her friends! She did move with a lower class of people than he would normally associate with. Annabel and Mottu, they were her neighbors, he could understand that; and Forttu the tavernkeeper, he was a jolly man, and one could understand that, too; but how would he feel if his wife were to spend long minutes chatting with Amita, and Rukmini, and Atmaram's wife, and Govind and Kashinath and Atmaram as well, when all he himself did was walk by them with no more than a courteous greeting? Could he, an artist in tune with the music of the spheres, ever be at ease with artisans and tradespeople?

What could he talk to them about, even if his Konkani improved? The tenor of his thoughts now embarrassed him. He reminded himself that their world had been his father's world, had been his world as a child, was his world now. His father would have chided him for his snobbishness.

Lying flat on his back, Simon examined anew the pros and cons of having Marie-Santana for a wife, much as he would examine the pros and cons of acquiring a rare stamp of dubious authenticity; each would involve a risk and some sacrifice. With a stamp, he would gain or lose some money; with Marie-Santana, he'd lose more than a bit of his prized independence. Here then was a more serious obstacle than friends whose world was circumscribed. His time would not be his own. Perhaps—and not just perhaps, but rather most likely—she would object to his spending as much time as he did poring over his stamps. Or to his playing the violin whenever he felt like it. Or to his spending two long lazy afternoons and one full morning a week playing bridge with the vicar and his cronies. There was also Angelinh' Granny, needing much care. And what would he gain? He tried to think, but the argument in his head went round and round, and he kept dozing off, awakening each time to the single, disheartening thought—it would not work.

He opened the window to let in the night, and breathed in once again the pervasive scent of jasmine. A corner of Angelinh' Granny's roof shone dully in the starlight. The jackals had fallen silent. Granny's garden lay empty, awaiting the dawn. He thought he'd stand there and wait, too, thinking of nothing, waiting till dawn broke and the morning sun again lured Marie-Santana out into the garden, but a bat hurled itself out of the darkness and missed his head by inches. Startled, he ducked, then shut the window. The clock struck three.

He sat on the edge of his bed, his mind a blank. He found himself getting sleepy. Settling down, he sighed, and rolled over onto his stomach, and in seconds was sound asleep. But when he awoke he remembered dreaming that he had been out in the garden, moving pots of brilliantly colored crotons from one spot to another. He did not remember ever having seen plants in such profusion. He remembered being told, "This one goes here, that one there." It had been a woman's voice, a strong yet gentle voice, but not his mother's. He did not recall seeing the woman's face. He remembered transplanting roses that did not prick his hands, roses that had been taken from a garden just three houses down the lane. He did not remember protesting.

23

THE DAY AFTER Lazarinh' had stopped by Marie-
Santana's garden gate, Amita, Govind the carpenter's
wife, returning from a trip into a neighboring village, was
treated to a most astonishing sight—their sturdy piebald
bull-calf, that she had raised almost from birth along with
her goats, was being driven up the lane that led over the
east hill to Goregão, and who was doing the driving but a
man in striped shirt and shorts, and even at that distance
she knew: who could it be but Lazarinh'? She tried to chase
after him but he was too far up the hill already, and she had
a child at the hip besides, and by the time Govind himself
had been found and had started up the lane with a friend
for company and protection, the sun's shadow had lengthened a full three feet to the east. The two had followed the
lane a good three miles into Goregão, taking what short cuts
they could, scrambling over rocks and scrub while keeping
the path in sight; and they had been told that yes, Lazarinh'
had been there, had been seen spending money in the village
market and in the tavern, but that he had entered Goregão
alone, sans calf. Sans calf, but certainly with money—fifty
rupees, more or less, the tavernkeeper said, in a wad of
crisp one- and five-rupee notes.

All this Govind recounted to his wife upon his return,

asking rather wistfully, for he was the kind of man who does not lightly think ill of another, whether she might not have been mistaken, after all? Was it really Lazarinh' she saw rustling their calf, and not some no-good migrant worker heading home to the jungle-covered Ghats?

"Wouldn't I know a *ghantti* if I saw one?" she retorted. "Since when do you doubt my word, the mother of your five children?" And she threatened to feed his rice portion to the pariah dog outside if he persisted in his questioning.

"So where is our calf?" she shrieked at Lazarinh' when she saw him come limping home later that night. "What have you done with it, son of the devil?"

"What about your calf, woman?"

"I saw you driving it over the hill this afternoon!"

"You saw me?! Then you saw the dog?"

"What dog, liar? There was no dog!"

"Is this the thanks I get," said Lazarinh', "to be called a liar, just because your eyesight is weak, and you saw no dog? Here I was coming home tired from work this afternoon, really tired, what can I tell you, and I see a calf running up the hill lane with a strange dog barking after it, and I've never seen that dog before but I know that calf, I see at once that it is your calf, which is like a sixth child to you, and I shout out as loud as I can, 'Ho, Govind! Ho, Govind's wife!' But you are nowhere to be seen, not you and not your husband, so I chase after the dog and the calf, over the hill, halfway to Goregão, and the dog turns away when I finally get to throw a stone at it, and rushes at me to bite me, and it's a big dog, so I jump on top of a wall for safety, and fall over on the other side, which is a good thing or else the dog would have bitten me and it would all have been on account of your no-good calf, but when the dog is gone and I climb on the wall again, your calf is nowhere to be seen. Now here it's night, and I return limping, my toes bleeding from stubbing them on rocks, my ankles swollen from falling off the wall, and you ask me where is your calf as though I, Lazarinh', whom the entire village knows from childhood as an honest man, as though I had stolen it?"

"The whole world knows you for a thief," she shrilled.

But he stood firm. "Where is your proof, woman?"

Govind's wife was rendered temporarily speechless, as a result of which Govind got very little to eat that night. "You should have been there with me to give him a beating, instead of wasting time and money in Forttu's tavern," she said, slapping his hand away as he tried to reach for a second helping of okra curry, a dish she knew he loved and thus had prepared especially to punish him with.

"I will tear him apart when I see him," Govind boasted, not to his wife but to the gurgling baby. "Limb from limb I will tear him apart, and feed his carcass to the jackals." He stood up and belched and lurched toward the door.

"If you go there now, he'll half kill you," Amita said. "And if you wait till you're sober in the morning, you'll be paralyzed by fear. Either way, we lose."

24

THE SPATE OF activity in Senhor Eusebio's garden did
not escape Josephine Aunty's attention, nor did Marie-
Santana's presence there. She accordingly increased the
range and frequency of her patrols, suspecting scandalous
goings-on.

Bits and pieces of dialogue filtered back to her ears,
much of it quite unsatisfying. "You need better soil," Marie-
Santana said at one point, as she kneaded a handful between
her fingers. "What you have here is mostly clay."

"You shall have it," Senhor Eusebio replied, and the
following day two lorryloads of garden soil were delivered.
Josephine Aunty, impressed, stood by and watched it being
unloaded.

"What now?" Senhor Eusebio asked Marie-Santana.

"I can get your garden started, but after that you'll need
to have someone working here regularly," she said. "Perhaps
one of Atmaram's daughters. The plants will have to be
watered morning and evening, seven days a week."

"I'll see that it's done," he promised. "But at least help
me supervise the whole thing."

"Between Granny and the housework, I'm short of time."

"I'll make it worth your while."

What could he mean by that? Josephine Aunty bent down to pluck a weed and study it intently.

"I'm not helping you for money, Senhor Eusebio," Marie-Santana said, nettled. "I don't have much use for money. For now, shall we just agree on where the plants should go?"

Later that week Josephine Aunty went to visit Annabel. "Has your 'Mariemana' then abandoned you?" she asked. "She's spending so much time helping the newest bhatkar."

"I sent her to him," Annabel said coolly. "He needed help."

"He's getting plenty," Josephine Aunty said. "And I heard her say she's not doing it for money."

But Annabel would not be provoked. "The planting will be finished by tomorrow," she said.

To Josephine Aunty's disgust, it was. The day after, heading home from market, she saw Senhor Eusebio out in his pajamas, watering can in hand. "Oh, but he's been truly hooked," she muttered. "A rich man watering his own garden—what will we not see next?" On coming closer, she saw he had stopped watering his plants and was looking instead at his favorite jackfruit tree in disbelief. Sidling up to the low stone wall that marked off the property, she saw three of the largest and ripest jackfruit that had hugged the trunk of the tree for days now lay shattered at his feet, caked in dirt.

"Ah, Senhor Euseb'," she called from the lane, "are you enjoying your garden?"

"And you, Josephine," he answered equally politely, "have you been to market?"

"I couldn't find what I had gone for," she said. "The vegetable vendors were all out of jackfruit. Could you perhaps spare me one of yours?"

"I would gladly have done so," he said, "but see what a terrible thing has happened. There's not a single ripe fruit left on the tree, large or small."

She clucked her tongue. "That one there was big as a pig," she said. "Forty pounds, at least. How did this happen?"

"Can't imagine. Just yesterday I was told this was a very healthy tree."

"Oh? And who told you that?"

"Marie-Santana did. She helped me finish repotting some roses, and I gave her half a jackfruit I had left over from last week. She tasted a segment and found it delicious."

"And she admired that tree?"

"Admired it? She said it was a joy to see an old tree that was still so fruitful. Fruitful, she said! Now this."

"Oh, Senhor Euseb'," Josephine Aunty said, "don't you see?"

"Don't I see what?"

"Never mind—I may have said too much already. Some people say my tongue runs away with me. Look at the sun—it's almost noon already! I'd better hurry home and get my cooking done."

SUMMER
1933

APRIL

25

"Too bad, Eusebio, your radio has given up the ghost," the vicar said. "Now all our news will be stale, since the Bombay papers are two days old by the time they get to us here."

"Don't be so quick with the last rites, Father Vicar," Senhor Eusebio said. "My radio may have seemed moribund, but dead it certainly isn't. All it needed was a new battery, and I got one in Panjim this afternoon."

"So we have news, after all?"

"From the Far East—Japanese troops have crossed the Great Wall, defeating much larger Chinese forces."

"*Deperdit numerus*—sometimes there's ruin in numbers. So does an effete and decadent civilization fall to a rising military power, and history repeats itself. I suppose the League of Nations will intervene?"

"The League can have little to say in the matter," Tendulkar said. "Japan has quit the League, remember?"

"The British lion must now beware," Senhor Eusebio said, "since sooner or later a Japanese general might set its tail on fire."

"They'd never dare," Simon protested. "The British Navy is far too strong, and even before I left Malaya, there was talk of strengthening Singapore's defenses. The British are preparing, but they're not unduly worried."

"If they're not unduly worried," the vicar said, "why are they now offering India a greater measure of self-rule? Out of the goodness of their hearts?"

Tendulkar guffawed.

"I scored a point for you, did I, Mr. Tendulkar?" the vicar said. "You liked that question, eh?"

"I couldn't have phrased it better," Tendulkar replied.

"I have sad news from Margão," Gustavo Tellis said. "It appears that there's a bad case of mumps in the family of Jacinto Furtado."

"Are you telling us this in your official capacity as regedor, or do you really know this man?"

"Neither. I just read the news in *O Heraldo*. I find such tidbits more interesting than what's happening in Manchuria. Come to think of it, a really bad outbreak of mumps in the Chinese army might have kept the Japanese away, something Chinese guns have failed to do."

"On the subject of keeping people away—" Senhor Eusebio began, but the vicar interrupted him.

"Is this more about mumps?"

"No, Father Vicar, it's about a boycott. In Leipzig last week, Nazi storm troopers slapped signs on the doors of Jewish businesses, warning that anyone entering them would be photographed. Part of a one-day boycott, they said."

"A boycott of the Jews! Why the Jews, when they represent so much of what's best in Germany?"

"Well, Hitler's minions don't seem to think they do. The Nazis have occupied Frankfurt's university and forcibly expelled all its Jewish professors, and Marxists as well."

"From a one-day boycott to expulsion of the Jews," the vicar said. "Back to the dark ages."

"There's more. They've seized Einstein's bank account in Kiel, all twenty-five thousand marks in it, and Einstein in Switzerland has hit right back, renouncing his German citizenship."

"Score one for Einstein," Tendulkar said.

"A grand symbolic gesture, but what use is it?" Senhor Eusebio said. "Hitler has been granted the power to rule as he likes for the next four years."

"What a godsent chance to shape the future," Tendulkar said, "if only he were wise and used his powers wisely. Now, more than ever, the world could use some stability."

"If," the vicar said. "If." He rose from the parapet and dusted off his soutane. "What a truly big question mark that little word 'if' can be."

26

IT WAS ARRANGED by Dona Elena that Senhor Teodosio should come by on Monday mornings and Thursday evenings to give Maria her music lessons, staying Thursday nights for dinner.

"I regret you'll miss your Thursday evening bridge sessions at the rectory," Senhor Marcelo said.

"Actually, it's given me an easy way out," Senhor Teodosio said. "I've been losing for weeks; after a while, losing becomes monotonous. And I still have Monday evenings and Tuesday mornings. It'll be a privilege to teach our little Maria, anyway."

"We also have some other business to take care of," Senhor Marcelo said. "You promised to take me with you on a hunt."

"I did?"

"Tigers. I hear there are tigers in the jungles of Salsette and Mormugão, and they come right up to the railroad tracks at night. Even near the sidings at Vasco da Gama, near the harbor."

Teodosio grunted.

"That makes it easier, don't you see?" Marcelo persisted. "We can rent a railroad car, park it on a siding, make it our base for the entire night. What do you say?"

"Marcelo," Teodosio said, "have you ever fired a gun?"

"I've gone hunting, yes."

"Fired a rifle? Against something big? Against tigers, a shotgun is like a peashooter."

"I'll take a rifle."

"Oh no. You take your shotgun. I'll take the rifle."

They set a date, later in the month.

On the day of the first lesson, as Maria eagerly awaited Senhor Teodosio's arrival, she hovered around her mother's Blüthner piano, running her hand gently over the keys and constantly wiping them clean with a cloth. Much to her surprise, Senhor Teodosio showed up with a beribboned mandolin.

"But I'd like to play the piano," she protested, as he presented her with the tiny instrument.

"My dear Mariasita," he said gently, his hand on her shoulder, "I'm aware of your preference. But I had a word with your mother, and together we've come to the right decision. A piano is a fine thing to have, no doubt, and your Blüthner is in excellent shape, considering how little it has been played, but how many homes have pianos in them these days? And how are they maintained? In the monsoon the hammers and dampers swell, the heat warps the wood, keys stick, pedals malfunction, strings rust and break. When you want these things fixed, there's no technician to be found, and when one does show up, he charges a fortune. A mandolin, on the other hand—the worst that can happen is, you break a string. A string you can replace yourself." When Maria still protested, he said, "I'll teach you to play and sing. Remember, you can take a mandolin to the beach or on a picnic—a piano you'd have to leave behind." What he neglected to tell her was that her mother had insisted on piano lessons in the first place, but he, never having played the piano in his life, had talked her into changing her mind.

Maria proved to be a good student, and one who practiced meticulously, remembering to count the *ands* clearly between the ones *and* twos *and* threes *and* fours. Her training was eclectic. The first scale she learned was C Major; the first tune, "Aloha Oe." "Con amore," said Senhor Teodosio, as Maria stumbled her way through that haunting Hawaiian melody; seeing her tremulous lip, he introduced her to the tremolo. The following week she went on to three songs about love, "Mississippi, River Blue," and later, to the latest hits from America—"Night and Day," "Smoke Gets in Your Eyes," and "The Song Is You." At parties she began to entertain requests for "O Sole Mio" and "Santa Lucia"; if importuned (and she was, repeatedly, by one or other of her aunts), she would oblige with "Turna a Surriento" as a first encore. For further encores she played and sang those perennial favorites, "The Lost Chord" and "The Holy City." The aunts wept, some openly, others fluttering their fans the better to hide their tears. For especially tender moments Senhor Teodosio taught her Paolo Tosti's "Goodbye," to which she later added a melancholy Portuguese *fado choradinho,* a weepy *fado* that tugged at the heartstrings. And Maria found a strange correlation: the more intense the tremolo, the more emotional the audience's response. This encouraging discovery helped her greatly to refine her technique.

27

ON A SUNLIT APRIL EVENING, Simon Fernandes went for one of his protracted walks, not toward the main road and the post office, but along one of the many lanes that wound along the side of the south hill. As he left the house, his only impulse had been to wander through a less-familiar section of the village and enjoy the balmy air; in minutes, however, he found himself standing in front of his childhood home. Pushing open the garden gate, he walked up to the front door and tried it. The door would not give, but one of the windows was slightly askew, and through the gap he saw sunlight pouring into the living room where the roof had caved in. He stood there a while, imagining himself a child, surrounded by toys. And he tried to imagine his parents as a young couple, doting on him. But the picture he carried in his mind was the picture of his parents in his adulthood; an older, even elderly couple. That image would not change.

He remembered his childhood in Kuala Lumpur as being happy; logic demanded that he had also been happy earlier in Tivolem. He must have had playmates; where were they now? Teodosio could not have been one; he was not of this village. Neither could Eusebio have been, he was older by far. Who then?

It was way past sunset when he turned back; twilight had deepened into a perfumed April night, and myriad stars lit up the sky. The lane wound past darkened houses, each with its own crowded little garden, each garden with its own retaining wall, its own wrought iron gate. The heavy scent of jasmine filled the air. This section of the village was strange to him, and though he knew some of the home-owners by sight, and exchanged brief pleasantries with them whenever they met, there were no names, no house numbers, no signs to tell him who lived where. He felt suddenly alone. The brilliant vastness of the sky increased his sense of isolation. He came to a house through whose well-lighted windows there came the sounds of revelry and laughter. Slowing his pace, he stopped by the gate. Instantly from within, unseen mongrels barked and scurried about. He heard voices approaching the door; not wishing to be caught eavesdropping, he hurried away. Other dogs now barked at his approach, marking his progress house by house, wall by wall, gate by gate, each warning growl and snarl reinforcing the message: "Stranger, keep out." Occa-sionally, a dog already in the lane prepared to challenge him, then backed off at his approach.

He decided to cut short his meandering and head for home. Turning left, he took a narrow uphill path that he felt might lead to his own lane; unexpectedly, it brought him face to face with Bald Uncle Priest's house. At this hour, the menace of its ghostly walls made him shudder. He thought of retreating; then, shaming himself, turned resolutely past it to the right. The lane now sloped gently toward his own place; he would have an easy stroll. There was no one else about. But when behind him he caught the quick scuffle of hooves—probably cattle that had strayed away from the cowherd and were now finding their way home on their own—he did not relish being in their way and quickened his pace. Still the sound came nearer. Alarmed, he turned to look, and found it was not several head of cattle but just one lone bull that was lumbering down the lane.

In the half light the beast loomed large. Simon felt fear crowding his chest but determined not to run. Instead, he walked as fast as he possibly could, but stopped just short of running; that way, he would at least maintain a safe distance. But the bull responded by breaking into a trot. "At least he's not yet charging," Simon said aloud. With a couple of hundred yards still to go, too far to run with any hope of outpacing his pursuer, he felt the need to reassure himself. "Not charging; no, not yet." He did not turn around, lest his fear increase and communicate itself, provoking an attack. He found himself speaking out loud again, words that had been alien to him until this moment: "God help me." And he knew he meant it. To have come back to Tivolem to be gored by a passing bull would strip his life of all meaning. He moved closer to the wall, giving God a chance and the animal ample room to pass.

In another few seconds the trotting bull caught up with him, was almost by his side, but instead of going on, slowed down to match his pace. With near panic in his heart, Simon forced himself to walk alongside the great ungainly beast. His fear gave way to elation as he strode down that long winding lane, sensing now that the bull, that symbol of strength and power, had run to him—to him, Simon Fernandes, the lonely one—for comfort and company. They were no longer each alone in their universe, two beings at odds with one another, but allies, each protecting the other. Approaching his gate, Simon was bold enough to place his hand lightly on the bull's back. It tossed its head, not slowing down, and, when Simon entered his garden, continued on its way.

That night after supper Simon Fernandes made a unique entry in his diary. This time he was little concerned with the mechanics of the day, with what victuals he had had to buy, how much he had had to spend. Instead he wrote:

"Was escorted safely home tonight by a passing bull. Or, maybe, for a short while it was I who was escorting him." And underneath that he scrawled: "After years of doubt I finally called on His name. His name! How easily fear makes believers of us all."

28

THE THEFT OF GOVIND'S CALF, and the problem of what to do about it, was the topic of profound discussion at Forttu's tavern for days and nights on end, even on the night of the full moon the following week when Mottu the mailman, having finished his rounds, went in there for only a second or two, he swears, and merely to inquire whether Forttu was expecting any important mail or packages in the next day or so. And when he came out, fortified by a single complimentary snort of Johnny Walker—"Just one, mind you, not the four that certain slanderous tongues say I have as a daily quota, God forgive them," Mottu said, "or they will surely fry in Hell"—he had emerged he said to find his bicycle, his sole source of income, gone, missing, stolen, and a figure much like Lazarinh's pedaling erratically far down the road, shirttails flapping in the wind.

The bicycle, besides being Mottu's means of livelihood, was also government property, so Mottu straight off went to the police in Mapusa. Presently a constable, with Mottu at his side, placed himself on a bench in Forttu's tavern, which like the forts and castles of old commanded the main entrance to the village. Alas, alas, for Lazarinh' when he staggered up that road at eleven that night—or at precisely 2305 hours, as the official records would soon show. The preserver of law and order showed no compassion even though Lazarinh' was carrying no loot and singing a raucous love song.

"What kind of miscreant do you take me for?" asked Lazarinh', as the handcuffs closed around his wrists right in the middle of the heart-rending finale to "Mariquinh', my Love." And turning to Mottu, he said, "Do I look like the kind of heartless evildoer who would steal the bicycle of a well-loved, much honored public office bearer like you?"

"You look like the kind of evildoer who would sell his own sister," interjected the policeman. "Luckily for your sister, you have no sister."

"My sister, if I had had one, would have been deeply hurt to hear you speak of me in such intemperate terms, o unbemedalled great one," said Lazarinh'. "You are the one who's truly lucky that I really have no sister, because if I had had one, and you had hurt her feelings by speaking ill of me in or out of her presence, I would have had to hurt your feelings in turn, possibly by kicking your noble posterior in public."

This metaphysical exchange might have lasted much longer had not, by an unfortunate accident, some say, the policeman's truncheon become disengaged from his belt, and his hasty lunge to retrieve it only caused the stick to bounce rapidly off Lazarinh's shins and buttocks, rat-tat-tat, thud-thud-thump, thu-thump, not once but several times. Fortunately, the stick itself suffered no irreparable damage. The policeman therefore returned it smoothly to his belt, but not before carefully testing it twice again against Lazarinh's buttocks—thwack! thunck!—to make sure it had lost none of its resilience.

The above version was pure speculation, of course, mere idle village scuttlebutt, based on the accounts of unreliable eyewitnesses. A far clearer light on what happened is shed by the official chronicle, the police log, which reveals that on the night and at the time in question one Lazar, aka Lazarinh', member of the public and palpable miscreant, while in a drunken state did enter into a loud and prolonged argument on civics with a wandering water buffalo that had defecated on the road; and after refusing to yield the right of way, and further becoming verbally and physically abusive, the said member of the public and known miscreant Lazar alias Lazarinh' got behind the said beast of burden and twice endeavored to push it off to one side, whereupon the said evildoer was soundly and repeatedly kicked by that otherwise docile and even-tempered animal, giver of milk, plower of fields, friend to all mankind. The log reveals that Lazarinh' was charged with theft and cruelty to an animal; it does not note the constable's reactions when days later the magistrate dismissed the complaint for lack of evidence, ignoring the affable buffalo that had been brought into court to buttress the story, and now stood to one side placidly chewing cud.

But Annabel was not one to give up. "We must tie up our statue of Saint Cornelius," she said to her husband.

Mottu winced. "For heaven's sake! Tie up a saint?"

"He's the patron saint of our village," she persisted, "and the patron saint of reformed criminals, and he's not called Saint Cornelius the Contrite for nothing. I've heard Angelinh' Granny say—bless her knowledge of these things!—that each time one ties up the statue of Saint Cornelius, stolen goods are mysteriously returned. In fact, Angelinh' Granny remembers that the one time they had a robbery in her house, when she was a child, the good saint remained tied up for days until everything that had been stolen was brought back."

Mottu looked dubious.

"Bad things happen to thieves who do not return their loot when Saint Cornelius wants them to," Annabel went on. "The longer the saint remains tied up, the greater his anger, the more his wrath is to be feared. Tell the baker we've tied up the statue and swear him to secrecy; that way he's bound to tell the entire village. And spread the word yourself as you make your rounds with the mail."

29

THE BAKER on his morning rounds thumped his staff with greater vigor than ever, bringing people scurrying out of their houses to hear what tidings he brought: Rukmini's famous milch buffalo had suddenly gone dry. The news produced a greater reaction even than the blighting of Senhor Eusebio's jackfruit tree. And it was not to be wondered at—that particular buffalo's milk, after all, discreetly diluted with water, met the needs of very many families, while Senhor Eusebio's prized jackfruit, exceptionally sweet though they were, were enjoyed only by the privileged few.

Josephine Aunty, properly solicitous, stopped by Rukmini's to commiserate.

"What a great pity!" she said. "A blow to us all."

"Ah, yes!" said Rukmini. "Kashinath is very upset. It's not just our customers, he says; what do we now give our children? But what can one do? Such is fate."

"It was the best milk in the village," Josephine Aunty said.

"So easy on the digestion."

"Far better than goat's milk."

Rukmini understood that in that single statement, Amita's goats had at once been discussed and downgraded.

"There's no comparison," she said.

"By the way," Josephine Aunty said, "have you seen Mar'-Santan' lately?" She refused to call her Mariemana.

"Two days ago," Rukmini said.

"Before your she-buffalo ran dry! Strange!"

"What's strange?"

"Oh, nothing," said Josephine Aunty. "You heard about Euseb' baab's jackfruit tree?"

"That was terrible. It bears the sweetest jackfruit in all of Goa."

"It did, but it may never again. You remember, Mar'-Santan' admired that tree. She told Euseb' baab the tree was fruitful. Fruitful, she says, fruitful, and—*dabhainz!*—the three biggest jackfruit fall down."

"Oh!"

"Very strange things have been happening around here since someone returned to Tivolem," Josephine Aunty said, "and not only to your she-buffalo."

30

AT MIDNIGHT on the third day of Saint Cornelius's bondage in the Mottu household, Annabel awoke with a start. She had heard a dull thump, and her first thought was that the statue of Saint Cornelius had fallen off its little altar. But on striking a match she found it was not so—the saint stood where she had left him, bound with strong twine, his head tilted in the same attitude of sorrow and resignation. "God forgive me," she muttered, holding the match closer for a better look into his glazed, reproach-ful eyes, until the flame licked at her fingers and she hastily dropped the match. It seemed to her then that the saint had given her a foretaste of hellfire for having tied him up, and she was about to untie him when she heard the sound again, and it was not anything in the house.

"Mottu!" she whispered, vigorously shaking her still-sleeping husband. "Mottu! Wake up! The thief is at the gate." And when he grunted and turned over she hissed again, "The thief! Wake up! The thief's outside! Go get him!"

Mottu, now wide awake, heard a scraping on the gravel path outside his door and rushed out, cudgel in hand, to where he caught the faint glint of metal by starlight. The bicycle fell to the ground with a clatter, and it was then that Mottu caught sight of the black-clothed figure turning to flee. With a blow of his cudgel he brought the man down. Thwack! Thwack! Thwa-thonk! went the club again as the figure scrambled desperately about on hands and knees.

"Mottu-u-u!" screamed the returner of stolen goods. "Stop! Don't you recognize me? I'm your neighbor Lazarinh'!"

"You lie!" cried Mottu, who knew exactly where the truth lay, but was not about to give up a heaven-sent advantage. "Take that for lying (thwack)! Lazarinh' does not dress in black (swish)! Lazarinh' does not steal—he told me so himself (thump)! Take that (double thump) for smearing the name of an innocent man!"

"O Mottu, Mottu!" cried the figure, "God bless you for believing in my innocence! But look closely—it is indeed me, it's Lazarinh'!"

"Aha!" cried Mottu, now getting a firmer grip on the cudgel. "So it's really you, is it? It's Lazarinh', come like a thief in the middle of the night, with my stolen bicycle, and dressed all in black like the devil himself?" And he raised his stick again.

"It's not what you think," said Lazarinh', leaping nimbly out of harm's way. "I had gone to a cousin's funeral in Assonorá, and having missed the last bus had to walk all the way home. You know how long that takes! By the time I passed Forttu's tavern, everything was pitch dark. Right outside the front door, would you believe it, I found your bike. In the middle of the road! In fact, I tripped right over it. If there were some light here you'd see where the pedal caught my shin. But when I tripped over it I didn't think of the pain—in fact, I felt no pain at all. My first thought was, Heaven be praised! This must be Mottu's missing bike! The thief has brought it back! That's what I thought. Lucky for him he got to leave it there before I arrived, or he would have caught it from me, I tell you! And how lucky is Mottu—I said to myself—that I was the first person to stumble across it, and not some half-drunken stranger with larcenous fingers! Then the bike would have been gone for sure! I must take it to Mottu right away, I said, without stopping to change from my funeral clothes, because this bike is definitely Mottu's, no doubt about it, and what's Mottu's must go back to Mottu as fast as possible, because that's the way Mottu delivers our mail."

"Hit him!" screamed Annabel, appearing suddenly in the doorway. In her left hand she held aloft a hurricane lantern, in her right a heavy frying pan. "Hit the misbegotten one!" she cried again. "Hold him till I can lay my hands on him!"

Seeing the enemy thus powerfully reinforced, Lazarinh' dove headfirst into some bushes, and though Mottu flailed about him with vigor, the cudgel became entangled in brambles, and his quarry fled into the night.

MAY

31

"WHY THE LONG FACE, Tendulkar?" Senhor Eusebio wanted to know. "Your hero Gandhi has been released. I'm pleased he's out; sixteen months is a long time for an old man to spend in jail. You, you should be delighted."

"I would be, too, if he hadn't started that fast."

"But it's not a fast unto death," Teodosio said. "He's fasting for just three weeks! Besides, if he gets his way, as he usually does, he will end his fast early."

"Three weeks will kill him," Tendulkar said darkly. "Just water, soda, and orange juice? He's in no condition for such an extreme test. Besides, he wants a promise—and action—that every Hindu temple in India will now open its doors to untouchables. Every temple! Do you think that's likely to happen, in three weeks? Three years? Or even thirty?"

"More likely in three centuries," Simon said. "Caste seems to be in our blood, though I myself am not at all a casteist."

"Of course you aren't," Tendulkar said. "None of us here are. But since you have no immediate family, I can safely ask you a hypothetical question. Would you allow a daughter, or a sister, to marry an untouchable?" When

Simon hesitated, Tendulkar cried, "You see? We think we aren't, when deep down we well may be."

"I would object to the marriage, Tendulkar," Simon said, "not from any bias but because of the consequences such a marriage would have. She and her children would be ostracized."

"Even by people she loved?"

"Even by people who loved her."

"Acerrima proximorum odia," the vicar said, to no one in particular.

"I happen to know that one, Father Vicar," Regedor Tellis said, laughing. "It's our nearest relatives who hate us the most. But let me make a deal with you. If you'll agree to stop quoting Latin proverbs, I'll get Tendulkar to agree not to quote from the Sanskrit. Sanskrit quotations are often very long, and even when they're short they take a lot of explaining."

"At least," the vicar said, "you did not threaten to get Tendulkar to fast."

"Our regedor loves food too much himself to ask someone else to give it up," Teodosio said. "But to get back to Gandhi. Some of his policies I agree with—the salt march, for instance. No government should have a monopoly on salt, a colonial government least of all. But this burning of foreign-made clothes, that was idiotic. If I burned these I'm wearing, I'd have to buy some more. That might make the British richer, but how would it benefit India?"

"You have misunderstood the clothes-burning bit," Tendulkar said. "The idea was to replace them with home-spun items. Like the salt march, clothes-burning hit the British in their wallets, affecting the mills and factories in Lancashire and Manchester; a bonfire whose light was seen around the world."

"Tonight, in Germany, people will be setting bonfires of a different sort," Senhor Eusebio said. "Students and Nazis have collected thousands of books they consider un-German, and they're being piled in the streets so they can be set fire to. Part of a national purification, that's what they call it."

"What an irony," Tendulkar said. "To purify India, Mahatma Gandhi fasts, and writes articles and books on social issues. To purify Germany, Hitler is going to burn books, especially those dealing with social issues. And he claims we have a common Aryan heritage?"

"The French seem to think he has more in common with the ancient Huns," Teodosio said. "Just a couple of days ago, *O Heraldo* ran an article that had appeared in a French paper, posing a quite fantastic question: 'What will France's response be if Hitler's troops at night occupy the Polish corridor, and other units cross the French frontier in motorized armored cars, cut our lines of communication, and penetrate a hundred kilometers into our country, while their aircraft attack our covering troops with gas and incendiary bombs?'"

"An interesting question," Tendulkar said, "but totally absurd, considering France's strength and Germany's weakness. Germany got drubbed just fifteen years ago. Hitler attack a powerful France? Never!"

32

"GRANDMOTHER," Marie-Santana said, "something's going on out there that's bothering me." The words came out of her slowly, painfully; she was not given much to complaining. Some vicissitudes of life, she had learned from observing her father, are best borne silently and with fortitude. "What cannot be cured must be endured" was one of his favorite sayings; she imagined that public opinion would qualify. But public opinion is formed by the people out there, in the outer vastness of the world; what one understands by the amorphous "public" should not include the residents of a tiny, close-knit village such as this, much less one's neighbors, much less one's friends. "It's like a whispering campaign, and I can't quite figure out why."

Angelinh' Granny, her gnarled fingers carefully sifting through a scattering of uncooked rice she had been tossing on a bamboo sieve, picked out a piece of grit.

"Tell me."

"People seem to be avoiding me. Just this morning, Rukmini was talking to Amita, who was out feeding her baby goats, and when they saw me coming, the two of them hustled the lot inside Amita's shack and shut the door."

"That's not like Amita at all. You're sure she saw you?"

"Yes, because she pretended very hard not to have seen me. And then I caught her peeking through a window."

"That's strange. And you've done nothing to offend her?"

"Not that I know of, nor Rukmini either. And Josephine Aunty—"

"She's just a gossip."

"I don't think she likes me. She simpers to my face, but I think she's spreading stories behind my back. Twice I've caught her whispering to Annabel, and each time they saw me they pulled apart—in a hurry."

"Hmm. Has Annabel been avoiding you?"

"Not exactly, but she's not as warm as she used to be."

"You asked her about it?"

"And she laughed. Said I was imagining things."

"You just might be. Wait a few days. Josephine may just be jealous. Before you came, she and Annabel were very close friends. Inseparable. Now Annabel spends much more time with you. Josephine must be upset." She took a pinch of snuff. "But to go around spreading stories. . . . What could they be about?"

"Granny, if I only knew! I seem to be neck-deep in trouble and have done nothing to deserve it."

"Trouble, child, is the sieve through which false friends fall," Granny said. "Annabel will come around, you'll see."

Marie-Santana lowered her head, making no reply.

"You're crying." Putting down the sieve she had been picking through, Angelinh' Granny rose unsteadily to her feet. "Facing away from me won't help. I know you're crying."

She held Marie-Santana in a bony embrace. "Let me find out what I can," she said.

And she tried. But no matter which of her visitors Angelinh' Granny asked—and they seemed to grow fewer by the day—they all professed ignorance.

33

O N Sundays at High Mass the Church of Saint
Cornelius the Contrite filled up by degrees. The poorest women arrived first, heads bowed, palms joined together,
feeling the presence of God, genuflecting before tiptoeing to
the font to dip their fingers in holy water and cross themselves, genuflecting again as they moved reverently up the
nave to where the gilded altars reminded them of heavenly
riches yet to come. They brought alms for the Sunday collection, but otherwise came empty-handed, bringing nothing
to sit on. Bit by bit they filled the greater part of the church,
occupying an area stretching from the communion rail that
marked off the chancel to the base of the marble pulpit.
Since they would spend an hour and a half on their knees
or sitting on the cold stone floor, they were the most wake-
ful and attentive part of the congregation. Women who were
less poor brought in whatever seat was most convenient to
carry—sometimes a low three-legged stool; sometimes a
worn pillow; sometimes a tiny wooden bench to squat rather
than sit on, barely a foot wide at best, and certainly no more
than four inches high. They placed themselves in orderly
rows between the truly indigent and the entrance to the
church, leaving enough of a gap so that even a casual obser-
ver would know who were the have-nots and who the haves.

The well-to-do sat on benches that were placed at the rear of the church. Dona Esmeralda, as befitted the grande dame of the village, had her place reserved for her—just within the church, close enough to the entrance to allow her to breathe in some fresh air, but far enough inside so she would not have to move if it rained. Dona Elena sat immediately to her right, but graciously yielded that place if Dona Esmeralda's son and daughter-in-law, Barnabé and Rosa, and their little son Angelo, were visiting. Then Rosa and the child sat between the two older women; Barnabé had to stand, with Senhor Eusebio and Teodosio, at the back of the church and to the right. Wealth is what separates us from Christ, a former vicar was fond of saying; and if proof were needed, he said, one had only to see how people placed themselves in church—those nearest the Blessed Sacrament were the poorest of the poor; but the rich distanced them-selves from it, voluntarily, seeking creature comfort. That vicar, unfortunately, was never able to stay long enough in any one parish to make his message stick; he died a sad-dened man.

The poorest of the poor, who sat or knelt up in front, seemed to be in constant flux, gliding silently up to a con-fessional and gliding back with folded hands and downcast eyes; gliding up to the communion rail and gliding back with head bowed lower still. In between, but never while the vicar was preaching, some of them might arise and tip-toe up to the poor box, to drop a coin in it and genuflect and light a votive candle at one of the four side altars. The most popular of these was graced with a unique piece of triple statuary—Saint Anne leaning protectively over her daughter the Virgin Mary, who was seated cradling the Infant Jesus in her arms; a most unusual scene, church his-torians said, because statues depicting Saint Anne and the Virgin Mary together generally do not include the baby Jesus. One or more candles in front of this much-revered group seemed always to be lit, and one also found there an occasional garland of marigolds, carefully placed at the feet of the Blessed Virgin by a pious Hindu supplicant seeking a child or grandchild.

The earlier of the two Sunday Masses, the Low Mass at six, drew a congregation of the working poor, not only because the service was short and they could then more easily tend to the chores of the day, but also because the homily was delivered almost entirely in Konkani. Almost, but not entirely; the vicar had been trained to salt his language with appropriate Latin phrases, not, as Senhor Eusebio once rather mischievously suggested, out of any desire merely to impress the *ignobile vulgus*—the vulgar multitude—but rather so as to give the congregation a sense of greater closeness to God.

The High Mass began promptly at nine-thirty, except on those days when Dona Esmeralda was late in arriving. On such days the sacristan waiting out in the churchyard would not pull on the rope he was holding, but would wait until the old widow, an elegant lace mantilla covering her head, was helped out of her carriage, wait until she had actually climbed the church steps and was preparing to cross the threshhold. Then, and only then, as she reached for the holy water with which to bless herself, would he give a measured tug on the rope lying ready between his fingers, so that the great bell gave tongue just once, boommm!, the urgency of its vibrations signifying that Mass was about to begin.

To reach the church in ample time, Marie-Santana left her house a little after nine, a fact of which Simon Fernandes was acutely aware. He had discovered it first by accident; while lounging in his balcão, he had heard the clanging of a gate disrupt the quiet of the morning and, turning his head to see what had caused it, had discovered his neighbor, dressed in a light blue sari, heading to church. He watched her move serenely down the lane; an hour and a half later, he placed himself in the balcão again, watching for her return. As she turned in at her gate he waved to her; but she had not seen him, and went straight up the steps of her garden and out of his sight. He made sure to be at his vantage point on subsequent Sundays, and then, in the middle of May, plucked up courage enough to be strolling casually down the lane at the precise moment when Marie-Santana was unlatching her gate.

"Good morning, Marie-Santana," he called, as she swung the gate open and stepped into the lane.

"Why, good morning, Mr. Fernandes," she replied, much surprised. "Are you going to church?"

"Yes, I certainly am," he heard himself saying, though that had not been his intention at all.

"Well, I'm pleased," she said. "I hadn't really thought of you as the churchgoing type."

"I have not been, for some time," he admitted, laughing, embarrassed a little by her frankness. "But once in a while I do surprise myself. Today, I thought—what on earth, why not?"

"Why not, indeed," she said. "Well, you must excuse me, I must hurry."

"I'll walk with you," he said, "if you don't mind."

She was taken aback; she had not expected this response. Men and women did not normally walk to church together; everybody knew that. Even with married couples, the women went first, the men sauntered after. By unspoken tradition the walk to church was a prelude to the Mass itself; some prayed, as though on a pilgrimage, and even those who talked, when they talked at all, did so in hushed tones. True, she and Simon had both grown up overseas, in less restrictive societies; if they could have walked to church together in Kuala Lumpur or in Quelimane, why not here? For the same reason that once inside the church she sat with the women and apart from the men—because the village had reclaimed her more than it had reclaimed him; of that she was sure.

"No, I don't mind, I don't mind at all," she said, "but it's not—" she fumbled for the word—"usual. Not by far. The men come to church just a bit later, you know, after the women are all inside."

"Oh, you can go in first," he said, "but it's a long walk, and I thought—I thought I'd enjoy your company."

She still seemed dubious.

"Well, if it makes you uncomfortable," he said, "if you think people—I'll—"

"No, no," she said, emboldened by his willingness to transgress. "Let's go."

But the lane was a river with tributaries; as they went along, from feeder lanes on either side came little streams of churchgoers, and to Simon's discomfort he found that Marie-Santana had been right, they were all women. Some of them greeted Marie-Santana, then gave him curious glances, looked back at her, then back at him, and then at each other with smiles and knowing looks, so that at last his spirit wilted. He felt he was being seen as a suitor, and he was not yet ready for that. Pretending that he had a pebble in his shoe, he stepped over to the side of the lane, and let Marie-Santana go on and the flood of women pass him by, himself arriving in time to see Senhor Eusebio step out of the brilliant sunshine into the darkened maw of the church.

Simon followed him in, but lost him in a crowd of men, all bunched up near the entrance to the church and over to the right. Unfamiliar as he was with the seating, he care-fully eased his way to the front of the group, to find himself standing directly behind Pedro Saldanha, who was kneeling at the base of the pulpit; he could go no further. To his left and up ahead at an angle he could see a mass of women seated on the floor; of Marie-Santana there was no sign. There he stayed for the duration of the Mass, eye to eye with a grotesquely carved bearded merman and two blue-eyed angels, the three bearing the weight of the pulpit on their heads; the altar he could see not at all, neither could he see the movements of the vicar and his acolytes. But he

heard all the *Dominus vobiscums,* the *Confiteor,* the *Kyrie*
and the *Gloria* and the rest of the half-forgotten words. At
the sermon, the vicar's voice from the pulpit above swept
him along with its oratory and its exhortations, so that
later in the Mass, at the *Domine, non sum dignus,* he felt a
welling-up inside of him, a thrice-repeated crying-out from
the top of his head: "Lord, I am not worthy that Thou
shouldst enter under my roof—yet say but the word and my
soul shall be healed." And he felt himself healed and was
glad to be in church.

Mass over, on his way out he dipped his fingers in the
font of holy water at the same time that a woman with head
bowed dipped her hand in it, and as their fingers inadver-
tently touched he saw it was Marie-Santana. He felt an
electric current surge up his arm then, even as her eyes
fleetingly met his, and she smiled. The press of people sepa-
rated them; he was jostled aside, and Senhor Eusebio of a
sudden was at his elbow murmuring, "Hello, old agnostic,
didn't expect to see you here of all people," and there was
no escape. Even as he chatted with Eusebio, he followed
Marie-Santana with his eyes. Most of all he wanted at that
moment to be with her, to feel that warm soft touch again.
To a question he did not understand he mumbled an answer
the other man did not hear. Marie-Santana did not turn
around, and by the time he and Senhor Eusebio reached
the road and began heading up the lane, she had crossed the
bridge over the nullah and was rounding a distant corner,
a quarter of the way home.

34

A FULL MONTH after Lazarinh' had escaped from
Mottu's wrath, Atmaram the shopkeeper's younger
daughter, the buxom one who now watered Senhor
Eusebio's garden, heard three coconuts fall to the ground
almost simultaneously an hour after sunset. Alerted by that
thud-tha-thump, she heard them roll toward her door and
rushed out to retrieve them, knowing from local custom
that any coconuts belonging to your landlord that fall and
roll to your door are yours to keep, especially if you have
helped in the rolling. But then the thought came to her—
three coconuts rarely fall to earth all at once on a windless
night, unless somebody is up there fooling with Mother
Nature. Looking up, she saw a man silhouetted against the
moonlight, clinging to the tree as motionless as a squirrel
that's spotted a cobra. *"Bapu!* O Father!" she screamed at
the top of her lungs, bringing the man shinnying down
even as her father came rushing into the yard.

"Badmash! Whoremaster!" cried Atmaram, for he had
recently returned from a visit to Bombay, and in that great
city had learned the right-sounding words to use at times
like these. Besides, he had rushed out thinking a stranger
was about to stain the family honor, and finding instead
that it was only Lazarinh'—for he recognized him in an

instant—out to steal the bhatkar's coconuts, he switched in relief from alarm to uncontrolled fury.

"Thief! Steal our landlord's coconuts, will you? Take that!" and he raised a coconut-frond club while Lazarinh' was still some six feet off the ground. Before he could strike, however, Lazarinh' bounced a coconut off his head, and once on the ground flung another at Atmaram's onrushing wife, who escaped injury only because she ducked under a clothesline on her way to battle.

"Ay-ee-eee!" cried Atmaram's wife, not missing a step.

Faced with this onrushing fury, now coming at him with eyes of fire and arm upraised, Lazarinh' darted nimbly past the shopkeeper, who was hampered by his unwieldy club. Hither and thither raced Lazarinh', dodging and weaving around the coconut trees, confounding the best efforts of Atmaram, his wife, and both daughters to catch him; he might even have gotten clean away had not their pi dogs joined the chase; one of them grabbing him by the ankle, Lazarinh' could not shake himself free.

The barking, screaming, cursing, and yelling brought a host of neighbors to the scene. But as they got in each other's way trying to pummel Lazarinh', he, reeling and crying out, worked his way ever closer to the nullah, into which he gave one mighty leap and once again fled into the night. Next morning he was back, defiant as ever, confident that the previous night's punishment would ensure his safety.

35

SIMON, looking at himself shaving one morning, felt the solution to a violinistic problem come floating unbidden into his mind. The problem had been worrying him for days; should he use downbow as marked in the music or upbow to avoid an unnecessary accent? He turned impulsively, preparing to call out, "I've got it, I've got the answer," but realized just in time that the person to whom he'd be addressing the remark had been dead some years already, and was even now resting in a quiet Catholic cemetery in Kuala Lumpur. The experience was not uncommon for Simon, this feeling that his father was around to talk to, and he wondered whether Michael in fact might not have planted in his mind the solution to the problem. Michael, after all, now not only had his own technical expertise to fall back on but also that of Tartini, Paganini, and Vieuxtemps, or whichever virtuoso violinist residing in Heaven he could persuade to play second fiddle in a quartet. Second violin, that is, to Michael's first. That man has an ego, Simon told himself, smiling, razor poised in midair.

Communication with his father came more easily to Simon now than when the old man had been alive; now there were no awkward silences, no hesitant beginnings, no brusque rejoinders, no hand cupped to ear asking for a phrase to be repeated. Whatever thought Michael or Simon chose to exchange was received as surely as the day's mail, and a good deal faster. One such message came to him after he had retired for the night. His father, whom he perceived to be walking by his side to the top of the Tivolem hill, stopped suddenly to say, "Find him."

"Find him?" Simon was astounded.

"Yes. He's your brother. You must find him."

"But," Simon said, "that's not the way you expressed yourself that afternoon in Kuala Lumpur. Then, if I remember right, you said you had no other son. John was dead. I remember it clearly, that's what you said."

And his father said, "I have a different view of things now. Just find him. Don't go to Africa yourself, but ask."

"Ask whom? Teodosio?"

"Ask him first. Later, if need be, ask her." Then he disappeared.

Simon woke with a start to find himself half-propped up in bed and sweating. Not wanting to question Teodosio directly in front of others, he sought him out in the afternoon before they all met at the bridge.

"In your travels around Mozambique, Teodosio," he said, "did you come across other Goans?"

"By the hundred. They were everywhere. Why do you ask?"

"I was wondering whether you'd come across a John Fernandes. He, too, was from Kuala Lumpur."

"I knew three Fernandes brothers in Beira," Teodosio said. "They ran a tailoring shop. And a family by that name in Lourenço Marques; they owned a bakery—baked good bread, too. Taught their child. She giggled when I taught her the English mnemonic for notes on the treble staff—Eat Good Bread Dear Father. But John, no, I met no John. Good friend of yours?"

Simon shook his head. "Let's say a distant relative. Very

distant." He smiled at his own secret joke. "How about in Quelimane? Did you hear of any Fernandes's there?"

"I was never in Quelimane, if you mean the town itself. It's pretty much a fishing port, import-export, sugar, sisal, coconuts, that sort of thing. I'd find no game there. Why not ask Marie-Santana? I hear she lived in Quelimane for most of her life."

"Somebody else suggested I do that," Simon said. "It's not that important, or I'd have asked you both earlier. Just a very distant relative I knew years ago."

Before going to bed that night, Simon sent a message out into the stratosphere. "I'll ask Marie-Santana when I'm good and ready," he said, "and not a moment before." That done, he lowered the wick in his bedside lamp to douse the light. It seemed to him the flame was a long time dying.

36

I T WAS that predawn hour of peace that comes when half the world has finally fallen into a profound sleep and the other half has not yet begun to stir. Into that time of suspended awareness the sound of the distant motor first insinuated itself into dreams and then turned them into nightmares. Like an ill wind the car sped through the sleeping village, its gears grinding as it bounced up the rutted road that wound over the hills toward Betim where, beyond the river, lay the capital city of Panjim. A car at that hour was a rarity; but even more than the straining engine, the startled villagers remembered that other sound—the high-pitched crying-out and yowling that sounded somewhere between a long-drawn-out "Mam-maa!" and the panicked bleating of a goat. Who was it keening in that car, and why?

It was a child from Goregão, the baker on his rounds told them next morning, a child who had been boarded at a school in that neighboring village, a child who the previous evening had climbed a *jambool* tree to pluck the luscious plumlike fruit, had filled his pockets and climbed higher still to the swaying topmost branches, where one had snapped, sending him crashing to the ground. They had found him at night, semiconscious, his skull fractured, and it was his cries and moans the villagers had heard as he was being rushed to hospital.

"The Angel of Death passed over our village," the vicar of Tivolem said from the pulpit that Sunday, "and we heard the flapping of his wings. The boy died, and we are left wondering why God allows such things. One might as well ask, Why did He not create trees with iron limbs? Why did He put in boys the quickness to climb tall trees, in men to scale the highest peaks from which to fall? We cannot begin to understand His ways, and must trust in His infinite mercy. Other than that, I have no answers. All I know is, when a dear one is struck down, whether young or old, infant or grandparent, it is always too soon. Much too soon." Carefully, he adjusted his vestments, knowing that all eyes, following the movement of his hands, would be reminded from whence he derived his authority.

"De mortuis—" the vicar said and paused, finger upraised, leaving the half-finished phrase hanging in air. "They say the child was good, and we know he was good. But of others, who are older and not quite so innocent, do we not also say the same thing? When we hear a man is dead, do we not praise him to the skies? And if that person turns up alive, do we not sometimes wish him dead? The same man, to be judged good or evil—is death the deciding factor? How twisted, how hypocritical then our judgments and our praise!"

The vicar's hands were white as they clasped the pulpit's marble rim. "Many good things will be said about us, too, when we are gone," he continued, "but only we and God will know whether we deserve such praise or not. And if we don't, by then it will be too late."

It seemed to Pedro Saldanha, standing with gray head bowed just inside the crowded church, as though the vicar had singled him out for that sermon and that admonition. Others in the congregation felt the same way; the vicar's eyes, when he turned their way, bore deep into their souls.

But Pedro Saldanha was overwhelmed. A humble and deeply religious man, he was known for kneeling during long stretches of the Mass, his knees burning through the cool stone floor, his arms outstretched in a symbolic crucifixion until he felt them no longer, feeling only pain. That Sunday, following the sermon, he knelt in prayer and remained kneeling, self-absorbed and self-crucified, long after all others had gone their way.

In their modest home his sister Geraldine waited lunch for him, anxiety replacing irritation as the hours passed and still he did not appear. She took the large wooden ladle from the pot and gave the curry another stir, feeding a bit of it to the scrawny tortoiseshell cat that turned and purred and rubbed insistently against her shins.

"Yes, yes," she said, when the cat turned away from the food. "So you'll wait for him, too. That's the way it is with the three of us, all growing old together, he perhaps fastest of all. But we too, cat; yes, even you, you with your nine lives."

She moved to the window.

"Sometimes you'd think I'm his mother," she said. "Perhaps our mother would have wanted that, that I should look after him so. But he. . . . We're stuck, unmarried—last of the family. No one after us to mourn our passing, pray in our memory. No one, but you."

The cat leaped onto the sill and looked down the lane, its tail swishing. "All right, so he's coming," said the woman. "Now I see him too." She went to the hearth and blew on the ashed-over wood to bring the flame back to life, feeling the heat flare against her face even as she drew back from the sparks and flying cinders.

"Hellfire," she muttered, remembering the vicar's sermon at the early Mass she had attended. Not that he had mentioned Hell—he seldom did; but he had spoken of the hereafter, which was close enough. But the priest who had been vicar long before him, that old priest had been able to work Hell and hellfire into every sermon he preached, no

182

matter what the text for the day. She had been a young woman then, terrified with the vastness of the afterlife, sleepless at the thought both of eternal bliss and eternal damnation. When the present vicar arrived, what she had liked best about him was he kept Hell in its place. Somewhere over there, but out of sight.

The garden gate creaked, and as she pushed the one chair back to the kitchen table, her brother entered the room. Silently she placed the pan and the clay pot on the table, and he sat and helped himself. He glanced approvingly at the curry, his favorite—yesterday's fish sauce, cooked in spices, chilies, and coconut milk, had been simmered down to a rich, pastelike consistency; a little would go a long way. He ladled three heaping spoonfuls of rice onto his platter, then slowly put some back.

She turned to face him. "It got to you that bad? Are we going to have fasting and abstinence now, in addition to prayer?"

"That vicar's got me thinking," Pedro Saldanha said. "You must have heard him at the six o'clock Mass you attended. Most priests would be happy to preach just one sermon a week, but not he. And what he said today is true! What will they say about me when I'm gone, Geraldine—and how little of it will be true? I never thought of it that way, not ever, and I've thought a lot lately about passing on."

"So? You're a good man; you've led a good and decent life."

"You think so? And is that enough? Not harming anyone, is that enough? And praying for hours—is that enough? No! I've got to go through the whole thing. I've got to see myself dead. Not really dead, but in my mind. Dead in my mind. And I've got to hear in my mind what they—you and they—are saying about me, now that—I'm gone. Then I've got to match the two—see if I've deserved the praise. Change my life, if I have to. Even now."

"Shall I heat the food again," she asked.

"No, it's fine as it is; yesterday's curry tastes so much better cold."

But in a moment he pushed the platter away and rose from the table.

"I must go to Mapusa," he said. "I'll be gone awhile." He began changing his clothes.

"You're wearing black? All black? Even the shirt?"

"It fits my mood." He did not look at her.

"If you're walking you'll be gone a good four hours."

"It may be five," he said. "I have much to do. But I'll be back before sundown."

But it was not quite three hours later that she heard the throbbing of an approaching engine and the unaccustomed crunch of tires in the lane. The cat leaped onto the sill, and Geraldine looked out the window in time to see a casket being taken off a hearse. "Mary, Mother of God," she cried in a panic, "not him!" and raced down the steps into the garden. But her brother was one of the two who were jockeying the coffin through the narrow gate.

"Who's dead?" she asked, her heart now loud in her ears.

"It's empty. Hold the gate!" he commanded, and with careful shuffling steps the men carried the coffin up and into the house. Into the sitting room they went, and set it on the two available chairs, right in the middle.

"Are you mad?" she cried, following her brother as he walked slowly around the casket, his hand following its plush-lined contours, "inviting bad luck and death on us like this, no one dead and this awful thing here in the house?"

"I want to see myself in my own coffin," he said. "I want to get the feeling, now, while I can do something about it." He paid off the driver of the hearse.

Outside, they heard a woman's voice at the gate, and Josephine Aunty rushed in breathless.

"I didn't hear the church bells toll," she said, then stopped, surprised. "You both—thank God! Then who?"

"Nobody," Pedro Saldanha said.

184

"Nobody's died?"

"Nobody."

"But—"

"Nobody's dead."

"Is anybody sick?"

"No!"

"Then why?"

"For your funeral," Pedro Saldanha said, exasperated, and Josephine Aunty fled, hysterical, the gate clanging after her as it swung repeatedly on its hinges.

He closed the shutters against the fading twilight. "I'm going to lie in it," he said. "There are candles wrapped in that paper. Light four and place them at the corners."

"I won't do it," his sister said. "You've never been quite like this before." And she asked again, leaning into his face, "Have you gone mad?"

"You may have to do it for me someday," he said. "Might as well practice now."

The candles lit, she left the room.

"Geraldine!"

She reappeared in the doorway.

"I miss the flowers."

"This room will be filled with flowers."

"Remember I like roses."

"I will remember. But if you keep this up, I may need the roses long before you do."

He was silent a while.

"It's no good," he said. "I can't see myself, not like this. Hand me a mirror."

She stood by as he watched himself intently for long minutes.

"It's no good," he said again. "It's not the same. Holding the mirror, looking at myself, it's not the same."

He climbed out.

"Are we done, then?" she asked. "Can this thing go back?"

He was looking at her with eyes of fire. Frightened, she backed away.

"Get in there," he ordered. The wall behind her, there was nowhere to go. But when, trembling, she finally began to climb in, he shouted, "No! Not in that flowered dress! Put these on!" and began to strip.

"God forgive me!" She wept, covering her eyes.

"What's the matter, woman? Never seen a man half naked before?" And he tossed her his clothes, standing there in his briefs.

Her dress bunched up as she pulled on the trousers; shirt and coat hung grotesquely from her shoulders. As she lay in the coffin, clothed now all in black, he handed her a crucifix. "Clasp your hands!" And he wrapped a rosary around them.

The cat leaped onto the rim of the coffin, mewing softly. Brusquely he put it out the door, then paced about the room, muttering to himself. Time and again he turned to look down at her, peering at her ashen face, but not seeing her trembling lips, nor the spasmodic shiver that shook her frame, nor the tears that rolled from her eyes, tears she did not dare unclasp her hands to wipe away.

"Not a word!" he admonished her, again and again, rapping on the side of the coffin. "Not a sound out of you! Not a peep! Not even a peep!"

Around midnight, when the tall candles had burnt low and he had fallen asleep slumped on the floor exhausted, she climbed out of the coffin and carefully led him to his bed. As she turned to leave, he suddenly jerked upright.

"We must build a chapel on the hill," he said, and fell back onto his pillow.

She shut the bedroom door, and, still wearing her brother's clothes, went out into the coolness of the garden, the cat turning and rubbing and rubbing yet again against her shins.

37

"HE'S A NICE MAN, that Simon," Angelinh' Granny said. "Much nicer than the other two." They had just finished their midday meal and Marie-Santana was clearing the table.

"He's a nice man, certainly," Marie-Santana said, "but I really don't know what you're talking about." She was tiring of these circular conversations, this constant return to the theme of marriage.

"You can't be all that naive," her grandmother said. "I saw him meet you at the gate a couple of Sundays ago and walk with you to church."

"He didn't walk with me, Granny, he just happened to be passing at the same time I was leaving the house."

"What a coincidence. When I was fourteen, a young man said the same thing to me as I was leaving for church. But I knew he was lying—he'd been waiting for me. Alas! He was just a boy. A year later, it was arranged that I marry your grandfather instead."

"Simon's just a neighbor." She kept her voice cool.

"Of course. I noticed you walked back alone."

"You stood there, by the door, watching to see if he would walk back with me?" Marie-Santana could barely control her anger.

"You watch over me, shouldn't I watch over you?" Granny's voice was plaintive. "Besides, I want your happiness. Simon is a good man; in all these years, there's not been a hint of scandal about him. He's showing an interest; get to know him! What's there to lose?"

"Must you ask? Only my reputation, and Josephine Aunty will see to that."

"Forget that busybody. How do you feel about him?"

"He seems all right."

"Simon has a clean reputation, a small fortune that he's retired on, and an obvious interest in you. If all you can say is, he seems all right, then tell me—why are you blushing?"

"Granny, for heaven's sake! All we've said is hello. So he walked a few yards with me on the way to church. He's a shy man, and I'm no Jezebel. I'm not going to chase after him, neither am I going to chase him away." She hoped that would be the end of the matter. But it wasn't.

"That's my child," Angelinh' Granny said. "Keep talking to Simon. But be very careful with that Euseb'. He has money to throw around and a shiny car to go with it. He gets proposals every week! If he approaches you, marriage may not be what he has in mind."

"Perhaps. I didn't tell you this, but last Friday, as I was walking to the Mapusa fair, he was in his garden when I walked by. Half a mile out of the village I heard a car honking a hundred yards behind me. Naturally I ignored it, though I knew it had to be him. But as soon as he came alongside, he stopped and offered me a ride."

"Was Lallu there?"

"No, Senhor Eusebio was driving himself."

"And you accepted?"

"I tried to turn him down. Said I needed the exercise. He said I could walk back but should ride in with him, since he was there already. I climbed in beside him, not wanting to be rude."

"And?"

"He was perfectly proper. Didn't touch me, didn't so

much as try. In Mapusa he came round to my side and helped me down."

"Did he make the trip just to be with you, you think?"

"Could well be—he's offered to drive me down before, but I've never accepted. This time he said he had some business to transact in town, and I had no reason to doubt him."

"Well, that's not a bad turn of events," Granny said. "Now we've got two moneyed men after you. Two out of three. Now go, you have things to take care of in the garden." Already she could hear Simon tuning up.

Senhor Eusebio was not the only one to offer Marie-Santana a ride on her weekly trips to the Mapusa fair. At nine o'clock on Friday a week after that incident, Marie-Santana, a half hour behind her normal schedule, had walked halfway down the long and palm-fringed road to town when she espied a cyclist riding somewhat unsteadily toward her. As the man approached, she saw it was Mottu; on recognizing her, he let go of the handlebars and waved enthusiastically with both hands. As the bike veered to one side, she held her breath, fearing he would fall.

"I'll give you a ride, Mar'-Santan'," he called out cheerfully. "You've still got a long walk ahead of you. Come on, get onto the crossbar."

"Thank you, Mottu, but it's a pleasant day and I'd rather walk," she said, as he stopped alongside. "Besides, I see you've already been to Mapusa. Why should you go back again?" Her suspicions were confirmed; she smelled liquor on his breath.

He made a face. "I've not been to Mapusa yet," he said. "I've been riding up and down this road for half an hour waiting for you, and now you say no?"

"Waiting for me?" she asked, surprised. "Annabel sent you?"

"No," he said, somewhat sheepishly. "That is—no. I just thought I'd spare you a tiring walk."

"Mottu, what's come over you? You're a married man; what would people say?"

He had stopped in the middle of the narrow road, with one foot on the ground. Now, with a bus approaching, they moved to the side. "And what would people say?" he echoed.

She resumed her walk, anxious to get away from him; he turned his bike around and rode slowly alongside.

"I'll tell them the truth," he said.

"The truth!" Her uneasiness increased. "The truth! And what might that be?"

"That you love me," he said.

"Mottu, are you crazy?"

"Don't call me crazy," he said, placing a hand on her shoulder. "A little drunk, maybe, but crazy, no. Not me! You love me, and we both know it."

"Take your hand off," she said sharply.

He leaned even harder. "Mar'-Santan', I'm going to do what I should have done when you came back. I'm going to kiss you."

She backed off and he lost his balance, so he had to steady himself with a foot on the ground once again.

"For shame," she said. "Think of Annabel."

"You never married," he said. "You waited for me, came back for me. And I—stupidly, I betrayed you, I got married." His face puckered; he was about to cry. "I don't want to think of Annabel," he said.

She watched him warily.

"Come closer, Mar'-Santan', love," he pleaded. "Annabel's not here to see us. Come, just one little kiss."

He turned the bike around as she backed away once more. "Just one kiss," he said again. "Annabel won't see us."

A rage seized her. As he leaned toward her again, she grabbed hold of the back of the saddle and pushed with all her might. The bike went off at an angle; she watched him teeter at the edge of the road; the next moment he and the bike had fallen into the field below. It was a four-foot drop, and Marie-Santana became concerned. She ran to the roadside to find him sitting, shaken but unharmed, on the freshly plowed ground.

"Are you all right?" she called.

He picked himself up without answering.

"We've been friends since childhood," she said. "You are a married man. Must you spoil everything now?"

"I'm ashamed," he said. "And drunk. I'm sorry. You won't tell Annabel?" He was weeping now. "If you tell her, I'll die. She's a good woman, Mar'-Santan'."

"This madness has to stop," she said curtly. "Go home, Mottu." She set off briskly toward town.

"Don't tell. Please don't tell, Mar'-Santan'." He was back on the road, his voice carried on the wind. "Annabel, my wife! Forgive me, my Annabel!"

"Did you meet anyone special, bai?" Granny asked when Marie-Santana got home that afternoon. She was in no hurry to answer; it was Granny's standard question anytime she went to the Mapusa fair. Carefully she showed off the rooster-shaped red clay water jug that was her sole purchase, turning it so its shape would be seen to the best advantage. When filled, it would cool boiled drinking water by evaporation; a slight tilt, and she could almost taste the sweetness. "Just the usual crowd," she said, adding, "but no one that mattered from Tivolem."

38

WHILE LAZARINH's fame as a petty thief and hood-
lum began to spread beyond Tivolem, it still did not
compare with that of older and better-known hooligans in
the surrounding areas. People wondered which of these,
then, was the brazen son-of-Shaitan who, on the third
Sunday in May, broke into the Church of Saint Benedict the
Beneficent in the hamlet of Aiconá, just two weeks before
Saint Benedict's famous annual feast and fair? It was an
hour yet to cockcrow when Apolinar', the church's aged
sacristan, preparing the darkened sanctuary for early morning Mass, shuffled to the main altar with lighted taper in
hand, genuflected, then raised his light to find—nothing.
Thinking that perhaps the vicar had moved the golden
candlesticks to the side altar, he turned in that direction,
only to see something that brought the cold hand of fear to
his heart: no trace of gold there either, but candles strewn
and trampled on the floor, vases knocked down, and Saint
Benedict himself—Saint Benedict, pride and patron saint
of the village—missing!

"Father Vicar! O Father Vicar!" Apolinar' called in a
choking voice and, rushing to the belfry, sent the great bells
pulsing into a clangor that shook the village awake.

Hushed were Aiconá's faithful as they moved through

192

the church, counting up the missing items. The gold candlesticks, the finely wrought candelabra, the exquisite censer that the vicar said came from the time of Vasco da Gama, the loss of these grieved them deeply; but the loss of the statue of Saint Benedict—Saint Benedict of the heavenly blue robe and the upturned visage and the mystical rapturous eyes—that loss left them truly orphaned.

Outside, the hubbub was immense. How could they celebrate their feast, the village women said, when their husbands would not be able to carry the statue in procession on their shoulders seven times around the churchyard, as had been done for centuries? Ah, but their saint would not forsake them, Apolinar' said, he would surely break free of the thieves and come back to his church and his people! And the sacristan had just begun to speak of the saint's great powers, of his many miracles, when his wife, having heard him tell those stories too many times already, suddenly began reciting the Rosary, and all joined in the responses.

With prayers, vigils, and a novena the distraught parishioners laid siege to Heaven, and the vicar declared he was going to keep the church doors open around the clock, so his people could take turns praying day and night, and Saint Benedict himself might—God willing—find his way back into his niche.

Nobody knows how the rumor started, but by the third night of the novena that Aiconá's villagers had begun, it was being said—even in Tivolem—that the statue of Saint Benedict would miraculously reappear in its usual place on the altar, some said on the eve of his feast, some said on the morning of the feast day itself.

The day before, crowds began converging on the church to witness the expected miracle, many coming from far-off villages, and not a few walking there from Tivolem. It was a pilgrimage of the devout and the curious! In the church, a thousand candles flickered and sank to *Pater Nosters* and *Aves* and *mea culpas,* and the sound of beating of breasts, while evening turned to night and night gave way to morning. Yet they waited, and prayed, and waited. Not till the Mass of the Feast had been celebrated, not till it was quite over and the acrid smell of fireworks filled the air, did the now disheartened faithful slowly drift out of the church, the niche on the altar still gapingly unfilled.

In the bright sunshine the fair awaited them, but they had no eyes for it. Still the vendors hawked and cajoled, held up their wares, and thrust bargains in their faces. So some children's wooden toys were sold, and models of squat churches made from sugar and painted a bright red and green, and a black lace mantilla or two, but there was not much doing anywhere, not even at the booth off to one side, where statues of saints and other religious objects stood arrayed on a cloth-draped table. Nothing much, at least, until the dark, full-mustachioed vendor began loudly hawking ointment, beeswax candles, and rosary beads he vowed had all been blessed by the Holy Father in Rome.

But the white-cowled women who gathered around at his call had another concern in mind, and having looked over those saints he had on display, and not finding the one they were after, the sacristan's wife finally thought to ask— did he perhaps know where they could find a statue of Saint Benedict?

"Indeed, I have one," said the man. "But it's not for sale."

"Could we at least see it," she persisted, "if you have it on hand and it's no trouble? It would mean a lot to us, just to look once more on his face, since our own statue was stolen just two weeks ago."

"Very well, then," he said, and reaching beneath the tablecloth carefully brought out a statue with upturned visage and rapture-filled eyes, one so delicately carved that it could have been mistaken for the stolen statue itself, had not this Saint Benedict been clothed in a robe of the richest crimson instead of heavenly blue.

Oh, the rush of people to see it!

"I'll give you ten rupees for it!" said a voice.

194

"It's not for sale," repeated the vendor.

"Fifteen!" cried another. And the women clamored, "It's for the church! A statue so beautiful should be in our church!"

"You have truly touched my heart," said the vendor. "It's my very favorite statue, and I've had it for many years, and it travels with me wherever I go. Of all the saints' statues, I like this the best, and I would not sell it to anybody, not even to the Holy Father himself, and not for all the money in the world; but since you say it is for your church, and this, after all, is the Church of Saint Benedict, it is right and proper that this statue should be placed on your altar, so I will let you have it for a mere hundred."

"Let me see it up close," said Apolinar', reaching forward.

"It stays in my hands," cried the vendor sharply. "Nobody touches it until I see your money!"

But the sacristan had already laid hold of the statue, and the two grappled for possession until Apolinar' let go with a cry, holding up his crimson-stained hands for all to see.

"Ayeee! Has this man cut you, Apolinar', my brother?" cried a woman. And turning to the vendor, she screamed, "What have you done to him, shaitan?"

But the sacristan, eyes bulging, could only point to the statue, where traces of a sky-blue robe could be seen beneath the smeared crimson paint. The vendor tried to hold on to the statue and run, and Apolinar' and the crowd tried to pull it away from him. Then, all of a sudden, they had wrenched it away, and—surprise!—the soup-strainer mustache was now on Saint Benedict, and no longer on the thief.

"Why, it's Lazarinh'!" cried a voice from the crowd.

Forgetting completely that the focus of their novenas and prayers and all-night vigils had been the simple return of the statue, forgetting that a miraculous return had been forecast for that very day, ignoring the fact that Lazarinh' had been the chief and only instrument of that return and thus might have been doing God's will, the crowd seized on him and beat him, shoved him, knocked him about, and would have very nearly beaten him senseless had not the police from Mapusa, who had been deputed to the fair and had been watching the fracas from just a short distance away, now decided that further punishment should only be legally administered. They therefore rescued Lazarinh' from the undisciplined mob and buffeted him soundly themselves as they took him first to the Mapusa head-quarters, and then to the district hospital.

39

SIMON FERNANDES sat himself at his desk and reached for an envelope containing stamps that had been issued in Hong Kong, but postmarked elsewhere, in any one of the so-called Treaty Ports of China. Three bore the bald visage of Edward VII; four the more regal mien of the reigning monarch, George V. More regal perhaps because more hirsute—George, King of England and Emperor of India, sported not only a fuller beard but hair on top of his head. One of the George V stamps puzzled Simon much; he could not decide, for the life of him, where it had been used: whether in Kowloon or Canton, or even—and this was an unsettling possibility—in Hong Kong itself? Only the letters *on* in the postmark were legible; the markings on either side were so faint they could be anything—*on* as in Hong Kong, which would make the stamp almost worthless; *on* as in Canton, which would be somewhat scarcer, but he already had that stamp in the very same shade, with a postmark from that port; *on* as in Kowloon, which would make the stamp considerably more valuable and desirable, and also fill an unsightly gap in his album. With these cogent factors in mind, he moved the magnifying glass back and forth, examining the stamp closely again and again, even using a pair of tweezers to hold it backward against the light, until the cancellation's faint markings became marvelously clear, taking on the shapes he wanted to see. With his eyes sidelining his conscience, he could now decide that yes, the stamp had indeed been used at Kowloon, and deserved an honored place in his collection.

He turned now to pleasanter matters—a set of Spanish stamps he had placed in a glassine envelope over to the right. It contained the three top values of Spain's Goya commemoratives, and it was these values that he chose to examine. Normally he saved this ritual for nights when the dogs were baying at the moon. Tonight was different. The set had been given to him in Kuala Lumpur in an elaborately sealed envelope as a joke, as he was about to board the train that would take him to Singapore en route to Goa. "It's a going-away present," his friend had said, a man who twitted him continually, "to show you there's more to stamp collecting than the British Empire. Enjoy them, old bachelor." Not till he was alone in his cabin aboard the freighter had he cut the envelope open. He was astonished then to see that the stamps showed Goya's portrait of La Maja, the voluptuous one—a full-fleshed duchess painted in the nude. Though he had been shocked initially, over time the model had become the object of his fantasies.

Tonight, through his magnifying glass, he focused on the face, the eyes, the mouth. Once again the eyes of the recumbent woman were wide open, and she was gazing unabashedly back at him. Tonight her face reminded him of Marie-Santana, down to the voluptuous smile, particularly in the light rust-brown, ten-peseta value that was closest to Marie-Santana's own coloration.

Simon was surprised he had not noticed that before. He tried to focus on the face and the smile, but his eyes kept following the contours of her body. La Maja resembled Marie-Santana in other ways, he found. The duchess, though of noble if not royal birth, was still, as portrayed in her nakedness, plebeian. Earthy. Accessible, even, though vicariously so. Big. Or rather, plump—an armful. Perhaps a bit more so than Marie-Santana, whose arms—he could not tell about the thighs—were not quite so fleshy. But he could imagine the breasts; yes, he could do that, imagining that was never a problem; he knew that if Marie-Santana were to lean back, lie down in fact unashamedly on a bed—what was there to be ashamed about, lying down in bed?—her breasts too would point east and west, even as the duchess's.

Had she been avoiding him lately? Had she sensed that he might think of her in that fashion, naked, lying on a bed, her bed, his bed, her arms crossed behind her head? Somehow, he had to declare himself. "Let me show you how I've secretly imagined you," he would say to Maja-Santana, if ever he summoned up the nerve and the moment were right. "Look at these stamps—that's how I see you, naked and chaste—naked and untouched." He realized then that he had fallen truly in love, though his thoughts ran to lust. He saw that he was running ahead of himself; he could not reveal his lust before he declared his love; and he could do that only if the moment were right, which he doubted it would ever be in that straitlaced village, and only if he summoned up the courage to say all he wanted to say, which he knew might well be never.

MONSOON
1933

JUNE

40

"WELL, have they climbed it yet?" the vicar wanted to know.

Senhor Eusebio shook his head. "Got close to twenty-eight thousand feet, then they were beaten back by the weather. So Mount Everest wins again."

"They'll never climb it," Teodosio said. "Takes them so long to get to the base and set up all those camps, and each time they set one up, wham! They get hit by a storm. The climbing season's over before they're quite ready for the peak."

"They found Mallory's ice ax," Senhor Eusebio said.

"Mallory? The name means nothing," Simon said.

"As a climber, one of the best. Nine years ago, almost to the day, he and a partner were climbing near the peak. Some think they made it to the top, but they just disappeared."

"That's something I'll never quite understand," Simon said. "To risk so much, train so hard, climb till the fingers are numb and the lungs and heart are bursting, and then the wind blows, a tiny rock slips, or an avalanche begins to slide, and all one leaves for posterity is an ice ax stuck where it no longer does any good. There are easier ways to achieve fame in this world."

"What makes you think they do it for fame?" Tendulkar

asked. "The climb is the challenge—no one's done it before. Mallory himself said, 'I climb it because it is there.'"

"Anyway, they're still up there, exploring possibilities," Senhor Eusebio said, "so they can try again in October."

"May be their last chance," Tendulkar said. "The Dalai Lama is said to feel that all that scrambling around amongst those high mountains angers the gods."

"Of course," the vicar said. "That's it! That's why the monsoon has struck."

"It's not quite like you," Tendulkar said, "to make fun of some other religion."

"Not of the religion, but of the practitioners," the vicar said. "I try to keep it down, but sometimes the urge is irresistible."

"The *Times* says Hitler is taxing bachelors," Senhor Eusebio said. "He's worried about Germany's low birthrate."

"At first I thought we had a non sequitur here, but I see I was mistaken," Tendulkar said. "A high birthrate is most definitely tied to irresistible urges. But a bachelor tax, if successful, could be bad news, especially for you, Father Vicar. The idea could be catching, and if Salazar adopts it. . . . Eusebio and Simon and Teodosio here could escape by getting themselves married, but you—you're trapped."

"It's not quite like you," the vicar said, laughing, "to make fun—"

"Only of the practice," Tendulkar interposed, slyly, "and not of the practitioner."

"News out of Lisbon," Gustavo Tellis said. "Three revolutionaries were caught red-handed with weapons and explosives."

"Revolutionaries against the revolution? We've come full circle. You're sure they were not monarchists?"

"That's the rub, and the irony of it all."

"The monsoon's up north already," Simon said, shaking his head. "It got all the way up there before it ever got to us down here! And we're right next to the sea. Just when does it start in the Himalayas?"

"Simon, I'm disappointed in you," Senhor Eusebio said. "You haven't been listening. All this feast of wit and wisdom being served up here, wasted on you. But to answer your question, the first of June."

"The monsoon is governed by the stars," Tendulkar said. "That's what the farmers believe. This year, they say, on the sixth of June, that's when our rains will begin. We have a couple of days to go still."

"And you, an educated man, believe them?" Simon said, incredulous.

"My nose is buried in books," Tendulkar said. "Their learning is tied to the fruits of the earth. Their feeling for the ways of nature never ceases to astonish me."

41

PEDRO SALDANHA, having eaten his dinner, was dozing at the table when he heard the sound: something quite heavy had fallen in his backyard and rolled over. A broody hen clucked a warning as Pedro came awake; he heard the ruffling of feathers, then an eerie silence. "You heard that, too, Geraldine?" Pedro called softly. His sister stood bent over the sink, frozen into immobility, her left hand clutching the pot she'd been scouring, her right hand still full of coiled coconut fibers dipped in ash.

"I'll go look," Pedro Saldanha said, rising, but Geraldine stopped him with a gesture. Outside the house, the silence was the silence of frightened animals on the alert. Brother and sister had much to lose—not just the flock of chickens that was Pedro Saldanha's joy, but a sow and her six piglets as well. All in all they represented money, good money, as they increased and multiplied—enough to ensure Pedro and Geraldine's present and a frugal future.

Pedro had been raising chickens and piglets now for close to eleven years; he sold them at the Friday market in Mapusa, though the plumpest chicks usually ended up in Dona Esmeralda's soup pots, sometimes in Dona Elena's, more recently sometimes even in Angelinh' Granny's.

"They pay you too little," Geraldine once complained. "You get much more when you sell them in Mapusa."

"They pay what I ask," Pedro answered, shortly.

"Mar'-Santan' pays you peanuts," his sister persisted.

"I ask her for peanuts," he said.

Pedro raised country chickens, but it had not always been so. On a trip to Bombay, when he first started, he had acquired a pair of leghorns, and a pair of Rhode Island Reds, the rooster a proud young cockerel that preened his black and red feathers and strutted around as the lord of his world. By the second year the hens were laying steadily, and since eggs as well as chicks were larger than the local product, he was able to sell both at a handsome price while still adding to his flock. And then came Lazarinh', turned fifteen, chasing a yardful of chickens out into the lane and driving the mother hens witless. They had never recovered, Pedro Saldanha maintained; and when a sickness struck, his entire brood perished. Now he was reduced to raising local poultry, the Rhode Island rooster replaced by a jungle fighting cock, just as tall, just as proud, black and red, and twice as quarrelsome. His size and his talons established his supremacy; it was he who each morning announced the coming of the dawn, leaving it to weaker vassals to spread the word.

The night of the incident in the backyard, the broody hen clucked loudly again and the rooster squawked, ruffling his feathers. Geraldine blew out the stub of candle by her side and peered into the darkness of the backyard. It was the night of the new moon. With heavy monsoon clouds drifting overhead, not many stars could shed their light. Worse, her view was obscured by a clump of banana trees, their broad leaves bowing and swaying in the freshening breeze. If anything else was stirring out there, she could not tell. Was it a stone, then, that had fallen off their crumbling wall? But if a stone, what caused it to fall, a heavy thing like that? Not a jackal; a tiger, perhaps?

Of a sudden, the yard came alive, rooster and hens flapping wildly about as they fought to become airborne, some making it to the roof; baby chicks cheeping, piglets squealing as they rushed from side to side. The old sow charged and connected; there was a thud, a grunt, a scrambling at the wall. Another loud thud, as of something falling; confused sounds receding in the lane. It was minutes before an uneasy quiet descended once again on the yard.

When at last Geraldine and Pedro felt it safe to go out into the yard, he with a flaming coconut husk in one hand and a cudgel in the other, the scene bore signs of the chaos that had prevailed. In one corner they found the piglets clustered trembling around the angry and victorious old sow; in another, the mother hens, with outspread wings, had brought their chickens under control. Two large stones had been knocked off the garden wall; chicken feathers were strewn everywhere; a banana tree had been bent askew, several new shoots had been trampled, and some had been broken off. But the animals, though still nervous, seemed safe, and welcomed them. The fowl clucked at the shadows thrown by the torch, but maintained their posts: the brooding hens with their eggs, others with their chicks. Only the old sow left her piglets and came noisily toward her master, the bristles on her neck and back still standing on end. He stooped down to pet her and found blood on her snout, and when he wiped it away with his hands, he saw the blood was not hers. Whatever intruder had jumped into that quiet courtyard had been given a reception it had not counted on, and would probably not come back again.

"Let's count the hens and chicks," Pedro Saldanha said.

They were all accounted for.

"Count them again."

"The hens are all here," Geraldine said. "So's the rooster. But one of the piglets is missing."

42

ALTHOUGH NEWS of Lazarinh's beating, arrest, and hospitalization did not make the local papers, noteworthy though it was, it did reach Tivolem the way important local news always does—with the thump-clank of tiny cymbals in a heavy staff announcing the baker was on his morning rounds. The villagers were immediately split into two dissenting groups.

"He got exactly what he deserved," said Mangu the coppersmith, and many agreed with him.

But others, led by Kashinath the barber, took the opposite view, insisting that what he got was not what he deserved— he should have been beaten half to death. "Crime must be controlled," Kashinath said, blowing the froth off a glass of coconut-palm toddy in Forttu's tavern. "What use are the police, what use are the judges, what use is the law, if criminals are routinely freed and roam about our streets? Since earlier thrashings have not taught Lazarinh' a lesson, the time has surely come to give him stronger medicine."

"The stronger the better," Forttu agreed.

Next morning the baker brought sobering news: Lazarinh's condition had worsened—he was dying. Dying!

"O my God!" said Mottu, but Kashinath scoffed.

"Lazarinh', dying? He has more lives than a cat."

Mottu, laughing nervously, agreed, then went off to Forttu's tavern for a comforting sip of Johnny Walker.

"Lazarinh' always comes back," Forttu told him over and over again, as Mottu sat hunched in a corner.

And the regulars there repeated, "Always, always! That's our Lazarinh'." And a man who had just come in from the marketplace said he had heard Lazarinh' had escaped.

Yet, next morning, there was the baker once more, thumping his staff with shrill urgency and telling everyone that Lazarinh' had died in the night. He had heard it himself at the bakery in Mapusa, from a man who had just come from the hospital.

Still unbelieving, they stopped the first bullock cart passing through.

"What news of Lazarinh'?" they asked.

"Lazarinh' is dead!" said the driver.

And the baker added, rather maliciously, that since Lazarinh' had probably died without benefit of clergy, his soul would surely fry in hell, and how did they feel about that now?

The village was devastated. Gloom blotted out the sun, and people on their way to the fields or to market gathered in knots to discuss the tragedy.

"That beautiful lad," said Mottu, "to die so young, in such a pitiful state!" And he shook his head in shock that such things should be.

"A tragic fate!" mourned Atmaram. "A fate I would not wish upon my worst enemy. And Lazarinh'—he was no enemy, he was a neighbor, a (yes!) a friend! Always ready to do you a favor, when one was needed! And what a climber of trees! Even the tallest coconut trees! If anyone needed coconuts—," and in a well-timed gesture he wiped an unborn tear against his sleeve.

"As a child he was always at my house," recalled Amita, stretching recollection to its limits. "And he would say, 'Govind's wife'—for he spoke like no other child, he was old and solemn for his years—'Govind's wife, are you going to give me a *laddu?*' And if I had no laddus as sometimes happened, then I gave him some other sweet. Or some gram, or a slice of ripe papaya, or even a piece of goat cheese or jaggery. He was like our own son—Govind and I could refuse him nothing."

Much praise was now lavished on the well-beloved newly deceased. Happy memories were evoked, eulogies were rehearsed, tears were shed! In the context of death, so final, so terrible, so utterly irrevocable, even the incidents of the calf, the bicycle, and the coconuts were construed as harmless escapades that had been vastly misunderstood at the time of their occurrence. The people of Aiconá were roundly and properly condemned for their heartlessness, their savagery, their inhuman cruelty in killing—in fact, in murdering (why had the good people of Tivolem been pussyfooting around that word?)—in murdering poor defenseless Lazarinh', standing proud and defiant, far from home and from those who would have protected him, standing in fact quite alone against a treacherous mob. And the point was raised: Hadn't he taken the statue back? Hadn't he refused to sell it? And wasn't it true that he was seized upon and beaten before he could get it to the church? Strong contrasts were drawn between the ethos of the two villages; things such as this lynching, it was agreed, could never happen in Tivolem, not in a thousand lifetimes.

It was Josephine Aunty who brought the discussion back to reality.

"When," asked she, "should we have the funeral?"

"Of course," said Forttu, clapping a hand to his forehead. "We forgot about the funeral!"

"It must be a proper funeral," Pedro Saldanha said. "I'll pay for the mass, and arrange for the confraternities."

"I have a little money," Josephine Aunty said. "I could pay for the band."

"I'll pay for the band," said Forttu, "and for the casket, candles, whatever is needed that Pedro Saldanha is not paying for. Josephine Aunty, you're all alone. Save your money—you may need it someday."

In the midst of all this, Annabel, who had been listening intently to all the to-and-fros, uttered a muffled "Lord forgive me!" and, making the sign of the cross three times in quick succession, whispered hoarsely, "Look!"

"It's a ghost!" cried Josephine Aunty, and they all crossed themselves, all except Govind and Amita and Atmaram, who, being Hindus, could scarcely invoke the same protection. Lazarinh' alive was one thing, but Lazarinh' the ghost appearing in Tivolem, bandaged head, swollen lip, bruised shin, and all, not waiting for night but facing them down in broad daylight—this was a type of haunting beyond all reason and experience.

"Mottu, get the vicar quick, with incense and holy water," cried Annabel. But Mottu saw the ghost was standing between them and the path to the church, and Mottu did not move.

They fell back a step, then, and would have turned and scattered had not the ghost also stopped.

"What's that thing jumping and shrieking in the bag in his hand?" asked Josephine Aunty. "What fiend has he brought us from Hell?"

With a piercing squeal the thing burst from the bag and raced toward them as if chased by the devil.

"Merciful God!" cried Annabel, and fell in a faint.

They flung themselves against the sides of the lane, and the thing flashed by, leaping over Annabel where she lay, and they saw it as a blur of gray and white, that's how fast it was moving as it sped past Marie-Santana, now coming up the lane toward them.

"Pedro Saldanha, isn't that the piglet you thought a tiger had taken?" she asked.

"By heaven, you're right!" he said. "And now Lazarinh's ghost has touched and defiled it."

"What ghost?" asked Marie-Santana. "Ghosts disappear—pouff! Look! This ghost is alive and is running away!"

"That's Lazarinh'!" shouted Atmaram. "That's the thief who steals our coconuts, who stole Amita's calf! Get him! Get the motherlover, the defiler of sacred places!"

Lazarinh' heard their shouts as they surged behind him, and gaining the road as the Goregão-Betim bus came groaning round the bend, he caught it on the run, barely ahead of their clawing hands; and the last they saw of him he was leaning out the rear door, gesturing obscenely and spitting into the wind.

That Saturday afternoon the vicar of Tivolem sat, pen poised in hand, thinking long and hard of the possibilities open to him for the evening's homily, and the sermon to be preached at Sunday Mass. Should he draw parallels between Lazarinho's reappearance after reported death, and the miracle of Lazarus called forth from the tomb? Could it possibly have come about to serve some higher unseen purpose, or was it perhaps due even to the intercession of Saint Cornelius the Contrite, who after all, as patron saint of Tivolem, looks after the spiritual needs of all local sinners? But if so, why did Lazarinho then steal the piglet? Or could it be that these two incidents, coming so soon one after the other—the statue in Aiconá, the piglet in Tivolem—could they be taken to mean that Lazarinho, the known and hitherto unrepentant thief, in his inmost heart and unbeknown to himself, really wanted to make restitution? Had he freed the piglet so it could run to Pedro Saldanha, or had it broken free? These were the questions that plagued the good vicar's mind and that he wished his parishioners to ponder.

But his curate, Father Pires, younger by far and more worldly in his outlook, gently said no. Whatever the judgment of posterity might be, at that moment Tivolem's fifteen hundred inhabitants, whether Catholic or Hindu, would not consider Lazarinho's reappearance to be one of Saint Cornelius's more laudable achievements. Not unless, the curate said, they had first been meditating long and hard in the depths of Forttu's tavern.

With a sigh, the vicar agreed, and preached instead on the general subject of minor mischief in youth, citing the case of the young man who asked Saint Ignatius to make him a priest, and when the saint took him into his own home for prolonged tutelage, the young man turned out to be an inveterate prankster. But with strict restrictions on the number of pranks that could be played each day—Saint Ignatius limited them to seven, the good vicar said—the youngster finally made it into the priesthood. And one of his first acts on being anointed was to write a life of the saint. So it is all right to indulge in youthful mischief, the old vicar said, provided it is of the inoffensive kind, and that ultimately you dedicate your life to God.

And that, Mottu the postman told Annabel his wife in a whispered aside, is exactly where Lazarinh' had failed, and for that he would come to a no-good end.

"Amen!" said Forttu the tavernkeeper, sitting three rows to the rear.

But Mottu kept his eyes up front, and the Mass proceeded.

43

WHEN THE FIRST RAINS failed to arrive even by
the eighth of June—they should have started on the
sixth, Angelinh' Granny had agreed—the voices of Little
Arnold and his friends could be heard as they went singing
in scraggly procession through Tivolem's winding lanes:

> *Saint Anthony where the bamboos sway,*
> *Cast rain upon our fields, we pray.*

Carefully avoiding the ruts, down the narrow bone-dry
lanes the children went, carrying symbolic rocks and small
flat stones on their heads, calling repeatedly on the miracle
worker for help:

> *Saint Anthony in the bamboo grove,*
> *Send showers to us from heavens above.*

Was the saint really in the bamboo groves, Little Arnold
wondered, and if so, what was he doing there? Finding no
ready answer, he and his friends continued to sing, turning
this time to a second, also-powerful ally:

> *Saint Isabel, good queen of the poor,*
> *Full knee-deep water we implore.*

Francisco Xavier Antonio Candido Pires, now in the seventh month of his assignment as curate of the parish of Tivolem, heard the children singing, saw them come down the lane, and stopped in his tracks when they ran up to him and crowded around to get his blessing. That blessing received, they went their way, and he continued his climb. He had a social call to pay, and a prospective site to explore. Though sweating profusely in the ninety-degree heat, he knew both tasks would bring him pleasure. He found pleasure, too, in the children's ditty, and began to sing it under his breath. At Granny's gate he stopped, counting the steep steps that led up to her place. She welcomed him warmly enough, but was plainly troubled. "Three days without a drop of rain," she grumbled, "and this is the first time in fourteen, fifteen years such a thing has happened."

"Bad for the crops," the curate agreed, accepting the scalding hot cup of tea Marie-Santana pressed on him at Granny's behest. He poured some of it from cup to saucer, blowing strongly across the top to tame its fire.

"Drink it hot," Angelinh' Granny commanded. "The hotter you drink it, the sooner it will cool you down. Lord knows, you come walking uphill in this weather, and at this time of day, you're going to need a lot of cooling."

Father Pires, good curate that he was, did as he was told, and endured the scald. He had stopped by because he had been told she was his second-oldest parishioner, not quite as old as Dona Esmeralda, but more or less housebound. Now he was beginning to like the crusty old woman.

"Our people are troubled," Angelinh' Granny continued. "They keep watching the skies. I do, too. Wouldn't you? Half the fields have yet to be plowed. The seed sits in our houses, waiting to be sown. I keep telling myself, God the All-seeing must surely know that our fields are thirsty now."

"He knows; I assure you God knows!" the curate said soothingly. "But in case He has forgotten, the vicar reminded Him this morning, wisely asking for just enough rain to meet our needs. To have asked for too much would have been as bad as asking for too little."

"Two hot days in a row should have sucked the rain clouds out of the sea already," Angelinh' Granny persisted. "And yet. . . . Mar'-Santan', child, go see if the sky looks like rain."

"Not a cloud up there, Granny," Marie-Santana reported. "The sky's as clear as when I checked it last, just an hour ago."

"Well, I must be off," the curate said, getting to his feet. "That tea was a great help."

"If you must. But you'll be baking out there. Don't know why anyone would want to climb to the top of the hill on a scorching day like this, especially you in that black soutane."

"I want to see the village from up there," he said. "There's talk of building a chapel on the hill. Pedro Saldanha—you must have heard. I want to see what it's like, up there."

He blessed them both at the door, and as he turned to leave, Granny asked him to bless the house. He murmured a quick prayer, promising to return with holy water to do it room by room.

Beyond the gate he turned right onto that part of the lane that wound past Dona Elena's house and led to the top of the hill. It was the siesta hour, and Dona Elena's garden lay still and deserted. Beyond the crotons and the jacaranda, the massed roses, the passion flowers and other flowering vines, the house slept. Father Pires realized he had escaped the need for another protracted visit and yet another cup of tea. He was grateful for this small mercy; sometimes he felt the training that future priests received in the seminary was quite inadequate; that besides doctrinal instruction and training in the rituals of Holy Mother the Church, they should also be given courses in how to hold down, or effectively refuse, endless cups of too strong, too milky, or too sweet tea.

Beyond Bald Uncle Priest's house, the lane branched off into a winding path that brought him to the upper reaches of the nullah. Ignoring the goatpath to the left that would have taken him to the crest of the hill, he crossed the nullah with some difficulty, stepping from rock to exposed rock, balancing himself on one and testing the other for stability before daring to take another step. Since the rains were late, there was not much more than a trickle of water here, but it was spread out, and he did not want to get his shoes wet, not when he still had so much steep climbing to do.

Father Pires now followed the stream to its source, a spring bubbling up between rocks into a limpid pool. The trees grew thickly here, not so much woods as a miniature forest. At his approach, a gray heron took wing and thrashed its way powerfully aloft. A kingfisher on watch froze itself into invisibility. Dragonflies ignored him, continuing to hover at the edge of the pool. In the upper reaches of a large old banyan tree a kutturr bird called hoarsely to its mate. Bulbuls warbled. He looked for, but could not see, their nest. A kite, riding the languid air currents up above, banked steeply, flapped its wings once, then dropped onto a tree, causing its topmost branches to sway. The kutturr and the bulbuls fell silent. The kingfisher stayed immobile. Father Pires became aware of his own loud breathing; the only other sounds to be heard were the burbling of the water and the buzz of dragonfly wings. Down by the spring, the priest squatted and, cupping a hand, scooped up and drank in the coolness of the water. It was sweet enough to warrant another swallow; then, dipping a handkerchief into the pool, he cooled his face, wiped the nape of his neck, and stood up to continue on his way.

The banyan tree towered above him; from its massive outspread branches, slender shoots reaching downward sought the ground. Some had already touched earth; of these, several had burrowed into the soil and anchored themselves and begun to thicken into secondary trunks, thick as a man's thigh; others, slender and ropelike, hung free, tantalizingly close at hand. He reached out and grasped one, testing his weight against it, remembering with pleasure the

218

thrill he had felt as a child swinging out from just such a tree over what had seemed like an abyss, yet may have been no wider than this stream. Making sure he was not being observed, he took three quick steps back, and was about to kick free of the ground when he heard a twig snap. Abashed, he let the shoot slip from his grasp, only to find the intruders were a cow and her calf coming down for a drink. But the fear of discovery was upon him, and, brushing by them, he resumed his climb.

Father Pires now found himself trudging up a trail that zigzagged ever more steeply uphill—the one Marie-Santana had used when she went looking for the boatman—a path made by goats far more surefooted than he. Their droppings were everywhere. There was no shade; only a few low-branching cashew trees dotted this section of the hill. At one point he sought to save himself a meander by climbing ten paces directly to the next level above; a hand's reach from that goal, he saw that he had misjudged the steepness of the incline; he could go no farther. With his knees bent, his palms flat against the warm tilt of the hill, he paused to catch his breath. Already his calves and thighs ached from the unaccustomed exertion. A quick look below showed him the peril he was in—a single slip could send him rolling downhill, perhaps to his death. By a strong effort of the will he calmed himself. He could not remain there forever, he had to make a choice—either to conquer the remaining bit of slope, taking his courage in his hands, or to slither down as best he could to the path below. He decided to press forward; he could not bear to look down once again. A silent prayer to his guardian angel strengthened his resolve.

Gingerly reaching down and easing off each shoe in turn, he tossed it to the path above; then, inch by inch, grasping at scrub and grasses and working his feet into any toehold he could find, he himself gained the upper path. There he stood and gave heartfelt thanks; it had been a close call. Nearing the hilltop minutes later he perceived what Marie-Santana down below had been unable to see—a massed bank of gray clouds glowering on the western horizon, and the threat of an impending squall.

On the plateau at last, he turned to look at the village spread out below him. The church itself, with its broad Portuguese-style façade—no spires—lay some way to the north, framed by a mass of coconut trees, its courtyard abutting the road. Somewhat nearer and adjoining the road, nestled in the shade of a mango tree, he could see the marketplace, where Jesus might have preached had He been around. And if Jesus, why not His curate? In the months since his arrival in Tivolem, Father Pires had learned the answer to that question: because Jesus had been fortunate— He had not had a vicar placed above Him to tell Him what He could and could not do. But the thought, impractical for now, could be tried out once he himself took over the parish, his parish. His parish? Recognizing the face of temptation, he murmured, "Get thee behind me, Satan!" and crossed himself.

This side of the church, partway up the hill and well off the main road where it branched west toward the coast, he spotted Senhor Eusebio's flat-roofed house and terrace and, next to the nullah, that landlord's holdings—the low, thatch-roofed clump of adobe cottages in which Atmaram and Kashinath lived with their families, with Govind as their neighbor. Over to the right, on a bylane and aloof from the rest of the village, lay the long twin roofs of Dona Esmeralda's centuries-old house. Farther up the lane that wound past Marie-Santana's garden, and a couple of hundred yards closer to where he stood, Father Pires spotted Dona Elena's elegant home. Senhor Eusebio and Dona Elena were engaged in a rivalry of sorts, he had discovered from church records; with Eusebio's return to Tivolem, they had begun celebrating the feast of Saint Cornelius in alternate years after Dona Esmeralda had dropped out of the picture, and each year the feast had been more lavish than the year before. He saw possibilities there for a little fund-raising—Pedro Saldanha's chapel-building funds might need supplementing.

Between Senhor Eusebio's home and Dona Elena's stood another group of houses whose occupants he could name—Angelinh' Granny and Marie-Santana (the wayside cross facing their gate was a clear marker); Annabel and Mottu, with their son Little Arnold; the gossip Josephine who lived all alone; the pushy violinist from Kuala, what's his name, Fernandes. The remaining homes he could not identify; they were half-hidden by trees, and the perspective from this height did nothing to jog his memory.

The task the curate had set himself this particular afternoon was finding on the crest of the hill the one spot that would be most visible from down below; and he wanted it also to be visible from the Arabian Sea, some ten miles to the west. He paced about the broad hilltop, but try as he might, a view of the ocean eluded him; not all the tea-spoonfuls of iodine extract his sister the doctor had made him swallow in his teens had helped add an inch to his five feet in stature. Right now, since longer legs were out of the question, he would have settled for eyes bulging atop his head, like a fly. He looked for a cashew tree to climb; the only tree nearby, a towering mango, stood some fifty yards or so to the rear, its branches too high for him to reach. Frustrated, he looked for a rock and stood on it, catching at last—eureka!—a glint of sun upon a dancing ocean.

This, then, he exulted, would be the spot on which his dream chapel would be built—Pedro Saldanha's chapel. Right here! Not just the villagers, not just the people using the road, but even voyagers on ships plying from Goa's ports to Bombay and then Africa and Europe would see it and pause, however briefly, to pray. To those returning from abroad it would be a welcoming landmark; to those leaving, a symbol of hope, a promise that someday they too would return. He looked west again, to where the ships would be—the storm was now pushing that much closer, the sea quite gray. He should be heading down.

Sunshine still bathed the hill on which he stood, however, as well as the village below, and he chose to linger a while. In the increasingly harsh light the contrast between hilltop and village was startling. Where he stood the grass had been baked brown by the sun, but down in the valley the trees and carefully tended gardens remained lush and luxuriantly green. He knew the green was deceptive; the umber fields that stretched beyond the church had only been partially readied, as Angelinh' Granny had told him; the untilled areas showed just how brown and parched the soil had really become.

At the cross in front of Granny's house a knot of people had begun to gather, and their numbers kept increasing. Seeing them drop to their knees on the hard and stony earth to pray for rain, he knew their anxiety, and wished he could ease it; rain was on the horizon and approaching rapidly; he could see it, they couldn't. He wondered whether this was what it felt like to be an all-knowing God—to be watching dispassionately, from a height, and then to face the eternal dilemma: seeing the present and the future as one, to intervene, or not, to save mankind from its fears and its folly. Free will, and all those endless arguments that went on and on, as the poet Omar said, "about it and about."

Perhaps God did walk the mountaintops; that's where Moses had found Him. That could also be why so many wise and holy men, Hindus though they were, went half-naked, he had been told, into the snowcapped Himalayas, seeking God, and sat there cross-legged, gazing into the face of Eternity, never wanting to come back. If one found Him there, why would one come back? To be God, up on a height, would be to see the unfolding of great and minor events, to see the comings and goings of antlike creatures, to see them lighting candles, burning incense, making impossible promises, trying to bend Him to their will—to see all this, this earnestness, these aspirations, this longing for the ethereal

222

and the sublime, and all the attendant foolishness; to see all this, and perhaps to smile, indulgently. A man, a child, seeing a group of ants all marching together in single file, might watch a while, and then go his way—or he might step on them and grind them into the dust. But God? Would God reach out a hand, and pick one out of the line of march— possibly a leader—and test him, as well as those now left behind? Or would He, too, at some point step on them all, and pulverize them? In the Old Testament, isn't that what He did?

The faint sounds of plaintive singing broke into Father Pires's musings and brought him back to reality; that, and the rising clatter of a swiftly advancing rainsquall. As the first warm drops splattered on his face—Heaven's blessing, was how he described it later—he knew exactly what his chapel, Pedro Saldanha's chapel, should be called: the Shrine of the Madonna of the Raindrops. He raised his arms in gratitude, a split second before the crackle of a lightning strike sent him scrambling down the slope, and the first great peal of thunder rolled from the black clouds surging above him.

44

Teodosio and Marcelo did not go tiger hunting on the date they had set. In fact, over the next few weeks they set and cancelled several dates because, as each one drew near, the hunter was called away on urgent and unavoidable business.

"Teodosio," Senhor Marcelo finally said, "all my life I've heard and read about shikaris and their wonderful exploits. In my imagination I've shot a tiger or two myself, you know how it is. Fantasies! Now here you are, a hunter with a proven skill with a gun, and you're willing to take me along with you on your next shoot. What a privilege! I beg of you, let's not let anything interfere with this next hunt I've arranged. Next month, Saturday, June 18, I've booked a railroad car to be placed on the outermost siding at Vasco, and we'll wait there until it's almost dark, and then go to a machan that will be built overlooking a tiger path. And I'll make sure you'll be there with me if I have to kidnap you."

So they went, the two of them, on the appointed day, looking (so Maria said) like a pair of overfed identical twins—Tweedledum and Tweedledum. Senhor Marcelo, too, was dressed in tall boots and a khaki outfit that a tailor had patterned for him after one of Teodosio's. No sooner had they gone than Dona Elena had some changes made in the great hall. The rare Oriental rug that for years had had pride of place in front of her grandfather's portrait was moved to another part of the room; a fresh grouping of antique chairs was tastefully arranged around the vacant spot thus created.

"But, Mama, what goes there?" Maria asked, pointing at the spot where the rug had been.

"I don't know for sure, Maria, but be patient," her mother replied. "By this time tomorrow that spot will be filled." She hummed a little tune.

That night the servants joined Dona Elena and Maria on their knees; together they meditated on all five sorrowful and five glorious mysteries of the Rosary, to ensure the hunters' safety. Although this exercise in piety took well over an hour—one or other of the servants had to be continually prodded awake—further precautions were taken. Candles were lit at the church and at the cross in the lane, each candle being replaced before it had quite burnt out. The night dragged on.

Next evening the men returned as they had left, by taxi, empty-handed and now greatly crestfallen.

"What happened?" Dona Elena asked, as the two hunters stood their guns in a corner.

"There were no tigers," her husband said.

"No tigers? I thought you had heard the place was crawling with them."

"My informants were mistaken. There were no tigers. Ask Teodosio."

"No tigers at all," Teodosio confirmed glumly. "We were grossly misinformed. It was a total waste of time."

"Some other time," Dona Elena said. "Perhaps you can go up to the railway depot at Collem, which is not close to the ocean, like Vasco, but much nearer the Ghat forests themselves. There you can try again; you're bound to find tigers there. Don't give up on your dream, Marcelo."

Strangely, these words, so lovingly uttered, seemed to depress them even more.

Dona Elena and her husband were well pleased with Maria's progress in music. They discussed with their cousins, on either side of the family, the possibility of having monthly musical soirees, where members of the younger generation, of both sexes, could mingle in a friendly cultural setting and get to know each other. That certain young people might fall in love was an outcome devoutly to be wished; and if by chance the wrong parties connected, that could be taken care of quite easily.

Unfortunately, before plans could quite be finalized, Senhor Marcelo came down with pleurisy. He was ill for days, with sharp pains in the chest that grew worse each time he drew breath.

Teodosio came to visit. "How do you feel?"

"Like one of your pythons got me. It's that bad."

"This python's not going to win," Teodosio said, easing himself into a chair. "You are."

Doctors came and went as his fever waxed and waned with the moon and the tides. One hundred and three. One hundred and four point five. One hundred and one.

The patient mumbled to himself. Dona Elena had placed a cloth steeped in eau de cologne upon his fevered brow when he suddenly gestured to her and whispered, "Elena!"

She bent low to listen. "Yes, Marcelo."

"Why is there nothing in front of grandfather's portrait, where the Chinese rug used to be?"

"It's waiting for the tiger skin you and Teodosio will bring back from Collem."

He clutched at the coverlet, moving his head from side to side. "There will be no tiger skin from Collem."

"Your dream expedition," she said soothingly. "You'll get to shoot them yet. Get well, Marcelo, love, the tigers are waiting!"

"That's why," he whispered haltingly, "that's why we're not going back there. They're waiting—always waiting. They were all around us at Vasco."

"He's delirious," Dona Elena said to Maria, who had just come into the sickroom.

"No, Elena, it's true," he said. "They were there. Three of them, padding and grunting around outside our railway compartment. Scared us both half to death."

"Don't talk now, dear Marcelo," she said, putting a finger to her lips. "Save your strength. You can tell us about it when you get well."

"Papa, there were no tigers," Maria said, ignoring her mother's signals to be quiet. "No tigers, remember? You told us so yourself. And Senhor Teodosio confirmed it."

"We made up that story," her father said, "because we were ashamed of what happened. I was scared to death. And Teodosio was sick." He stopped to draw breath, and winced. "He was sick all over the place. If a tiger so much as coughed in the dark—and they were doing that every now and then, sometimes just under our window—his stomach turned."

"Hush," his wife said, this time putting her finger to his lips, but he pushed her hand away.

"Then two of them turned on each other, snarling and roaring and slamming into our compartment in their fury. It was terrible. That's when Teodosio had an accident."

"What sort of accident?" asked Maria.

"Our brave hunter wet his pants?" Dona Elena exclaimed, laughing. "What about all those safaris in Africa?"

"Fairy tales. He admitted it—the only hunting he's done has been over here, shooting rabbits and waterfowl."

"And he fooled us all. Wait till I tell Dona Esmeralda."

"You can't tell her, not her, nor anybody else," Senhor Marcelo said. "I promised him I wouldn't tell, and if I hadn't been so deathly ill, I wouldn't have told. But I couldn't go, having lied, without telling you the truth."

"It was a very small lie," she said, "and it didn't hurt anybody. So hush again. You aren't going—we must stop this foolish talk. Now I'll go get you your chicken soup and your conjee, and by morning you'll feel a whole lot better."

"Now that's a very big lie," he said, "but I do feel better already. Chicken soup and conjee, chicken soup and conjee, a man could get well just so he'd never get to see either of those again."

He seemed to rally as he sipped at the broth and the gruel, and soon drifted into a fitful sleep.

The intermittent but measured tolling of church bells broke the news to the villagers of Tivolem, and carried over the surrounding hills to neighboring settlements. People hearing the mournful sound knew: "He died!" and the women crossed themselves. Relatives and friends living nearby came over immediately; messengers were sent to alert those living far away. Teodosio was absent; believing that his friend was mending, he had gone off on a day's hunting trip.

Senhor Marcelo's body was placed in a coffin in the drawing room; this barely done, mourners began to arrive, mostly on foot, the more affluent in bullock-drawn carriages, a few in cars. Dona Elena, silent in her grief, sat by the coffin with Maria at her side, accepting the brief hugs and the prolonged embraces, the salt tears and the murmured expressions of condolence. If she sensed that some of these were hypocritical, she gave no sign of it. The room kept filling up; as more people came, the wreaths were piled high. In the unbearable heat the women fanned themselves discreetly, causing the tall candles to flicker. Sweat mingled with the heavy scent of flowers and perfume and burning candle wax to assail the senses. The prayers droned on, in Portuguese and also in Konkani, so the poor and illiterate would not feel excluded.

With Marie-Santana by her side, Maria wept and composed herself by turns; she broke down when her aunts embraced her—the news had reached them late—and when her cousins arrived. A line of mourners waited to pay their respects; Teodosio, dazed, arriving late and out of breath, worked his way to the head of the line, took Dona Elena's hands in both of his, held them an instant before being

228

pushed aside by the next in line; but though she acknowledged his words of comfort he wondered whether she was aware it was him. Maria left him in no doubt; when he turned to her, she rose and put her head on his shoulder and let it rest there until he gently sat her down again. As he went off to stand a little to one side, people remarked (and Josephine Aunty more so than others) how much more a friend of the family he had become in the short time he had been teaching the child.

Already a dozen mourners were sitting outside on the balcão because there was no more room in the house. Nearby villages had sent in their confraternities—besides members of the elite, who regarded it an honor and a privilege to serve, the groups included solemn, sunken-cheeked men, drawn from the ranks of the poor, who still wore their scarlet and white-lace surplices with the ease born of familiarity. This day their numbers were impressive—they knew their presence would be acknowledged in cash and with generous portions of wine. Some had attended an earlier funeral, and already been so rewarded. If their breath smelled, nobody noticed.

When the vicar finally arrived; when he and Father Pires had led the prayers and the responses in Latin; when the moment of parting drew inexorably nearer, Dona Elena's flushed cheek betrayed a heightened emotion. As six male relatives moved to take their places as pallbearers, she gave a quick cry, "Marcelo!" and lunged to embrace him; Maria clung to the coffin, crying despairingly, "Papa! No, no, Papa!" before falling in a faint. Gentle hands helped them up, sustained them in the long walk down that room, past the mass of faces, those staring tear-filled eyes. Somewhere up ahead a brass band began to play Chopin's "Funeral March"; to those measured beats, the solemn cortège walked a mile to the church and the burial plot.

The vicar's lengthy sermon included an emotional eulogy: Marcelo had been benefactor, exemplary Catholic, doting husband and father, dear and respected friend. Teodosio, there and not there, listening and yet not listening, became aware that in both sermon and eulogy the priest had repeated a Latin text from the Mass: *In memoria aeterna erit iustus; ab auditione mala non timebit.* And Teodosio drew solace, as was intended, from that comforting and timeless truth: For the just man is indeed remembered forever, and he need fear no evil tidings.

"Dust unto dust," Teodosio murmured at the gravesite. A welter of Latin phrases spun in his mind: *requiem aeternam; lux perpetua.* His was the last trowelful before the gravediggers set to work.

45

THE WALK to and from the church on Sunday mornings
had developed a pattern of its own. Simon would catch
up with Marie-Santana some time after she had left her
house; they would part company much before they reached
the churchyard, so she could go in first. After Mass he
would linger awhile on the church steps, chatting with
Senhor Eusebio; she would slow down near the little
bridge, or stop to chat with a fellow parishioner, until
Simon happened by. It was a game they played with the
gossips, and they enjoyed playing it.

One Sunday morning, hearing Marie-Santana's gate
clang by prearrangement fifteen minutes earlier than usual,
Simon left his own house a minute later and to his surprise
found her still there, waiting for him. The hour being early,
the lane was deserted. The look on her face startled him;
she had been weeping.

"I want us to stop by Amita's," she said. "I want you
to see something that's troubling me deeply. Then we need
to talk."

"Why Amita's?"

She did not answer him, but led the way. At Amita's,
three of the children were playing outside the door with the
baby.

"Their faces," Marie-Santana said. "Look at their faces."

"The black dots?"

"Do you know what they are?"

Simon shook his head.

"All of Amita's children wear those spots," she said.

"So?"

"Rukmini's four children wear them, too."

"I may be dense," Simon said, "but I still—"

"I didn't know what they stood for either, until Josephine Aunty told me yesterday. They're talismans painted on a child's face to make the child look ugly and thus ward off the evil eye."

"I still don't see why that should bother you."

"Because Amita and Rukmini have been avoiding me for quite a while now. I didn't know why, but now it seems obvious—they think I am the one that has the evil eye."

"Marie-Santana, but that's absurd!"

"Still, that's what they believe—that I can bring harm to anyone or anything I praise. And it hurts, it hurts me deeply, because more and more people are beginning to believe it, too."

"I don't, and Granny doesn't, I'm sure. And we should know."

"I have a few good friends left still," she said. "But you can count them on one hand. Besides you and Granny, there's the vicar, and Dona Elena, and Annabel. Thank God for all of you, and especially for Annabel—she's been like a sister to me."

46

As her neighbors gathered by the cross to pray for rain, Angelinh' Granny, too frail to walk down all those steps, watched all the preparations from her own threshhold; then, beads in hand, she joined in the prayers and the long-drawn-out singing of the litany, her hoarse voice hardly audible even to herself. With the house at her back, she could not see the hilltop, but she saw the sky turn a threatening black, while slanting, brilliantly clear sunshine still bathed the scene before her. In the middle of *Alma Redemptoris Mater* the rains came, and the smell of the drinking earth was incense wafting to heaven.

Next morning, aging men the color of burnt clay carried wooden plows on their shoulders to the fields, where oxen were then yoked to the plows in pairs; and Little Arnold on his way to school stood transfixed as he watched the men plodding behind the bulls, turning red earth to shadowed gold. The great common field had long been divided into smaller squares and rectangles by bunds of mud a span or so in height and almost twice as wide; each time the bullocks came to one of these, the men lifted the plowshare out of the ground and set it down again into the soft soil on the other side. Little Arnold knew where the family strip was, and waited as the oxen patiently plowed it; and when they were done, he watched the women sowing rice seed in graceful sweeping arcs, handful after handful till the strip was done. And he still stood rooted there till the oxen came back again, dragging a plank on which a man rode to press the seed down into the soil with his weight. The watching child wanted to share that bumpy ride, to feel the soil give way beneath him, the lumps collapse, but he saw from the sun that he was late for school already and ran right up to the door of his classroom and still got scolded for his lateness.

Day after day dark towering clouds blew in from the ocean, and howling winds and Tivolem's hills and Saint Anthony in the bamboo grove together swept them up into cooler air. People cast an eye on the approaching storms and quickened their pace, but not till the first lightning bolt hissed out of the blackened sky and its deafening thunder-clap made their hearts jump did they think to open their umbrellas or begin their mad rush to shelter. By then the wind was slamming windows shut even before servants could get to them, and grape-sized raindrops drove the livestock home. For more than a week rains blanketed the village, cascading off rooftops, leaking into Dona Elena's kitchen, finding new chinks in Dona Esmeralda's old twin roofs and driving that lady frantic, flooding Senhor Eusebio's rooftop terrace and seeping into his house, stripping the earth from Atmaram's coconut trees and toppling one of them almost onto Govind's roof, turning lanes into streams and the once-dry nullah into a foaming torrent. In the fields the squares between the retaining bunds were submerged in water; beneath those bright vermilion lakes the seed began to sprout. Yet Angelinh' Granny kept working her beads because Saint Anthony's feast was still days away and she did not want the saint to slacken off. He rewarded her faith. Not until June 14, the day after his feast, did the skies clear. Then the sun shone bright, the fields grew thirsty again, and Angelinh' Granny began working her beads harder than ever.

Her fellow villagers were less worried. With the feast of

Saint John the Baptist coming on June 24, they knew the saint would see to it that the broad and deep well at each house, by now already half-full (except Angelinh' Granny's, which was deeper than most), would by that date have been filled almost to overflowing. Else, how would the villagers go in neighborly groups from house to house, singing hymns in the saint's honor, jumping into each family well and swimming around in it with joyous abandon as though they had just been baptized in the River Jordan? It was a day of celebration, Saint John's day was, and many of the menfolk would be more than a little soused, having found it difficult to resist the tiny shots of cashew liquor that would be pressed on them by each household; and on this one day Josephine Aunty would be particularly so, even though she claimed she hardly touched a drop of that same feni from January through December, and took only a tiny sip on feast days and birthdays, at funerals and on anniversaries, and on other days of singular merit.

This Saint John's Day, Josephine Aunty stood next to the parapet of Angelinh' Granny's well, and there in the water six feet below her was Forttu; also swimming happily around were Govind, and Kashinath, and Braganza the postmaster, he the only one wearing pink bathing trunks that came down to the knee instead of plain white shorts or a loincloth. The well had sides of rough-hewn stone, and was no more than some twelve feet across, so all one could do was kick off from one side and glide or dog-paddle one's way to the other; unless, that is, one swam like Marie-Santana.

Off to one side, clinging to a cranny with his left hand while reaching out tentatively to the center with his right, was Mottu. The mailman was a weak swimmer, and the water was deep; having dared to jump in, he had panicked on surfacing and then immediately made his way to the side, spilling water out of both sides of his mouth like a ship steaming into port. He held on to the crevice for minutes, content to watch others jump in one after the other. Only when Forttu was in the well with him did he take a deep breath, puff up his cheeks like a bullfrog, and push against the wall with his feet, easing himself toward the other side. The glide went well until he remembered to use his arms; then he splashed himself almost to a standstill before he had quite reached the center. "Keep going!" cried Forttu, but Mottu was turning in fear with his mouth wide open and swallowed a great draught of water. Still, he managed to fight his way back to the side again, where he stayed puffing and panting, making a great show of kicking up bubbles with his feet while clinging gamely to the wall.

Little Arnold, standing on the parapet near Josephine Aunty with two dried yellow coconuts tied to his back, had watched his father thrashing about, seen the panic in his face, and found the sight less than reassuring. Here he was, all of six years old, about to jump into that yawning abyss for the very first time, right into those forty feet of clear water, so clear that when the surface was still one could see the small turtle swimming far below, and sometimes even a water snake lying on the bottom; and if his father was having so much trouble down there, after all those years of holding his nose and jumping in feet first, what was the point of jumping in when one didn't know how to swim at all, even though one was no longer a baby but really six years old, and had coconuts on one's back to keep from drowning?

"I'll hold your hand," Marie-Santana said, climbing on to the parapet beside him, and Josephine Aunty drew in a sharp breath of disapproval because Marie-Santana should not be jumping into that well at all with all those men down there just waiting to see her dress go ballooning up over her head. But Little Arnold backed off, even though he knew Mar'-Santan' Aunty was the best swimmer in Tivolem, where most women did not swim at all. He had seen proof of her prowess in that terrible cloudburst when Atmaram's coconut tree, its base eroded, narrowly missed falling on Govind's house, when the stone quarry that had been cut

236

into the hill on Tivolem's western edge had been filled to overflowing and people had gone to look at it in wonder, all that water forming a great lake in the side of the hill, rocks and trees towering up on all sides, the water deep red at first but, after settling, clean and inviting and frighteningly deep, and Marie-Santana alone of all the people standing gazing in wonder there had decided to jump from the highest rock wall, dress and all, and had swum back and forth—dog paddle, frog kick, back float, and even the Australian something, lifting her hands clean out of the water, the way the feringhee did—fifty times and more the length of that quarry, until even he and Uncle Simon, the last admiring onlookers, had gone home, leaving her no option but to clamber out as best she could.

People had criticized her then for swimming in public, some by saying, "What do you expect? She has been corrupted by living overseas"—overseas being understood to be ever a den of iniquity—and others saying, "She was born over here, she should have known better," and Josephine Aunty saying sometimes the one thing and sometimes the other, depending on who she was talking to.

Little Arnold admired the way Mar'-Santan' Aunty had climbed so fearlessly onto the quarry wall, her toes curling over the edge, and the way she had jumped into the water in one fluid movement, her skirt tucked tight between her knees, her left hand holding her nose daintily and not the way Uncle Forttu did; by contrast, Uncle Forttu seemed gross, though he was a load of fun when he wanted to be. She had jumped in with her right arm raised high above her head, so that when her toes hit the water and the spray splashed upward every which way and her body went under and the great green bubble sizzled where she had been, one could still see her hand sinking ever more slowly beneath the surface, until only the tips of her fingers remained visible. Little Arnold wished he could do all these things, but knew he could only do them after he had learned how to swim, and his mind told him that until he had learned how to swim it would be foolish to go jumping into quarries and wells that deep even with Mar'-Santan' Aunty holding his hand, coconuts or no coconuts. Besides, this was Saint John's Day, and he heard Josephine Aunty say half-aloud that only men were supposed to jump into wells on this day, and he didn't want to be the one to get Mar'-Santan' Aunty in trouble by getting her to jump into the well with him after she had already done the wrong thing once by going swimming in the quarry.

But though Little Arnold hung back, Marie-Santana jumped into the well just as Forttu was climbing out. Mottu was chagrined; since the time she had rebuffed his drunken advances on the Mapusa road, he had stayed out of Marie-Santana's way; yet here she was, in the same well with him, and no way out for him but to leave, thus drawing attention and losing face. The other swimmers, who had pulled over to the side, stayed there clinging to the wall while she surfaced; seeing Forttu preparing to jump in again, she too got out of the way, and stood quietly treading water off to one side. Though she was facing away from Mottu, he was sure she had seen him there in the shadows.

"Watch, child," Forttu said on the parapet, handing Little Arnold a small white conch. "Toss it in."

Little Arnold tossed the shell in and watched it spiral slowly below the surface, its progress distorted by the water still sloshing to and fro. Forttu at his side stood watching it too, a kingfisher waiting for the right moment to swoop, until suddenly he snatched a quick deep breath and gripped his nose and jumped, folding his knees and feet beneath him, and the surface of the well when he hit turned into one huge roiling bubble, and there was Forttu's head going down right in the middle of it, and as the bubble subsided he flipped himself over, the soles of his feet white against liquid green, the shell far below now invisible but still slowly spiraling down, and Forttu fast as a turtle in hot pursuit. He came up triumphant and gasping for air, the conch

238

held high for everyone to see, and Little Arnold forgot his fears long enough to cheer.

Then Forttu clambered out once more, and stood smiling encouragingly right beside him, and said, "Come on, let's jump." Little Arnold wanted to jump in right then, his heart said jump but his knees said no, and his feet being closer to his knees pulled him back from the brink.

"Pinch your nose shut," Forttu said, and Little Arnold did, and the next thing he knew Forttu had picked him up with a hand beneath each armpit and had tossed him right in the center of the well. Little Arnold saw the water rush up at him, leaving him no time to cry out. He closed his eyes the instant the well swallowed him; but the next second he opened them to see bubbles sprouting in front of him, bubbles flashing by him, bright bubbles, brighter by far than water. He felt water in his mouth and tried to spit it out. Two hands he could see, in front of his eyes, pumping furiously up and down, up and down. Two feet he could feel hard at work, knees jerking up as far as they could go. At his back an irregular thumping, a tugging at his waist—the coconuts a pair of hands yanking him back to the surface. The water getting brighter and lighter. Much lighter. He had not known water so blue could so quickly turn so green.

Mottu by the wall watched his son break the surface and flounder around in a circle, getting his bearings, the yellow coconuts at his back bobbing along with him. Little Arnold sputtered; but seeing the sheltering wall and friendly faces at hand, he paddled their way, making more noise than progress.

"Come, come!" Govind coaxed, and Kashinath too reached out an encouraging hand, a hand that was ever so gradually withdrawn as the boy fought his way toward it. "Come!"

When just a stroke or two away, Little Arnold lunged for Kashinath's shoulder, missed, and went down gulping water. But the coconuts pulled him up again, and with a quick flip of the wrist Govind was at his side, guiding him deftly to where he could get a grip on a crevice. He clung there, panting, not letting go, lips trembling a little, as Forttu jumped in again, and after him Kashinath, and after him Mar'-Santan' Aunty in her dress that was now clinging to her so tight she no longer had to tuck her skirt between her knees. Each time they jumped in, Little Arnold shut his eyes against the spray, and the shock wave pushed him against the well wall, and the great bubble that crested in the center reached out to him and first buoyed him up so he took a sharp breath and then bobbed him up and down, while myriad tiny bubbles prickled against his feet and belly and burst against his chest.

"Over here, Little Arnold," Marie-Santana said, "come over to this side." She was treading water right next to his father. Mottu and she exchanged glances; she gave him a cool smile. Little Arnold let go, felt himself go under, turned clawing to the wall till he found his fingerhold once again.

"Don't be afraid," she said. "Push your feet against the side. Come on, push! The coconuts will help you float." Still he shook his head.

She kicked off and glided halfway across, where she once again treaded water, just out of his reach. "Look! No hands. It's easy. I'm close to you now. Come on, I'll catch you. I'm right here!"

Marie-Santana stretched out her hands to him and smiled, and the child let go of the wall, and once again the agitated wavelets rippled out in all directions as he struggled to reach her.

"Move your feet, Little Arnold. Kick! Kick!"

Annabel and Josephine Aunty, watching up above, clapped their hands as he inched forward. Little Arnold looked up at his mother and laughed, forgot to keep up his puppy stroke, and promptly sank beneath the surface. When he came up he found not only Mar'-Santan' Aunty there ready to help but also his father, concerned for him and no longer afraid for himself.

240

Little Arnold felt good. "You'll swim like a fish," Marie-Santana said, backpedaling till she was again just out of his reach. "Come on, let's see if you can catch me."

When the time came, he did not want to leave. "You see, there's nothing to swimming," Mottu said to him once they had clambered out of the well and were heading home to lunch. "Nothing at all. You saw that yourself. Keep your mouth and nose above water, work your hands and feet. All you have to do is keep moving."

Mottu was unusually preoccupied at dinner that night. His thoughts were on what had happened in the well that morning; his jumping in, and Little Arnold on the parapet, and Marie-Santana appearing out of nowhere. Forttu could have taught the child to swim; Forttu was always teaching others how to swim; but no, Marie-Santana had to climb up beside Little Arnold and hold his hand and try to get him to jump. Even when the child had refused, and she had jumped in by herself, and he, Mottu, had turned his face half away so she would not think he was there gaping at her in the well, hoping to see whatever there was to see, Marie-Santana had swum round and round within inches of where he was clinging to the wall, and when her face came out of the water for air and her mouth was open, so were her eyes, and she was looking at him. Then when Forttu had tossed Little Arnold in and the boy was dog-paddling as any novice would, she had swum to where he, Mottu, was and had treaded water and called the child to her. Or was she calling him? Now he was sure she was. All that jumping in, those fancy strokes, showing off for whom, if not for him? And when she treaded water, bobbing up and down in her tight wet dress, tempting him with her mango breasts—a mating dance, that's what it was. And that smile—how brazen, with his wife standing there at the parapet. The changeable minx! He should have given her a sign, perhaps a secret sign that he was on to her game and willing, as she was, even with Annabel there at the mouth of the well, looking down.

Mottu had had his share of feni that day, before going into the well and after coming out of it, and also before sitting down to eat, but now that he had finished eating and the cashew liquor was a warm glow in his stomach, he leaned forward and poured himself some more. He felt masterful; let Annabel object if she dared.

"You've not said a word during dinner," Annabel said to him. She had been watching him throughout the meal, and he had as carefully avoided meeting her gaze. "Didn't you like it?"

He seemed not to hear; he had decided to ignore her. Her womanly intuition working at peak level, his wife drew her own conclusions. She sent Little Arnold off to do his homework, then without preamble came right to the point.

"If you so much as look at her sideways, I'll kill you," she said.

"Me look at her?" Mottu said, startled that she had read his thoughts. "Look at whom? At her? Mar'-Santan'?" He laughed hollowly. "She looks at me," he said, drumming his right forefinger on his chest. He saw at once that she did not believe him.

"In the well," Annabel said. "I'll drown you in the well."

"Can't see how," he said. "You're scared of the well, and can't swim a stroke."

"That'll make it that much easier," she said.

He puzzled over that, but made no reply. He could not see how it could be done, without her being down in the well with him, and he took a last large swallow of feni to clear his mind. But of this he was sure—if she were even halfway serious, she'd find a way.

Later that night, after he had fallen asleep alone in bed because Annabel had busied herself banging pots and pans about in the kitchen, he found he had acquired miraculous powers. With a single arching step he was able to cover as much ground as if he had done the running broad jump; he was gliding through the air in slow motion. Not quite believing what he had just accomplished, he stepped forward lightly again, and covered more ground still. He tried three steps and found himself soaring. Exhilarated by success, he sought a tough challenge, and found it in the steep incline that led to Granny's house. Starting from the top step of his own balcão, he felt three easy leaps would place him squarely in front of Granny's door. And so it was. The first took him to within inches of his own garden gate. Landing lightly on the ball of his left foot, he bounced off it high enough to clear the gate and land on the other side of the lane. A slight kick off the toes of his right foot and he had cleared the garden wall and was skimming along inches above Angelinh' Granny's stairs; when he felt he was losing altitude he moved his feet lightly in a scissoring motion and began to soar once again.

Now, standing by the front door of Granny's house he turned, and his own house seemed very far away and below him. Nevertheless, he regained his own porch with just one upward leap and a graceful swoop. He felt so good about having done all this that he turned and looked about to see if there were witnesses.

Marie-Santana was standing in Granny's balcão, where he himself had been just seconds earlier; she was looking directly at him and smiling, and as she waved he could see that her dress was wet and tight from swimming and it clung to her figure like onion skin. She put her hand to the side of her mouth so her whispered words would carry more clearly: "Move your feet, Mottu. Come on, move! Quick! Let's see if you can catch me."

He saw then, as she swayed seductively to and fro, that to reach her he would have to leap over his own well, where Annabel was now standing squarely on the parapet, daring him, arms akimbo.

JULY

47

"STRANGE NEWS FROM PORTUGAL," Senhor Eusebio said, "via, of all places, London. The BBC said today that Lisbon fears a coup. Two jailed rebel officers have escaped from an Oporto prison, and that's given the government the jitters. Hear this: a bulletin said the ministers of war, the interior, and the navy are taking steps—I jotted this down, it sounded so precious—'to dissipate the revolutionary atmosphere that enemies of the government have been displaying lately.' And it's not just the ones they arrested last month that they're referring to. I think they mean you, Tendulkar."

"Aquila non capit muscas," the vicar said. "Eagles don't bother killing flies. No offense meant, Tendulkar. Old Latin saying."

"None taken."

"I only meant that, as an intellectual Gandhian, you're really quite harmless."

"You're making it worse. I should hope that some of my ideas at least would be mildly subversive, in a nonviolent sort of way."

"You'll get your head shaven, Tendulkar, at the very least," Senhor Eusebio said. "Don't say we didn't warn you."

"If we, the elite, don't speak up, who will?" Tendulkar

demanded. "Must we always walk in fear, biting our tongues? Our ancestors weren't this way. We've had incidents here, just decades ago—the Rané rebellion. We were teenagers then, all of us; you, Father Vicar, excepted."

"True, I was already a priest," the vicar said.

"That time, Portugal sent the crown prince himself to put down the revolt," Tendulkar said. "So what happened? The Ranés retreat into the jungle, he follows them. He bivouacs and leans his back against a tree. He moves, and wham! There's a bullet where his head had been. Minutes later he lies down, his head on a pillow. He turns, and another bullet slams right into the hollow his head had made. And a man riding up with a flag of truce brings him a note: 'We could have killed Your Royal Highness twice in a single evening. Why don't you make peace and go home?' And go home he does, very sensibly, having first granted amnesty and made peace."

"Ah, but those were different times," Teodosio said. "The monarchy treated us as equals back in those days. We elected representatives to the parliament in Lisbon and shared in our own government. All that has changed. Now under Salazar's dictatorship, we deal with the Colonial Office; we're just another colony."

"There's also the matter of semantics and attitude," Tendulkar said. "On paper, we're all Portuguese citizens, never mind that we are Indians—or Goans, if you insist, Teodosio—by birth and descent. But they classify us three ways: those of us who speak no Portuguese are classed as *indigenas* or *nativos*. This infuriates me. Are the people of Portugal not also indigenous or native? And those of us who do speak Portuguese are patronized as being *assimilados*. This infuriates me even more; should we be praised for being assimilated into a lesser culture? And the third and topmost group is defined as 'Portuguese and people of Portuguese descent.' Is this not racist, and yet we must accept it?"

"We must, because they have all the guns," Simon said.

"That's where you're wrong, Simon," Tendulkar said

passionately. "That's where you're dead wrong. How many guns does Gandhi have? He wouldn't touch a gun if you handed it to him. Yet, he's shaking the British Empire to its foundations. Moral authority is what unarmed people have, and the Mahatma is showing us how to use it."

"Well, to get off on a different tack," Eusebio said, "an American scientist has invented an iconoscope that can send pictures through radio waves. So in a few years we'll all be able to sit home and watch our own picture show."

"May it be long in coming," the vicar said, "because when that's a reality, it will mean the end of all human intercourse."

"Father Vicar," Tendulkar said solemnly, "I believe that was a most unfortunate choice of words."

"Have you seen Mottu's new bike?" Senhor Eusebio asked.

"How could we miss it?" Teodosio replied. "He's riding it all around the village, drunk and sober, ever since he got it."

"It's strange, the way he's behaving," Tendulkar said. "Something's bothering that man. I knew he liked a drop or two, but now he's drinking much more. The other day he sat outside Forttu's tavern for half an hour, grumbling that the place was closed. Perhaps you can talk to him, Father Vicar."

"He hasn't been near me in months," the vicar said. "Still, I could try."

"If he should fall off his bike, Forttu will get the blame," Tendulkar said.

"More likely it will be Marie-Santana," Teodosio said. "You must have heard the rumors."

"About Marie-Santana having the evil eye? Eusebio's jackfruit, Rukmini's she-buffalo?"

"Nobody knows why those jackfruit fell," Simon said angrily, "and to blame it on Marie-Santana is stupid. Naturally, she's hurt by all the talk."

"Stupid, and very unfair," the vicar said, "since there's little she can do to challenge it. Perhaps, Eusebio, you yourself can come up with a reason why the fruit dropped overnight."

"Bats," Senhor Eusebio said, scratching at his chin. "Bats could have done it. They're everywhere."

"Good try," Tendulkar said. "In fact, jolly good try, as your friends the British might say. But some will still ask, why did the bats only strike after Marie-Santana praised the tree? And why didn't they eat the fruit, instead of just knocking it down? Our people will still say, evil eye."

"It could have been Lazarinh'."

"Was he here at the time?" Teodosio said. "And even if he was, why would he do it? He'd eat the jackfruit, not leave them rotting in the mud."

"Good point, Teodosio," Senhor Eusebio said. "Normally, he would have eaten them. But he could have done it out of spite, because I would not let him be my gardener."

"He could have done it, of course, I grant you that," the vicar said. "But we just can't accuse a man without some tangible evidence."

"I have a thought about Mottu being in his cups," Tendulkar said, still pondering the mailman's recent behavior. "I wonder if there isn't a woman at the back of this, somewhere."

"Pshaw!" Senhor Eusebio said. "He's a family man."

48

"IT'S TIME WE FOUND YOU A HUSBAND," Granny said. "This Simon thing seems to be going nowhere."

"I wish you'd stop," Marie-Santana said. "There is no 'Simon thing.' And when I want a husband, I'll find my own." She was reminded of a piece of music that fit her grandmother's exhortations perfectly. Introduction and rondo, that was it. No, introduction and rondo capriccioso.

"There certainly is a 'Simon thing,'" her grandmother said. "When he strolls by each Sunday morning at the precise moment you open the gate, when he walks with you halfway to church, I think we have a 'Simon thing.' When Josephine comes and asks me if Simon comes to visit, when she knows for sure he doesn't, there certainly is a 'Simon thing.' And when, after all these weeks, he still hasn't said a serious word to you, the 'Simon thing' is going nowhere. If he's a shy man, draw him out."

"I'm not desperate yet, Granny; I'm all right. The right man will come along." She nearly added, "It could be Simon."

"That happens mostly in fairy tales," her grandmother said. "Perhaps when you were a child I told you too many of them. Princes don't come riding by, pumpkins don't turn into coaches. We are poor—you have no dowry. You're getting older. That's the reality. We have to start looking now."

"I don't want to be marketed like a she-goat in heat."

"You make it sound vulgar. It's the way things are done—arranged marriages work. Look at mine, it lasted forty years."

"I heard Grandpa drank and the two of you fought a lot."

"No more than other couples. And we still made a life. I have no regrets, neither did your grandfather. Look at your parents—that too was an arranged match, or didn't you know it."

"They fought a lot, too. It used to drive me crazy."

"Of course they did. Flint and steel, that's what couples are like. Either one without the other is cold and as good as dead; together, they strike sparks and light a fire. That fire is life. But behind the fights there must be respect."

She rose from her chair to hobble about the room, then paused. "I know about fights," she said, looking directly at her granddaughter. "But in all our family fights there was never an insult—not to our son, not to each other, except once. And your father and mother were the same way— they never struck each other down, nor you either, with blows or with words. That's what holds a marriage together; that's what builds a family—respect and affection, more than love. Without respect—"

"And can you guarantee respect?"

"More than when people fall in love. Then, 'Do you love me?' is the constant question. That's love? That's selfishness! And if the answer is 'no, I don't love you,' that sort of love dies. But the foundation of respect lies in thinking of the other person, and not only of the other person, but of the consequences—of the future. Do you know what it is to hurl an insult at a spouse or a child? It's like a poisoned arrow; one can apologize, and pull the shaft out, but the poison remains. Or like the sting of a wasp—one pulls out the stinger and the barb stays in the flesh. And sometimes the one who's struck is so small and so defenseless there's no way to fight back. Or protect oneself."

Marie-Santana, now pensive, maintained her silence.

"The poison always remains," Granny said, her voice gone quite tremulous. "People forget that. And then, should something happen, should the other party leave or die, there's the guilt, which lasts forever. I hear people say, 'If only I'd known. . . . If only I hadn't said that.' By then it's too late." She was weeping now. "I said to your grandfather, I said to him once, 'You should eat cowdung.' I don't remember why I was so angry then, I was so very angry that my anger made me say it, but when I saw the shock on his face, I hugged him and cried. He forgave me. He's been dead some forty years, but those four words that I hurled in anger still haunt me, though I took them back immediately."

"He forgave you," Marie-Santana said softly, her arms around the weeping old woman. "Don't torment yourself any more! He forgave you, and it happened more than forty years ago!"

"Guilt is forever," her grandmother said.

"You must have loved each other deeply."

"Loved? It was an arranged match, remember—we did not know each other until we met. But the people who arranged it had asked around, found out about him, about me, about our families. That tells one a lot—as the older trees grew, so do the saplings turn out. Our love bloomed after we married. But love before marriage can be blinding; one asks no questions, but is certainly told a whole pack of lies." She paused, then asked, suddenly and fiercely, "What happened to your inheritance? The man who stole it—you trusted him. Were you in love with him? Had he promised to marry you? You're flushing—I must have guessed right."

"You're going off on a tangent." Marie-Santana rose and left her grandmother's side, visibly upset at the turn the conversation had taken. "I don't want to talk about it."

"He took you for everything, and you standing by with

your eyes closed because you loved the scoundrel. That's probably what happened, isn't it? Tell me the truth, now—isn't that it?"

"It's over and done with."

"And still you wait for love. Tell me his name, tell me what village he comes from."

"Granny, he's not a Goan, he's an Anglo."

"I'll put a curse on his head."

"Granny, enough!"

"Thank God not all men are such rats," Angelinh' Granny said, but Marie-Santana had already left the room, and the sound of her anguish could be heard through the house.

49

THE LEARNED VICAR of the Church of Saint Cornelius
the Contrite, pastor of Tivolem and father confessor to
his flock, was taking his late afternoon stroll as usual, but
instead of stopping at the bridge, where Senhor Eusebio
and Simon Fernandes were already waiting for him, he
chose a circuitous route that took him into the very heart
of the village. He did not mind being stopped every few feet
by well-wishers—not just his regular parishioners but their
Hindu neighbors as well. In fact, he seemed to relish the
experience, particularly when little children out playing in
the street were urged by passersby to run and kiss his hand
and ask for his blessing. It thus took him a while to get to
the particular lane he was seeking, but once there he opened
the heavy leather-bound tome he had been carrying instead
of his usual breviary and began reading it as he plodded up
the now somewhat steep incline. Every now and then he
would stop, read a passage aloud to himself in Latin, and
chuckle.

One such pause occurred by chance not far from Marie-
Santana's house, right next to a window whose curtains,
though drawn shut, had rustled faintly at his approach, as
though stirred by an invisible wind. Stopping beneath that
window, the vicar not only chuckled but laughed long and

hard, shaking his head the while. He had barely resumed his stroll when a gate creaked open behind him and the slap-slop of scurrying slippers told him the bait had been taken.

"Father Vicar! Wait! Wait for me!"

"Ah Josephine, my child," he said. "What a surprise! Were you home, then?"

"I was making some cheese, and I've brought you some. It's from Amita's goats' milk, and you know what excellent milk they give."

"Indeed. I thank you."

"You are reading a book, Father Vicar."

"A fascinating volume about the ancient church."

"And it makes you laugh?"

"For a reason: it's about penance. We live in truly soft times, Josephine."

"I don't understand, Father Vicar."

"Naturally you don't. What's the most penance I've ever given you? A decade of the Rosary, a Sorrowful Mystery or two, maybe? Something you can take care of in five or ten minutes? Well, they were tougher in the old days. Why, here's a penitent, a woman of about your age, who had to go on her knees from her own village to a shrine some twenty miles away, and over a couple of hills, too. It took her months! What do you think of that penance, eh? Do you think it was too harsh?"

"She must have deserved it," said Josephine Aunty stoutly. "Those old Church Fathers, they knew what they were doing."

"Indeed they did. Perhaps I should follow their example more closely, and make more severe the penances I assign. Yes, oh yes, quite a bit more severe. Thank you, Josephine, for giving me such a fine idea."

She blanched. "Father Vicar, that woman—the one who had to kneel her way over the hills—what was her sin? Had she committed adultery, or killed someone?"

"Oh, she had killed, all right—she killed a reputation.

254

The sin of calumny, it says here. Seems she had an evil tongue—falsely accused a neighbor of being a witch. Fortunately, this was at a time when women accused of being witches were no longer being burned at the stake. So it was a bit like saying, today, that one's neighbor has the evil eye. It's a terrible thing when one goes around making such accusations."

"My curry," she said. "I left it on the fire! Forgive me, Father Vicar, but I must run!"

"The fragrance fills the air," the vicar said. "Ah, all those delicious spices! Go. Meanwhile, I shall enjoy your cheese."

"Anquis in herba," the vicar muttered to her retreating back, promptly translating the phrase from force of habit. "Snake in the grass."

At her garden gate she turned to wave.

"I'm glad we agree on tougher penance," he called, before turning to resume his stroll. "That's truly a fine idea."

From behind the wrought iron scrolls she flashed him a venomous look.

50

ON THE MORNING OF FRIDAY, the twenty-eighth of
July, 1933, at a few minutes to eleven o'clock, an
official-looking registered letter arrived at the Tivolem post
office with the rest of the mail from Panjim, addressed to
the *Excelentíssima e Ilustríssima*—the Most Excellent and
Most Illustrious—Senhorinha Maria Santana Pereira, in
care of the similarly Illustrious and Excellent Senhora
Angelinha Pereira, Tivolem, Goa, India Portugueza. Turning the envelope over and over in his hands, Postmaster
Braganza noticed the elegantly angular writing; the word
Urgente scrawled to the right of and just below the address,
underlined twice and followed by two exclamation marks;
the five red lacquer seals, each with its own signet ring
imprint, spaced ever so carefully along the flap on the back,
to prevent any possibility of tampering; the splash of colorful Mozambique stamps on the front, the postmark from
Quelimane. He remembered that Simon Fernandes, special-
ist though he was in stamps of the British Empire, still had
a side interest in the stamps of Mozambique; and the postmaster made a mental note to tell him that Marie-Santana,
the most illustrious and most excellent, might now be able
to give him a few of the newest. That settled, he called for
Mottu and sent him off posthaste to deliver the letter.

A letter such as this was a rarity in Tivolem, and Mottu would normally have relished the importance that came with delivering it. Taking a letter to Marie-Santana, however, was another matter; after Annabel's threat, he had begun avoiding his neighbor as much as possible, and only spoke to her, always briefly, in his wife's presence. Still, the letter had to be delivered, and seeing as how it was the most important piece of mail to reach Tivolem in months, he naturally rode his bike first to Forttu's tavern to share the news. The tavernkeeper, having examined the envelope as closely as the postmaster had done earlier, announced that it had probably come from a wealthy old dowager who was naming Marie-Santana in her will, or from the dowager's lawyer—or from the lawyer for some other heir, threatening to sue. He then rewarded Mottu with a larger than normal shot of feni and sent him on his way.

In the normal course of events, Mottu, having reached the lane that led to his own home and Angelinh' Granny's, would have gotten off his bike, as any prudent bicyclist would, for the ride from then on was sharply uphill. That morning, however, with the cashew liquor inside him, he felt exceptionally strong and daring, and the letter was urgent, so as the slope grew steeper, he rose from the seat and stood as he pedaled, forcing the bike up the lane against terrain and gravity, gaining ground by moving diagonally from one side of the lane to the other and back again, the bicycle rising and falling as it crisscrossed the double row of ruts. Finally, drenched in sweat and proud of himself but quite out of breath, he stood ringing his bicycle bell triumphantly by Marie-Santana's gate. True, she had kept him at arm's length for weeks, but this time she would have to face him; he was there on business, representing the government.

She hurried down the steps, with Annabel following.

"A letter from Mozambique," he cried. "Urgente." He handed her the envelope, his manner now properly official. "You'll have to sign the receipt. You'll have to sign the receipt, right here on the line, where it says 'Recipiente.' Be sure, Mar'-Santan', to sign your name in ink, the way the sender has it—Maria no hyphen Santana. If you don't, we'll have a problem."

He waited, somewhat impatiently, while the women went into the house for pen and ink. When they returned, Marie-Santana handed him the signed receipt, the envelope in her hand still unopened.

"Look at all those stamps, and those seals," he said. "Mar'-Santan', aren't you going to open it?"

She was in fact more than anxious to open it, but only in private. Having looked at the handwriting and recognized it, she just stood there, the envelope in her right hand, tapping it lightly against the knuckles of her left. She could guess at the contents; it almost certainly contained news of Fernshaw, dead or alive. The simple act of opening it not just in Mottu's but in Annabel's presence, good friend though she was, would instantly trigger questions she was not prepared to answer.

"The letter," Mottu insisted, speaking again in his official capacity as mailman. "It could be very important."

"I'll read it later," Marie-Santana said, almost absently. She decided to bluff it out. "It's from a friend in Quelimane, a lady almost as old as Dona Esmeralda. It can't be that important—all those stamps are just her way of making sure the letter gets through to me."

Mottu, disappointed, turned his bike around.

"Thank you all the same," she said. "That was a lot of trouble, coming up here especially for me."

He mounted the bike, his fingers clutching both brakes.

"Mottu, be careful!" Annabel cried.

He waved at them over his shoulder, and, although he was not pedaling, the bike began to pick up speed as it went freewheeling down the bumpy lane, Mottu standing up on the pedals now and again each time he saw a pothole coming.

"I don't know why he has to ride down the hill, when it's so dangerous," Annabel grumbled. He's showing off, she thought; still trying to impress her, the fool.

258

"It's a fine new bike," Marie-Santana said, "and I remember him riding up and down this slope when he was a child. He loved to show off. He'll be all right, you'll see."

They went back into the house.

Mottu at that moment did not share Marie-Santana's sense of confidence. The bike was still gaining speed as he rounded a curve, even though he was working both sets of brakes, and he regretted not having jumped off while he could. Worse, he could see three of Amita's goats ahead of him, scampering about the lane. He shouted and rang the bell furiously, then jammed on the brakes, hoping they would hold and not just pop out on him. The bike swerved sharply, throwing him halfway across the handlebars, then skidded to the right till he fell off.

When he picked himself up, his first thought was for his bicycle, now lying a yard or so down the lane. The front wheel was quite askew; gripping it between his knees, he yanked hard on the handlebars, trying to correct the misalignment. When he had it almost right, and could do no more, he limped the rest of the way down to the post office, the bicycle wobbling by his side.

Postmaster Braganza was busy at his desk, preparing to send off a telegram. "Well, do you have the receipt?" he asked, without looking up. Getting no answer, he raised his eyes. "Good God! What happened to you?"

That afternoon, Annabel summoned the bonesetter from distant Aiconá, in preference to calling in the doctor from nearby Goregão. The man arrived at a quarter past eleven that night, having walked all the way. He found Mottu groaning in bed, gently felt his left leg and thigh, then prodded and probed more deeply, pronouncing no bones broken. But he suggested that the root of a certain bush be procured next morning, ground down into a fine paste, and applied to those areas that still remained painful; he then accepted a fee of two rupees, respectfully declined a shot of feni, and went his way. Mottu continued to groan awhile, then fell asleep, but Annabel remembered that her husband had not fallen off his bike even once in all the long years of their marriage until now; with the sound of Marie-Santana's voice churning in her mind, she stayed awake for hours, troubled in body and soul, pondering the sequence of the day's events.

51

MARIE-SANTANA thought it unusual when she first saw Little Arnold make the sign of the cross, since it was not yet the hour of the Angelus, and he was playing marbles at the time. The second time she saw him do it, a day later, he was playing cricket, and he was the batsman, and she had just joined three spectators on the sidelines. It was a deadly serious contest, she could see, with just one player a side, and it seemed to Marie-Santana the two sides were less than evenly matched. Little Arnold's opponent, the bowler, was a child perhaps a year older and rather heavily built, and Little Arnold's bat, made from a cut-down palm frond, was much too big for him to wield. Fortunately, the ball was made from a bundle of discarded socks that had been sewn together, so no hurt would come to the child even if he got hit with it.

Little Arnold saw the ball come curling through the air; it was a high and tempting lob, a once-in-a-lifetime chance to smack the ball right with the center of the bat and send it soaring up into the sky, higher than the coconut trees around him. With his feet planted squarely apart, he took a mighty swipe at it crosswise, missed, and the follow-through almost sent him sprawling on his face. Just before the next

ball was bowled, Marie-Santana caught him crossing himself again—and this time he was looking directly at her.
Seconds later the ball curved past his bat and rolled into the
coconut tree that served as his wicket.

"Out!" cried the bowler, as he did a victory dance. For
Little Arnold, the match was lost. Letting his bat fall to the
ground, he crossed himself again, twice, in quick succession,
and began to cry.

As Marie-Santana approached to console him, he turned
to run. "Not so fast, Little Arnold," she said, her suspicions
aroused. "When you grow up, do you plan on becoming a
priest?"

"No, Mar'-Santan' Aunty, I don't want to be a priest,"
he said, squirming in her grasp.

"But I see you making the sign of the cross so beauti-
fully," she said, bending down and wiping his tears, talking
soothingly, face to face. "That's a wonderful thing to do.
Very, very religious. Can you tell me why you do it, Little
Arnold?"

He was silent.

"Do you do it when you see Josephine Aunty?"

"No," he said.

"Or Amita or Rukmini or Angelinh' Granny?"

"No."

"But you do it when you see me?"

He would not meet her eyes.

"Why?" she insisted, shaking him roughly.

"My mother says—" he said and stopped, sobbing once
again.

"And what does your mother say, Little Arnold?"

"My mother says you have the evil eye," he blurted out,
and in the instant that she gasped and slackened her hold
he was off and running.

"My dear Marie-Santana," said the vicar of Tivolem, "I've
heard those stories too, for some little time."

"And from whom?"

"From here and there. In my role as vicar I harvest hints of whispers, echoes of echoes."

"And, Father Vicar, you've done something about them?"

"I have tried."

"And the result?"

He sighed. "I'm not sure. Some belief systems are hard to acquire, and others are hard to shake."

"And this is hard to shake? What's hard to acquire?"

"The system that focuses on the integrity of all human beings; on compassion; above all, on charity in our personal dealings and judgments."

"And your advice to me?"

"You can consider yourself accursed or blessed," the old priest said. "The choice is yours."

"Accursed I can understand," she said. "But how blessed? Accused of having the evil eye, how blessed?"

"People believe you have the power to harm, but, if so, you also have the power to heal," he said. "That's part of their belief system. I too have power, by virtue of my ordination and the robes I wear and the tonsure on the back of my head. My words, my prayers from the heart, and the blessings my hands bestow, are directed to God, and fall on the spiritually famished like manna from heaven. But there are times when my tongue speaks, my hands bless, but my mind and heart are elsewhere. Words and gestures are then like placebos—and like placebos, they often work with those who believe."

"I still don't see—"

"Listen closely," he said. "You can try denying that you have the evil eye and hope that people will eventually believe you. I pray that you will succeed. I will certainly help. But such rumors usually feed on themselves. Besides, those who think you have the evil eye will not easily change their minds. So be prepared for this: sometime, someday, someone you praise will bring illness on himself within hours, perhaps within minutes—a violent headache, a stomach-ache, even high fever. It could be an adult or a little child, it will make no difference—you will be blamed. Then you will have a choice. You can say, 'I had nothing to do with this, you brought it on yourself,' and let the person suffer, or you can tend to the distress, and take the imagined evil eye away."

"I don't know the first thing about it," she said. "I could never get away with it."

"Think back to your childhood. Ask your grandmother. Then do whatever needs to be done."

"But this is feeding on superstition," she said.

The vicar rose and went to the window. "Superstition, belief, faith," he murmured. "The line is ever so finely drawn. There are so many doubts, so many questions! Sometimes I wish I could talk to Christ on these matters. No, that would not do; I'd be quite speechless in the glory of His presence. Saint Augustine, then? No, I could not cope with him at all; he'd drag me into arguments that are way over my head." It seemed to Marie-Santana, as she waited for an answer, that the old priest had wandered off into a world of his own where she dared not intrude. "Perhaps, perhaps then, Pius X," the vicar said. "Yes, he'd be the one. I wish I'd met him before he died. A parish priest most of his life—he'd know what to tell me. Once, when I was down by his tomb beneath Saint Peter's in Rome, I tried. . . . There were people around, it was difficult to commune; Anglican nuns—they would have laughed at me. . . . And I'd ask Peter and Paul, if I could find them— Paul, first as Saul of Tarsus, and then as Paul the Apostle." His voice trailing off, he turned from the window.

"Tell me, Father Vicar," Marie-Santana said. "This business of the evil eye, and the taking away of the evil eye— how does it conform to the teachings of the church?"

Carefully he pulled out his watch. "My, my!" he said. "It's time for my afternoon breviary already. All these unanswered questions, that do so crowd the mind! I'm so glad we could have this talk. Go in peace, my child."

She bowed her head to receive his blessing, and kissed his hand, and waited to leave till he had left the room.

52

THE SUN WAS already riding low when Marie-Santana, back from her visit to the vicar and busy now with her roses, espied Dona Elena strolling down the lane from her ancestral home. Their meetings had always been pleasurable, and Marie-Santana, welcoming the chance of a pleasant chat, straightened up and brushed a hand across her forehead.

"O Marie-Santana!" Dona Elena said. "Busy gardening?"

"Oh, yes, Dona Elena! And you—enjoying a stroll?"

"Just down to the road. It's been such a lovely day, I thought I'd take a short walk. You know about Annabel's boy?"

"Little Arnold? What about him?" She became plainly perturbed.

"He's been vomiting badly since he came home from play this afternoon. Josephine told me just minutes ago."

"Oh!"

Dona Elena reached out and took Marie-Santana's hands in hers. "You are my friend," she said. "It pains me, as it will pain you, but I must tell you what they are saying."

"That I gave the child the evil eye," Marie-Santana said, reddening. Her mouth felt dry. She moistened her lips.

"You know?"

"Little Arnold blurted out that Annabel thinks I have

266

the power. I watched him playing this afternoon; he got sick, I get the blame." She looked her friend in the eye. "Dona Elena, you were not just strolling down to the road now, were you?"

"I wasn't. If I hadn't found you in the garden, I'd have knocked on your door. I felt I should come by and forewarn you."

"You'd do this for me? I'm grateful. But then—you too think I did it? Cast the evil eye?"

"Heavens, no. But others do; unfortunately, we live in a sea of ignorance."

Marie-Santana clenched her fists. "Josephine I can understand," she said. "And Mottu has his problems. But Annabel! My special friend! It's like a betrayal. How could she?"

"Think back to the time Mottu brought you a registered letter," Dona Elena said. "Once one accepts the concept of evil eye, every coincidence becomes cause and effect. He was riding his new bike; you admired it; you even told Annabel he was an expert bicyclist. Seconds later, he fell off and hurt himself. If you were Annabel, what would you be thinking?"

"That it was time Mottu cut back on the feni."

"If you were Annabel, with her background?"

Marie-Santana's lip was quivering. "Do you know the anger and hurt I feel?"

"I feel with you," Dona Elena said. "You are caught in an unfair trap. The child has a fever, they should send for the doctor; but because they think it's evil eye, they won't. What if you don't go, and he gets worse? But if you go, and he gets better, they will say, 'See, she has it, she gave him the evil eye, and she took it away.' Perhaps, in time, we'll be able to sort it all out. But meanwhile, what do you do?"

Marie-Santana thought back to the option the vicar had laid out—that she accept the imaginary power and turn it to good. But turning it to good by accepting it also meant scarring herself for life. Not Dona Elena, not Dona Esmeralda, nor Simon nor the vicar nor Senhor Teodosio would shun or fear her; but what of the others? Was she prepared for that? To have people turn away, make the sign of the cross, each time they saw her? Even retrace their steps, and go the other way? She didn't have to go to the child; there was no law that said she had to. On top of it all, she'd have to face Mottu and all his craziness, something she couldn't talk to Dona Elena about. Let them call the doctor! Wearily, she turned to her neighbor.

"You don't have to go to the child," Dona Elena said, "you don't have to, if you don't want to. I'll back you up."

The sound of Dona Elena's shoes crunching gravel in the lane had not quite died away before Marie-Santana stood before Mottu's house. As she prepared to knock, Annabel opened the door. She had been weeping; had she also been watching?

"I was hoping you'd come," said Annabel, sounding greatly relieved. Mottu was not to be seen; neither was Little Arnold.

Marie-Santana said only, "Where is he?"

Annabel ushered her in. "In the bedroom. He's been looking forward to playing a cricket match tomorrow, and if you don't take the fever away it'll break his heart."

"I'll pray over him, if that's what you want," Marie-Santana said, "but I must tell you now I have no powers at all, none whatever, for good or evil. I haven't made Little Arnold ill, and I didn't cause Mottu to fall off his bike."

She could see right away that Annabel was far from convinced.

"Whatever you say. But please! Please take care of my child. I'll bring you the hot red chilies and the salt and the pieces of alum, and then I'll bring him to you."

But when she did, the child just stood cowering behind his mother.

"Well, Little Arnold," Marie-Santana said, "you have a cricket match tomorrow, I think?"

268

He nodded, his eyes averted.

"Then we've got to get you well," she said, "so you can play. The whole team is counting on you. And next week we have a big day coming up. Not only another cricket match, but Sandow the strong man is coming, and there's going to be a bullfight. . . . So much excitement, and you've got to be there."

Swiftly, she went through the ritual: the sign of the cross made loud and clear in the name of the Father, the Son, and the Holy Ghost; the stream of "I Believe" affirmations; the salt, the alum, and the chilies clutched in her right fist drawn carefully from head to foot, front and back and down each side; the three Hail Marys each beginning with a clearly-mouthed Nomon Moriye, the rest mumbled sotto voce.

"Amen!" said Annabel, as Marie-Santana ended with a blessing and three sharp pats on the back. "Say Amen, Little Arnold!"

Little Arnold was a child transformed.

"He's ready to go play now," said Marie-Santana. And to the child, who now was smiling broadly, she said, "No more vomiting!"

"May I practice in the garden, *mãe?*" he said, reaching for his cricket ball. "I'll bowl against the side of the house till the sun goes down—we've got to beat that other team tomorrow."

"This is all in the mind," Marie-Santana said, after Little Arnold had gone into the garden. "I hope you understand that. There's no such thing as the evil eye, and even if there were, I haven't got it."

"Don't tell me there isn't," Annabel said, bristling.

Marie-Santana turned to the door.

"Don't go away angry," Annabel said, suddenly softening. "Please understand, he's our only child. If Little Arnold should get sick like this again, we'll want you back."

"You'd be better off sending for the doctor."

"The doctor? Whatever was bothering Little Arnold,

you rid him of it in a minute. No doctor works that fast or that well."

"I'll come, if it will help," Marie-Santana said wearily. It seemed to take her forever to walk the few paces back home. The vicar had been right after all.

AUGUST

53

"TENDULKAR, this isn't the best of news I bring you," Senhor Eusebio said. "Gandhi—"

"I know," Tendulkar said. "The Mahatma, his wife Kasturbai, secretary Mahadev Desai, and thirty others were arrested at one-thirty last night, at the ashram in Ahmedabad."

"You knew?"

"Bad news travels fast. Sometimes, by telegraph."

"There were sixteen women in the group. I'm surprised— that's half the total number."

"Well, you shouldn't be," Tendulkar said. "Women know that when it comes to raining blows on the head with a metal-tipped bamboo staff, the British Raj does not choose between the sexes. And still the women volunteer, taking their share of *lathi* charges, and suffering their share of broken skulls."

"If I were Gandhi, I'd keep the women home," Simon said. "It's not right that they should be beaten in the streets."

"That's hardly for Gandhi to decide," Tendulkar said. "It's up to the women, don't you think? If we, as men, deny them a part in the political process, is that fair? Look at us here, sitting on these parapets day after day, discussing all manner of political issues. Where are the women?"

"Women join our group? It wouldn't work," Senhor Eusebio said. "There'd be a scandal of sorts, most certainly."

"But if we believed they should, believed in the political and intellectual equality of the sexes, we'd take that risk, don't you think? A little bit of scandal wouldn't hurt all that much? We're meeting here in public, for heaven's sake. Nobody could accuse us of staging an orgy. So I ask again, why aren't the women here?"

"Dona Esmeralda's too old," the vicar said, "and even if she weren't, she and Dona Elena would rather meet with us in an elegant drawing room than be seen sitting on the stone parapets of a public bridge. Social status, social customs certainly affect their attitude."

"And Amita and Rukmini?"

"*Capistrum maritale.* Matrimonial bonds. And social custom. Even if women wanted to join us here, their husbands would not let them."

"So we're back to the men again. Is it that we think women's views are not worth listening to, their minds not worth cultivating? In Gandhi's vision of India, Marie-Santana would be here by our side, and some of the others, too, speaking and being listened to as equals."

"It amazes me," Senhor Eusebio said, "that Gandhi can whip up so much turmoil in British India, while we across the border remain untouched. Are the British bad taskmasters, compared to the Portuguese? That was not my experience with them in the Persian Gulf."

"They've created their own political problem," Simon said, "by practicing democracy at home, and wherever else they themselves settle, but denying it to their nonwhite colonies. Look how Canada, and Australia, and South Africa, even tiny New Zealand, have now all become autonomous dominions, while India, by far the most populous, is still being denied self-rule. But the very notion of democracy is like a yeast; let even a bit of it slip into a pot, and things begin to bubble."

"But what about the calm in Goa?" Teodosio asked. "Do

we really have political peace here, or is it apathy? The Portuguese have ruled us now for four centuries. For the first hundred years they had their moments of glory, but since then? Perhaps by association we too have now become sheeplike and lethargic and indifferent to progress."

"The times will change," Simon said. "Those of us who go abroad, we always come back, like the pebbles that children hurl into the sky. Some pebbles fall on soft ground and make a tiny dent, and others fall on hard rock and knock off a little chip. But we make a difference, we do. It may just take longer here in Goa."

54

"YOUR ANGER IS EATING YOU UP," Granny said. "I cannot bear to sit here, day after day, and see what's happening with you. Today's the limit! It was bad enough in May, when it was just Josephine and Amita and Rukmini spreading rumors about you; you got over that in time. But now that Annabel's doing it as well, you've been angry and crying all evening. May she break out in boils." They had finished dinner and Granny was preparing for bed.

"I'm angry because I'm hurt, but I don't wish her ill," Marie-Santana said. "Annabel—"

"Don't mention that name in this house."

"But you mentioned it first. Should I just go tear out her hair?"

"No," Granny said. "Give her the evil eye instead. Do it deliberately. Walk up to her and tell her she's beautiful and tell her why you're doing it—so that she might turn into a toad overnight. It might even work. She deserves it. Sheesh! What a horrible woman."

"If only I were someone else, I'd have no problem with that," Marie-Santana said. "Thanks for the idea, anyway." She tried to put it out of her mind, but it would not go away. Realizing it had immense possibilities, she spent some time exploring them.

The sight of Annabel and Josephine talking in the lane next day gave Marie-Santana the opportunity she needed. She walked right up to them and smiled an innocent smile and saw both neighbors cringe.

"Annabel," she said directly, with no pretense at small talk, "when I told you yesterday I didn't have the evil eye, that I didn't make Mottu fall off his bike or Little Arnold start vomiting, you didn't believe me, did you?"

"Mar'-Santan', of course I didn't."

"And Josephine Aunty, those jackfruit that fell off Senhor Eusebio's tree, you say my eyes and my words knocked them down? And I made Rukmini's she-buffalo go dry, too?"

"That's what other people are saying. I—"

"I didn't believe I had the evil eye," Marie-Santana said, cutting her short, "but you were both right. I do have it; I can do fantastic things with it, and I'll prove it to you, from this lane, right there in your own gardens. Show me the most beautiful plant you have, Josephine Aunty, the one you love the most. Is it that *mogra* over there? What marvelous flowers it has, and how richly scented! Look, I have praised it; by morning it should have shrivelled, don't you think? And this coconut tree from Annabel's lot that's leaning over us—move away from beneath it, Annabel—I'm going to praise this incredible crop of coconuts I see up there, and I don't want them to come raining down on your head. What wonderful coconuts! Creamy, refreshing coconuts! The best coconuts one can find anywhere! By morning they will litter the ground, and their insides too will have shriveled. And your houses! Josephine Aunty, don't go! No, I'll not ruin your houses—I'll be merciful and call them ugly, because if I praise them, the roof will surely come crashing down on you as you lie sleeping. Annabel! Why are you rushing inside, Annabel? Why have you slammed your door shut?"

Angrily she stalked up to the house and pounded on the door. "If no bad things have happened in your garden by

276

tomorrow morning, what will you believe then? Will you and Mottu give me back my name? Will Josephine?"

Nothing stirred within the house. She beat on the door some more. "My name!" Marie-Santana cried again. "My name, which you both have ruined. Will you give it back?"

She turned at last to go home and saw Simon standing outside the gate. "Bravo!" he said. "I heard that! Those two are not going to sleep tonight."

He thought she would stop and he would comfort her, but she rushed past him, unable to control her tears.

55

When Angelinh' Granny, dozing in her rocker, had finally fallen asleep, Marie-Santana pulled out a by now well-creased envelope and once again read over the letter from Quelimane. It had been a struggle to keep its contents to herself, with Granny always so close at hand, reading her thoughts. The questioning had started immediately.

"You receive an important registered letter, and I have to hear about it from Josephine? Why couldn't you have told me?"

"It's from my friend, the old Makwa chief, the one with the uncatchable goldfish," Marie-Santana teased. "Remember him?"

"A likely story! I'm the old Makwa chief in this house, and you should talk to me as freely as you seem to have done to that old man in Mozambique."

"I'll tell you, I promise. But later."

"It's about that man," Granny said. "It's got to be about that man. An important letter—I can smell it." Getting no clear answer, Granny shuffled off toward the kitchen, her slippers slip-slopping against the tiles and the soles of her feet.

Marie-Santana did not take long to reread the letter,

because it was brief, and she had the contents memorized. The lie she had told Annabel—that the letter came from an old friend, an old lady, a lady as old as Dona Esmeralda— now embarrassed her; on reflection, the subterfuge seemed to her pointless, and a sign of her own enduring weakness, born of her fear of being questioned, fear of the village's collective curiosity, of Josephine Aunty's tongue in particular. It had been easier to lie, to buy time to think, even though she had recognized the handwriting immediately as being that of an aged lawyer, long her father's crony. Now, having reread the letter, she read it yet once again, as if to draw comfort from the sense, perhaps, that in that town of Quelimane there was still someone she trusted, someone who cared. But the action that the writer expected of her? She had agonized over that question ever since the letter had arrived; in fact, had agonized even earlier about what she should do. Over the past few years, ever since she had uncovered John Fernshaw's perfidy and he had disappeared, she had asked herself, what if? What if, at last, he were found?

The letter said he had indeed been found. He had been found not in Quelimane but far to the south in the capital city of Lourenço Marques. And he had been found operating not as John Fernshaw but as J. J. Ferniss, sole proprietor of a flourishing import-export business. The lawyer now asked for instructions: Should he proceed against Ferniss/Fernshaw for fraud and embezzlement, have him arrested, tried, and jailed? The litigation might take months, and her presence would be required, the lawyer wrote, adding that in view of the large sums in question, the trip would be worthwhile, especially since she had such a clear-cut case. With Fernshaw now affluent, she could recover her losses in full; of that the lawyer was certain. Based on this certainty, and also because of his own long association with her family, he offered to advance the funds she might need for her trip back to Mozambique, if monies were at all needed.

Marie-Santana tucked the letter into the bosom of her

dress and, taking care not to disturb Granny, slowly went down the steps to the garden, walked all the way to the far end of her grandmother's little plot, and turned at last to face the aging house. She thought of the old lawyer's advice and the money she would gain if she filed suit and won. And what if she lost? There was always that possibility. Should she consult Simon? She decided against doing so; he had enough to do helping her cope with allegations of the evil eye.

As for winning—a personal hurt would be avenged, but would it be eased? Old wounds would be reopened. And the money? What would she do with it? She remembered the good times she had had in Quelimane, not just the little luxuries but the comforts of everyday life. Those were the days when work of a menial sort—her father would have chided her for that word—had been something she did not even have to think about, far less have to do in order to survive. If the lawyer were right—and she had absolute faith in his judgment—she could now with a stroke of the pen break free of her present circumstances; build a better house, a better life for herself and Granny, have as many servants, even, as Dona Esmeralda, if she so desired. But the question that kept intruding into her mind was whether that recovered wealth would bring her greater happiness. In Quelimane, surrounded as she was with choice material possessions, had she not wanted more? And because she had wanted more, she had needed Fernshaw, had needed his managerial skills, had been blinded to the fact that the profits he promised and so freely produced came out of funds he was siphoning out of the family fortune. Her youthful and at the time insatiable desire for a better life: was that not why Fernshaw had triumphed?

Granny had few wants and few material needs, Marie-Santana realized. Granny herself had posed the question: What use would she have for money at her stage in life? She herself, young as she was, since returning to the village, had seen her needs diminish in number. Where once she

280

would have craved that new pair of shoes, even with a dozen barely used pairs still lying in her closet, she now went barefoot in the house some of the time, in the garden most of the time. The first time she had ventured outdoors without her sandals she had winced, her soles gone soft, at the sharp reality of each pebble on the path; now she took comfort in the warm graininess underfoot.

Granny's prized possession was her rosary; she fretted more if she mislaid her beads than if the roof leaked. Marie-Santana recalled the one time since her return when she had mentioned, wistfully, that had she had the funds, she would have used them to improve the old house. Her grandmother had been aghast. "Improve it? You mean change it? What would you change in it? The family home, that's been this way for generations? Every room in it, every stone, holds memories for me, and for you, but especially for me. After I die, do what you like, but change it now?"

With her grandmother once more asleep on the balcão, Marie-Santana strolled slowly back through the garden, lingering a while among her father's weathered old roses, touching a scarlet petal here, stopping to breathe in a fragrance there, unmindful of the butterflies flitting all around and the bees and yellow jackets that began to hover at her approach. She stopped at last among the yellow roses, delicate and velvety and subtly aromatic, in all the garden her father's favorite bloom. She asked herself what her father would have done. As a businessman, the lawyer's advice might well have made sense to him; what, then, of his philosophy of life? She stayed there by the rose perhaps five minutes, perhaps ten, lost in thought; then, her mind made up, she slowly returned to the house.

Angelinh' Granny came awake as Marie-Santana started up the steps. "About the letter, Granny," Marie-Santana said. "They've found him."

"Found him? The crook? You couldn't tell me that?"

"I have been asked to make a decision and needed time to think. Papa's lawyer wants to know if I want the man jailed."

"A stupid question. Of course you want him jailed. Will you get your money back?"

"I'd get it back if I sue and win."

"Then have him jailed and sue him. The sooner the better."

"This doesn't sound like you at all," Marie-Santana said, surprised and disappointed by her grandmother's vehemence. "The money's not important anymore; he squandered all of mine, and anything he now has he must have stolen from a dozen others. I don't want even an anna of it. Let others sue! Can you accept that? And what would I gain by throwing him in jail?"

"Do you care for him?"

"No."

"It sounded as though you did. But since you don't, let me tell you what you'll gain, aside from the money. Justice for yourself and the others he has cheated. Revenge—and retribution. That's the way of the world."

"Most certainly, but that would not be Papa's way," Marie-Santana said softly. "That would not be Papa's way at all." Wearily, she eased herself onto the stone bench facing her grandmother.

"My son sometimes took leave of his senses," Angelinh' Granny said. "Or so the world thought. Why should I be surprised if his daughter thinks the same way? I'm only an old woman, and got carried away. You're right—the money's not important. Do whatever will bring you peace."

56

LITTLE ARNOLD'S CRICKET MATCH against boys from a neighboring village—an event of almost global significance in their eyes—was going to be played on the very outskirts of Tivolem, down a dirt road to a clearing that was perhaps seventy yards across and surrounded by a sparse coconut grove. Neither team expected or wished for a grown-up audience. The adults now streaming toward the clearing, they knew, would leave after watching the two events that were to precede the game: feats of strength by the "Indian Sandow"—the real Sandow being Britain's wax-mustachioed answer to America's Charles Atlas—and a fight between two trained bulls. One of them was Vittol's, which made the fight special; Vittol was the best trainer of bulls in all of Goa.

Marie-Santana looked around the clearing. She saw Annabel approach, smiling, and she was glad. The day after she had pounded on Annabel's door, Annabel had come to her to apologize, the coconut palm unscathed. Their friendship had been precious to them both; they had embraced and wept. Now they stood side by side, comfortably, watching the crowd grow. Besides people from the adjoining villages, half of Tivolem was already at the scene when the Indian Sandow arrived, riding atop a lorry laden with paving stones. Just inside the clearing, the engine sputtered and died. Sandow leaped out and cranked the engine mightily, but it refused to start. The driver called on him to crank it again; but still the engine would not catch. The strong man turned to the crowd and salaamed.

"My God, I thought he'd be built like a potbellied wrestler, but look how lithe and muscular he is," murmured Forttu.

At six feet, Sandow towered over the villagers. "I need five men," Sandow said, "to push the lorry closer to the center of the clearing. Ten yards will do it. I'd do it myself, but I must save my strength. Five strong men with strong backs—where are the strongest men in Tivolem?"

He looked at Kashinath.

"Not me," said Kashinath. "I'm only the village barber. You need strength, take Forttu here. Look at the size of him; besides, he's used to lifting heavy things."

"Go on, Uncle Forttu," cried Little Arnold. But Forttu declined as well. Yet, five men were found, strong laborers in the fields, and the bronzed muscles of their shoulders and backs rippled as they got behind the lorry and pushed. Then, because it would not budge an inch, five more men were added, who spat on their hands and spread dirt on their palms to get a better grip. The third time around they placed their backs against the tailgate. Still the lorry would not move.

"Only ten yards!" coaxed Sandow. "Ten, fifty, a hundred rupees each, if you can do it! Go help them," he said to Little Arnold, who had been hopping up and down excitedly and needed no further urging. They tried to move it, then, with Little Arnold's powerful help, and much laughter and many sly digs and catcalls from the spectators; but try as they might, the lorry stayed solidly in place.

"Well, do you still want the show to go on?" Sandow asked the crowd.

"We do!" they cried. "We most certainly do!"

"Then I guess I'll have to move the lorry myself," he

284

said. "But, to spare my arm muscles, I'll just have to pull it with my teeth."

"With his teeth!" cried the baker, who had been among those who had failed in the attempt. "An elephant could not move that thing just with its tusks."

The crowd quieted down as the muscleman prostrated himself in prayer. Then, stripped to his loincloth, his muscles glistening in the sun, he set about his task. With both ends of a rope attached to the lorry, the center gripped between his teeth, he leaned forward till his face seemed just inches from the ground. His clasped hands were before him; the fine tension in his biceps, his shoulders, his back and thighs, his calves and feet down to his toes, made him seem like an ancient statue come to life. Long seconds passed; sweat dripped off his face and gleamed bright on his body. As the tension grew, the lorry creaked and leaned forward, then settled back again. The crowd groaned. The rope stretched tight again till it hummed, and still the lorry did not budge.

Aahhh! went the crowd as Sandow slipped; quickly, he regained his balance. The rope stretched taut once more, and this time—slowly, magically, as if drawn forward by an irresistible force—the lorry began to move. They began to applaud, then; by the time he had the lorry up to walking pace, the children were running wild with excitement. The crowd cheered again when, turning around and placing himself in harm's way, he leaned against the front end and slowly brought the juggernaut to a halt. By the time he had lifted a boulder tied to his braided hair, bent a metal bar into a near-circle, and leaned against and bent back a sword whose point had been placed squarely against his breastbone, his assistant had collected a fair amount of money.

For the climax, Sandow now lay on his back, arms by his side, while the assistant prepared to drive the stone-laden lorry onto his chest. "I can't bear to look," said Annabel to Marie-Santana, as the lorry inched up to Sandow's barrel chest but failed to climb it. Nervously, she grasped her friend's arm and held on tightly.

The driver backed off, then came forward again at a slightly faster speed. The women shielded their eyes; the crowd gasped, then cheered. The wheel had climbed onto Sandow's chest and, after an agonizing pause, had backed off it, and he now stood before them, salaaming, folded palms touching his forehead.

"If only I could make money that quickly and easily," said Govind the carpenter, watching the coins come raining from the crowd. "He's made more in an hour than I make in a month."

"I'll make you a sporting offer, Govind, my friend," said Forttu. "You go lie down in front of that lorry and let the wheel go up on your skinny chest, and I'll give you twice as much money as Sandow has collected so far. Think of it—twice as much! And I'll throw in all the coconut-palm liquor you can drink, every day, for the rest of your life. Or I could pay the money to your widow, which you may prefer."

But they were interrupted. "Here comes Vittol!" cried Little Arnold. "Here they come, he and his bull. Ohhh!" And indeed, from the other side of the clearing, Vittol the trainer had entered, walking proudly; his champion fighting bull trotted beside him, small, lithe, and all muscle. As the children ran forward to escort them, Vittol shortened the tether and the two marched briskly around the clearing, the bull snorting and tossing its head to the applause. Vittol then took up his station in the center, his back to the sun, and the bull, snorting again, came alongside, gently rubbing his head against his master's side. The children giggled nervously; only Little Arnold was bold enough to ask, "Can I touch him, Uncle Vittol?"

"From over here," said Vittol, and Little Arnold reached out, timidly touching the bull's side and stroking its forehead and muzzle while his friends crowded around.

"Don't be afraid; he likes it," said Vittol, as the bull tossed its head and stretched out its neck to be scratched;

286

but before the boy could reach out again, the bull had snorted and now stood tensed, muscles quivering, facing the old dirt road.

"They're here!" cried Forttu as, to a beating of drums, the challenger appeared, with a noisy group of hangers-on, his powerful black bull restrained on either side by men holding ropes.

"Stand back!" the man cried. "Stand back! Make way for the best, the fiercest fighting bull in the whole world. This is going to be a short fight—that is, if Vittol and his month-old calf dare show up at all."

"We're here ahead of you, we've been here and waiting," said Vittol, "waiting so long we thought you weren't coming. But now I see why you're late—you had to round up six strong men to drag that frightened creature of yours even this far."

The crowd laughed, for while Vittol's bull now stood poised and ready, his rival was bellowing and bucking from side to side in a frantic effort to break free. But despite Vittol's bravado, Kashinath's faith was shaken.

"Vittol's bull is not going to win this one," the barber said, shaking his head. "Not this one."

"What makes you say that?" asked Mottu, who stood to lose a bit of money.

"Look at him! He stands barely shoulder-high."

"So what's new about that? Vittol's bulls are always much smaller than the bulls they fight, and yet time after time they have shown us that size is not everything."

"True, it isn't," said Kashinath. "But if it's power you want, look at the other bull now." And indeed, the black bull was putting on an impressive display, alternately pawing the ground, bellowing, and tearing up the soil with his sharp, curved horns.

"What are they fighting for, Forttu?" asked Marie-Santana.

"Four sacks of grain, to begin with," said the tavern-keeper. "Vittol and the challenger have put up a sack apiece, and the village has added two more. And there's some money. Winner takes all."

"I have bet on Vittol's bull to win," said Mottu, sounding now much less sure of himself.

"You can see you were too hasty," said Kashinath.

"I think not," said Forttu. "Vittol's bulls have not lost a fight, not in fifteen years. But here comes Senhor Euseb'. Let's ask him what he thinks."

"Perhaps we should ask her instead," whispered Kashinath, nodding toward Marie-Santana. "Whichever bull she fancies, with her evil eye, that'll be the end of him."

"I'd bet on Vittol's bull, without question," said Senhor Eusebio when they asked him.

"You would, Senhor Euseb', but you haven't?" said Mottu.

"Yes, yes, I have," said Senhor Eusebio, somewhat testily. "I've bet a whole rupee."

"That doesn't show much confidence, Senhor Euseb'," teased the taverner. "You'd raise your bet a little, maybe? Say to ten rupees? One hundred?"

"A bet is a bet, no matter how small," said Senhor Eusebio, laughing. "But a big bet, now—that's a gamble. I never gamble."

"And that's how the rich stay rich," muttered Mottu, watching the landowner amble on.

"Sh!" said Marie-Santana as the two bulls were freed of their tethers and now faced each other, a bare ten feet apart. For long seconds they stood motionless, the small cool champion and his fractious opponent, each taking the measure of the other; then, as the big bull once again pawed the ground in challenge, kicking up dust, Vittol's bull lowered its head, snorted, and charged—and the big black bull swerved sharply aside, turned tail, and charged the crowd.

"Sandow! Sandow!" cried Little Arnold, and the crowd took up the frantic cry for help, but Sandow was nowhere to be seen. Seldom has such a big man climbed a coconut tree so fast! Vittol's bull, having gained the field, stood

288

stock still, watching the other careening about. Crouched behind Sandow's tree, Little Arnold saw the bull turn and come trotting his way; panicking, he bolted across the clearing. With a bellow the bull thundered after him. Quick though Little Arnold was, the bull was faster. Annabel screamed and clung to her friend in terror, but as the boy dodged, Marie-Santana broke free, then hurled herself forward with the shriek of a banshee.

"Run! Run!" she screamed at the child as the rogue bull stopped in its tracks and turned to meet her challenge. The moment's respite was all Little Arnold needed, but it was not quite enough for Marie-Santana. Fear now gripped her heart. She found herself alone, almost in the center of the clearing, no help at hand, no friendly trees behind which she could dodge to avoid those deadly horns. Her surroundings fell away from her; in her universe there was now only the bull, and she herself, and not quite ten feet of ground between them. Balanced on the balls of her feet, prepared to run to left or right, Marie-Santana became aware then of her mind as a being outside of herself, instructing her what to do. Avoiding sudden movements that could trigger a charge, she eased herself out of her encumbering sandals and pushed them to one side. Then, her eyes still fixed on the bull, she stooped and reached her hand to the ground, searching desperately for a stone, a pebble, something solid to throw. It worked with dogs, she knew from experience; you reached for a stone, and any dog confronting you would turn and run before your hand so much as touched the ground. But the bull did not budge, and her hand came up with just a handful of sand and grit, the bull not pawing the ground but snorting and shaking its head. She threw the fistful of sand, then, and with the wind at her back it caught the bull in the face and eyes and it stood there confused, snorting and blinking, while the crowd shouted for her to run; but instead she picked up more handfuls still and peppered the bull in the face, forcing it to back away slowly from the unexpected fury of her attack and finally to turn completely away, and the crowd cheered; but the mind that was outside Marie-Santana told her now was the time to run, the bull was about to swing around and charge, so she ran as she had not run since a child. In those childhood games of tag, fleet of foot as she was, she had eluded her playmates with ease; but now it was the bull, not Mottu, who was at her heels and gaining. She twisted away, and the onrushing beast swept past; as it turned and stopped, her fear was now tinged with elation. She had survived; she could do it again. The trees were closer now, and though the bull stood in between, all she had to do was twist and run and twist again. She no longer felt alone. She became conscious of movement in the crowd, of men looking for stones, of the bull's owner and handlers coming up with ropes and falling back as the bull ripped up the earth again with hoof and horn.

She dodged the next charge, but the second time around she tripped over the sandals left lying on the sand, and though she recovered, the bull caught her a glancing blow as she sidestepped and dropped her to the ground. The crowd rushed forward then, shouting and reaching for stones in a soil where there were none; but all that Marie-Santana could see was the bull, standing over her with bloodshot eyes, frothing at the mouth and snorting horribly.

For a long moment she looked him in the eye. "Dear God," she prayed, "let this be quick." She did not hear the distant bellow then, but she heard a thundering of hooves, felt the earth tremble, and in an instant Vittol's bull was in her range of vision, was bearing down on them, had hooked his horns under the challenger's belly, and tossed him in the air. The black bull rolled as he landed and tried to strug-gle to his feet, but there was neither wind nor fight left in him. Vittol's bull stood guard by Marie-Santana, snorting, watching, just watching, then trotted back to his master as the black bull rolled painfully onto its side, breathing heavily.

A dozen willing hands lifted Marie-Santana up and

caressed her face, her arms, her being. Though bruised and shaken, she was not seriously hurt.

"What gave you the courage to rush out like that?" Forttu asked in admiration.

"I saw a child in terrible danger," she said. "And— maybe—at the back of my mind I thought of my father, and what he would have done. I've always wanted to be like him, wanted him to be proud of me."

"Your life must have passed before your eyes," Govind said, "when you were down on the ground. What did you think, when you saw that big black bull ready to kill you?"

"I thought, first, Angelinh' Granny needs me," she said. "And then I prayed."

Some, including Annabel, agreed they had seen her lips moving in prayer. Others claimed to have seen her actually talking to the bull; and Josephine Aunty went so far as to say that Mariemana—'Marie my sister', not Mar'-Santan' any longer—had even reached up to stroke its face. But while no one else had seen that gesture, all from Tivolem agreed that, once Vittol's bull had come thundering for-ward, full tilt, the black bull's fate had been sealed, and Mariemana was as good as saved.

57

THE KNOCK ON THE FRONT DOOR was furtive but insistent. Who could it be at that hour? As Angelinh' Granny snored peacefully on in the next room, Marie-Santana, despite her fear, groped for matches and finally got a candle lit at the door.

"Who is it?"

"It's me, Simon. Open up!"

At the sound of his voice she was at once relieved and concerned—relieved it wasn't a stranger; concerned that what had brought him there was bad news; that he had been hurt, or was somehow in trouble. Carefully she slid back into its wall socket the heavy wooden beam that she drew each night to bar the front door, and opened the door a crack.

In the dim flickering light she could see he was distraught. "I heard what happened," he said. "I came as soon as I heard."

"Simon, it's after eleven o'clock! It could have waited! Did Josephine see you come?"

"Her house is dark," he said. "And I couldn't wait. You could have been killed, Marie-Santana."

"But it didn't happen. Little Arnold is safe, and I'm safe, too, thank God."

"I thank God, too," Simon said. "More than you know." His hands were trembling. "Is Granny awake?"

"No."

"Then come out onto the balcão. We have to talk."

"Not now, not at this hour. I'm not dressed."

"We have to talk," he said. "If not now, when?"

"In the morning. I'll be out watering the garden at seven. If you pass by then, we can talk across the garden wall."

"I must talk to you in private," he said. "There are people about at that time. Josephine especially."

"We'll get to talk, I promise you. Now go, before all this whispering wakes Granny up."

"I'll be awake all night," he said, "thinking of you."

"I hear Granny stirring," she lied. "Please go!"

He waited to go down the steps till the wooden safety beam had been slid back in place. Her ear to the door, Marie-Santana heard the garden gate pulled softly to, heard the latch drop in place; waited until all sound of the receding footsteps had ceased. "He loves me," she whispered to herself, as a warm flush suffused her body; she leaned back against the door to let the sudden dizziness pass. "He loves me. He loves me."

Blowing out her candle, she continued to lean against the door in the darkness, letting time flow by. Her mind was a whirl of emotions as the events of the last few hours crowded back on her. She had looked death in the eye and survived; in seconds she had gone from local undesirable to village heroine. And now Simon. . . .

She tried to quiet the beating of her heart. Did she love him? She did not know; for the past few years she had resisted even the idea of falling in love. On the other hand, looking back, she realized he had been much in her thoughts lately, and not just because of Granny's prodding. She listened of course for the violin; but if the violin were silent, and she were engaged in some tedious chore, such as drawing water from the well or doing the daily wash, she found herself wondering where he might be and what project might be engaging his attention. Certainly these were signs of more than casual interest on her part. As for him, she knew now that he was in love with her; had he wanted to propose? And she had sent him away!

The moment would not have been right, she decided, not at that hour, not in the dark in the balcão. She would want to see his face when he proposed; and it would have to be when he—when they both—were not under the stress they were in that night. But he was such a shy man, of course, his courage might fail him; he might never get around to declaring his love, preferring instead to woo her with his violin, through those constant amorous serenades with which he filled the evening air. That's what he had been doing, she realized, these past few months; when she had been out in her garden, and he playing the violin in his home, some at least of those love songs had been from the heart, for her. Perhaps even when he did not quite realize what he was doing. And if the serenades continued, would she not find a way?

She checked on her grandmother, still fast asleep and snoring lightly, then went back to her own room and slid under the coverlet. She had barely done so when the snoring stopped.

"I always liked that Simon," Angelinh' Granny said. "Fine man. Very fine man. Your parents would have approved."

"Granny!" Marie-Santana said sharply, but all she got back was an answering snore.

That night Marie-Santana had repeated nightmares, in which the big bull slobbered over her. In some of these dreams she was naked; in all, she was saved by the thundering of hooves, and woke sweating in the stillness of the night to hear Angelinh' Granny snoring. In the fourth nightmare the dream changed: the charging bull reared up, and stood on its hind legs, and took off its bull-mask, and the face that was revealed, contorted and evil, was Josephine Aunty's. And Josephine Aunty said, "Your life in this village is still ruined. The world believes you have the evil eye. Go, and leave Annabel alone."

But the savior bull then came up, and that bull was Angelinh' Granny, and Granny's hair shone with a silver light. And Granny said, "Don't listen to her; you have a choice. You risked your life to save the child—the whole village now loves you." And Granny vanished, to be replaced by Simon, who put his violin to his chin, and said, "I love you and will stand by you. Tell them the truth, that you are as normal as the rest of us. They will believe you." But before he could play, Josephine Aunty said, "No one will believe you. I'll twist everything you say and do. I will hound you forever."

Marie-Santana, remembering her talk with the vicar, gathered up her inner strength and said, very clearly and firmly, "If you do, you will grant me power, power over the village, power to do good where you wish to do evil, power beyond your control. Is that what you want? Then do your worst!"

Then Josephine Aunty, putting on her bull-mask once again, dropped back onto all fours and slunk away. And Marie-Santana called to her retreating back, "No matter what you do, I, not you, will win."

The sound of her own voice awakened her. She felt strangely calm. Angelinh' Granny stirred in the cot in the next room, saying sleepily, "Did you call, bai?"

"You must have been dreaming, Granny dear," Marie-Santana said. "I'm right here. Go back to sleep."

From that time on, whenever she was asked by friend or stranger about her role in the bullfight (and she was asked time and again), Marie-Santana's version of what she had said and done in those last few desperate moments differed somewhat from the account she had given on the day itself.

"Sure, I thought of my father and of Angelinh' Granny, and I prayed," she would now say. "And then I thought, if only I had the evil eye, I could look that black bull right in the face, and praise him, and he would shrivel to nothing.

You saw what happened. It wasn't me, but Vittol's bull, that got him. Was that the evil eye?"

No, said Kashinath and Amita and Rukmini; not the evil eye, but Vittol's victorious bull had been the instrument that saved her.

"A powerful instrument," Josephine Aunty added. The village agreed.

58

SIMON SHAVED AS CLOSELY AS HE COULD, and dressed with care; he had already, waking and sleeping, mentally rehearsed the words he would speak to Marie-Santana. He waited, as planned, till he saw her at work in her garden; then he walked down the lane with as firm a step as he could muster. Approaching Marie-Santana's gate, he found himself ambushed.

"Mr. Fernandes, out so early! Did you hear the news?" Josephine Aunty gushed, bobbing up in her garden out of nowhere. "Mar'-Santan' saved Little Arnold's life yesterday. Such courage, defying a raging bull!"

"I heard it, and I know I couldn't have done as much," he said. He spoke haltingly, groping for the unfamiliar Konkani words. The fears he had expressed to Marie-Santana the previous night were realized—they would not be able to talk freely after all.

"No one could have, certainly not that Sandow! Sheesh!" Josephine Aunty made a gesture of intense disgust. "When the bull charged, that man went up a coconut tree faster than a toddy tapper. Not even a monkey! But Mar'-Santan'— you should have seen her! She's out in her garden; why don't you ask her?"

"I was about to do that," he said, chagrined, "but only

297

for a moment; I'm heading for Mapusa." That was the first excuse that came to his mind; as long as she was around and eavesdropping, he needed to be careful. "Marie-Santana!"

Marie-Santana, who at the first sound of Josephine Aunty's voice had suddenly busied herself with her roses, now looked up, as though surprised.

"That was a wonderful thing you did," Simon called out. "Wonderful! Brave and wonderful!"

She came to the gate to greet him. "Josephine Aunty might have done it, too," she said, "had I not jumped in first." Josephine, accepting the possibility, simpered modestly. To Simon, Marie-Santana said, "Do you want to come into the garden?"

He shook his head. "I have an errand to run." Switching to English, he dropped his voice to a murmur: "I was afraid this would happen. We can't talk here—not now, not like this. She has the hearing of a bat on the wing."

"I'm sorry," she said softly. "Tonight at seven, then, by the bridge. I'll be walking back from Mapusa."

"Don't be late," he pleaded. Then he said out loud, "Every last detail. I want to hear it all." He turned to Josephine and said in the vernacular, "To risk her life like that—"

"She came this close to death," Josephine Aunty agreed.

"You had better get started," Marie-Santana said carefully, her back to Josephine. "There's no telling what that woman will be thinking if you dawdle much longer. We'll meet at seven."

"Well, I must be going," Simon said cheerfully, addressing both women.

"If you'll wait just a minute," Josephine Aunty said, "so I can put on my sandals, I'll walk to Mapusa with you."

He had to think quickly. "And I would have enjoyed your company. But did I say Mapusa? A stupid mistake— I'm going to Panjim."

"Then I won't go to Mapusa today, after all," Josephine

Aunty said. She seemed disappointed. "It's a long walk, and I'll wait till I have someone to walk with. But before you go, can I at least offer you a cup of tea?"

"Not this morning, thank you," he said, "I don't want to miss that first bus to Betim."

He waved to them both in turn, then walked briskly down the lane, hoping Josephine Aunty had not seen through the charade. "Malevolent pest," he muttered through clenched teeth as he headed for the bus stop.

The day dragged. He had no business at all to take care of in Panjim, yet here he was, at not quite eight in the morning, wandering through the narrow lanes of the residential quarter of Fontainhas, all because of Josephine. It had seemed a plausible excuse at the time he came up with it, trying to outwit a busybody—Josephine Aunty thinking "he's dressed up because he's wooing Mar'-Santan', but since he's pretending he's going to Mapusa, let me call his bluff," and he himself countering with "but I'm really going to Panjim." It certainly seemed to have allayed her suspicions. But it had been a whole lot of trouble to go to, this trip by bus and gasolina to Panjim, a pointless trip, a wasted day, and he felt foolish for having gone through with it. But there was Marie-Santana to think of, he reminded himself; Josephine's tongue had done her enough harm already. Things would be different once he and Marie-Santana were married; Josephine would have nothing to gossip about. But when would that day be? He was having trouble enough just getting Marie-Santana alone so he could declare himself.

The peacefulness of Fontainhas calmed him down somewhat, the flowerpots in the windows matching the tiny impeccable gardens and the cats on the ledges watching him with quiet interested eyes, reacting with pleasure when he reached up and tickled them under the chin; by the time he turned and made his way to the municipal gardens his anger had quite drained away. He decided to while away the day in that pleasantly exotic setting, thinking of the future; if he left at four he'd be in Tivolem in plenty of time to meet with his cronies and then with Marie-Santana.

In Tivolem he found the group at the bridge already in session. "You missed all the excitement yesterday," Senhor Eusebio said, wagging a finger at him. "Not just Sandow, which was exciting enough, and the bullfight, but Marie-Santana saving the child. That was something to see! What kept you away that was so important?"

"I was practicing," Simon said, somewhat sheepishly.

"A strongman show and a bullfight, and you stay home and practice? What are you practicing for?"

"Music is a demanding mistress—that's all the reason one needs. Now tell me what happened."

"Well, for one thing, there was no bullfight. When Vittol's bull charged, the challenger turned and ran straight into the crowd, horns lowered. We scattered, fast as we could, in every direction."

"That much I heard last night, from Forttu. He says you ran past him faster than a rocket at the feast of Saint Cornelius."

"And he's right. The only thing faster than me was Sandow. We didn't see him go flashing by till he was half-way up that coconut tree."

"We have misjudged him," Tendulkar said. "He didn't climb that tree to escape, he did it so he could bombard the bull with coconuts. He just didn't climb high enough."

They laughed.

"And Marie-Santana?" Simon kept his voice level.

"Ah, Marie-Santana—she ran too, but when the time came, she was magnificent. The bull chased Little Arnold and we froze, but she went after it with just her bare hands. Stopped the bull dead, while the child got away. Bare hands, and presence of mind—throwing sand in the bull's eyes by the handful, just like that."

"Marie-Santana has guts," Regedor Tellis said. "Raw

300

courage she has in plenty. Teodosio, she did the kind of thing you might have done, had you been there."

"Ah, but I would have had my gun," Teodosio said. He had just returned from one of his hunting trips. "Without my gun I'm not quite sure what I could have done. My knife would have been useless."

Simon, drinking in the generous praise for Marie-Santana, the endless recountings from various points of view, the half-embarrassed, half-boastful claims of who had been the nimblest to escape, or the most fearful, still kept looking furtively at his watch. He had heard all he needed to hear; Marie-Santana was indeed a heroine. Why couldn't they now just go?

"Brother Simon must have a special appointment this evening," the vicar said, rising and stretching to end the session. "I've never known him to check the time so frequently before."

"There must be a lady involved, eh, Fernandes?" Gustavo Tellis said familiarly, amid general laughter. "Yesterday's heroine, maybe?"

It was just before six—he had an hour to kill. With a touch of bravado he said, "You'd like to know, wouldn't you, Tellis?" There was a hint of laughter in his voice. "Then why not hang around? I'll be meeting the lady here, at seven."

"I'm not that stupid," the regedor said, still laughing. "If you had a rendezvous, would you be telling us about it, and would you be having it in such a public place? No, you have some other scheme in mind. You can tell us about it tomorrow."

The sun that had been hanging like a ball of red fire above the Arabian Sea had dropped below Simon's horizon, daubing the clouds to the west in brilliant hues of orange and crimson and purple. In his impatience, Simon had left the bridge and was now walking along the road to Mapusa; in the reflected light it stretched out before him, at this hour quite devoid of traffic, a straight, dark ribbon fringed on either side by coconut trees. Where the trees narrowed in the distance there appeared a dot, that in time turned into the figure of a woman, and even in the deepening dusk he knew from her walk that it was Marie-Santana.

He went forward briskly to meet her then, the words and phrases he had been rehearsing all that day now swirling through his head. But as she drew nearer all the fine speeches he had so carefully strung together left him; he took her outstretched hand in his and could only stammer out a greeting.

"It's all right, Simon," she said, her left hand at his elbow. "Take your time. I'm listening."

He drew a sharp breath. "I—"

He could not speak, his confusion deepening.

"Simon," she said, slowly and soothingly, "this thing you've been wanting to talk about so much, is it—about us?"

"Yes, it is," he said. "It's about you—and me." He paused. "Marie-Santana, I'm not much good at this; my violin speaks of love more eloquently than my tongue. It's—about being together. Forever. Marie-Santana, I want you to marry me."

He watched her face anxiously.

"Marie-Santana, will you?"

She, anticipating a proposal, prepared for hesitations but not for the swift abruptness of it, now found herself playing for time. "I am more than flattered," she said. "That you should ask—I feel honored. You are very special to me, Simon. I admire and respect you, have done so from the day we met."

"Then it's yes?"

"It's not a no," she said gently. "But it's not yes, either. At least, not yet. Marriage is for life, and to agree to that we'll need to know each other better. Much better. There's a part of my life you know nothing about; I've hidden it from the world. And there's a part of your life I know nothing about, because I haven't asked. We haven't talked. But at least now we can make a start."

"And for that we must spend more time together." Simon began to speak more rapidly. "I shall call on Granny tomorrow. Once I tell her I'm courting you, we won't have to worry about Josephine's foul tongue anymore."

"Don't call on Granny yet," she said. "I urge you to wait awhile. Let us take it by degrees."

He seemed nonplussed. "You think she will object?" he said, his anxiety deepening.

If only he knew! She smiled inwardly. "On the contrary, Granny thinks highly of you. She has told me so, time and again." She did not tell him in what context. "But I want us to be sure of ourselves, first, and then we can let the world know. We will then see if Josephine's tongue still wants to wag."

She sat herself on the parapet of the bridge and he sat down beside her. "I cannot promise you happiness," he said.

"Happiness is something I cannot even promise myself," she said, clasping his hand in hers. "Should I then be upset you can't promise it to me?"

"I can promise you comfort," he said. "Companionship, of a sort. Some caring, a lot of affection, and love."

"Simon," she said, softly. "You have just offered me four intangibles that no one has offered me before. Any one of them by itself would make for a good life."

"I have a good life in mind. But if we hit bad times, I would hope to make them better."

Immersed in thought, she made no reply.

"My asking you to marry me," he said, "this cannot have come as a total surprise. At some point you must have sensed my interest. I'm not an eloquent man, Marie-Santana, but my seeking you out—even the walks to church that gave me so much pleasure. . . . You must have sensed I had feelings for you. Did you not think that some day I might—ask?"

"I put it at the back of my mind," she said.

"And why?"

"Because in my circumstances it seemed impractical."

"I don't see why. I have enough for us to live on."

"Oh, it's not the money. I've not had money, then I've had it, and I've lost it; either way money's not made much of a difference. But I have Granny to think of, as well as myself."

"I'm not asking you to leave her," he said. "If I had a home of my own she'd live with us; since I don't, we'll naturally live at her place. After all, it's your place, too. And two can look after her better than one."

She rose and they walked slowly toward the village. "I'll still have to think about it," she said.

He stopped, and turned her so she faced him. "Are you at least a little pleased that I asked?" he said. "Give me a sign—any sign—so I don't torment myself tonight."

She hesitated, briefly. "I am more than a little pleased," she said. "But you must know, at this moment, although I like you, and I like you very much, I do not love you. Not yet, anyway."

"Loving me doesn't come easily. Few people do. Will I see you tomorrow?"

She leaned over and kissed him on the cheek. "Yes."

He tried to hold her and draw her to him but she pushed him gently away.

"Tomorrow," she said coolly, touching her hand lightly to his cheek before turning away. "Tomorrow."

He watched her as she walked toward the marketplace, the dusk enfolding her but not erasing her image; then, when she was well out of sight, he walked in her footsteps, not noticing the shuttered shops, nor the glint of light in Forttu's tavern, nor how he had turned into their lane, but breathing in her imagined fragrance with every step he took, his heart singing.

That night the full moon had the dogs abaying, but in Simon's rented home La Maja remained untouched, unwatched, in her thin glassine envelope. Instead, Simon took his violin from its leather case and its silk wrappings, and went out into the cool of his balcão; and the village and all the creatures in it slept well that night, because the music he sent out toward Marie-Santana and the stars was a soft and rapturous serenade.

SEPTEMBER

59

"WHAT NEWS ON THE INTERNATIONAL FRONT?" the vicar asked.

"The Nazi Congress has convened in Nuremberg," Senhor Eusebio said. "They say in Berlin that no German emperor was more enthusiastically acclaimed than Hitler when—"

"Enough of this Hitler already," Teodosio said. "Anybody else in the news?"

"Roosevelt. His financial program is causing such hardship that resistance is increasing by the day. Protests could soon turn violent—very violent, the way they see it in Washington."

"A bad time for America," Simon said. "He's feeding it some very bitter medicine."

"A bad time for America in more ways than one," Tendulkar said. "See how the arms race with Japan is heating up."

"Thousands of miles of ocean between them," Teodosio said, "and they are in the middle of an arms race?"

"*Anima mundi*," the vicar said. "It's the spirit of the world."

60

"THEY'LL BE TALKING ABOUT US," Marie-Santana said, "if they're not talking already. We keep running into each other daily like this—here at the post office, the bazaar this morning, Atmaram's store last night—they'd be stupid to think it's just coincidence."

Simon nodded. "But if we stop meeting and talking altogether, who knows what other stories they might come up with."

"So why go through all these charades here?" she said. "Why not go instead to Panjim? We can be alone there, even in public; can visit the municipal gardens when the military band is playing, or the Cine-Teatro to catch a movie; and the library is not too far away, either."

"The movie house," he said. "That's an idea! The matinée, tomorrow afternoon."

"It's an old film," she said, "so old it probably is scratched half to pieces."

"Who cares? We'll be together."

"I might care," she teased. "It's not every day I go to the movies. I deserve a clean print whether I watch the movie or not."

The next day dawned cloudy and wet, but by ten a brisk westerly wind had blown the rain showers through Tivolem toward the Ghats, letting the sun shine through. Marie-Santana fed Granny her noonday meal, then stopped to say hello to Josephine Aunty, who had quickly emerged at the clank of the gate.

"Are you going out?" Josephine asked the traditional neighborly question.

"I have an errand to run," Marie-Santana said. "It shouldn't take too long. And you—are you enjoying the breeze?"

"I'm enjoying the music," she said, waving a languid hand toward Weathervaneman's house, where Simon Fernandes was playing a concerto slow movement with quiet intensity. "I wish I knew what that was."

"I have no idea," Marie-Santana lied. "You'll just have to ask him."

"Sometimes he plays divinely. Surely you must think so, too."

"Oh, sometimes, certainly. We can hear him very clearly up in our house—you can, too, I suppose. Well, I'm already late, I must be going."

"Perhaps I'll come with you."

"I was hoping you'd look in on Granny," Marie-Santana lied, thinking, "I'm getting good at this." And she felt no guilt; Granny had shown she could cope with the pest. "I'll be gone most of the day."

"I'll look in on Granny later," Josephine Aunty said. "For now, I'll just listen to him play."

Simon, seeing her solidly posted there, wishing she'd go away, continued playing for a good fifteen minutes, switching finally to a ferocious sawing away at technical exercises calculated to drive her indoors. Minutes after she had fled, he put away his instrument and, changing swiftly into his going-out clothes, walked briskly away from her house toward the hill. Passing Dona Elena's, he turned left onto the lane that led toward Dona Esmeralda's stately mansion, then turned left and left again, circling around to where Marie-Santana waited at the bus stop. But when the bus arrived, and he found her an empty seat, he could not sit beside her—he had to stand all the way, his hand gripping the backrest, his thigh rubbing against her arm as the over-loaded bus bounced and swayed over the uneven road. "We need roads that are kept in better shape," she said. "And I thank God for what we have," he replied.

As they arrived at the Betim crossing, she saw the big launch already full of passengers, ready to cast off. "I'll race you," she said, and they rushed to catch it, breathless from laughter, as the warning whistle sounded. By the time they reached the launch, crewmen on the dock had released the hawsers and were pushing against its side, angling it away from the pier.

Seeing the widening chasm opening up before her, Marie-Santana stopped short, but Simon already had one foot on the gunwale and had grabbed hold of the rail. "Come on," he said, "we can still make it." With his left hand firmly gripping her elbow, he helped her leap on board. Her heart beat against her breast, a frightened bird. Now that she was safely on the launch and looking down at the water bubbling alongside, she became aware of the risk they had taken. People had been crushed between boat and pier in just such circumstances; others had drowned. It was something only the very young and foolish would have done, or those in love. The launch gathered speed; she snuggled up to him against the increasingly chill wind blowing in from the ocean, and he held her close. In the crowd they went unnoticed.

They were late for the movie but it mattered little. The film was in Portuguese, a language he had long forgotten. An elderly female character was a busybody who functioned much like Josephine. The similarity was superficial, how-ever; she was a well-meaning gossip whose mischief was incidental rather than premeditated; this much he could gather on his own. Marie-Santana had to translate the dialogue for him, and this he enjoyed immensely—her warm breath against his ticklish ear. An elderly mestiço woman behind them, annoyed by the whispering and by seeing their heads constantly together, hissed malevolently, "Silêncio!" then seconds later tapped him sharply on the shoulder with her fan, saying, "Não posso ver!" But when they scrunched down in their seats to give her a better view of the screen, she apparently lost all interest in the movie, leaning instead obscenely over the backs of their seats to see what they were doing.

Marie-Santana giggled. The woman adjusted her glasses and peered more intently. Simon turned to stare at her and she stared right back. Her eyes were enormous. Simon narrowed his to slits. She turned away, muttering, "Caneco insolente!" The racial insult passed him by. Marie-Santana's giggling became uncontrollable. From farther down the aisle people turned to shush them.

"Let's go," Simon said. "We've had our share of entertainment. Meeting this battle-ax was itself worth the price of admission."

They strolled awhile in the municipal gardens. As the evening shadows lengthened, jasmine buds began releasing their heady perfume. Beneath an ancient Arabian palm he said at last what he'd been meaning to say all day: "I love you. I love you so much sometimes it seems my heart is bursting. You say you do not love me yet—but that itself gives me hope, hope that someday you will learn to love me, too."

She had to choose her words carefully. How could she tell him that she already felt she loved him, but was afraid of that love? Would he understand?

She said, "I have learned to be leery of love. I loved someone once, in Quelimane, and it turned out very badly. At the time, I said never again. Never."

"He must have been quite unworthy of you."

"I thought the world of him," she said, "and so did my parents; he worked in our family concern. An Englishman, he called himself; but my father said he was really an Anglo. John Fernshaw, literally a fair-haired boy."

"You don't have to talk about it unless you really want to," he said.

"I want to get it over with." She paused, finding it strange that Simon had not reacted to a coworkers name, then decided to try again. "The name 'Fernshaw'," she said. "It's not familiar to you?"

"Not in the least bit. Should it be?"

"I thought it might, because he told us stories of working for a while in the civil service in Kuala Lumpur."

"Never heard of him." Simon's tone was firm.

"If it's any help, 'Old Bartlett' was his immediate boss."

"That's strange—Milton Bartlett was my boss, too. But I never heard of Fernshaw, and Bartlett never mentioned him. But if Fernshaw told you they were together, he may have been transferred, or may have quit, well before my time. When did he join your company?"

"In 1918. He came to us straight from the War. My father trained him, trusted him, made him assistant manager. He learned the business and he learned it fast. Later, when my parents died, I promoted him to manager—not because he had told me he loved me, but because he was efficient, a wizard at figures, and I needed him. I had no experience, no skills, remember. The promotion itself almost doubled his salary."

"And you, yourself, you fell in love."

"At twenty-seven, and naive, I was an easy mark. He must have known. The business prospered—I felt I'd picked a winner. I told him we should marry."

"Oh, my poor Marie-Santana! Had he seduced you, then? Is that why you are telling me all this?"

"No, he hadn't, Simon—but it wasn't for want of trying. The first time, when I pushed him away, he said, 'Who can see us? We're all alone.' And I said, 'God can.' And the next time he said, 'What if I don't believe in God? Who can see us then?' And I said, 'I can see myself.' That stopped him.

312

He knew then that I would not settle for lovemaking as a substitute for marriage. But he was cunning. He said, 'I can't marry you, not yet, not the way things are—people will say I married you for your money. I'm saving all I can, but it's not enough.' So I gave him a raise. Then I gave him another."

"And he wanted more."

"He asked me to make him a partner. I agreed. All the time he had his hand in the till. By the time I found this out, the firm was deeply in debt. Fernshaw disappeared. I closed the business, sold the house, worked for the next three years to pay off the debts, every last one of them. Then I scrimped to save for the passage home, to be with Granny. Thank God, I found not only Granny but you as well. Perhaps Fernshaw did do me a favor, after all."

"He certainly did me one," Simon said. "I just wish you'd been spared the suffering that came in between."

"Life for me will balance itself out," she said, "if I give it half a chance."

"And I'll give it the other half. I'll make it up to you, I swear it, as much as is in my power. I'm surprised you can speak of Fernshaw at all without great bitterness."

"Oh, the bitterness was there. For a while I even wanted revenge, and I tried to track him down. Then I found the anger was eating me up, not letting me get on with my life."

"And you never found him."

"Me, myself, no." Then she added, impulsively, "But John Fernshaw has been found."

"The letter from Quelimane? The postmaster told me it was plastered with stamps."

She hesitated a moment. "My lawyer wrote to say that John Fernshaw is now J. J. Ferniss, head of a flourishing import-export business in Lourenço Marques."

"So you'll sue to recover?"

"It's crossed my mind. But no, I'm letting the matter drop."

"You're still in love with him, then?" Simon sounded desolate.

"Far from it."

"Then you're taking the Christian way."

"If you want to call it that. I just don't want to sue. The money I lost was my own. The money he now has is tainted. It belongs to some other victim, and perhaps to more than one. I want no part of it."

"Even if it leaves you penniless?"

"Even then."

He was silent a moment. "I too have been looking for someone who hurt the family," he said. "Not in the same way, but he hurt us deeply all the same. Since you lived so many years in Quelimane, there's a chance you might have met him."

"Try me—I remember names and faces."

"A John Fernandes, also from Kuala Lumpur?"

"Not ever. My turn to ask: should I have?"

"There was a slim chance. John is my younger brother, who ran away from home years ago. A ne'er-do-well, but I loved him then, and still do. We all loved him, but it was pretty one-sided, except that he loved our mother. When she died, he ran. Wrote me once some six years ago, weeks after our father had died, but John did not mention him anyway; may not have known, of course. Still, not mentioning my father—his own father—that hurt. But what could I do? All I had was this brief note postmarked at Quelimane, with no return address. Said he'd struck gold. Never wrote again. If you'd met him, at least I'd have had some news."

"I can understand, I think, his not writing to you," she said. "He may have been quite ashamed. I myself didn't write to Granny for years. I'm sorry I can give you no news of him at all. A John Fernandes, I'd have mentioned him to you right away, the very first time we met, if he'd looked at all like you."

Simon, gazing into her eyes, felt a sudden fear clutching at his heart. The man who had cheated her in Quelimane, with his stories of "Old Bartlett" and the office—

314

"I hope John Fernshaw didn't look much like me either," he said, hoping it would sound like a joke.

"Typical Anglo-Saxon," she said. "Tall, almost six feet; fair; blue eyes, sunbleached hair. That sound like you?"

Simon paled. He thought, my God, not him. I have found him at last, and it's the worst possible news—his shadow falls between me and Marie-Santana, between us and the future, us and all happiness. But the notion that his brother would have cheated the very woman he professed to love was too shameful to be true; for all his faults, John would not have stooped so low. Still, Simon felt soiled. It's a coincidence, he told himself; many Anglo-Saxons would fit Marie-Santana's description of the man. Not ready yet to probe further, he forced a smile, saying, "From your description, if John Fernshaw were my age, we'd be mistaken for identical twins."

"Absolutely."

They laughed, and gratefully he let the moment pass.

He wanted to take a gasolina across the river but she, noting his sudden gloom, drew him toward the river beach instead. "Perhaps Shankar will be there," she said.

"Shankar?"

"A boatman my father knew. He owns a special canoe."

"It will take that much longer."

"We have the time," she said, "and it's a wonderful experience. Today, what's the hurry?"

Shankar was at the strand, his boat moored, quite empty of passengers. He came forward immediately to greet them. "Ah, my especial bai! Welcome once again. We can leave at once."

She looked at Simon.

He handed her in. "Of course. An especial it shall be."

To Shankar she said, "You remember."

"How could I forget? It's in my blood—against the tide, then with it. Only, this time, regrettably, I cannot do it."

"And why not?"

"It's slack water," he said, grinning broadly. She laughed.

"What was that about?" Simon asked.

"Some advice my father gave Shankar when he was a young man, a small hint about the best way to row across a tidal river."

"And no doubt a lesson drawn on real life. Your father must have been a practical philosopher."

"Perhaps he was," she said wistfully. "He never talked much to me. But his presence by my side, his strong presence, meant more to me than perhaps even he knew. When I was a child, Granny tells me, we always crossed the river in this same canoe, my father by my side, my mother and grandmother facing us. Since returning from Africa I've crossed and recrossed the Mandovi three times already, not counting our trip by the launch; this is the fourth. Each time it's been in this canoe. And today, for the first time, you're with me, and there's no tide to row against. The wind is down; the river's like glass. Perhaps it's symbolic— this crossing with you could be the very best crossing of my life."

61

THE NIGHT Simon and Marie-Santana returned from
their trip to Panjim, he had spent an hour after dinner
in the semidarkness of his balcão, playing a series of soft
love songs—Schubert, Tosti, Toselli, Friml, Romberg—not
on his regular violin but on the fine Amati his father had
left him, an instrument whose very tone was meant for
love. And he ended the serenade with "Vilia," pianissimo,
the faint throbbing notes mirroring the tenderness in his
heart. At last, the violin put away, he lay flat on his back
in bed, staring at an almost invisible ceiling. On that blank
screen the camera of his mind projected the scenes of his
future—Marie-Santana and he, yes, Marie-Santana and he
himself, laughing and loving for time without end. With so
much happiness within him, why then was he having so
much difficulty drifting off to sleep?

Candle in hand, he went in search of the note his brother
had written him, years earlier. He had to see that phrase
again, where John had mentioned having struck gold. Perhaps reading it again, this one time, the note would yield up
some of its mysteries. Not just the main question—where is
John?—but the one that now nagged even his subconscious:
What gold had he struck? Gold as in the legendary gold of
Sofala and Ophir, or the real but minimal gold to be found

in the alluvial deposits of Quelimane? Or figurative gold, perhaps, in the person of a young heiress, naive and vulnerable, because recently orphaned?

He found the note where he always chanced upon it, in a large stash of papers he was forever sorting. Dripping hot wax onto a corner of the table, he then pushed the candle firmly down on the spot and held it there, waiting for the wax to set while he read the stark message over and over again. "I am well. I hope you are too. I've struck gold." Nothing there to give him a clue as to what his brother meant. Wearily, Simon put the note down on the table. John's image now floated before his eyes, John still aged twenty-three, though he would be forty by now; the note itself seemed to rise up from the table and alternately hover near and then float away from his eyes. He realized with a start that he was asleep on his feet and in danger of knocking the candle over and burning himself. Prying it off the table, he headed off to bed.

When he found himself walking up the path to the top of the hill, Simon, expecting a voice at his elbow, saw instead his father waiting for him on the plateau.

"So you found him," Michael said.

"I did?" Simon, breathing hard, stopped climbing.

"You found your brother."

"I found someone called John, yes."

"That's not what I meant. You found John Fernshaw, or J. J. Ferniss, your brother."

"Now wait a minute," Simon said. "Through Marie-Santana, I found one John Fernshaw, a different person altogether—an Englishman or an Anglo, I believe, who claims he worked in Kuala Lumpur with a man who happens to have been my boss. And can tell stories to prove it."

"Stories John heard you tell at our dinner table. Don't play games with me, Simon. I can read you as easily as you and I can read a piece of music."

"All right," Simon said. "I admit it. John Fernshaw could be my brother."

"It's not a 'could be'," Michael said. "The evidence is in. There can be no more 'could be's' about it. Fernshaw alias Ferniss is your brother."

"You're too insistent," Simon said. "It could be true, but it may not be—we still don't know for sure. Fernshaw could have heard the stories anywhere. And you're assuming John changed the family name, but we don't know for sure that he did."

"The more easily to pass off as an Anglo? He'd have liked nothing better," Michael said. "From Fernandes to Fernshaw, Fernshaw to Ferniss, each a very simple change."

"That it is."

"And each time bringing in a good bit of money. Striking gold, I think, is what he called it the first time around." Michael dug in his pocket and produced John's note.

"You took that from my desk?"

Michael ignored the question. "This gold that he struck in '27—isn't it Marie-Santana's inheritance he is talking about?"

"I've thought about that," Simon said, "and I don't like what I think."

"You've got to tell her, then. You'll lose her if you don't tell her. You've got to! You yourself must tell her the truth."

"After I've checked on it further," Simon said. His father said nothing, waiting.

"Am I not tormenting myself enough with this," Simon said, "that you must torment me, too?"

Still his father was silent.

"The shame of it," Simon said a moment later. "The utter, terrible shame of it. A blight on the family."

He thought he heard Michael say, "The greater shame would be for you not to own up." But Michael had disappeared. In the next breath Simon called after him, "And you've got it all backward! If I tell her, then I'll lose her.

Why would she marry the brother of the man who ruined her life?" Still, Michael did not come back. "I'll make it up to her, I promise you I will," Simon said. By then he was rolling downhill, helplessly rolling, shouting "I'll lose her! I'll lose her!" into the unforgiving wind, until the wetness of his pillow and his own wrenching sobs shook him awake.

62

"YOU ARE SHINING UP THAT POT AGAIN," Angelinh'
Granny said. "Allow yourself just one more scrub, then
ask the genie what you'd like to know."

"I'd like to know about Simon's family," Marie-Santana
said, carefully setting the brass pot down in the sink and
turning to face her. "Everything you know about them."

"I knew Simon's grandparents and his parents," Granny
said. "God-fearing people. Good to their neighbors. Michael
and Faustina used to visit, and she and I often walked to the
Mapusa market together. Oh yes, and I liked little Simon.
He used to call me Enginh' Aunty then, couldn't get the
word right, and your grandfather would tease me, saying,
'You're a real Engine Aunty—always full of steam.' Once
they moved to Kuala Lumpur, we lost touch."

"So you know nothing about his younger brother?"

"Oh, we knew he was born because they used to write
home, to Michael's parents. The letters thinned out after the
grandfather died and stopped altogether after she followed.
When the children were almost grown, a cousin of ours
who had met them in Kuala Lumpur gave us news. That's
the last I heard, until Simon himself came to visit years ago."

"You didn't know the brother had run away?"

"No. Nobody told us."

Marie-Santana now chose her words carefully. "Something odd happened a few days ago, Granny, when Simon asked me if I had met his brother in Quelimane. I said if they had looked anything alike I would have remarked on the resemblance. And he looked startled. I could swear he was about to say something, and then decided not to."

"Mar'-Santan', child, perhaps he was going to tell you that his brother looked nothing like him at all. Not like the rest of the family at all. Fair and tall, that's what my cousin said he was, fair and tall, like an Anglo, and not like the family, not even in his behavior. Is something wrong? You seem very upset."

"No, not at all," Marie-Santana said. To avoid her grandmother's anxious scrutiny she turned to the sink and picked up the pot once again. Simon must have suspected, after all. He may have more than suspected; from her description, he may have known for sure that John Fernshaw was his missing brother. She set the pot firmly down on the floor of the sink to control the trembling of her hands.

"You are upset," her grandmother said.

Marie-Santana heaved a great sigh. Would Granny never stop? This was the wrong time for an inquisition; she needed to be alone, needed time to collect her thoughts. She decided not to respond, but found herself answering anyway. "If I'm upset, it's for Simon's sake. It must have been a blow to his parents, and to him, having a son and brother who was a total misfit."

"This tall and fair misfit," Granny said. "Could this be the man—Ferncoss, Ferngloss, whatever—you knew in Quelimane?"

"I've told you, and I've told you over and over again," Marie-Santana said, now quite irritated, "that the tall and fair man in Quelimane was actually an Anglo. An Anglo-Indian, Granny, not one of us." If she repeated it often enough, it might even turn into the truth.

"But supposing it is as I think, Mar'-Santan'," Angelinh' Granny said, slowly and carefully. "It wouldn't be the first time a fair Goan has passed himself off as an Anglo. Turn around now and face me again—this is important. Supposing the man is really Simon's brother; you realize, if the news got out, that shame would settle on his family? Could you marry Simon then?"

"Supposing, supposing," Marie-Santana retorted, suddenly angry. "It's not true, so for me the question does not arise. But since you asked, would you?"

"I would. Cain was Cain, Abel was Abel. Simon is Simon, no matter what his brother turned out to be."

"Simon is Simon," Marie-Santana repeated softly, her anger now gone. "That part certainly is true. As for his brother, was he the man? I don't know, I really don't know."

"Then ask him. Do you have a picture?"

"I'll have to look."

She left the kitchen on that pretext, even though she didn't have to look, she knew exactly where the photograph was. But she was not in the mood to bring it out now; what she wanted was an end to the questions her grandmother was preparing to throw at her. While rummaging noisily through one drawer after another, she heard Granny adjusting a chair here, putting down a utensil there, shuffling about the kitchen as much to use up the time as to mask her own unease. Marie-Santana felt guilty then, for not sharing her inmost fears more openly; if there was comfort to be found anywhere, she would have found it within those aged and wrinkled arms. In escaping to her room, even with so plausible an excuse, she had shut out love.

"I'm going off to sleep," Granny called from the door, and Marie-Santana stopped all the pretense and went to her then, threw her arms around her and let the tears flow.

A good hour after her grandmother had fallen asleep, Marie-Santana, back in her own room, turned up the wick in her kerosene lamp and took out the family album, looking at Kodak Brownie snapshots of her father, her mother, herself, and the one picture of John Fernshaw she had saved because of who he was standing next to in the Quelimane office—her parents; John Fernshaw, a good six inches taller than his employer, blond, smiling, his pale eyes staring directly into the camera.

"I'll show this to Simon," she said, half-aloud, as she doused the light. "Not his brother—dear God, Simon is Simon, certainly, but let this not be his brother."

But it is, her mind told her; it has to be. Those stories John told, about his boss and Kuala Lumpur, he must have heard them from Simon. If Simon were asked, casually, about Old Bartlett, he too might come up with the same anecdotes. But would that make them brothers? Hadn't Simon as good as denied it? If she challenged him now, might she not lose him? Not a brother, not even a coworker; he had denied knowing any Fernshaw at all, and as for some of the office stories, Fernshaw may have been one of Bradshaw's assistants before Simon's time. That was it, that had been the possibility Simon himself had raised, and it was the most logical explanation; one of the strange coincidences of life.

Sighing, she settled back to sleep.

But what if?

She could not rid herself of the arguments; sleep, usually so faithful an ally, was a long time coming. Lying on her back in the total darkness, her imagination took hold. "Out of my life!" she hissed, fists clenched, addressing a shadowy Fernshaw hovering menacingly near the ceiling, "I put you out of my life once, and you're back?"

The figure moved.

"Out!" she cried. "For God's sake, let me be."

"Bai," came Angelinh' Granny's voice from the next bedroom.

Marie-Santana forced herself to be quiet.

"Mar'-Santan', bai!" She heard her grandmother sit up. "I'm all right, Granny. Do you need anything?"

"I heard your voice."

"I must have been dreaming. I'm all right, I'm fine; go back to sleep."

She waited till she heard her grandmother settle in again and cover herself.

"Simon will rid me of you," she said, silently this time, to the shadow still stirring near the ceiling. "You can't be his brother. I'll confront him in the morning, your picture in my hand."

Fernshaw disappeared. Relieved, she drifted off into a profound sleep. But by morning her resolve had given way to renewed fears.

63

MARIE-SANTANA started the long trek to the river at sunrise, her mind in a turmoil. "God give you a good day," the fisherwomen called, as they trotted past at long intervals. "God grant you grace," she answered mechanically. God grant me grace as well, she thought; I need it, I need it, I've never needed it more than now. John Fernshaw's photograph rested in her purse; she had not had the courage to show it to Simon yet. She was not sure she ever would; she was no longer sure of anything. She trudged on. Two hours later, at the first glint of water, she stopped: what balm was she hoping to find there, by the banks of the Mandovi? At best, she would find Shankar, the boatman. With luck, if no other passengers were already seated in his canoe, she could ask once more for an especial, a trip, alone, to the far shore and back again. And what would that produce? Her father's voice, yielding sane counsel in her fragmenting world? She had evoked her father's calming presence once before; who was to say it could not happen again?

A quarter of a mile farther down the road, where the steep declivity began, the panorama of the city opened up before her. On the far bank directly ahead, an empty dock awaited the arrival of the Bombay steamer; some distance to its left the palace of Adhil Khan, Muslim ruler of Goa at the time of the Portuguese conquest, stretched like a tawny cat by the road that ran the river's length far as the eye could see. Behind the palace and partway up a steep rise, the white façade of the Church of the Immaculate Conception surmounted a zigzag series of steps; beyond its towers the houses on the Altinho clung to the heights. In the morning light the city revealed itself in ascending pastel layers, its perspective mirroring the flat horizontal strips in Persian and Moghul miniatures. On Marie-Santana's side of the river and some miles downstream, the fortress of Aguada brooded over the estuary, as breakers from the Arabian Sea moved lazily in, to topple in long thin foaming lines on the shallows of the sandbar.

A gasolina had started its oblique run from the city to the jetty she was approaching; the big launch, tied up at that same jetty, would not begin plying until later, when the volume of passengers had picked up. It had been about to pull away from that same spot when last she'd been there with Simon; she remembered the last-minute exhilarating run, the momentary indecision, the warm supportive grip of his strong hand around her elbow as he helped her leap safely aboard. Once again she felt herself glowing. But the mood did not last; she doubted that her happiness would, or Simon's for that matter. If Fernshaw were indeed Fernshaw—but what if he were Simon's brother? Then, if the case broke, and her name and her parents' appeared in the papers, shame would attach to Simon, as the brother of an accused swindler; would attach even to her, though she was a victim. And people would talk, about her, about John, about why she had been so closemouthed about what had happened to her in Quelimane. Josephine Aunty could be counted on to spread the gossip far and wide, hinting, perhaps stating for a fact what was blatantly untrue, that John and she had been lovers, or that he had fathered a child, that the child had been aborted. And Josephine would not be alone; hadn't the gossip turned so many others against her? Would she herself have the strength to face this down? Would Simon? Or would their marriage founder on the rocks of slander and suspicion? It may not come to that, Marie-Santana reassured herself, adding, Your mind is running ahead of itself. All you need do for now is establish Fernshaw's identity. All you need do is confront Simon. Steel yourself, she added. But she couldn't.

On the river bank a few boatmen were already hustling for customers. There was no sign, as yet, of Shankar.

But at nine, he was there.

"An especial, once again, Shankar," Marie-Santana said quickly, cornering him before he could begin calling for customers. "From here to the Panjim shore and back again."

"You must love the river, bai," he said, "to want to make this long journey without even setting foot on the other side."

"It calms me down. And it gives me time to think."

He helped her into the canoe, then eased it into the river. The slack tide had just ended; the ebb tide had not yet gathered momentum; it would be an easy trip.

"Your friend is not with you," he remarked, bending to the oars, as she sat chin in hand, looking off into the distance.

"No," she said, still facing away.

He had to steer carefully, to avoid the empty canoes bobbing close to shore.

"And from what you said, bai," he ventured, "your trip this morning, back and forth alone, just like that, has something to do with a weight on your mind?"

"A decision I must make, and it's not an easy one."

"Then it concerns—him?" His voice conveyed so much empathy, she could not be offended.

"Yes. There's something I feel I should know, and it's something I don't want to know."

"Back and forth across the river," he said. "In search of an answer to a question to which you do not want the answer. A question that cancels itself." He feathered the oars, briefly, then dug them into the water again.

"Back and forth," he said again, "like life itself."

"Is life, then, a question that cancels itself?" She found herself drawn deep into a dialogue she had not counted on.

"Not exactly. But our lives themselves are like the crossings and recrossings of a river."

How true, she thought, and smiled wanly.

"No sooner have we reached the far side than we die," he said, "but no sooner do we die than we are born again, and must now row once more to the other bank." He paused to catch his breath.

Her thought had been different: One crossed and, on the other bank, ended up where one had started from.

"Always it's the other bank," he said, "through all our existences, till we achieve oneness with the All-Pervasive One."

"In my religion," Marie-Santana interposed, "once you have reached the other bank, that's where you'll find Heaven—or a far less pleasant place."

"Hinduism then is somewhat kinder, bai," he said, smiling. "We Hindus are given more chances than one."

"I like your notion of life as crossing and recrossing a river," she said, "but I have always thought of my life as being itself a river. Where the river melts into the ocean, that ocean itself could be the All-Pervasive One; the crossings would then be over."

He laughed. "Perhaps. But think carefully: that blending of sea and river is not an end, but part of a cycle." He was pulling more strongly now, to counter the growing current; the canoe glided smoothly between the powerful strokes. "A river loses itself into the sea; the sea turns its waters into clouds which become rain which becomes the river yet once again. Life followed by life followed by life; death but a transition from one form of life to another to yet another."

"You think a lot."

"The river gives me time, bai. I wait and I wait, and the mind must occupy itself, and even when I'm rowing, the people I ferry give me things to think about."

"And I, have I given you something to think about today?"

"Yes. There's a sadness about you this morning that's different from your sadness the day you came looking for me at Betim. Then, you were searching for your past; and now?"

"Now, a portion of my past has caught up with me."

"You've been hurt?"

"That's true."

He watched her closely, saying nothing. She dropped her eyes. She put her arm over the side and dragged her hand through the water, marshalling her thoughts. The strangeness of the situation got to her; here she was, alone in a canoe, talking to Shankar as she might to a priest in the confessional, except that she was not confessing to any sins. She could have talked to the vicar just as easily, not in the confessional but still in private, and he would have been understanding, of that she was sure; yet she had not done so. Like Granny, he was too close to her; and he might, in an unguarded moment, have mentioned it to the curate; priests were human, after all. And if the curate? While Shankar. . . . Confiding in Shankar was much like confiding in a stranger—his life and hers touched only at those rare intervals when she was riding in his canoe. And they had no friends or acquaintances in common; there was no one she knew that he could share her confidences with, even if he wanted to. His silence at that point encouraged her.

"I'm afraid that, because of that hurt, I in turn may hurt someone," she said.

He did not answer immediately. She hesitated, not knowing whether to continue.

"That question you have in mind," he said at last, and paused, reversing his stroke and slowing the canoe to let a dhow slip serenely by, its lateen sails angled to catch every

330

puff of breeze. "Whatever that question may be, I have a question for you, too."

"I'll try to answer it."

"Is the person who once hurt you more important in your life than the one you may hurt now?"

"The person who hurt me is out of my life," she said, after a moment's hesitation. "But he is casting a very long shadow."

"The earth casts a long shadow on the moon, too, but the shadow passes and the moon shines brightly as ever."

"As my chance for happiness grows, this shadow grows darker and more threatening," she said, surprised at her own persistent gloom.

"Even as the demon's shadow threatens to swallow the moon in a total eclipse. Our village people drive the demon away by gathering in the streets and setting off firecrackers and yelling and banging on pots and pans."

"But to me the demon's shadow is very real," she said. "It has nothing to do with folk mythology. I have known this demon for several years, and no amount of screaming, or banging on drums and pots and pans, has yet driven his shadow from me."

"Then let me change the picture to one I know something about from experience—a flood tide at full moon. Once caught up in it you cannot easily escape its power."

"So you share my pessimism."

"Perhaps not, bai. Your father years ago advised me to row against the tide. And you see I do it still."

"He would have been pleased, as I am."

"The question is, why did your father say what he did?" He paused, but she remained silent, waiting for his explanation. "Surely what he meant was, use the tide, don't just fight it or go along with it. Even a flood tide has currents in it, he said; one can choose a current as one can choose a sliver of one's past; or one can use even the weakest of eddies to turn one's canoe completely around."

"A complete turnaround," she exclaimed. "My father

said that? Use even the weakest of eddies to turn completely around?"

"The very words your father used," he said, very gently,
"when we were having a similar conversation in this same
boat, all those years ago. Only, then, I was the one who was
troubled, and he was asking the questions and supplying by
far the better answers."

"I hear him as you speak," she said at last, her voice
tremulous. "In your voice and in your words, I hear him
quite clearly. Someone told me, when I told her about you,
that surely you carry his memory in your heart."

He nodded, deeply moved, and rowed on in silence, letting her grapple with her own emotions. At last she raised
her eyes to meet his.

"This question, the answer to which you fear," he said,
feathering the oars once again, and watching her intently,
"what if the answer is offered you, without your even asking; what then?"

She seemed not to have heard. But the question had set
her to thinking. She had assumed, since time was passing
and Simon was avoiding the issue, that eventually she would
have to ask him; was afraid that in her anxiety she might
even confront him; and if that happened, what would his
answer be? Shamefaced admission? If she shamed him,
where would it get her? And if he denied it outright, denied
Fernshaw was his brother, denied even knowing him, could
she accept that without reservation? If the denial were false,
would that not poison their relationship? And supposing
the denial were true, might a suspicion not linger in her
mind? Worse, might Simon, deeply hurt, not turn against
her? What if, on the other hand, what Shankar suggested
really came to pass; what if, even before she asked, an
answer were proffered, might that not resolve her dilemma?
Show an openness on Simon's part, where she feared con-
cealment?

With Shankar still watching her, the canoe drifted and
the current took hold, turning the bow toward the mouth of

the Mandovi. A mile downstream, she could see the breakers vainly battling the waters of the river.

"If the answer is offered—" she said, and stopped.

She had wanted to say, "I will welcome it," but found herself struggling once again with the conflict within her; not to know was painful enough, but to know could be more painful still.

He slipped an oar into the water to reangle the boat, so carefully it made no sound. Then he repeated his question: "What if it is, bai?"

"Then I will not need to hear it," she said, suddenly animated. "I will not need to hear the answer at all. The offer will be the eddy that turns it all around—the question will then have canceled itself. Shankar, back to Betim."

"Turn back? So soon? And the trip to the Panjim shore?"

"Now quite unnecessary. Back to Betim," she said. "You have found me an eddy. The debt you feel you've owed my father has been more than fully repaid."

64

As MARIE-SANTANA walked up from the Mapusa road at twilight, she saw a lone figure seated at the bridge over the nullah; Simon had been waiting, she hoped for not too long. The feeling akin to euphoria she had experienced after her talk to Shankar that morning had long since disappeared, to be replaced by a more tempered optimism— Simon would volunteer the information she sought. He would. It could not be any other way. "What if he did?" the boatman had asked, forcing a conclusion. Now, suddenly, the question reversed itself. What if he didn't? She put the thought out of mind.

Simon had not spotted her yet; he was facing toward the village. At last he turned his head, and came forward to greet her. Fighting an impulse to run to him, Marie-Santana did not quicken her pace.

He stopped short, standing there awkwardly before her, not daring to take her in his arms. "I have spoken to the vicar," he said, "not here at the bridge before the others, but at the parish office." He reached for her hand. "Everything's set."

His words sustained her mood. Not everything's set, not yet, she thought, but it soon will be. After you tell me what you know about John Fernshaw. What she heard herself say instead was, "The banns will be read?"

"From the pulpit, beginning next month." He cleared his throat, dropped his voice a notch, and declaimed, imitating the vicar's resonant tones: "Be it known that one Simon Fernandes, bachelor, born and resident in this parish—"

"And Marie-Santana Pereira, spinster, also of this parish," she cut in, laughing.

"Having declared their intention—"

"Now have plans to make," she said, suddenly sober. "Our engagement first, right away."

"Yes, yes! I'll have the ring picked out tomorrow."

"You've no idea how happy this will make Granny. She'll want to bless us. When shall we tell her?"

"Tonight, if you like. And we'll set the date for next week."

"Then tomorrow we'll go to the jewelers in Mapusa. I'd like to get you your ring, too, at the same time. And Simon—"

"Yes, Marie-Santana."

"Our engagement will be just a simple ceremony before friends."

"But a proper engagement for all that, with brown jaggery and crisp fresh coconut chunks and chick peas, and firecrackers exploding in the lane."

"And after the banns, the wedding. It'll be a good wedding, Simon."

"The best."

"It'll have to be simple," she said. "I can't pay for the best."

"But I can."

"I can't have people say I'm marrying you for your money."

"And I can't have people saying I'm a skinflint, either. You'll have as many bridesmaids as you want."

"I want just one. Annabel."

"Then Annabel it will be, your matron-of-honor."

"And a flower girl."

"With flowers from your garden. And Little Arnold as a page boy. We'll invite all your relatives."

"I only have Granny. And you? You must have some in other villages?"

"Not that I know of, not here in Goa."

Not here in Goa, true, she thought, but somewhere out there, there's John. She noticed he had chosen his words carefully; he had said nothing about John, had not even mentioned the name. John was not in Goa, John was God knows where; but why would Simon not even try to find him before the wedding?

Her doubts resurfaced. With the Fernshaw issue unresolved, next month was close. When would she have the courage? She disengaged her hand. Hesitantly, she said, "The banns next month—"

"Is that too soon?" he asked, sensing her unease. "I thought you would be pleased."

"But I am."

They were strolling away from the village. Dusk had settled on the valley, and a cool light breeze stirred the jasmine in her hair. He reached out a hand to touch the tiny loop of flowers. "Unfair advantage," he said, caressing her hair and breathing in the fragrance, "doubly unfair, when you already have me in your power."

His voice lulled her. "What a wonderful day this is turning out to be," she said. "One of the best in my life. I have found you, the kindest and gentlest of men. And now, look, we have a lover's moon."

"No more special nor beautiful than you."

She blushed. "And to think that you were once so tongue-tied."

"Knowing you and loving you has changed me, Marie-Santana. And it has changed a lot of other things. My world's full of a magical singing."

"And before?"

"It was a dark and lonely place, except for my music. Even the stamps didn't help."

"My world was dark and lonely, too, except for Granny. Not even Annabel. . . ." her voice trailed off. "Loneliness has been the sad reality, for me, the past half-dozen years and more, until you came into my life and brought along your music."

"You have me now; your lonely days are over."

"The banns still have to be read," she said. "And after the banns we'll have three more months to wait."

"Three more months in which someone can object, or you can change your mind."

"I've made up my mind."

He turned to face her. "I love you," he said softly, his hands on her shoulders.

"I see people coming," she said, gently pulling away, as two figures that had been crossing the fields now climbed onto the path. Were they neighbors? From their walk she guessed that they weren't; had they been, news of their tryst would soon have spread all over the village. Not that it mattered anymore, now that Simon had spoken to the vicar.

They strolled side by side in silence, close but not touching. After they pass, she thought, after they pass he will tell me, and get it over with.

"God grant you a good night," the strangers called as they walked by.

"God grant you grace."

"I'm so full of happiness," he said to her, "I must keep dreaming."

"You said something earlier," she teased, "but we were interrupted. What was it again?"

He took her in his arms and kissed her. "Does that answer your question?"

"I want to hear you say it."

"I do love you."

"Then kiss me again."

He looked around.

"There's no one coming," Marie-Santana said.

It was a while before they walked back to the bridge.

"I've been thinking," Marie-Santana said. "Thinking a great deal—about us."

He stopped, dismayed at her tone, now suddenly grown somber. "I'm listening."

"We haven't talked," she said. "In all this while we still haven't talked seriously about some things that matter."

"It's not too late."

A voice warned her she should not throw her happiness away; she should let the question slide. Still, she heard herself ask, "What do you know of me?"

"Enough to want you for my wife."

"And the things you do not know?"

"They do not matter."

They resumed their stroll.

"And why don't they matter?" she asked, suddenly.

"Because it's the past. Marie-Santana, is something wrong?"

"No," she said. "No. Nothing."

"Is there something you want to tell me?"

"Me, no. Do you?"

"Since this has turned into confession time, let me confess that I have my fears, have had them for quite some time."

"You want out?"

"For your sake. More and more it seems that through me our marriage could be touched by scandal."

"Oh?"

"And it's best you be prepared, as I'm preparing myself. It concerns someone you know—John Fernshaw."

"His having been found troubles you?"

"It's who he might be that troubles me. You told me he talked about his civil-service days in Kuala Lumpur and mentioned people I'd worked with. I told you then I didn't

know him, that there was no Fernshaw in our office in
Kuala Lumpur."

"And that's not true?"

"It is. Absolutely! I've never known a John Fernshaw.
But what if I knew him, without knowing it, under a different name?"

She waited, saying nothing. "Perhaps you should sit," he
said, motioning toward the parapet; he himself continued
to stand. "The thought has crossed my mind that he could
be my brother, recounting as his own the stories he had
heard me tell."

Again she waited for him to continue.

"If Fernshaw is my brother," Simon said, still choosing
his words carefully, "if he's arrested or even charged, word
will get into the papers as to who he really is, and shame
will attach to my family. To me, for being his brother; to my
parents, for having spawned him; and to the village as well,
by association."

"I'm not pressing charges."

"You told me that. But others may. Then, if you marry
me, shame will attach to your family as well. You, even
though you were the victim, will be blamed as the cause
of it all."

"Shame cannot come to my family through you or
through John," she said. "Shame to my family can only
come if I myself perform shameful actions. And that hasn't
happened yet."

"I must be sure," he said. "I must be sure that John
Fernshaw and my brother are not one and the same person.
Or that they are. I have to know."

She opened her purse. "I have a picture here with me,"
she said, "I've been carrying it about for a while, not knowing quite how or when to show it to you. He's standing
right next to my parents, but the moonlight's hardly bright
enough for you to make out his features."

Simon's hands trembled as he studied the ochre Brownie
print she had handed him. In the pale light the tall man's

features were indistinguishable, but his stance told Simon all he needed to know. He cleared his throat, opened his mouth to speak, then fell silent again. He groped for a handkerchief, sweating profusely. He's suffering, she thought; and a second voice said, So let him suffer. But she dismissed this, still remaining silent, giving him the time he needed.

At last he turned to face her. "We have a problem," he said. "Marie-Santana, I'm ashamed—Oh God!—what you said happened in Quelimane—"

"Don't!" she exclaimed, placing her hand to his lips. "Don't say it." She rose and turned away, so he could not see her face. If she was crying, she was crying silent tears. He could not tell. But he read the turning away as a gesture of rejection; it seemed that with the mere mention of his brother's misdeeds their dreams of happiness had been shattered forever. He wished now he had heeded his dead father's advice, and told her what he had suspected weeks earlier; he would have lost her then as he was losing her now, but at least her hurt would have been less. He could not let her go, not like this, not ever.

"Mar'-Santan'—"

He'd never called her that before. "Mar'-Santan', love!" He wanted to reach out and enfold her in his arms, yet feared her reaction. Despite his father's prodding, he had never been close to a woman before, neither emotionally nor even physically; now his inexperience galled him. Timidly, he touched her on the shoulder; she did not stir.

"Have I lost you, then?" he said, hoarsely. "You will not hear me out?" Silence.

"Mar'-Santan'?" His voice was a whisper.

"I too had figured things out," she said, turning to face him, her mouth trembling. "Though I couldn't be certain. Granny told me she heard that he was nothing like the rest of your family. Not at all like you. I had a question, about who John was, and whether you knew, and whether you were going to tell me or risk having it a dark secret in our lives. That question has cancelled itself—John does not matter. What matters now is that, once you were sure, you wanted to tell me. That's what matters to me most. Even though you were afraid, you, of your own will, were going to tell me."

She could no longer control her sobs. Her face in his shoulder, he held her close, wordlessly, and softly caressed her hair, waiting for the trembling to subside.

EPILOGUE

"SIMON NOT HERE AGAIN?" the vicar said. "If he keeps this up, not being here could become a habit."

"As it will, once he's married," Tendulkar said. "From now on, we should only accept into our group those bachelors who promise to remain bachelors."

"On pain of?"

"No need for a penalty if they marry," Postmaster Braganza said. "Marriage will provide all the pain they need."

The vicar cut into the general laughter. "You're a one to talk," he said, "when you're a prime accessory to marriage."

"I am? And you can prove it?"

"Yes, indeed. Without your postal facilities, few love letters would get through."

"And what about you, Father Vicar?" the postmaster counterattacked. "You read the banns, perform the ceremony. . . . You've read two of Simon's banns already."

"Ah, but I'm a proponent, not a cynic," the vicar said. "As an aide of the Almighty, I try to make sure that marriages are made in Heaven."

"I, although a cynic, also have a solid defense," the postmaster said. "True, the post office makes sure the love letters go through, but we also preserve a balance—we also forward other documents—even news despatches—that could ruin a marriage, or even the prospect of one."

"You mean the news about Simon's brother," Teodosio said. "Sad. Who would have thought it! A messy bit of business, and bound to get messier, is the way I look at it. In Simon's place, I'd want to hide."

"But he's not to blame, and he's not hiding," Tendulkar said. "He's busy making the arrangements. And here he comes toward us now, with Marie-Santana, no less."

"To judge by the way they're sauntering, our lovebirds are in no great hurry to get here," the vicar said.

"Marie-Santana's probably on her way to the Mapusa fair," Senhor Eusebio said. "Goes there every Friday."

"Or she may be coming to join us. We should certainly welcome that. A woman to liven up our discussions."

"Don't count on it, Tendulkar," Teodosio said. "His brother's not the only problem the two of them face. Josephine has a new campaign going."

"She lost on the evil eye. Now what's her weapon?"

"Caste, the first stone. She claims he's not a Brahmin, hence Marie-Santana should not marry him."

"But surely Marie-Santana is aware of his caste?"

"Then we should applaud the two of them," Tendulkar said. "It takes courage to break that barrier."

"It certainly does," the vicar said. "And the two of them have all the courage that's needed. But they'll be within earshot in a moment; it's time we changed the subject."

"Before we do, one last question," Tendulkar said. "With all the problems and obstacles they face, Father Vicar, do you have a Latin phrase to fit the situation?"

"But of course, and I thought you'd never ask. In fact, I have three. I have one for Josephine: *Antevictoriam ne canas triumphum*—do not sing your victory song before you've gained the victory. I have one for our pair of lovers: *Amor omnia vincit*. Not always true, but in your case at least, we hope that love will conquer all. And I have one for the rest of us, and I include those in the outside world who are mighty and now rule over our destinies: *Vanitas vanitatum.* Vanity of vanities. Do not hunger too much after power and glory, for in time those, too, shall pass."